PRESIDENT PORFIRIO DIAZ

DIAZ

BY

DAVID HANNAY

KENNIKAT PRESS
Port Washington, N. Y./London

DIAZ

First published in 1917
Reissued in 1970 by Kennikat Press
Library of Congress Catalog Card No: 77-112804
ISBN 0-8046-1071-1

Manufactured by Taylor Publishing Company   Dallas, Texas

GENERAL EDITOR'S PREFACE

THE author of this volume has here combined an appreciation of a man remarkable in his generation with a lively picture of an American republic, still little known to us in Europe ; thus fulfilling two objects of this series. President Diaz's achievements as a statesman, though important to his contemporaries, appear to have had only a passing value. But he is worthy of note by the student of the nineteenth century, since he brought his country to a more respectable prominence and to greater prosperity than it had enjoyed since its original conquest by the Spaniards ; and he also induced many outside its borders to take an interest, however mercenary and uninformed it may have been, in the country he governed so absolutely and for so long a period. For his own corner of the world, indeed, he was truly a maker of the nineteenth century. He is also interesting as a type, a particularly favourable type, of the *condottieri* who flourish and then vanish so rapidly on the Central and South American scene. Mexico itself, though so near a neighbour to the United States, is still the most mysterious to us of all the American countries. Perhaps it has never yet outlived the wonderful tales brought back to Europe of Aztec cities and civilisation and the exploits of Cortes, the most chivalrous of all the Spanish adventurers. Mr. Hannay has kept for us some of the mystery in his descriptions of the country's wild rolling uplands and of the mediæval adventures of his hero and his hero's adversaries in this land of sudden surprises. He has also made the people and the land more real and living to us at a time when they have become specially interesting in the politics of the world.

BASIL WILLIAMS.

September, 1916.

CONTENTS

	PAGE
GENERAL EDITOR'S PREFACE	v

CHAP.		
I.	INTRODUCTORY	1
II.	THE BEGINNING OF A CAREER	29
III.	THE FRENCH INTERVENTION	53
IV.	THE RISE TO THE FIRST RANK	86
V.	THE POLITICIAN	117
VI.	THE FIGHT FOR THE PRESIDENCY	144
VII.	THE FIRST TERM	177
VIII.	AN INTERIM	207
IX.	PRESIDENT FOR GOOD	237
X.	THE INDIAN PROBLEM	265
XI.	ANARCHY WELLS UP	290

BIBLIOGRAPHY	307
CHRONOLOGY	309
INDEX	315

DIAZ

CHAPTER I

INTRODUCTORY

José de la Cruz Porfirio Diaz, known to all the world as President Porfirio Diaz, was born in the city of Oaxaca, capital of the State of the same name, in the Republic of Mexico, on, or within a few days before, the 15th of September, 1830.[1] He was baptised on that day in the cathedral. No Spaniards nor Spanish-Americans of that time would willingly have incurred the least risk that their child should die unregenerated by the water of baptism. It is highly probable that the future President was born on the day on which he was baptised, or not more than three days earlier.

His father, José de la Cruz (Joseph of the Cross) Diaz, is said to have been a pure-blooded Spaniard, but in the former Spanish colonies everyone in whom a strain of Indian blood is not too marked to be overlooked ranks as white. When Porfirio had become

[1] The letter "x," which is now used by the Spaniards only in words of Greek or Latin origin adopted late in the history of their language, was formerly employed to represent the sound "sh," which does not exist in Castilian, but is common in the Indian tongues. The Indian pronunciation of the President's birthplace would be Oashaca, and of his country Meshico. But the Spaniards do not like the sound and have in practice replaced it by the guttural "j," which is a strong "h." They write Oajaca and Mejico. We keep the spelling we first knew and therefore mispronounce both ways.

the foremost man in Mexico, his flatterers discovered that José de la Cruz descended from one of the conquistadores. The President's enemies indeed were ready to affirm that he was the bastard of a priest. The first assertion is only an example of a world-wide folly, and the second may be dismissed as a specimen of Spanish-American political polemic. In an account of his " Parents, Childhood and Youth," published with his consent and aid by Genaro Garcia in 1906, the President's father is stated to have been a poor and illiterate man who worked as the " dependiente " of a firm of traders. The word would be applied to a porter or workman of that level. He ranked, in fact, a little above the class of the " peones " or agricultural labourers, who in colonial times were, and in practice still are, serfs in Mexico. He was at least personally free. In 1808 he married Patrona Mori, the daughter of Mariano Mori, an immigrant, or son of an immigrant, from Asturias in Old Spain, and of his wife Tecla Cortes, a pure-blooded Mixteca Indian. The marriage was performed at the village of San Sebastian Etla in Oaxaca. After working for some years in the Sierra de Ixtlán, José took his half-Indian wife to Xochistlahuaca in the province of Tlaxcala and the bishopric of Puebla de los Angeles. Here he became a squatter or homesteader on a piece of virgin soil. In one respect at least José resembled his son. He was a hard worker. Though he had no capital, and could neither buy machinery nor hire much help, he contrived to plant his little holding with sugar-cane, and he added a small store to his cane-growing. After a few years he had something saved and something to sell. With the proceeds of his hard work he returned to his native province Oaxaca, bought a little piece of ground which he planted with " maguey," the aloe from which the native liquor pulque is tapped. To provide an outlet for the produce of his " magueyera " he opened a wayside inn, a " mesón," at the town of Oaxaca, and further undertook to act as farrier and veterinary surgeon. José de la Cruz, who is also said to have been at some time farrier in a cavalry regiment, was plainly a handy man.

Porfirio, who does not appear ever to have used his father's " font name " (*nombre de pila*), was the sixth child and eldest surviving son of these worthy people. Another son, Felix, who in later years shared his fortunes, was born after him. But in 1833 the father died. No man not a politician or capitalist and usurer had much chance of making money in Mexico in that age of anarchy. The death of the laborious father plunged his family into years of hard struggle with sheer hunger. Patrona Mori made an effort to keep the " mesón " going, but had to give it up. If it were not that the Mexican needs little and that the widow had inherited some small handful of money from her husband, it would be hard to see how they survived. By untold miracles of thrift and work, aided by the kindly heat of the sun, which makes fires rarely necessary and warm clothes a superfluity in Oaxaca, Patrona kept her own head and the young heads dependent on her above water. She had relatives among the beneficed clergy, then the wealthiest class in Mexico, but they do not appear to have given her much help, if any.

By one means or another, at the cost of sacrifices more or less cruel, Porfirio was able to get some primary education. He was placed with a carpenter whose trade he picked up while attending school, probably not for long hours nor with exact regularity. At the age of fifteen he was placed in the local seminary (Seminario Pontificial). The mother, besides wishing, as was natural, to see her son " wag his pow in a pulpit," knew that it was far easier to provide for ten men in the Church than for one out of it. The licentiate Dominguez, his godfather, who was then a canon of Oaxaca, and who later on was the bishop, appears to have given Porfirio some aid. But the lad, who was somewhat restive in the seminary, had to eke out his allowance by doing odd jobs of carpentry. During the years of studies in the seminary he had an interval of military drill. 1846 and 1847 were the years of the war with the United States, and Oaxaca raised a militia battalion. It was known by the not very martial name of the " Peor es Nada," which may be translated as " nothing would be still worse." It consisted wholly of boys. At this time Porfirio had the advantage of attending a course of lectures on " tactics " and " strategy " given at the local Institute of Science and Art by Lieutenant-Colonel Ignacio Uria. In the hope of seeing more service than was offered to this corps he tramped to Mexico, but too late to share in the war. On the whole he showed himself a lad of spirit and resource, as when he provided himself with a fowling-piece by buying a rusty gun barrel from a rag and bone shop, fitting to it the flint and steel of a broken horse pistol, and mounting it on a butt of his own construction. The historian does not record whether he ever fired his patchwork weapon, or if so, what happened. As Porfirio survived to use more scientific weapons, it is probable that he never put his handiwork to a hard test. He drilled his fellow-schoolboys, as other

INTRODUCTORY

warriors are said to have done, maintained discipline by rough and ready methods, and used his command so as to render himself a serious pest. Imprisonment for a month in the seminary cell was the reward of one of his achievements. In short, he was as absolute a nuisance as only a healthy boy ought to be.

In 1849 he had finished his course at the seminary. What he had learnt was no doubt a trifle, but he had decided that he was not of the wood of which priests are made even in Mexico. To the great wrath of his godfather, the Canon Dominguez, he refused to take orders. His mother wept and argued in vain. Porfirio had his way, and the last ten Mexican dollars of his father's poor hoard were spent in buying law-books for him. He had decided to take to the law. The intention was so far put into execution that he attended the lectures of his future chief in war and politics during many years, the Zapoteca Indian Benito Juarez, then professor at the Institute of Oaxaca. He even passed his first examination in Civil and Canon Law in 1853. But in that year events occurred which decided that the future of Porfirio Diaz was to be spent in winning fame, power, and wealth in the saddle and by the sword. If the story is not to be a meaningless series of unintelligible incidents, we must first understand what was the condition, social and political, of Mexico when his career began, and this we shall never be able to do if we do not go back to the antecedents of the Republic, not of course for the purpose of giving a history of the colonial period, but in order to comprehend what were the inherited beliefs and tendencies which inevitably conditioned the minds and acts of the republicans.

Englishmen and Americans have often been less

than just because they have expected what was not to be hoped for from the Spanish-speaking peoples of the New World. They have generally begun by assuming that if the Mexicans have not behaved as they themselves would have done, the explanation of the difference is to be sought in the mere vice or folly of individuals. Vice and folly have abounded in Spanish America, but when we are judging the conduct of persons, fair criticism requires that we should allow for what they have inherited in thought and habit from the three centuries during which they were colonies of Spain.

A Spanish colony was everything which an English colony was not.

The men who founded the English colonies in America differed in origin and character. But there were certain points, and those of the most vital order, on which they were similar. They came from a country which had for centuries been a true commonwealth, a united nation. They had been accustomed if not to actual participation in the work of self-government, at least to the sight of it. They were equally accustomed to the thought that they had a share first in the making, and then in the administration of the law. And then they came under a certain influence of a religious character. Their doctrines, their dogmas, their ideas and preferences in Church government were not the things which mattered. Beliefs and theories might die, or undergo inward changes in spirit, without affecting the radical unlikeness which divided the English from the Spanish colonist. If we except the few Roman Catholics who found a refuge in Maryland, the English colonies, north, middle, and southern, were settled by men who, whether they came from England or from Scotland, or were Palatines or French Huguenots, had all alike crossed the line between the Holy Roman Catholic and Apostolic Church and the Protestant world. For them the Reformation in all its manifestations had swept away the rising circles of teachers, rulers, intercessors—the Heavenly Host and the earthly hierarchy—which hung over the mediæval man and spread between him and God. Salvation to them was not to be won by acceptance of an ancient divinely inspired authority, by obedience to its orders, and humble reliance on its wisdom, but by each of them by their own faith and conduct and the will of God acting directly on them. That the types of character produced and fostered by this revolt against authority in the infinitely important sphere of religion were often unamiable and sometimes eccentric to absurdity, are propositions nobody need take the trouble to deny. *Es irrt der Mensch so lang er strebt*. The essential truth is that Protestantism tended to foster the capacity to think and act for yourself on all sides of life. The men and women who would not throw the task of saving their souls on an inspired priesthood, who read a book and drew their own deductions, would not be the passive flock of a mundane authority in the business of government.

These colonists, predisposed as they were to develop and act freely, came to an open field. The thinly scattered tribes of Indian warriors and hunters whom they found in front of them could neither assimilate with them nor resist them effectually. Therefore they could exercise no influence on the European intruders on their forests and their hunting grounds. A further and a most vital difference was that the

English colonists came with their wives and children to form communities, and to till the soil.

When we turn to the Spanish colonies we meet at once with the exact opposite of every one of these conditions, moral or material. Spain was not a commonwealth, a nation. It is only becoming one in our own time. In the age of the conquest it was a collection of kingdoms, countships, and lordships which were held together because the same prince was the sovereign of each of them. And these various parts were socially divided into classes of nobles and non-nobles, town and country, Old Christians and New Christians, who came from converted (for the most part forcibly converted) Jews and Moors. The old Christians were clean in blood, and the new were unclean—stained by admixture of Jew or Moor.

The reader, who may have heard of the power of the mediæval Spanish cortes, the vigorous municipalities and provincial institutions of old Spain, may be surprised to hear that the people had no practice in self-government. But it is true. Whatever may have been the case in the earlier Middle Ages (and a good deal in the way of restriction would have to be said on that point), the confusions of the later fourteenth and the whole fifteenth century till the accession of the Catholic sovereigns had disintegrated cortes and municipalities alike. The Spaniards had been saved from mere anarchy by the royal authority alone. The town councils were little more than ornaments, self-electing, or confined to a few families. All effective power was in the hands of royal officers. As for the law, it was an art and mystery confined to the lawyers, who were the most useful agents of the King. There was no jury in Spain.

INTRODUCTORY

When we turn to the Church as it had developed in Spain, we see an art and mystery belonging to the clergy. The laymen, with the exception of a few who were effectually weeded out by the Inquisition, left the doctrines and the dogmas to the clergy. For themselves, they were taught to believe explicitly in the Church and implicitly in all the Church held to be true. What the King wills is the law. What the Church propounds is the truth. These were the two fundamental principles of Spanish government. When a Mexican viceroy told his subjects that their duty was not to think but to obey, he was stating the accepted orthodox rule. Religion for the Spaniard was in the main the performance of certain acts and ceremonies, the participation in certain material means of salvation which the priest alone could provide. To suppose that this double yoke was imposed by force on a reluctant people would be to misunderstand Spanish history altogether. The royal authority was accepted because it was their one protection against anarchy. The Church was obeyed because it alone by its wonder-working sacraments and its absolutions could save them from hell fire. Orthodoxy was the honourable distinction of the old Spaniard of clean blood. Heterodoxy was the brand of the inferior race, the unclean class. No submission to the Church was other than honourable. To dare to think for yourself was dangerous and shameful.

Now if a people with these ideas and rules of conduct had come to " the Indies," as the Spaniards always called their possessions in America, bringing their wives and children for the purpose of tilling the land, they would not have brought with them the elements of a self-governing polity. But they came as soldiers, as adventurers in search of fortunes to be made rapidly by the sword, and to be taken back to be enjoyed in Spain. With few exceptions the first comers laid their bones in the New World after begetting a larger or a smaller number of children by their female Indian captives. The Government was so far from encouraging real settlement that it put obstacles in the way of the colonist after the first work of the conquest. It feared the formation at a distance of strong communities, because they might be tempted to consult their own interests rather than those of the home Government. The very merchant who wished to go in order to look after his affairs had to obtain a permit, which was given him for a time, and only on the production of a written certificate from his wife that she consented to his absence. He was not to be allowed to take her lest he should be tempted to remain. The aim of the State was to found a dominion wherein officials and soldiers should direct the labour of a native population so as to produce a great revenue for the Crown. That Spaniards continued to go is true. Sometimes the King was tempted to allow emigration to develop some mining industry and augment the royal share of the bullion. Sometimes he was weak. At all times his officials were corrupt and could be bribed. Men who shipped as sailors or soldiers in the galleons deserted and escaped up country, where they knew they were sure of good pay.

There were differences between the colonies, though they were not great. As our business is with Mexico, it will be enough to speak of " The Kingdom of New Spain," to give the proper official title. When it was finally settled it extended from Central America in the south to a vague frontier on the north, from Upper

California across to Florida. Five distinct elements of population were scattered over this vast territory—the Creoles, the Mestizos, the Mulattos, the Zambahigos, and the native Indians.

By the Creoles are to be understood the descendants of Spaniards who had, or were by general consent considered as having, no mixture of Indian or negro blood. "*Criar*" in Spanish is "to breed," and, properly speaking, whatever the Spaniard brought to the Indies and cultivated there—his own race, his horse, his ass, his cattle, pigs, poultry, and plants—was *criollo*. The combination of Spaniard and Indian was *mestizo* (mixed). When the diminution of Indian labour and the desire of the home Government to spare the native population led to the introduction of negro slaves, there came the mixture of Spaniard and black, who is the *mulato*. The *zambahigo* was the half-bred Indian and black. Mulattos and Zambahigos (from which comes our Sambo) were less important in Mexico than in some other Spanish colonies. Finally there were the native Indians of over a hundred tribes speaking dialects of sixteen languages. For long they formed the bulk of the population.

The Spaniard did not find a free field when he came to Mexico. The native civilisations of America were no doubt, as Gibbon says, "strangely magnified" by the conquistadores who first saw them. Still the Mexican Indians cultivated the land, built towns, and had a social order not very inferior, if it was at all inferior, to that of the Spaniards themselves. Mere hunters and savages, "Indianos bravos," were met only in the far north and south. In the central mass of the kingdom of New Spain the natives were "Mansos" (tame) or "Pueblo" (village) Indians.

They diminished before the Spaniard, but they did not perish utterly, and after a time they began again to increase. They were in various degrees capable of some civilisation, and not all were at any time enemies to the Spaniard. On one point the histories of the Spanish conquest of Mexico and the British conquest of India touch one another: Cortes won by combining under his banner many tribes which were in revolt against the tyranny of the Aztecs, just as the East India Company always found native allies and willing subjects. The army which took the Aztec Tenochtitlan, the city of Mexico, consisted mainly of Indians. Friendly relations and a certain interpenetration of the races, not only in blood, but in character, were possible as between Spaniard and Indian. Some of the native races maintained a measure of national existence. This was particularly the case with the Zapotecas of Oaxaca, to whom Benito Juarez belonged entirely, and the Mixtecas, from whom Diaz descended through his mother. It should be noted, too, that a mixture of Indian blood is held to fortify in Spanish America and in modern times carries no stigma. The mixture of negro blood was always a discredit, for it was considered less natural.

So far we have considered only those parts of the population which belonged by birth to Mexico. But there was another, and one of commanding importance by its direct action and by the consequences of its work. This was the " Peninsular " or Spaniard from Old Spain, who came generation after generation, partly to recruit but mainly to govern—as civil officials, as soldiers, and as Churchmen. In the eighteenth century, when the Bourbon dynasty had modified the policy of its predecessors, they came freely

INTRODUCTORY

as traders. Then they commonly married in the country, and their children recruited the Creole or the Mestizo elements. But it is as a governor, an official, or a priest that the Peninsular best deserves notice.

The mere framework of Spanish colonial government need not be described at large. There was a viceroy, commonly a great noble, who was preferred because his rank, his family connections, and his estates at home were guarantees that he would not try to make himself king. Beside him, rather than below him, was the *audiencia* (the " hearing "), composed of lawyers, the *oidores* (or " hearers "). It was the viceroy's privy council, and it was a law court from which there was an appeal to the Supreme Council of the Indies at Seville. When it sat as privy council the viceroy presided. When it sat as a law court its president was its chief. When the viceroy's term of office was over, the audiencia had a right to inspect and pass his accounts. It could make a report on his conduct while in office. The audiencia was in fact a check on the viceroy, and if he died in office it administered until his successor came. Under these two was an organisation of officials who need not be named. They were necessary subordinates and could easily be paralleled from British India, or any Crown colony. The Church was fully organised with archbishop, bishops, lesser clergy, monastic orders, and Jesuits. No more need be said of it now except that, by grants from the popes, the regalities of the Crown were great in Mexico, and its control of the Church was complete. The King was " Lord High Constable of the Christian Army."

The machine was after all but a machine capable of being used for good or for evil. The spirit of the direction was the vital question. The first truth about it is that the Spanish colonial Government was the very faithful representative of the distrust felt for all the elements of the Mexican population by the rulers at home. It may be said to have been wholly composed of Peninsulares with a few exceptions. The natural love of the Spaniards for a place under Government was a strong influence no doubt, but the main reason why the Spanish Crown filled all offices by men it sent out was the abiding dread lest the colonists should render themselves independent. There was a real reason for this distrust. The Spanish Law of Trade, like our own Navigation Laws, aimed at restricting the whole trade of its colonies to the mother country. This was of course a grievance, and led (as the Navigation Laws did in New England) to wholesale smuggling. But there was another reason and a more potent one.

When the Government of the King in early days had to settle its hold on the Indies with few troops it made use of a very old device. It handed the Government of the Indians to *encomenderos*. The encomendero held his power as a trust *in commendam* for life, or for a term of years, or during pleasure. He was in fact a zemindar who controlled the Indians for the King, raised revenue, and took his dues. By a process with which Europe was once very familiar, the life or temporary office became an hereditary property. That the King was the only owner of the soil by grant from the Pope and by conquest was a maxim which figured in law-books. That he had the right to revoke the encomiendas singly, or altogether, no lawyer doubted. But the right was one thing, and the might was another. Whenever there was the merest suggestion of a revocation, a threat of rebellion was automatically

INTRODUCTORY

produced. The encomendero was so completely the master of his Indians that they would follow him in a revolt. He did not wish to rebel if he was let alone, but if he was to be deprived of his holding he would make a fight. The King of Spain was early as helpless in the presence of the opposition of the united encomenderos as any king of the eleventh century would have been if faced by a universal refusal of homage by the Crown vassals. When menaced by that peril the Spanish kings yielded. They made a struggle. Their Laws of the Indies have been praised for the provision they contained to protect the Indians from ill-usage. The intention was honourable, and every credit may be given to the good-will of the King. In Mexico the laws did produce some effect. They helped to save some Indian communities from extinction by forced labour in the mines. They secured some measure of protection for Indian towns and endowed them with communal lands known as "*ejidos*," *i.e.*, exits. But no injustice is done to the King if we assume that he and his advisers were quite as anxious to clip the wings of the encomendero as to protect the Indians. Now, if the Indies were to be governed by the Creoles, the officers must, for lack of any other body from which to take them, be sought in that very class. Therefore all offices were filled from Spain. The encomenderos, predecessors, if not actual ancestors, of the "hacendados," the overgrown Mexican landlords of to-day, with their five million or even twenty million acres of land, were left in possession of their power over the rural Indians, and the Government was directed by officials from Spain.

Mexico was not without the germs of what might have been, or perhaps only looks on paper as what might have been, a political organisation. There were town councils (*cabildos*), and there were occasions in Spanish colonial history when delegates from a number of these councils were assembled in a convention or a cortes. But cabildos and cortes alike were the reflections of the worn-out institutions of the mother country. The town councils were self-electing. The outgoing members at the end of their year of office named their successors, who at the close of their term repaid the compliment. So a quiet rotation of office was kept up between a select number of privileged families. Such as they were, they would have provided the machinery of a vigorous colonial system of self-government if there had been any wish for one. But there was not. Segregation, isolation, a secretive life for family and town, have always been notes of the Spaniards. They have never shown a good capacity to combine for any political purpose—have always been inclined to personal, family, and local rivalries and distrusts. Their virtues are individual, not social, and every effort at combined action brings out their vices. Therefore they have been passive items in the hands of King and Church while the monarchy and the hierarchy were vigorous. When the life ebbed from these institutions there was nothing to take their place except the absolute necessity for some form of rule among gregarious men. Therefore a Spanish colony fell into anarchy qualified by the temporary predominance of some man with a stick. The tragedy of the whole race at home, as in the Indies, has been that many of the best and most honest among them could find nothing better to do than to fight contumaciously and pitilessly for the only kind of social and political principle they knew—

the King and the Faith—in other words, for the dead and the dying. Old Spain was at least directly influenced by the great living communities about her in Europe. In the isolation of the kingdom of New Spain there was nothing to counteract the faults of the race, and everything to exaggerate them.

Education could hardly be expected to exist in such conditions. There were universities in Mexico, but they were limited to droning over the scholastic philosophy in its dotage. A few exceptional men here and there might apply themselves to botany or some other scientific subject. But there was no training for the community, nor even for a class. It would have been no great evil that the mass of the population learnt nothing except to repeat their catechism and "Ave Maria" by rote, if those who were supposed to be schooled had had a substantial education. But except in the Jesuit schools, where the upper class was taught some Latin, there was nothing beyond an endless ringing of the changes on "Ens" and "Essentia," a perpetual rattle of disputation over unrealities, in phrases which the Inquisition had tested and found orthodox. The candidate for a licentiateship of laws had to read the text-books and codes, at least after a fashion. But his training was also one in mere disputation on points and in terms laid down for him. The debauching loquacity of the modern Spaniards and Spanish-Americans, the deadly readiness of all of them to pour out torrents of grammatical sentences which express no genuine conviction and mean nothing, and the predominance among them of the "attorney species" are the ruinous inheritance left by generations of a so-called education in mere gabble to the exclusion of thought and of the study of things.

Where in all this conglomeration of fragments were to be found the elements of a polity ? Only in the royal authority, which all by virtue of an inherited instinct revered even when they were provoked into resistance by a personal grievance. Outbreaks of disorder were not uncommon in Spanish America during the eighteenth century. A vague tendency to think that the land belonged to those born in it was to be noted from time to time—the forerunner of the revolt which began in 1810. But these outbreaks were not directed against the monarchical principle of the State. Men took up arms and rioted when a trade monopoly granted by the King became intolerable. In Mexico city there was one triumphant explosion when a reforming viceroy attempted to stop the sale of " pulque " in the interests of sobriety. But when the grievance was removed all went back to the old order. The nature of these transient outbreaks may be illustrated by an incident which occurred some thirty years ago in Spain. It was a year of drought, and the inhabitants of a village in Valencia were menaced not only by a total failure of their harvest, but by the drying up of the wells of drinking water. Their church possessed a crucifix of peculiar sanctity. It was taken out and carried through the fields by a procession with candles burning and singing of hymns. No rain came. At last on the third or fourth day of these pious exercises the villagers became overwrought. Being now worked into a " rabieta," a spasm of mad rage, they stood the crucifix upside down in the market place, they covered it with filth, they kicked it and threw stones at it, they abused it in the choicest terms of Spanish blasphemy, which is not mere cursing and swearing, but truly blasphemous. In the middle of this crazy scene down came the rain as it does in those parts, advancing in sheets and spouts and hurling the dust up before it. And then the people saw how useless the image was, and they were prepared to listen to a Protestant missionary ? Quite the contrary. The people of that village only concluded that the Lord had been moved to pity by the sight of the extremes to which their suffering had driven them and had at last sent the rain. They were more persuaded of the miraculous virtues of the image than they were before. So the discontented colonists who forced the King or his viceroy to give way remained as convinced as they ever had been of the royal goodness.

But now suppose that the belief in the sanctity of the royal authority—the medium which held together the individuals, classes, and races which made up the pudding-stone of a Spanish colony—began itself to disintegrate, what would, what must, follow ? The whole mass would have of course crumbled, and when the process had gone far enough the pebbles or flints once embedded in the worn-out medium would sink into a heap. And that is precisely what happened in Mexico. Various causes had been at work all through the eighteenth century to dissolve the bond. There was an increasing sense of grievance in the Creole and Mestizo classes. As they were recruited by immigrants from Old Spain and grew stronger, they began to resent the exclusive possession of office by the Peninsulares and the insolence of the official class. It was a common observation down to the day when Spain lost the last fragment of her colonial empire that the non-official immigrants soon came to sympathise with the Creoles, and that their children were Creoles out and out. The official Peninsulares were not only harsh administrators and generally corrupt, but they were socially insolent. In the seventeenth century they already avowed their doubts whether any of the elements of the native population were entitled to be considered as rational beings (*gente de razon*). The Creoles, they said, sucked in the Indian vices with the milk of their Indian nurses. The Mestizos were the offspring of vicious women—a bastard race. The Indians were children. Resentment of this official insolence began to extend timidly to the royal authority itself. Then Charles III. struck a terrible blow at the loyalty of the leading Creoles when he suppressed the Jesuits. The company in Mexico, as elsewhere, had aimed with great success at monopolising the education of the moneyed classes. The arbitrary cruelty of the treatment meted out to them shocked their old pupils. The mass of the population was not much affected, and the Jesuits had many enemies among the bishops and the other religious orders who helped to destroy them. The King had ample support at the time, but the sanctity of the whole Church suffered by this brutal crushing of a great order, and the King's authority was inseparable from that of the Church. Then came the example of the revolt of the English plantations and the help given to them by the King of Spain in alliance with France. Wealthy Mexicans who visited Europe and immigrants from Spain began to spread the ideas of the French *philosophes*. The Inquisition strove to exclude the writings of Rousseau, Voltaire, Raynal. The community was against it, and the " enlightened " officials whom Charles III. sent out were no friends to the Inquisition. The King honestly desired to remove the worst faults of his colonial administration. Something was done, and a real stimulus was given to the material prosperity of the colonists. But it is an old observation that resentment against evils always finds expression when the sufferers are beginning to enjoy relief. Charles, a man besotted by a conviction of the divinity and omnipotence of his office, was always sawing the branch between himself and the trunk of the tree. In order to improve his means of defending his colonies against British attack he permitted the formation of a Creole and Mestizo militia. Spanish army officers, who had as little right as they well could have to look down on any kind of troops, laughed at the " milicianos." But these bodies provided the framework of the " patriot " armies of the immediate future.

The French Revolution re-echoed in the New World and found discontent stirring below the surface. There was still no actual disloyalty to the Crown. " Viva el Rey y muera el mal gobierno " (" Long live the King and death to the bad government ") was the first watchword of the insurgents throughout Spanish America. In the King there was no help. The wretched exhibition of themselves given by Charles IV. and his family covered the once sacrosanct royalty with contempt. Spain was dragged along by France. War with England cut Mexico off from the peninsula. Unmistakable signs that the Spanish rule was nearing its end began to appear. One of the later viceroys, Iturrigaray, entered into a plot with the Creoles to establish a colonial self-government. The system of administration elaborated by Charles V. and Philip II.

was for the last time justified of its children. The audiencia suppressed the viceroy and sent him back to Spain, where he died in prison. When Napoleon endeavoured to seize Spain in 1808 Mexico remained loyal to Ferdinand VII. But it began to act for itself, and there was nothing to prevent its independence. Spain had no troops in the colony. The armed forces were composed wholly of native militia. The old colonial Government had become a skeleton held together by wire. When the French invaded Andalusia in 1810, and the conquest of Spain seemed to be inevitable, Mexico might very well have fallen away as did Buenos Ayres. It remained loyal for another ten years because the Creoles and Mestizos were suddenly threatened by a revolt of the Indians.

The explosion was directed, indeed, by a Creole who was acting in combination with other men of his own class—the priest Hidalgo. He had been much influenced by the philosophy and the "sensibility" of Rousseau. He had worked for his Indian flock and had great popularity among them. Some schemes which he framed for their good were brutally destroyed by the colonial Government. It was on that provocation that Hidalgo began to organise his conspiracy. The Government got wind of what was going on and made some arrests. Hidalgo, seeing that it was now or never, revolted at the head of his Indian followers not nominally against the King, but against the Administration. What was to have been a general colonial movement became a race conflict. Hidalgo himself went through the evolution familiar enough in the terrorist time in France. In the passion of the struggle and in rage against the injustice of his opponents he became convinced that the only way to

INTRODUCTORY

protect the oppressed was to slay the oppressors. His philanthropy turned bloodthirsty, and he led his Indian followers into a general massacre of Creoles and Mestizos. In the presence of this peril the menaced classes rallied to the audiencia and the royal Government. The Indian revolt was put down and Hidalgo executed. His enemies said that he died asking pardon of God and man for his sin in letting the mischief loose. It is equally likely that in the reaction of feeling probable in so emotional a man he made this confession of sin, or that his enemies invented it for him.

Whatever Hidalgo may have said or felt, it is only too true that his insurrection was the beginning of infinite misery for Mexico. He was succeeded as a patriot leader by another priest, the Mestizo Morelos. When he too was put down and executed, other chiefs were found to continue a partisan warfare in the mountains till 1820.

The legend of Mexican history is that this struggle was a fight for freedom against Spanish oppression. The sober truth is that the ten years from 1810 to 1820 were filled by the first Mexican Civil War. Spain could for long send no troops, and she never sent more than a few. Her resources were almost wholly devoted to attempts to hold or to reconquer South America. The combatants of the ten years' war were Mexican parties. If that statement is disputed, the proof of its truth can be conclusively given by a mere statement of the circumstances in which the independence of the country was finally declared.

In 1820 a Spanish army, which had been collected near Cadiz for transport to South America, revolted at the instigation of Liberal officers. The Constitution drawn up by the Cortes in 1812 during the Peninsular War and suppressed by Ferdinand VII. was restored. Now this instrument of government was odious to the clergy chiefly because the men who made it were known to aim at the secularisation of the Church land. So far the higher clergy in Mexico, who were generally Peninsulares, had been loyal, though a large proportion of the parish priests, who were often Mestizos, and the friars of native origin were patriots. But when they found themselves threatened by a Radical and " godless " Government in Spain the higher clergy also became patriots. In combination with the Creole military leaders, whose loyalty had worn away to nothing, they proclaimed the independence of Mexico. The Spanish Government fell without a blow. A few soldiers from Old Spain held the fortress at San Juan de Ulloa for a time simply because the Mexicans had no naval force, and the castle stands on an island opposite Vera Cruz. But the viceroy himself had to sign the document which announced the end of the Government he represented.

If the Creole landowners had possessed any of the qualities of an aristocracy they could have made themselves masters of Mexico in the years between 1810 and 1820. But they were a mere class of persons of fine manners who at their best were amiable and admirable in their family relations, while at their worst they were debauched and addicted to gambling to the verge of insanity. There was no institution in Mexico except the Church, and that also was divided and lacking in faculty for government. If a revolution is the substitution of one Government by another, then the declaration of independence did not accomplish a revolution in Mexico. It was simply a formal recognition of the already patent fact that the only principle of government known to the Mexicans of all shades was dead, and that nothing was left save the innate gregarious instincts of the human animal. On that foundation a new social and political order was to be built.

The thirty-five years which passed between the declaration of the independence of Mexico and the beginning of the career of Porfirio Diaz cannot be said to have seen even the first steps in the progress of the work. They were full of mere anarchy. Presidents rose and fell at the rate of about one a year. It could not well have been otherwise. No Mexican was any longer aware of a reason why he should obey what was supposed to be the Government for one moment longer than he saw occasion, or than he was restrained by lack of means, or by terror of instant death, from setting out to become himself a Government. After the ten years of war, between 1810 and 1820, the land was full of armed factions. They had a free field in a thinly-inhabited country full of mountains which invited the guerrillero and the bandit. Even if a history of a chronic state of disorder were possible, this is not the place to make the attempt.[1] But, when we look steadily across the confusion, certain tendencies, if not exactly political principles, are seen to have been implied in the conflicts of contending factions.

The words " Federalist " and " Centralist " which figure largely in the controversies of those times did

[1] The reader who wishes to become better acquainted with the barren contentions of little self-seeking men may be referred to Vols. VIII. and IX. of " The History of the Pacific States," by Mr. Hubert H. Bancroft.

really stand for something. The framers of the first Mexican Constitution made a slavish imitation of the Constitution of the United States. They were the Federalists. From the beginning there were Mexicans who foresaw that this form of government would not suit their country, if only for the sufficient reason that there were in Mexico no " States." Its provinces were not political entities, each with its own history, character, and training in self-government, as were the thirteen British colonies which combined to form the Union. These critics maintained that the only government the Mexicans understood was one by a strong central authority. What they really wanted was a continuation of the Spanish viceroyalty and audiencia, but composed of Mexicans working in the interests of Mexico. Here was a genuine political issue very fit to be settled by political methods and argument. The career of President Diaz goes to show that these dissenters, who were known as Centralistas, were right. If Mexico could have produced Jays, Jeffersons, and Hamiltons they would in all probability have written, not a " Federalista," but a " Centralista."

The issue was not debated politically, but was turned into a downright scuffle of kites and crows. It is substantially accurate to say that whoever was at the head of affairs for the time being (having put himself there by armed revolt) tended to be " Centralista " because the name went easily with the widest possible exercise of authority. The Spaniard is naturally " *mandon*." We may translate the word by " Jack in office," but only with partial truth. The " mandon " is not only a conceited creature who makes the most of his office. He is always a potential tyrant to whom no words come so easily as " Aqui mando yo " (" I command here "), and who enforces obedience by the most brutal or even bloodthirsty methods. Every " mandon " is persuaded that the whole abstract authority of the State resides in his person, and that not only all opposition, but all independence of judgment, is rebellion to be punished by death. The history of Mexico is full of bloodthirsty " Jacks in office." But a perfect readiness to suppress and to kill is not enough to make a strong Government. It is quite capable of promoting sheer anarchy by provoking, or absolutely terrifying, men into armed resistance for their safety's sake. Mexico offered a fine field for insurrection. The natural answer to the Centralist " mandon " was the provincial Federalist, who raised the standard of revolt, of course in the name of Freedom. When beaten he fled into exile if he escaped being shot. When he was victorious he tended to become Centralist and " mandon."

In so far as real political parties existed the Centralists may be said to have consisted of the landowners of Spanish descent and the Church, which was naturally on the side of authority. Now there were certain conditions which did tend to solidify the Mexican hurly-burly into a fight over material things. The old Spanish rule, working by class and private laws to divide that it might govern, had established its Fuero (forum) Militar, and its Fuero Eclesiástico (the military and the Church franchises). The reader must remember that in its original sense the word " militar " had nothing to do with the professional soldier, the member of a standing army. The Brazo Militar of the mediæval Spanish Cortes—the Military arm—was composed of the nobles. In Mexico the landowners had been assimilated to the Brazo Militar of Spain. They were justiciable only in their own " forum." But so great is the power of a name that the army, because it is " militar " in quite another sense, had been allowed to share the franchise of the nobles of the Middle Ages. We are sufficiently familiar with the rights and immunities of the Church in our own history to make it superfluous to explain what was meant by the Fuero Eclesiástico. Mexican Churchmen claimed all that the Churchmen who resisted our Henry II. had called their rights, and they actually possessed their privileges. The separation from Spain had even increased their power, for it took the authority of the King, which in Spanish America was great, from off their necks. Army officers and priests could not even be sued for debt except in their own courts.[1]

Army and Church were always more or less " Centralista." Therefore it became a great object with the Federalists to abolish their franchises. As the Church was immensely rich, owning, it was calculated, a third of all the wealth of Mexico, hostility to its legal privileges inevitably went hand in hand with a longing to secularise its property. The conflict had risen to its acute stage when Diaz entered public life as a follower of Benito Juarez.

[1] The British reader may be surprised to be told, what is none the less the fact, that these class franchises survive in Spain itself. An army officer can be sued for debt only before a military court. A very few years ago a retired army officer who had committed a murder in very horrible circumstances was tried by a military court which sentenced him to death.

CHAPTER II

THE BEGINNING OF A CAREER

WHILE the day on which he could begin his active career was approaching Diaz continued to work at the law, taking pupils to support himself and his mother. In the meantime he had before him a proof that men could rise to power by the pen and word as well as by the sword in Mexico, though the country was given up to military violence. There also the story of Bertrand and Raton has been known in public life. The craft of the "attorney species" has not seldom made a tool of the mere fighter. In after years and when he was President he was always ready to confess that his first "patron" was Don Marcos Pérez, a pure-blooded Indian, a judge and a professor of law at the Institute of Oaxaca. By the friendly offices of Pérez he became well known to the leader whom he was destined to succeed as ruler of Mexico, the Zapoteca Indian, Benito Juarez, who had risen wholly by the way of the law. Juarez had been, and when Diaz first knew him was, governor of the State. It must be borne in mind that the foundation of the power of a party leader in Mexico has commonly been a local influence. He becomes what is known in the slang of Spanish politics as a "cacique." He practises "caciquismo," and on that fulcrum he works his lever. The cacique and his caciquismo are not of necessity evils. Given a sound moral atmosphere and good political instincts, and there can be no better taking-off place for a public career than the support of a man's neighbours in his native place or his chosen home. Mr. Chamberlain might quite fairly have been said to have been cacique in Birmingham, Pym and Hampden were caciques before him, and when Cromwell was called King of the Fens nothing else was meant. But when the moral atmosphere is bad and the politics are faction the case is altered. A local leader rises by intrigue, corruption, or violence. Specimens of both kinds abounded in Mexico. Many of the chiefs who figured in the ever-recurring crises of the chronic anarchy were no better than brigands who levied blackmail in money or votes at the head of their following of " plateados," so called because their clothes and the harness of their horses were adorned with silver (*plata*). A plateado was a Claude Duval highwayman, or gentleman brigand, as distinguished from a low footpad. Intriguer and blackmailer might unite in the same person.

Juarez is allowed to have gained his power by exceptionally fair methods. The fact that he despoiled the Church has perhaps created a prejudice in his favour in certain quarters. But it is generally allowed that he had been an honest lawyer, that his political course was consistent, and that, unlike the majority of his contemporaries, he, though not indifferent to his interests, did not accumulate a fortune in office. His Indian blood no doubt helped him, but it was a legitimate advantage. The Zapotecas of Oaxaca had not been degraded to the miserable level of serfdom as the native tribes of Central Mexico were. They were hillmen, robust and courageous— often yeomen landowners working for themselves. Fr ench officers who campaigned among them during

THE BEGINNING OF A CAREER 31

the " intervention " found them less servile than other Indians, and saw in them a better appreciation of law and order and common honesty. We are entitled to believe that if they trusted Juarez they did so for creditable reasons and that their preference was to his honour.

In the company of these Indians Porfirio found himself happier than under the control of the clerical authorities of the seminary. He records in his diary that " My intellect first expanded under the heat of Liberal principles, and I developed and improved in philosophical studies."

In 1854 Diaz could not enjoy the advantage of direct personal guidance from Juarez. The Governor of Oaxaca had been driven into exile in the United States by the " mandon " who was then at the head of the Government, so called, of Mexico. This was the once notorious and, if he had not been so greedy and so capable of brutality, the amusing Antonio Lopez de Santa Ana. This personage was the perfection of his type. He had the dignified personal appearance, the grave gesture, the innate faculty for bearing himself with an air of good manners, which in the men of Spanish race (he was a Creole) often cover the most complete intellectual and moral nullity. There was nothing in his handsome head save the kind of cleverness which can be wholly disassociated from judgment. In his character there were vanity, greed, and an element of animal courage which increased his powers for mischief. In 1853, when Mexico was smarting from the disasters of the war with the United States and was sick of incapable anarchists, he had been invited to make himself Dictator in the wild hope that he would give the tortured country its long-desired good government. He had never shown the least proof of ability to satisfy that wish, but the others had been every whit as bad, and none of them had lost a leg in fight against a foreign enemy. Now Santa Ana had, and on the strength of that superiority he had been accepted as Dictator with the quality of "Highness." In some villages he was even proclaimed as the Emperor Antonio I. A hankering after monarchy had never died out in Mexico among those who were more concerned to enjoy the protection of a strong Government than to upset whatever Government there was for their own advantage. Once in the saddle he applied the only methods of administration he understood—suppressions and military executions. He quarrelled with some of those who helped him to rise, accusing them, truly enough no doubt, of corruption, and driving all opponents out of the country as far as he could. The familiar reaction followed. A Centralist was hectoring in the capital. The Federalists took up arms in the outlying provinces. The first blow which Diaz struck in a civil war was given in opposition to Santa Ana.

In 1854 his Highness the Dictator was busy putting all dissentients within his reach under lock and key. The friends of the exiled Juarez were the natural victims of these measures of precaution. No one of them was more distinctly marked out for arrest than Don Marcos Pérez, and he was accordingly confined in a tower of the convent of San Domingo. The Dictator's vigilance was not unreasonable, for already the Liberal opponents of his rule were in arms in the Mixteca hill country to the west of the city of Oaxaca under the command of one Herrera. The mass of townsmen in Mexico habitually behave as our own ancestors did in the Wars of the Roses. They recognise the armed man who is in possession for the time being, reserving their right to go over to the other side if only it can make a successful forcible entry. Political partisans who are temporarily reduced to silence by hostile force within the city plot to introduce their own friends from the outside. At such times those who, like Don Marcos Pérez, are " caracterizados "—that is to say, marked men—must expect to be subjected to precautionary arrest. At such times, too, young and active men like Porfirio Diaz earn the good-will of the side they elect to fight for by adventuring to keep up communications between the plotter within and the warrior without the walls. The future President began his career by a feat which would be quite in place in the biography of Chicot. We have the story told in the future President's own words.[1]

He tells how when Don Marcos was arrested the " fiscal " (*i.e.*, public prosecutor), Pascual Leon, was instructed to prepare the indictment. Now it happened that Señor Leon owed money to Diaz and was tardy in his payments. The creditor had therefore a good right to drop in at the fiscal's office, avowedly in pursuit of the debt, but with other aims, as he plainly says. Don Pascual avoided the unwelcome visit, and Diaz was left alone for a space. All is fair in love and politics. The fiscal in the hurry of his retreat had

[1] I quote from the official biography written by Dr. Fortunato Hernandez. " Un Pueblo, un Siglo y un Hombre " (" A Man, a Century and a People ") (Mexico, 1909). This is an official book published in reply to " Porfirio Diaz, la Evolucion de su Vida " (" the Evolution of this Life ") (New York, 1908), by Don Rafael de Zayas Enriquez, a decidedly candid friend. Dr. Hernandez says that he takes this and many other passages from the "unpublished work " printed by Don Matias Romero " in the same simple, concise and veracious form in which General Diaz dictated it to the shorthand writer."

left his papers lying on his desk. Porfirio's legal education qualified him to select those which were best worth looking at. In a very few minutes he had made a number of notes likely to be useful to Don Marcos. The question was how to convey them to him.

The prisoner was confined in the monastery of San Domingo. His cell was in the lock-up of the building wherein delinquent friars were shut up. This house of correction, known as the turret (*torrecilla*), projected from the main building into the yard of the sacristy. It was lower than the body of the monastery. The walls were thick. The cell, three metres long by two wide, had a door with a wicket in it through which a prisoner could be watched, and a window high up on one side, barred heavily in the middle of the thickness of the wall. The cell was in the top storey of the torrecilla, and below was a door opening on the courtyard. Sentries were posted inside both at the door of the cell and at that which gave on to the yard. The monastery was occupied by a detachment of Santa Ana's partisans. There was only one way of communicating with Don Marcos, and that was by dropping on to the *azotea* (the flat roof of the turret) and then lowering oneself to the level of the window. The sill was broad, and whoever could reach it could find a footing on it and steady himself by holding the bars. There was a shutter on the inside of the window, but it had an opening at the top. In order to get at the azotea of the turret it was first necessary to reach the roof of the monastery. To come at the higher roof it was necessary to climb the outer wall of the garden and then climb over certain lower outbuildings. This was the adventure reserved for Porfirio.

THE BEGINNING OF A CAREER 35

He might have been unable to achieve it single-handed, but he had the best and most trustworthy of comrades in his brother Felix, now and at all times till death divided them. Felix, commonly known by his nickname " El Chato " (*i.e.*, " Flatnose "), had always been the comrade of Porfirio in every escapade or hunting excursion in the Sierra. They were both athletes and cragsmen. The feat presented no more difficulties than were sufficient to stimulate them. With a well-tested lasso, hemp sandals on foot, or barefoot, they could surely reach the highest roof, and once there the rest was plain sailing, on a conveniently dark night.

The time was chosen, and under cover of darkness the brothers reached the four-metre-high garden wall. One standing and the other climbing on his shoulders, the thatched covering (or *barda*) of the wall (it was, one gathers, built of adobe, mere sun-dried brick) was soon reached. Whichever got up first held a rope for the other. Felix dropped down to scout for a possible sentry in the garden. None were stationed outside the building, a fact which does no credit to the officer in command. Then the way to the roof of the monastery bakery along the barda was flat and safe. The bakers were at work and were singing to lighten toil. " Quien canta sus males espanta," which may be rendered by " He who trills scares away his ills," is a sound old Spanish proverb. The noise they were making drowned all others for the bakers. The brothers passed unheard from the roof of the bakery to the roof of the kitchen (then empty), thence to the roof of the quarters occupied by the provincial, the superior of the house. From a small kitchen standing there it was but one pull up more to the monastery roof. The climb was no obstacle to men accustomed to use the lasso. The noose was deftly tossed over some solid projection. One held the rope while the other swarmed up. Whoever was up first put his back into it to pull up the other. The President uses the very idiom. " Haciendo cuadril," he says. Now the " cuadril " is the haunch bone of an animal. *Hacer cuadril* is to plant the heels firm and pull with weight and muscle, in the language of the muleteers. The mule can show them how to do it when in one of his frequent fits of obstinacy.

Sentries were stationed on the roof, but they proved no obstacle. Porfirio and his brother learnt of their existence, not by seeing them, but by the sound of their voices as they called one another up, " Centinela, alerta " (" Watchman, watch "). But if the repetition of the call keeps the men awake at their posts it tells a listener where they are and where he must go to avoid them. No sentry was posted on the roof of the turret. Those who were on the roof of the main building were probably squatting in corners out of the wind wrapped in blankets. For that or for some other reason they kept so little watch that the brothers could untie a long rope fastened to the clapper of the convent bell and tie it to a battlement. This was to provide themselves with an alternative line of escape if the alarm were given below and their retreat by the garden side were cut off.

They dropped quietly on to the solid roof of the turret, and while El Chato watched above, Porfirio was lowered by the lariat they brought with them to the level of the cell window. A Latin phrase whispered through the airhole in the shutter told Don Marcos that a friend was at hand. Standing on the window cill and gripping the bars, Porfirio gave his news to the prisoner and heard his answers. The President does not report the matter of their talk, but it is to be presumed that it had reference to more than the law papers of Don Pascual. Messages were sent to friends outside. Then the adventurers returned as they came after replacing the bell rope. And the feat was repeated for three nights. How they contrived to free the lasso when they had lowered themselves by it on their return is a question which the reader may ask, but it is one for which there is no answer. The services of a friend inside would account for all, but none is mentioned. One thing is certain, and it is that no man who rose to be ruler of a State in the nineteenth century, outside of the adventurous world of Spanish America, could boast of such a feat.

Though the matter of these conversations is not reported, we may be tolerably sure that it had reference to a plot for handing over Oaxaca to the opponents of Santa Ana, who in January, 1854, had drawn up the Plan of Ayutla, so called from the place where it was proclaimed. It was one of a long series framed to secure the future good government of Mexico. The Dictator, though he was beginning to be hard pressed from all sides, held his ground as yet. In December of that year, being perhaps inspired by the recent shining example of Napoleon III., Santa Ana called for a plebiscite in which the free and independent voters of Mexico might decide whether or no they preferred to be regenerated by him. On these occasions, or their like, the line taken by respectable people in Spanish and Portuguese America is one with the answer of the Oxford undergraduate who, when asked to sign the Thirty-nine Articles, replied cheerfully, " Oh ! yes, or forty if you like." [1]

The President tells us that until the very day of the voting he was not sure whether he would " characterise " himself by voting openly against Santa Ana or be content with abstaining. The offhand remark of a friend that abstention was the course which would naturally be taken by those who were afraid stung his spirit. The friend—whose name, Francisco de Enciso, deserves to be recorded—must have part of the credit for the bold act which marked Diaz at least in the local world of Oaxaca as an intrepid partisan. In

---

[1] It happened to me some years ago to travel by sea from Santos in Brazil to Buenos Ayres with a very well bred and intelligent Argentine man of business. In answer to a question of mine concerning a political matter, he replied politely that he took no interest in it whatever. When a young man and in the illusions of credulous youth he had shared in a political movement, which of course entailed fighting. When it was over he reflected that he had been very young, very foolish to risk his life for the sake of a gang of intriguers who meant no good to anyone but themselves. Since then he had left politics alone. Another Argentine of the same stamp told me, smiling the same smile, and making the same indication of the shrug of the shoulders, a barely perceptible movement, that a shower of rain (he was a cattle breeder, an " estanciero," and the country was suffering from drought) was of infinitely greater importance than any Presidential election. The profound mistrust which Spanish-Americans of good social position and honourable personal character feel for all politics may have had a share in the reserve of both these gentlemen, though they trust us more than they do most men, for they rely on our honour (" la palabra Inglesa "), a confidence which for us is a great asset. Yet my acquaintances were really stating a point of view. The respectable Spanish-American acts very much like the Arab quoted by Mr. Kinglake. When his burnos becomes intolerably verminous he puts it on an ant-hill and the ants eat the pest. So in Spanish America, when the politicians in office go too far, the moneyed men who suffer too much provide this or the other military politician out of office with the means to make a " pronunciamiento." They finance a revolution. The Arab can shake the ants off when they have done their work, but it is not so easy to shake off the politicians. This attitude of the industrious non-political world of Spanish America must be borne in mind if we wish to understand how so much bad government has been tolerated ; why revolutions have been so common ; and also why, in spite of bad government and revolutions, these countries have grown in material prosperity and increased in population. The political strife is largely a game played by a class, and the working community goes on its way, leaving the chiefs and swordsmen to fight among themselves.

the heat of his resolution he came to the room where the book for recording the votes was lying open, and there with his own hand, and avowing his deed in a loud voice, gave his vote for General Alvarez, " the hero of Ayutla."

The next step was to hurry from the room and the town. Indeed, he received a warning note from another friend, one Maldonado, telling him that the authorities were already talking of his arrest. A third friend, a member of the dominant faction, warned him verbally in the streets to be off. The wine, in fact, was now drawn and must be drunk. Nor was Porfirio anywise unwilling to do what was needful. An open display of preparations for flight would perhaps have hurried his arrest. He had to get on horseback without letting the enemy see what he was preparing to do. No great fortune is required to keep a saddle horse in Mexico, and he had one. Wearing a deceptive air of indifference, he led his horse unsaddled to the water outside the town. A friend hid saddle and bridle in a buck-basket and sent them down to the water covered by clothes as for the wash. Then Porfirio saddled and rode off to join the Indian Herrera, who with a small and ill-armed band of Indians was already in arms for the cause in the neighbouring hills. It was not unlike an incident in a story by Mayne Reid, but then the Captain wrote about Mexico and knew it well. And now Diaz was fairly launched on the career which was to make him master of the Republic and earn him the respect and confidence of the statesmen of Europe and America.

The first weeks of his new life were more arduous than successful. Santa Ana's party was strong enough to break up Herrera's band. Diaz had to take to hiding, but the tide was going against the Dictator, and the partisans of the plan of Ayutla were able to get possession of the city of Oaxaca. A redistribution of offices naturally ensued, and Diaz was named sub-prefect of the district of Ixtlan. It was a small post given as a beginning, and was to all appearances not a promising one. The Indians of Ixtlan were considered to be of a very unmartial character, so much so that they were exempted from military levies as being of no use.

Every Mexican armed force consists of two elements—the directing body of fighting politicians, or mere brigands, and the rank and file of Indians. The latter are simply pressed. Every political party has at one time or another promised to give up the *leva* (*i.e.*, levy) of Indians and replace it by a fair conscription. No party has ever kept the promise. The Indians are too broken, too cowed, too torpid, and too divided to resist. They submit, and their women come with them to forage, cook, carry burdens, and provide the only army service corps which Mexican armies have possessed. A Mexican army is in fact a temporary artificial tribe which camps or marches with its swarm of women and children. So long as they are paid and fed, these Indians obey and show a good deal of passive courage. When not paid or fed they desert. They pass over in masses from the losing to the winning chief. A Mexican victory usually meant the incorporation of the mass of the beaten side in the ranks of the victorious army. The directing element of the beaten side, the officers, were shot wholesale after the battle. With such soldiers actions tended to be fought at very long ranges, and the result was reached through desertion, and not by blows.

The Mexican of all shades can fight fiercely in certain circumstances, or when his passions are aroused. But he fights best behind stone walls, or in trenches, where his Indian passivity enables him to endure much hammering without a sense of excessive strain on the nerves. As for passion: what passion can a pressed Indian feel for contending political generals and political terms which are to him meaningless? He suffers patiently when he cannot desert, and will meet death in the shape of a military execution with an air of complete indifference. M. de Kératry, who served in the French " contra-guerrillas " during the Maximilian adventure, writes as if he had been shocked by what seemed to him the brutal callousness of the Mexican guerrilleros of Indian blood whom he saw shot in large numbers by order of the redoubtable Colonel du Pin.

It will be seen that to be appointed sub-prefect of a district where the Indians—the Indiada in Mexican phrase—are of such notoriously poor quality that nobody had a wish for their services was no great promotion. And Diaz was soon called upon to bring help to the party. The Plan of Ayutla included the abolition of the Fuero Militar and the Fuero Eclesiástico. When the Republicans, as the opponents of his Highness the Dictator called themselves *par excellence*, gained possession of the city, they of course proclaimed the Plan. The officers of the 4th Regiment of Horse, and those of the 10th of Foot, which were stationed in Oaxaca, were offended at the prospect of the loss of their privileges, and on second thoughts reproclaimed for Santa Ana. The Republicans were driven out. Diaz was called upon to come to the help of his friends with the Indiada of Ixtlan. The enemy was for the moment too strong for them, and Diaz found himself compelled to go back to his district and disband the Indians he had pressed. But this eclipse did not last long. Santa Ana's folly was ruining him, and he was soon in flight. The Republicans recovered Oaxaca. Juarez came back as governor after a period of semi-starvation in the United States.

He and his colleagues of the Republican party now set to work, to organise their followers, who had hitherto been mere guerrillero bands, into a National Guard for the purpose of swamping the regular army. Hereupon the professional army officers, some of whom had acted against Santa Ana, joined forces in a body with the equally menaced Church. And now began a fair fight on a true political issue. On one side were the Liberals, intent on an abolition of military and clerical privileges, and on the other were the menaced army officers and priests who constituted the Reaction. The place of Porfirio Diaz was with the former. Juarez, we are told, had begun by offering him a major's commission in the National Guard about to be formed. He declined the offer on the modest ground of unfitness, and preferred to remain as sub-prefect of Ixtlan. As he did actually accept a commission as captain in the National Guard in December, 1856, we may assume that he was not held back by diffidence alone from taking service at a slightly earlier date. His native sagacity must have shown him that the foundation of real power in Mexico is a local influence. He remained in his district to win it, and he gave his first proof of his capacity to manage his countrymen by obtaining an appreciable amount of useful service in the field from the Indians of Ixtlan. From that fact we may perhaps conclude that if they had been of small military value hitherto the reason was not so much that they were more pusillanimous than others of their race, but that they were more recalcitrant to the press. It may be remembered that the parents of Diaz had lived for years in the Sierra de Ixtlan, and he had relations there.

Without undertaking to go into details of the confused period of the overthrow of Santa Ana, we must note rapidly that the victorious Republicans obtained possession of the capital. Their first President was Alvarez, the hero of the Plan of Ayutla. He proved but a transient President, and was quite out of place when he was no longer playing the guerrillero on a hillside. Comonfort succeeded him and formed a Ministry in which Juarez was Minister of Grace and Justice. The career of Comonfort is unique among Mexican Presidents, for he ended by making a pronunciamiento against his own administration. He was a moderate Conservative who had been driven to join the Liberals by opposition to, or fear of, Santa Ana. His conduct shows that he was prepared to go a certain way with them in reform, for he allowed his Minister of Grace and Justice to pass the law called after him " Ley Juarez," which abolished the Military and Ecclesiastical Fueros. But it would appear that when reform was seen to be developing into a confiscation of the Church's property Comonfort became frightened. He turned over to the Reaction, was overwhelmed in the confusion he created, and fled abroad. We may apply to him the scoffing lines written on the Archbishop of Paris, Louis de Noailles.

> " Cy gît Louis cahi caha
> De oui et non s'entortilla,
> Puis dit ceci, puis dit cela,
> Perdit la tête et s'en alla."

The united Clerical and Military parties obtained possession of the city of Mexico and the central mass of the country. Juarez, who as Minister of Grace and Justice was also President of the Supreme Court, and by the Mexican Constitution entitled to replace the President of the Republic in case of death or disappearance, was recognised as his successor by the Republicans. He made his way through various hazards to Veracruz, from whence he directed the ensuing three years' strife with the Reaction, or Conservative alliance, headed by that Miramon who was destined to be shot by the side of the Archduke Maximilian. Partly because he had the support of the United States, which recognised him and allowed its naval officers to intervene in his favour, but not a little because his position at Veracruz, the chief port of Mexico, enabled him to intercept the customs revenue, Juarez was first able to hold his ground and then to advance against the capital.

While the general struggle was running its course in the centre and north Porfirio Diaz was steadily fighting for the common cause in the south, and was incidentally qualifying himself to succeed Juarez as "cacique" in Oaxaca. The company of National Guards he commanded was raised in Ixtlan, where the hillmen would follow him, but nobody else. His party was predominant in the State till August of 1857, when the Conservatives, led by a Spaniard of old Spain, Cobos, who had carried a natural faculty for guerrillero warfare to Mexico, burst in on them from the north, and beat them badly at Ixcapa. In this action Diaz was severely wounded by a musket bullet in the leg. The wound laid him up for four months, and the bullet was, for lack of a competent surgeon,

THE BEGINNING OF A CAREER 45

not extracted till 1859. It was then taken out at La Ventosa by an American naval surgeon whose ship was protecting the workmen engaged in laying a road across the isthmus of Tehuantepec.[1]

Even before he was cured he had resumed service. It is characteristic of Mexican history that his chief in this part of his life was the Mejia who made a third with Maximilian and Miramon before the firing party at Querétaro. At Santa Catarina when Republicans and Conservatives were contending for the town, and on the battlefield of Jalapa, where Cobos was defeated, he distinguished himself as a subordinate. "The torrent of reform," says the future President's biographer, Señor Escudero, in his "Historic Notes," "was advancing in waves of blood to overwhelm the past." The Republicans gained ground, and, after Jalapa, Porfirio Diaz was named Governor and Military Commandant of the district of Tehuantepec.

The isthmus of Tehuantepec lies at the south-east end of Mexico, where it meets dense tropical forests, and the Central American republic Guatemala. The town and administrative district of the name lie on the south side of the isthmus. Geographically they occupy a section of the great Mother Range (the Sierra Madre), which stretches along the Pacific shore. The administrative district is of considerable size (500 square leagues), but they are square leagues of rugged hill and tropical forest, inhabited at that time by 60,000 Indians and half-breeds. When the inhabitants were not torpid and utterly indifferent they were much under Clerical influence. Juarez, who was making head with difficulty against Miramon, could

---

[1] This road was an American venture and was a forerunner of the Panama Canal. The scheme was quashed by the Senate.

spare Diaz but few men and no money. On the contrary, the new Governor was expected to raise revenue and help the general cause by receiving and forwarding arms to be imported from the United States. The whole force given him for the performance of these duties was 150 men.

The enterprise was, however, not quite so hopeless as it looks on the bare statement of these facts. Most of the inhabitants of his government did not care for either party, and if they would do nothing to help him they would do nothing to hinder. The Conservatives had their hands full elsewhere, and could send no force against him; and there was a third condition—a universal one in Mexico—which was much in his favour. However stagnant life might be in the valleys of the Sierra Madre, the scattered towns and villages had vivacity enough to keep alive local rivalries. The county town, as we may call it, Tehuantepec, was in a chronic state of dissension with the town of Juchitan. The first was Clerical and was in the hands of a party calling itself the Patricios, the Patriots, or Patricians, for the word can be used in both senses. Probably for no other reason than because Tehuantepec was Clerical, the town of Juchitan took the other side. Diaz chose the latter as his headquarters, as was to be expected. The place was for other reasons convenient to him. It is near the sea-shore, and therefore well placed to receive stores from the United States, whereas its rival lies inland.

Diaz held his government for two years, 1857 to 1859, gathering in what money was to be obtained and dashing out in swift raids as occasion served. He swooped down on the Patriots or Patricians of Tehuantepec, who were clumsily preparing to fall on

THE BEGINNING OF A CAREER   47

him, and sent them flying. For this service he was promoted to a majority. The promulgation of a new law which abolished the old military commandantships in March, 1858, and replaced them by " political districts " made an alteration in the name, but not in the character of his functions. Another success against the local Clericals at La Mantequilla earned him a lieutenant-colonelship. And then he did his party a material service.

A considerable convoy of arms imported from the United States had been collected at Juchitan. It was to be sent on to the Republicans. But Juarez could send no troops to protect it, and Cobos, who still held Oaxaca, got wind of so useful a prize. He prepared to make a raid into Tehuantepec and lay hands on the weapons. They would have been valuable to the Conservatives, who, owing to the hostility of the United States and the occupation of Veracruz by Juarez, were cut off from supplies and were much distressed. The Government at Veracruz learnt or suspected the intention of the Conservative leader, and orders were sent to Diaz to destroy the arms rather than allow them to fall into the hands of the enemy. But Diaz would not submit to that necessity without an effort, and he contrived to pass the arms across the hills with the help of his friends at Juchitan. While the convoy was making its way to the persons for whom it was intended, he at the head of his little force beat up the quarters of the intruders from Oaxaca and delayed them effectually. By the end of 1859 he had made himself master of the town of Tehuantepec and had earned his colonelcy. He was now able to come to the help of his friends elsewhere. The political district of Tehuantepec was to Diaz what the Eastern Counties Association was to Cromwell.

The Republican forces in Oaxaca were under the command of General Ordaz, who was struggling with Cobos for the possession of the city. Diaz having now beaten down the Patricios, raised 500 Indians by the usual process of the press and marched to join the Republican general. The venture was not at first a successful one. When Diaz moved out from Tehuantepec, his old Juchitan friends, who formed a large part of his force, proved recalcitrant. They were ready to serve in their own country, but were not prepared to go out of it on an expedition which might keep them from home for an indefinite period. Diaz had to quiet a mutinous outbreak on January 10, 1860. The danger was, however, averted only for a few days. Cobos, who appears to have known his business, was not the man to allow the two Republican officers to unite their forces at their leisure. He took the sound course and marched rapidly to fall upon them while still separated. On January 21 he attacked Diaz at Mitla. When the Conservatives were seen coming on, the sulky Juchitans ran away in a body, and Diaz suffered a smart defeat. Fortunately for him the approach of Ordaz drew Cobos off. He turned to deal with the new enemy, and was in his turn beaten. This timely intervention gave Diaz space in which to rally his following or such part of it as had not gone back to Juchitan. He joined his fellow-Republicans, who were now under the command of Salinas, for Ordaz had been killed in the encounter with Cobos.

The death of Ordaz was a bad mishap for the Republicans. His successor proved, if not disloyal, at

THE BEGINNING OF A CAREER 49

least captious and dilatory. Cobos was allowed to pick himself up. All armies of the guerrillero kind reunite almost as readily as they scatter, and the Conservative leader could rally on the city of Oaxaca. While he was restoring order in his following the Republicans were wrangling. The civil representative of the Government, Diaz's old friend Marcos Pérez, endeavoured in vain to stimulate Salinas to activity. They quarrelled, and Diaz strove to pacify the dispute. He refused to put his superior officer under arrest at the request of Don Marcos. Then Juarez sent a new general, Rosas Landa, to take the command. But his choice was singularly ill-judged, for when Cobos took the offensive again Rosas Landa fairly ran away, and the Republicans were beaten out of the field. Diaz and Salinas, who held together, took refuge in the mountains of Ixtlan.

After such a disaster the Republican forces would appear to have been decisively disposed of in the State of Oaxaca. And yet in August of this very year Diaz and Salinas were in possession of Oaxaca city, and Cobos it was who was hiding in the hills. The victories of loose guerrillero armies are indeed commonly barren, since they are not gained in the execution of a comprehensive, well-thought-out plan. Moreover, it not uncommonly happens that the desire to put booty in a safe place, or to obtain some private fruit of victory, or even only to enjoy a little rest, disorganises the victorious side as fully as if it had been beaten. Cobos was unable to follow up his successes, and was forced out of Oaxaca because his party was losing ground everywhere, his funds were running dry, and his men were deserting him.

The victory of his cause in his native State completed the first period in the public life of Porfirio Diaz. The beginning of another was marked in a significant manner. In 1860 he received his commission as colonel in the regular army, which had now been reorganised by Juarez. The new model no longer enjoyed the invidious privilege of the Fuero Militar, but it was none the less the greatest force in Mexican politics. When Diaz passed from the National Guard, to which he had hitherto belonged, and became an officer of the standing army, he, as it were openly and officially, took his place as a candidate for the Presidency. Not, of course, at once, but when the opportunity should come. It was natural, and we may even say inevitable, that when he became colonel he also became deputy in the Congress summoned by Juarez. We must not say he was elected, because no such thing as a free election has ever been known in any of the republics formed out of the fragments of the Spanish colonial empire—nor yet in Portuguese Brazil. If Diaz came to Mexico city in 1860 as deputy for the district of Ocotlan and also as colonel in the Oaxaca brigade of the national army the reason was that the Ocotlans received a *congé d'élire* permitting them to choose him.

During the last stage of the war he took an active share as a subordinate under Ortega in the field. He was present at the battle of Calpulalpam, where the organised forces of the Conservatives were finally broken. But an overthrow of this kind did not by any means entail the total defeat of the party. The Church was fighting for everything which could stimulate it to struggle. The Ley Juarez had deprived it of its "fuero," which it was bound by all its principles to consider a gross outrage. When Juarez became

President of the Republic his Minister of Grace and Justice framed the Ley Lerdo de Tejada—that was his name—by which all the property of the Church was confiscated. This measure was one of immense importance for Mexico. Its effects are felt to this day, and we shall have to come back to it. For the moment it is enough to point out that the Ley Lerdo de Tejada not only secularised the lands of the Church, but that it took all land in Mexico out of mortmain. The spoliation, as the Conservatives were bound to call this measure, affected not the Church alone, but the Indian towns, which found themselves deprived of the common lands which had been secured to them by the old Spanish Laws of the Indies. If, therefore, the Indians rallied to the cause of the Church with the cry of "Religion y Fueros," they were not acting from mere bigotry, nor were they fighting only for the abusive privilege of the clergy. Their own interests were threatened. The priest and the Indian had a common cause.

They found a leader in Marquez, a pure-blooded Indian of the Sierra de Querétaro. The man was a savage who killed with joy. He fairly earned his title of "Tiger of Tacubaya." But he was a vigorous guerrillero leader. The French officers who saw him later on judged that he had even the qualities of a general. And he had the further considerable advantage that he was an Indian chief who could rely on the loyalty of his tribesmen. Though Juarez was in possession of the capital and had summoned a Congress, a great part of the country was in the hands of the Conservatives. In June, 1861, Marquez made a dash at the capital. Diaz was compelled to leave his place in Congress and join Ortega in the field.

Marquez was driven back. His loose bands of guerrilleros were at a disadvantage in the open. He was beaten at Jalatlaco and then again at Mineral del Monte. On the first occasion Diaz attacked without orders and won a distinct success. The Conservatives were described as defeated and their army as scattered. But the reader will understand that, as usual, being defeated and scattered by no means entailed being brought to submission. Marquez's guerrilleros did not make a point of honour of holding a position. They relied on wearing their enemy down, and they knew very well that the few thousand more or less disciplined troops at the disposal of Juarez were utterly unequal to the task of occupying their hills. They divided when hard pressed, only to meet again miles off. The Conservatives were masters of much of the country, and Marquez was in arms when a new and a strange chapter opened in the history of Mexico.

CHAPTER III

THE FRENCH INTERVENTION

WHERE the carcass is there will the eagles be gathered together—and the vultures. The weakness and anarchy of the late Spanish colonies marked them out as a tempting prey for armed adventurers. Squatters came to the territory north of the Rio Grande, Texas, and then, not without reasonable grounds of provocation on the part of corrupt and brutal Mexican officials, tore it away. The slave power in the United States saw an opening for the extension of slavery in Northern Mexico. By the end of 1849 the Republic had been deprived by force of, or had sold, all its belongings beyond its present northern frontier. Small adventurers nibbled, or tried to nibble, bits of Central American or Mexican land. The Englishman who knows of the Cacique of Poyais only from Thackeray may be excused for believing that he was an invention of the novelist. But Gregor Macgregor was a flesh and blood reality who has his column in the " Dictionary of National Biography." He tried to conquer and to found a State. The mining camps of California bred imitators of the Cacique in some numbers. There was Walker, known in rhetorical phrase as the Grey-Eyed Man of Destiny. Quite a small world of filibusters made inroads, launched companies, and commonly ended before a firing party. Their doings are recorded in Mr. H. H. Bancroft's " History of the Northern Mexican States,"

Vol. II., with copious references to authorities. It is a point not to be overlooked that the French among the miscellaneous swarms of fortune hunters in California cast their eyes on the province of Sonora, at the northwestern end of the Mexican frontier. Schemes for founding a French colony in Sonora were evolved and advertised. Napoleon III. himself did more than play with them. The object was to work the mines, which had been profitable under Spanish rule, but had been neglected since its fall. Two attempts to seize on the much-exaggerated wealth of the province were made by French adventurers under the leadership of the Comte de Pindray and the gentleman of Provence who bore the imposing name Gaston Raoulx, Comte de Raousset Boulbon. The first died in mysterious circumstances—by his own hand or by murder at the hands of his mates. The second, a young *décavé* who had run through a fair patrimony in a few months, had written a novel, said to be very bad, and a good deal of such verse as poetasters wrote with Lamartine and Alfred de Musset before them as models, was intent on making a great deal of money by a gambler's throw. He was shot by the Mexicans in 1854. They may stand for the eagles.[1]

The vultures cannot be better represented than by Jecker of the notorious bonds. It is to be observed that this financial adventurer, who was at last murdered by the communards, was in partnership or league with Raousset Boulbon. European capitalists

---

[1] The reader who may care to investigate this odd backwater of American history will find quite interesting matter in the story of his captivity, told by M. Vigneaux, one of the companions of Pindray and Raousset Boulbon, and in the rather frothy but amusing life of that person by the Marquis de la Madelène. There is another by a M. de Lachapelle, which I have not seen.

THE FRENCH INTERVENTION   55

had been very imprudently ready to lend money to the Spanish-American States. The facility with which the transient chiefs of these communities were for a time able to raise loans had a good deal to do with promoting their spendthrift wars. The money was of course scandalously wasted, and much of it was stolen by the predominant generals of the day. A large part of the diplomatic correspondence of other nations with Mexico was concerned with the reclamations of defrauded and disappointed creditors. To them were to be added the incessant complaints of foreign merchants, who suffered from robbery disguised as forced loans, or robbery naked and unashamed. In reality these victims suffered a good deal less than native Mexicans. After all, they had their Consuls and Ministers to speak for them, while the dictator of the day had his reasons for not going too far against the possible dispensers of loans, or the Governments from which he might have to ask a safe refuge. After a time honourable financial houses declined to have anything to do with such creditors. Then the rulers who came and went were driven to make bargains with mere money-lenders of the Jecker stamp. Miramon, the Conservative President expelled by Juarez for one, made a bargain with Jecker. In return for a little money down he acknowledged a huge sum of debt.

I do not propose to swell these pages by even the briefest summary of the diplomatic history of the French intervention in Mexico. It has been often told and can be conveniently read in the " Expédition du Mexique " of Captain Niox, or, better still, in the " History of the Second Empire," by M. Pierre de la Gorce. But it is not an irrelevancy in a life of the man who was to put Mexico in an honourable position, at least for a time, to give some account of the "bochorno," the sweltering puddle of hot mud, from which he pulled his country. We will leave aside the dreams of Napoleon III., the fantastic delusions of the Spanish Court, the queer mixture of Quixotic vapours and Sancho Panza-like gross common sense of Prim, the wrongs of the British Embassy as told by the Minister (Sir Charles Wyke), the fictions of the French Minister (M. de Saligny), the produce of a disorderly imagination coloured by financial speculations, and the *tripotages* of the Duc de Morny. In 1861 the War of Secession was coming on in the United States, and they for a time were neutralised. Then all the vague ambitions, the self-deluding and deluded greeds of the Raousset Boulbons and Jeckers, ran into the river of dreams of "regeneration of the Latin race" and creation of a barrier against the ambitions of the United States (very rashly avowed) which flowed through the loose imaginings in the head of Napoleon III. The practical result was the French intervention in Mexico and the ghastly story of the Empire of Maximilian.

Yet it was not all the folly of a *songe creux*. There was just enough reality in it to provide a solid basis for the vapours to settle on. We shall have evidence from the campaigns of Porfirio Diaz himself that multitudes of Mexicans would gladly have reconciled themselves to obey a strong, intelligent foreign Government, which would keep order and administer with an eye to the good of the country. There was, too, the Church, maddened by spoliation. There were the Indians, aggrieved by the confiscation of the communal lands. If the work had been done honestly,

THE FRENCH INTERVENTION 57

if the Church had been fairly treated as far as fair treatment was possible in such a case, and the Indian commoners justly compensated, the throwing of the lands held in mortmain into " general circulation " might have been a gain for Mexico. But it was not honestly done. We need not take too high a tone to the Mexicans. Considering how Henry VIII. spoiled the English monasteries, how barons and lairds ravened the Church lands in Scotland, what was done in France during the Revolution, and in Spain after 1833, we can leave the Mexicans to do the preaching for themselves. The fact must none the less be recorded that a swarm of pillagers, fraudulent purchasers, politicians, and generals in search of booty settled on the confiscated lands. No part of the produce was devoted to the public good. The victims were sore and angry. The victimisers were thieving, scuffling, intriguing, and lying.

The mass of quiet townsmen and the peasants of Indian blood who had some property bowed, not unwillingly, to the foreign rule as they did to the unending patriots, all more or less sanguinary, who proclaimed this or that, and raised the banner of revolt. If there had been no United States, or if the Secession had succeeded; if Maximilian had not been a weak-willed and vaguely romantic person who lived in a perpetual performance of private theatricals; if the Clerical party had had sense and statesmanship; if the mass of Mexicans who longed for peace and security would have acted instead of waiting to be saved by some Heaven-sent good government, the empire might have been established and the Archdüke might have died at a great age on what was absurdly enough called the throne of Montezuma. As every one of these conditions was lacking, it was just a frantic adventure.

In the spring of 1862 England and Spain had withdrawn from what they had meant should be an attempt to recover debts, and France had been launched on what was in plain English a scheme to conquer Mexico thinly veiled by professions of a wish to enable its people to decide their own destinies undeterred by the " menaces of demagogues." General de Lorencez was at Orizaba with some 6,000 French troops. He had been joined by a few hundred Conservative guerrilleros—lean and sun-dried scarecrows, half naked, armed with lances and mounted on their wiry nags. They and their usual tail of women and children gave the French no very high opinion of the military quality of the allies they were to find in Mexico, according to the highly-coloured promises of M. de Saligny. The Zouaves and Chasseurs d'Afrique in Lorencez's little army had seen just such a " smala " before. The Mexican forces sent by Juarez to watch and oppose the French were commanded by General Zaragoza, with whom Diaz was now serving as brigadier in the Oaxaca contingent.

The French basis of supply was at Veracruz. This, the principal port on the Gulf of Mexico, lies on the sea front of the Hot Land (the Tierra Caliente), which is a strip of marsh some sixty miles wide, swarming with yellow-bellied mosquitoes and reeking with fever. The inner border of the Tierra Caliente is formed by the river Chiquihuite. Beyond the river begin the slopes of the great snow-capped mountain Orizaba. Here is the starting-point of the Tierras Templadas (the Temperate Zone), well cultivated and containing well-built towns—Córdoba, Orizaba, and others. The

THE FRENCH INTERVENTION

Tierras Templadas rise by a gentle slope till they are cut by a barrier of high and precipitous hills running from north to south—the Cumbres, or Heights. The Cumbres can be turned, but the country was roadless and little known to the French. The yellow fever of the Tierra Caliente had been so fatal to them that they had drawn every man they could to the front. Guerrilleros were pestering their communications, which were but ill guarded. If Lorencez had endeavoured to turn the Cumbres he would have marched into the air.

In the circumstances the French general would have done better to remain at Orizaba till the means for a further advance were provided. But he had the natural desire of a soldier to distinguish himself. And then he had been assured by M. de Saligny, whose advice he was told to take, that he had only to show himself in the interior in order to be greeted with effusion by the mass of the Mexicans. He knew, too, that there were Conservative bands in the field and that they were threatening General Zaragoza. So he decided to advance, relying on the vast military superiority of his soldiers and the promises of M. de Saligny.

Behind the Cumbres lies the lofty tableland of Anahuac, the Cold Lands (Tierras Frias) of Mexico. Two passes lead from the town of Orizaba to the plain of Anahuac—one by the Cumbres de Maltrata is only just practicable by wheeled carriages, and very difficult. It leads to the town of San Andrés Chalchicomula. The second goes by the defile of Acultzingo, from whence the road is open and easy to the very Clerical town of Puebla de los Angeles, which was the prize he aimed at. The pass is a staircase flanked by precipices, almost impossible to turn, and providing two most defensible positions at the Great and Little Cumbres, the two parallel chains forming the range. It may be confidently asserted that if such a position had been held by Prim with half the Spanish soldiers who had just gone back to Cuba, or by 2,000 Boer marksmen, Lorencez would not have forced the pass by a front attack, not even if he had been prepared " to cloy the jaws of death." But he was opposed by pressed Indians who had received a mere veneer of drill, who had never been taught to hold a position solidly, and who were commanded by men who were officers only because they had received commissions. The patriot troops had just given a proof of their quality. The first brigade of the Oaxaca contingent had been sent to take quarters in the tithe barn of Chalchicomula. They shambled into the yard, men, women, and children, bringing with them a convoy of gunpowder. The explosive was thrown down at the " grace of God," and the women set about cooking their husbands' dinners. The natural consequence followed. The gunpowder caught fire and blew up. The brigade, the women, children, horses, pack mules, and the tithe barn were dashed to pieces. Yet that brigade passed for one of the best in the Mexican army. It had served under Diaz and was partly raised by him. It would be pure waste to spend words over the action of April 28 when Lorencez forced the pass. Enough that eight companies of the 2nd Zouaves and six companies of the 1st Battalion of the Chasseurs a pied rushed a position 600 metres high defended by some 4,000 men and 18 guns, with a loss of two killed and 32 wounded.

Lorencez may be excused for thinking after such an

experience as this that he could safely rush at anything held by Mexican troops. When Zaragoza fell back on the town of Puebla the French general followed him nothing doubting. But he was mistaken. The Mexicans, Indians, and mestizos were not cowards. When they were stationed in solid stone buildings, loopholed, they could stand well. Puebla is a typical Spanish-Indian town, full of solid houses and massive convents, and defended on the east by outlying forts. The proper approach is on the western side, and so Lorencez had been told by a Mexican officer who joined him. In his contempt for such soldiers, and his overweening confidence in his own men, he simply marched along the Orizaba road from the east, and rushed at the forts on May 5. He had no battering train, and what guns he had—light field-pieces—were fired at too great a distance to produce any effect. Of course no impression was made on the forts. The French, marching up to unbreached walls, lost heavily, and were brought to a standstill. Diaz contributed materially to their final repulse by a well-timed and well-directed sortie against the flank of their line. A violent storm of rain came down. Lorencez fell back with a loss of 16 officers and 156 men killed, 19 officers and 285 men wounded. Zaragoza hardly went too far when he said that the French general made his attack *con torpeza*, that is to say, in a very clumsy manner. But the victorious Mexican's report grows almost lyrical over the valour of the French soldiers, and it is easy to see that the general was much and agreeably surprised by his victory over " the first soldiers in the world."

Diaz himself was honourably candid as to his own feelings. When in later years he dictated his reminiscences he frankly said : " The victory was so unexpected that we were surprised indeed by it, and as it appeared to me to be a dream I bivouacked that night on the field in order to confirm the reality of the event by the dumb testimony of our enemy's dead and those of our own forces ; by the talk of the soldiers round the fires, and the distant glow of the enemy's camp."

The French did indeed inspire such a profound respect for their fighting capacity in the open that no serious attempt was made to harass them during their retreat to Orizaba. General Zaragoza did, it is true, follow them in time and at a safe distance, but he made no attempt to force on an action. The siege of Orizaba which he proceeded to form when he had been reinforced amounted to very little more than a passive watching of Lorencez's little army from a long way off. General Zaragoza showed a well-grounded prudence in abstaining from more active measures. The result of the one offensive movement of the Mexicans only proved their utter unfitness to meet the French at close quarters. Orizaba is dominated by a hill, the Cerro Borrego. When an attempt was made to seize this position on June 14, and by a large Mexican force, it was shattered by 140 soldiers of the 99th of the line commanded by Captain Detrie. The Mexican force was composed of 2,000 men of the division of Zecatecas, who were counted as the best drilled in the Mexican army.

From early in May, 1862, till the beginning of March, 1863, the war was at a standstill. The French were receiving reinforcements and were preparing to advance. Juarez was doing all that was in his power to organise a national resistance. General Lorencez reopened, and kept open, his communications with Veracruz until he was recalled and replaced by General (afterwards Marshal) Forey. Diaz, who had been promoted to general of brigade for his services on May 5, was appointed Military Governor of the Veracruz district. There was, however, very little for him to do. The only forces available for operations against the invaders were the guerrillero bands formed of men who had lived by civil strife. They were mere brigands, whose highest achievement was to butcher stragglers, and, when the luck favoured them, to cut off a very small detachment. They were perfectly ferocious, and they excelled themselves in cruelty to those of their countrymen who were known, or were only suspected, to sympathise with the French. Against them the foreign authorities organised the notorious contra-guerrillera led by Colonel du Pin. This body was recruited mainly among the broken men—beachcombers, deserters from ships, bullies and ruffians of all nationalities, and no scruple—who have ever hung about the Gulf ports. Du Pin fought the Mexican guerrilleros with their own weapons, and proved to demonstration that European vagabonds led by a French officer could equal the vilest excesses of native ferocity. No good was to be done for the one side or the other by such methods as these. Diaz might well prefer, and did prefer, to take his share in a more honourable kind of warfare.

While the French expedition was being raised to an adequate strength by drafts from Europe, Juarez was preparing to defend his Government. The method he took was perhaps the only one available in the existing circumstances. He concentrated the arms and the men he could scrape together at Puebla, and decided to make a stand at that fortress. A place besieged is a place taken unless it can be relieved from the outside, and, as the President's power to collect another army capable of forcing the French to raise the siege they were certain to undertake was *nil*, it follows that the forces shut up in Puebla must sooner or later be lost. The case would seem to have been one for acting on the maxim of Sir William Wallace—who loved better to hear the lark sing than the mouse cheep—for refusing to shut men up within walls, for relying on a policy of wearing the French down by skirmishes and stopping their advance by threatening their communications. So undoubtedly he ought to have behaved if he could have relied on the support of the whole population of Mexico. But he could not. The mass of the people was passive, and a good half of those who were prepared to act—that is, the Clericals—were bitterly hostile and were co-operating with the French. To hold Puebla strongly, make a long defence and so gain time, was on the whole the best course to follow. So some 15,000 men were thrown into the town and there awaited the advance of the French. The President's policy was to some extent justified by the fact that not a few of the Conservative leaders rallied to him when it became clear that the country was about to be invaded by a French army. Their patriotism was possibly stimulated by a shrewd suspicion that a Government supported by a serious force might be strong enough to put a stop to the profitable game of pronunciamiento-making. Yet they must be credited with having subordinated party to country without renouncing their principles, for no sooner had the French army retired before the menaces of the United States in 1867 than most of them who survived took up arms at once in the old quarrel. In 1863 there was a faint possibility that all the Conservatives would follow their example, and there was a good deal to be said for giving time to time—*dar tiempo al tiempo*, as the Spanish maxim (much acted on) has it. Zaragoza having died in the interval, General Ortega was appointed to conduct the defence.

The siege of Puebla was even more creditable to the Mexicans than the repulse of Lorencez's feeble attack on May 5. They held out from March 16 to May 17, and then did not surrender till their provisions were exhausted. We are told in the reminiscences of Diaz that he and several other of the generals present urged Ortega to take a line which would have been more spirited, and if successful vastly more effective, than a pure defence. He says that when Forey's army of 26,000 men was closing round the town it advanced in two columns, one on one side and the other on the other. Diaz and the generals who thought with him implored their chief to strike at the head of one of the columns. It does appear a tenable proposition that an army of 15,000, or according to the French of 20,000, which possessed the advantage of acting on interior lines and of being covered behind by the town, might have spared men enough to concentrate a superior force at a point of attack to deliver a shrewd blow at the French while they were coming into position. Ortega would take no risks and refused. His advisers retired, some of them grumbling audibly that they were condemned to be caught in a trap and compelled to surrender sooner or later.

The President's memory of that council of war may be frankly accepted as correct. Subordinate officers who cannot give the decision, and who therefore would not be held responsible if it were taken and failed, have always been ready to urge the adoption of a bold course on wary commanders-in-chief. On the principles Diaz was no doubt right, and yet it may well be that Ortega was not wrong. The attack from the centre to the circumference by the lesser on the more numerous army is no doubt a brilliant manœuvre, but unless it is performed with rapidity and precision it will infallibly be disastrous. The Mexican army had not been trained to observe what Collingwood called " the nice concert of measures that are necessary to success." If Ortega had tried to play the great game of Rossbach and Leuthen and Salamanca, it is, considering the quality of his troops, eminently probable that he would have been heavily beaten, and then Puebla would have fallen at once. The cautious line he took had at least the merit of making it possible to hold the French back for two months and so give time to time.

M. Pierre de la Gorce, in his " History of the Second Empire," tells us that when the first reports of the siege of Puebla began to reach Paris (by steamer, for the Atlantic cable was not laid at that date) the name of Zaragoza—the Spanish city, not the Mexican general—was much in the mouths of critics and also of nervous friends of Napoleon III. There was just enough similarity between the two sieges to save the comparison from being altogether one of the Macedon and Monmouth order. There was, however, one great difference. The capital of Aragon was defended in 1808 by its inhabitants and the countrymen of the neighbourhood, who took refuge within its walls. Puebla was defended by its numerous garrison. The

THE FRENCH INTERVENTION 67

city was perhaps the most levitical in all Mexico—the very centre and headquarters of the Clerical party. Whatever sympathies the townsmen had were rather with the enemy outside than with the defenders within. But as usual these sympathies were entirely passive. Forey gained nothing positive by them.

The prominent part which Diaz took in the two months' resistance laid the foundation of his fame. Until now he was only one of a large body of political and semi-political generals and colonels, who were collectively a pest. When the siege ended he was well on his way to become a national hero. We must therefore dwell a little on his actions and look with some attention at the place where they were performed.

Because Puebla " of the Angels " was, and from the first had been, above all a Clerical city, it abounded in massive buildings. Its sixteen convents and many of the secular houses within it had been erected in the most flourishing ages of Spanish colonial history. Building material was abundant, time was no consideration, slave and serf labour was obtainable in unlimited quantities. In these conditions the Spaniards constructed as if they were building for eternity. They brought with them an excellent tradition of masonry, inherited, not from the so-called Arabs, whose work in that kind was far from good, but from the " obras de Romanos," the works of the Romans at Mérida, Segovia, and Tarragona. They made admirable mortar, and then they held the rule that " Lo que quita el frio quita el calor " (" What keeps out the cold keeps out the heat "). A thick-walled house is warmer in winter and cooler in summer. All this stonework would have crumbled into dust within a few hours under the fire of the guns which have thundered in the ears of all the world since August, 1914. But Forey had no such battering train. The massive old Spanish walls were quite equal to the strain of resisting his field-pieces and his eight " canons de 12 de siége," with their reserve of six of the same calibre. Nor had Ortega been negligent in preparation. The forts on the west and south and the city walls were looked to. Of these no more need be said. Forey was warned by the experience of Lorencez and made his attack from the east, where the city lies most open. Ortega had foreseen that this would probably be the side to be assailed. He had made a fort of the penitentiary which stood outside the walls. It was named the San Javier (*i.e.*, St. Xavier). But the real defences were within. Barricades had been solidly constructed, house walls loopholed, mines laid. He meant to fight from barricade to barricade, and to force the enemy to pay heavily for every advance. It was a reasonable calculation that Forey, whose reinforcements must reach him across the Atlantic, could not afford to be "a general at 10,000 men a week." The French officer would perhaps have done better to begin where he was forced to end, that is to say, invest the town and starve it out, standing ready to scatter any forces which might come to its relief. He would have got the place quite as soon as he did, and would have lost fewer men—a consideration of some weight for a general who had only 26,000 with whom to dominate a country four times the size of France. But this thrifty course would have been painful to an army which, justly enough on the whole, had no great respect for the military qualities of its opponents. So he fixed his headquarters at the convent of San

THE FRENCH INTERVENTION 69

Juan on a low hill to the east of the town, and prepared to clear the way by taking the San Javier and then effect a quick storm.

It is not necessary to give a detailed account of the siege, but only to show the theatre on which Diaz was to win distinction. As regards the general operations, it is enough to say that the besieger's force had no difficulty in disposing of such relieving force as Juarez was able to send; that the San Javier was stormed, the city walls occupied; and that then the real fighting began inside. This stage lasted till April 7. During that period the French had lost one general and seven officers killed, 39 officers wounded, 56 soldiers killed, and 443 wounded. A casualty list of 545 in an army of 26,000 may not appear very serious. But the progress made was little, and the historian of the Mexican expedition, Captain Niox, has to confess that this fighting amid loopholed walls, over mines, and under falling roofs tried the nerve of the soldiers. It made, he confesses, " une impression facheuse sur leur moral." Forey turned the siege into a blockade and waited till hunger compelled the Mexicans to capitulate.

Diaz was in the thick of the fighting during the last days of March and the first of April. The portion of the line particularly entrusted to him was composed of the convents of San Marcos and San Agustin, which lie respectively north and south of one another, and the block of houses between. Puebla is built in straight streets cutting one another at right angles. The houses in the oblong blocks, known as " manzanas " in Spanish, are closely joined and inhabited in flats. The President's reminiscences supply a lively picture of a passage of street fighting.

The French advanced till they were in possession of the hospice facing San Marcos, and were piercing the walls in order to bring a gun to bear on the buildings opposite. The ground floor of San Marcos was occupied by shops on either side of the " zaguan "—that is to say, the porch and passage which led into the courtyard, the central " patio " of the building. The door had been solidly barricaded with flagstones taken from the ground of the zaguan and the courtyard. An opening had been made through the wall at the back of the yard to allow the defenders to come and go without exposing themselves in the open. When the French had pierced the wall of the hospice, they fired into the San Marcos and beat in the front of the shop to the right of the porch, and attempted to rush the building. They advanced to blow in the door of the zaguan, did not succeed, and then they forced their way in through the shop.

" There was," says the President, " one anxious moment when the fury of the French charge into the courtyard struck my soldiers with panic so that they went so far as to attempt to run, but the narrowness of the opening in the wall would not allow them all to get off. At that moment I fired a little mortar which I had in the yard loaded with grape shot, and let them (*i.e.*, the French) have it near enough to singe their beards [*a quema ropa* = burn their clothes, the equivalent of the French *à brûle pourpoint*]. It scared them sufficiently to make them leave the courtyard they were just about to occupy, and they ran back into the porch."

One of the Zouaves in the attacking party made a rush at Diaz, who stopped him by hurling a revolver into his face. He fell, either from the force of the

THE FRENCH INTERVENTION 71

blow—which was no doubt severe, for Don Porfirio was by all testimony a very strong man—or because he was wounded at that moment by a shot. The President never indulges in the Munchausen vein and generally gives ample credit to his friends and subordinates. On this occasion he records the stout help given him by one of his corporals. He adds a biographical detail which deserves to be repeated for its candid simplicity. The revolver was a second-hand one and out of order. It had been bought in a pawn-shop, he tells us, " for at that time our pecuniary circumstances were bad." [1]

His soldiers now rallied and forced the French out. The fighting went on for three or four days. The French brought guns and tried to master houses here and there by forcing their way into front rooms and firing into and across the patios. The result commonly was that they brought the roofs down on their own heads. For though the walls of these old buildings are extremely solid, the frequent earthquakes which afflict Mexico have taught the wisdom of making the roofs light so that they collapse easily without injury to the shell of the house. The inhabitants who cannot get clear away in time take cover in the thickness of the walls at doorways. Diaz contrived to hold the San Marcos. When the French renewed the attack and again tried to burst into the building through the shop, he prepared a trap. Holes were made in the

[1] For the benefit of possible book-hunters and curiosity-seekers in Spanish-speaking countries I will put a note here which my experience tells me will not be superfluous. The adjective " *viejo* " (old) means second-hand. A *libro viejo* or *pistola vieja*, like Don Porfirio's in this case, is a second-hand book or pistol. When what is sought is a book or pistol or any other article interesting for its age the curio-hunter should be careful to ask for a *libro antiguo* or *pistola antigua*. The Spaniards never err in their use of the words, and the blunders of foreigners, who usually do, are the cause of innocent merriment.

roof and hand grenades were dropped on the intruders. They were once more driven out. Diaz tells us with perhaps a touch of not ill-natured malice that the officer who commanded the final assault, when deserted by his men and called on to surrender, replied in the legendary Cambronne formula " The Zouaves never surrender ! " Nevertheless he did when it became clear that he would be shot if he proved contumacious.

The President's narrative is on the whole borne out by the French version of the story given in Captain Niox's History.

A few days of this work convinced Forey that he would lose more men than he could afford to spend if he continued in his attempt to take the town house by house. He suspended these attacks, sent for heavier guns from the French men-of-war in the Gulf, and confined himself to beating off the feeble efforts of the Mexicans to relieve the garrison and to menacing the outer forts. When the would-be relieving army had been routed by Forey's subordinate Bazaine at San Lorenzo and the provisions of the garrison were nearly exhausted (though it was afterwards shown that the townsmen had hidden considerable stores of food), Ortega tried to obtain a capitulation and the honours of war. Forey insisted on surrender pure and simple. The Mexicans laid down their arms after destroying their ammunition. Diaz was one of the 26 generals, 303 field officers, and 1,179 company officers who fell into the power of the French. It was quite in accordance with the established rules of Mexican warfare that a large proportion of the common soldiers taken were at once incorporated by the Conservative leader Marquez, who had joined Forey, in his own ranks.

Of the officers, many were sent to France, from whence they were subsequently allowed to return on the understanding, or in the hope, that they would join Maximilian. Some did take that course. A large proportion of the prisoners contrived to escape within a few days. Diaz was one of those who succeeded in getting away. At a later period he was accused of having broken his parole, but he always denied that he had given it, nor could it ever be proved that he had.

When free he hurried to report to Juarez at Mexico city. Don Benito saw that after the fall of Puebla and the rout at San Lorenzo he was in no position to offer further opposition to the advance of the French on the capital. He removed his Government northwards to the famous old mining city, San Luis de Potosi. Diaz, whose rank as general of division was confirmed in October, 1863, was commissioned to raise troops in the province of Querétaro. " The city of Mexico," said Juarez, " will be just one town more in the possession of the French." He was perfectly right. The occupation of the capital had no effect whatever on the other cities and provinces of the Republic, which had never followed its lead and enjoyed local independence. The French had apparently forgotten the teaching of the Peninsular War and the utter uselessness to them of the occupation of Madrid. Forey left Puebla on June 4, and occupied the capital on the 12th. He met with no opposition. All the townsmen asked was that he would not allow Marquez to enter the city. When they were assured that they would be protected against the " Tiger of Tacubaya " and his cut-throats they decorated their houses and welcomed the French with effusion.

A parody of Napoleon's scandalous proceedings at

Bayonne in 1808 now followed. A miscellaneous assembly of notables was held, and it offered the "Crown of Montezuma" to Maximilian. The vote of this scratch collection of mere insignificances was made to do duty for a national choice. It was not what Napoleon and Maximilian had hoped for, but they had committed themselves already. The Emperor of the French could not go back without covering himself with ridicule. After the repulse at Puebla in May, 1862, the honour of the French arms had to be vindicated. A foolish enterprise was to be persisted in because it had been begun. A provisional Government conducted affairs in the name of the Emperor Maximilian till he should arrive—that is to say, it professed to be the Government of Mexico wherever a French garrison was in possession on the line of communications from Veracruz to the capital and in a few places to right or to left. Everywhere else the government, as far as there was any, was conducted in the name of the Republic and of the President Juarez.

The unhappy Archduke and his still more unhappy wife, Amélie Charlotte of Belgium, reached Veracruz in May, 1864, *en mal hora*, in an evil hour for him and for her. He came with the remnant of a loan raised by the help of Napoleon and burdened by a heavy financial obligation which he was totally unable to fulfil. He was bound to support the French army of occupation out of a non-existent revenue. It was the French army which had to support him out of its military chest, which again had to be filled from France.

The essential folly of the whole venture was made manifest from the day that the Archduke reached his capital. There were many Mexicans who would have accepted a good Government from Maximilian so long as they were not called on to make efforts or undergo sacrifices to help him. There was only one body of persons in Mexico who would or could have given him effective support. They were the Clericals, and their help was to be had on their terms only. The conditions they would have imposed may be fairly said to have been all that Hildebrand or Boniface VIII. would have claimed or Pius IX. would have insisted on if he could. They asked for nothing less than the entire subordination of the State to the Church, the restoration of all Church land, the suppression of all freedom of worship and opinion. Now it was manifestly impossible for an Austrian archduke to submit to such demands. It was still more impossible for Napoleon III. He would have helped the Church if it had allowed him, but no ruler of Frenchmen could dare to make so abject a submission to Clerical pretensions. The Mexican Clericals were not amenable to reason. They would not listen; they scorned all appeals to show moderation and accept facts. They would assert and demand all as a right not to be discussed.

As it was impossible to work with the Church, Maximilian had to fall back on efforts to win the support of the Liberals. When he tried to govern as a Mexican ruler, he soon came into collision with the French. When he supported the French, he offended the Mexicans. Add to this that the United States would never recognise his Government, though he debased himself to humble solicitations. When the cause of the Confederacy declined and fell, it became obvious that the Union would insist on the withdrawal of the French troops. So long as they remained they could easily scatter the armed mobs which were called Republican armies ; but they never succeeded in driving Juarez over the border, though he was so hard pressed as to be forced to send his family for safety to American territory, and while he remained in any corner of the country, though it were only in some out-of-the-way hiding-place in the deserts of Chihuahua, the Republican Government was in being.

No more need be said of the war in Northern Mexico. The field of activity assigned to Porfirio Diaz was in his native South. In October, 1863, he received a commission which had perhaps more to do with his future importance than any other incident in his career so far. He was appointed to take 2,800 men raised in the North and to march across Central Mexico to Oaxaca. His command was to be known as the Army of the East and was to include the provinces of Guerrero, Puebla, and Oaxaca. To reach his command he had to pass the line of communication of the French army, watched as it was by 30,000 men, including the " traitors " who had joined the invaders. In so far as the necessity for avoiding armed forces was concerned, the difficulties of the feat were not very formidable. Thirty thousand men are but few to watch vast spaces of country thinly inhabited and full of mountains. Allowing for his own knowledge and the help of local guides, allowing, too, for his freedom from the embarrassment of a heavy train of artillery and ammunition wagons, to avoid an intercepting force was a comparatively small matter. The real difficulty rather began when the French line of communication was crossed, and the march had to be completed through mountains covered by dense forest where no roads were, and when even local

THE FRENCH INTERVENTION 77

knowledge failed so utterly that it was necessary to march by the compass and explore as he went. The considerable powers of endurance of the Mexican Indian soldiers were sharply tested, and there was probably no passage in his life in which Don Porfirio benefited more by his early love of sport on the hillside and practice as a cragsman.

A glance at a fairly good map will do more to make the march intelligible than any amount of words. The starting-point was at Amalco, to the south of Querétaro. From Amalco it was necessary to take a sweep out to the west and then round south by Molinos de Caballero, Aguangueo, Orocutia, Laureles, Los Arcos, Almaloya, Soltepec, and Zacualpam in order to avoid the French force stationed at Toluca, to the south-west of the city of Mexico. From Zacualpam Diaz and his little army had to turn south-east to reach Oaxaca. In front of them was Tazco or Tasco, a small place held by a native force under French command. Diaz did not think it necessary to avoid this obstacle. On October 26, 27, and 28, he assailed and took it, capturing a supply of useful weapons. From Tazco he marched by many places of names exotic and sonorous—Tepecuacuilco, Atlixtaca, Ixcatiopa, Xilaca-yoapas, Huitezco, south-east to Oaxaca. The reader who follows the route will see that it led across, and recrossed, several chains of mountains, hills which go to make up the great Sierra Madre, many rivers which are in fact mountain torrents, and across much sub-tropical forest.

It was not till the end of November that Diaz, marching like the knight-errant of the Spanish ballad, " De Sierra en Sierra, por orillas de la mar " (" From hills to hills by the seashore "), reached Oaxaca, where he found a state of things very characteristic of a country distracted between anarchy and foreign invasion. So far the provisional Government, or the French generals, without whose direction nothing could be done, had been too busy in the centre and the north to pay attention to the south. The Southerners, Sudeños in native speech, were well disposed to stay quiet so long as they were left alone, and Cajiga, the Governor of Oaxaca, with his secretary, Esperon, had in fact made an arrangement with the provisional Government whereby the State agreed to remain quiet if it were not attacked, and to await the taking of a national vote. In plain Castilian this meant that Oaxaca would fall into line if the provisional Government could rid itself of Juarez—provided, of course, that the local interests of local politicians were fairly considered. The intrusion of Porfirio Diaz, a man with local connections, at the head of an armed force recruited so far away as Querétaro and the still more distant provinces of Sinaloa and Sonora, was most unwelcome to Governor Cajiga and his secretary, and indeed to all who preferred a quiet life.

When the Governor met Diaz he began by pointing out that the large powers given to the General were unconstitutional—a common malady with " powers " in Mexico—and went on to ask whether he intended to make use of force. Don Porfirio states in connection with a later passage of history at Oaxaca that it was his custom to use ferocious language in order to spare himself the painful necessity of taking harsh measures. So he answered in, as we can imagine, a significant tone that he certainly would use force against the French and all traitors. The hint was plain and effective. Cajiga and Esperon travelled

THE FRENCH INTERVENTION 79

rapidly to Mexico, leaving the State of Oaxaca headless. Constitutional pedantries were out of place at such a crisis. Diaz stepped into the Governor's place, and appointed as his secretary his trusty friend, Justo Benitez. All lovers of a quiet life accepted these irregular, but in Spanish America normal, proceedings with passivity.

Don Porfirio now began to organise the three provinces put under his command to take an active part in the war. Another glance at the map will show that Puebla, Guerrero, and Oaxaca were of the highest importance to the national Government for a reason apart from the revenue they could contribute to the general treasury of the Republic. They flank the whole line of communications from Veracruz to the capital, and from the capital to the Pacific coast at Acapulco. So long as they remained in the hands of the Republicans they constituted a perpetual menace to the provisional or imperial Government and tied down a large proportion of its troops. If they had been patriotically zealous they could have made it impossible for Bazaine, who had succeeded to the command of the French army when Forey was recalled in October, 1863, to carry out operations against Juarez in the north. If they had no such influence the reason simply was that, as Diaz shows very plainly in his reminiscences, the people were not zealous. When the Empire had fallen because the only prop which upheld it—namely, the French army—had been withdrawn in obedience to the menaces of the United States, it became the custom to speak of this war as a struggle between the outraged patriotism of a whole people and a foreign invader supported by a few traitors. The reality was very different. The war was a struggle between a French army which was absurdly unequal in numbers to the task of occupying a country of 769,000 square miles in size, full of rugged mountain chains, on the one hand, and on the other that part of the population, which had ever been in arms against some Government, and which had ever used those same mountain fastnesses as places of arms and of refuge. The mass of the population was passive and would do nothing to help or to hinder either side except under pressure.

As the Republican army could not be organised into an effective force for offensive operations, and as the French were too busy elsewhere to advance, months passed before anything happened. Moreover, a French army could not move like an encampment of Bedouins, using its women as army service corps, and going, as the sailors might say, "flying light." It needed a battering train and the usual impedimenta of a regular army. Now the south and south-east of Mexico are separated from the centre by rugged mountain country, in which the roads were mere tracks, often mere beds of torrents winding between upright cliffs of bare rock, and crossed by "barrancas" or precipitous-sided beds of rivers, and cañons, sheer fissures of great depth. There were places on the line from Mexico to Oaxaca where it was necessary to wind for three or four miles in order to get from one side to another of a narrow valley. The indispensable preliminary to an advance on Oaxaca was the construction of a road, and to that Bazaine applied himself. The campaign at the end of 1864 and the beginning of 1865 was made up of the construction of the road and the fall of the city.

During the first half of 1864 Bazaine confined

THE FRENCH INTERVENTION 81

himself to pushing his outposts down to, or a little beyond, the 18th degree of latitude. By this measure of precaution he covered the province of Puebla and confined Diaz to Oaxaca. The French advanced, road-making as they went along. They found no difficulty in obtaining native labour for pay. On the contrary, the population welcomed them, and complained bitterly of the exactions of the Republican leaders. If Diaz had had the measure of active support which Mina and other guerrillero chiefs found in Navarre and Catalonia during the Peninsular War, he would have made the French pay dear for every step in that advance. There was no lack of effort on his part. In August, when the French attack was beginning to develop, he dashed at them fiercely and on the best guerrillero principles, making false attacks to cover rapid marches across hill and dale, and falling on posts he had selected for attack. But when it came to actual hand-strokes his men would not stand up to the French. Even when he caught a small detachment of his enemy bathing and assailed them, they seized their rifles, fought naked, and the Mexicans were beaten off. General Brincourt, who was in immediate command, drove the Republicans before him and advanced to within sixty miles of Oaxaca. He was convinced that he could get the town by a quick attack. Bazaine, however, thought the advance would be premature till the communications were opened by the making of the road. Brincourt was ordered to establish an advanced post at Yanhuitlan, and withdrew his main force. Bazaine reserved the occupation of the city for the time when it could be done solidly, and for himself.

Both sides now fell to work with spade and pick,

the French at road-making and Diaz in the fortifications of Oaxaca. Mexico gained lasting advantage from the road, but the fortifications turned out to be of no use even for their immediate purpose. The fact was that the position of the Republican general was a hopeless one. Many of his subordinates were deserting him. Officers of high rank went off either to submit to the Emperor or to take to guerrillero fighting, with its attendant advantage of contribution-raising. Throughout the whole campaign, which ended with the occupation of Oaxaca by the French in February, 1865, the national guards of the smaller towns either refused all obedience to the Republican Government and stood aside from the struggle entirely, or they openly joined the Empire. This was in fact the period when the Republican Government was at the lowest and when Maximilian could claim to be gaining ground. The Civil War in the United States was at its height. General Sherman had not yet exposed the hollowness of the Confederacy by his march from Atlanta to Savannah. Many Mexicans of note who had hitherto remained loyal to the national cause now made their submission to Maximilian. Among them was General Uraga, under whom Diaz had served in earlier years. Uraga made an attempt to draw him over to the cause of the Empire. If he had succeeded he would have rendered his new master appreciable service. The adhesion of the Governor of Oaxaca would have carried with it the submission of the whole south of the country and a valuable addition to the resources of the empty treasury of the Empire, and that without the need for any sacrifice of men or money on the part of the new Government. Maximilian and the Mexican advisers

THE FRENCH INTERVENTION 83

he drew about him would have had good reason to rejoice if such an important gain could have been made without the aid of the French. They were very restive under the dictation of Bazaine.

Uraga sent his son Luis with a letter to Diaz. We cannot suppose that this was the actual beginning of their correspondence. Luis Uraga would hardly have been sent into the lion's den unless some security had been given for his safe return. There is no probability, and there is certainly no evidence, that Diaz ever meant to desert his party. But he may have been not unwilling to take advantage of an opportunity offered him by the other side to affirm his loyalty. Uraga's letter, which reached Oaxaca in November, was plausible, and it gave Diaz reasons of an honourable, or at least of a decent, kind why he should follow the example set by the writer. The converted Liberal general pointed out that the Republican armies were all scattered and that a prolongation of guerrillero warfare, with its usual accompaniments of raids and extortion of contributions, could bring nothing but misery on Mexico. He protested that he was not asking his friend to give his aid to a French annexation of Mexico. He declared that if he thought the national independence to be menaced he would have continued to resist to the last. But he was convinced that the independence of Mexico was quite safe under Maximilian and that a constitutional monarchy offered the best of guarantees for good government in the future. The letter was indeed written with all the instinctive understanding of a Spaniard or superior stamp of Spanish-American how to say what you have to say with the air becoming to a gentleman and with dignity.

The weakness of Uraga's plea was one of which he was perhaps not himself conscious. The deadly readiness of men of Spanish blood to confound the fine word with the substantial fact may have misled him, as it has done, and daily does, many others. There was nothing in the general's letter (nor was there in the notorious facts of the case) to show that Maximilian's Government could live for six months if the French army were withdrawn. Without its aid the Emperor would be even less able to support himself than the native Presidents who had come up and had gone down at the rate of about one a year. If he had not known this, why did he endeavour to recruit bands of Belgian and Austrian soldiers of fortune?

Now, even if we refuse to allow Porfirio Diaz the credit of having acted on principle and from patriotic feeling (which we have no right to do without evidence) he was certainly a man of sufficient native sagacity to see what was patent to others. If the Empire was wholly dependent on the continued assistance of a French army, it was a farce to talk of national independence. And, unless there was a guarantee for a continued French occupation, no one who joined Maximilian could have any security for the future. Don Porfirio professed his belief in the final victory of the national cause and declined to take Uraga's advice.[1]

It would not be worth while to go into the details of the fall of Oaxaca in February, 1865. The measures which Don Porfirio had taken to put the town in a

[1] I have not thought it necessary to quote the letter he sent in answer to Uraga's. It is verbose, and is written in the involved gerundial style of modern Spanish-speaking officialdom. The mere wording of the document was probably due to Justo Benitez.

THE FRENCH INTERVENTION 85

state to be defended, and most especially his destruction of a number of houses for the purpose of depriving a besieging army of cover, had caused deep offence. Desertions grew more frequent, the townsmen were sulkily hostile, there was no prospect of help from without. Indeed, the only support Don Porfirio had was a small mounted guerrilla led by his brother El Chato. When Bazaine had once drawn his lines round the town there was nothing to be done save to surrender. It may well be that if Don Porfirio had not ridden out to surrender on February 8 he would have been betrayed by some of his followers.

CHAPTER IV

THE RISE TO THE FIRST RANK

WHEN Diaz, accompanied by two of his officers, presented himself at Bazaine's headquarters, the marshal came to what was in the circumstances a very natural conclusion. He thought that the Mexican general was about to do as many of his countrymen had recently done—namely, make his submission to the Emperor. On the face of it there was no other explanation of a hurried surrender. Yet we have not only the assurance of Don Porfirio himself, but a long succession of patent facts, to prove that Bazaine was entirely mistaken. The Mexican general surrendered because he knew that his garrison was not to be relied on, and he took the most unusual course of coming out with the white flag himself because he could not trust any of his subordinates not to play him some ugly trick.

Bazaine, we are told by Don Porfirio, showed very bad temper when he was forced to see that he was in error. He accused his prisoner of having broken promises given at Puebla, and more than hinted at a firing party. Diaz denied that he had given his parole in 1863 or that he had ever promised to join Maximilian. A reference was made to the record taken when Puebla had surrendered, and it was found that Diaz was right. He had not only refused to give his parole, but had declared that he would not adhere to the Government set up under cover of the French

THE RISE TO THE FIRST RANK 87

intervention. Bazaine was not the man to be deterred from strong measures by formalities. But in February, 1865, it was becoming clear that the French must look carefully to their going. He abstained from taking a course which would have tended to scandal. The garrison of Oaxaca was disposed of in the usual way. The local levies were sent back to their homes—nothing loth. Those who had been drawn from the north were either sent back, or were incorporated in the Emperor's unpaid and barely disciplined Mexican levies, from which they in due course deserted, sometimes in whole companies with their officers at their head. Diaz was sent to Puebla, well treated but closely watched.

At Puebla he remained till September 15 of 1865. After the disastrous, the indeed all but ridiculous, end of his command of the Army of the East, it might well seem that his career was over even in such a country as Mexico. Yet he stood higher than ever in the estimate of his party. His failure was not due to any fault of his own. He would have fought if his men would have followed him, and amid the many and scandalous defections of 1864 he had been found faithful.

Don Porfirio does not say it, nor is the thing one of those which men freely say, but we may safely assume that he was well content to remain for some months quietly in Puebla under charge of the Emperor's Austrian officers. There was for the moment little good to be done in the field, but a man of his knowledge and experience must have felt confident that an opportunity to reappear with effect would present itself before long. The decisive events of that quiet interval did not take place in Mexico. They were the occupation of Savannah by the Federal general Sherman in December, 1864, and the surrender of Lee at Appomatox in April, 1865. The full significance of the march from Atlanta to Savannah may not have been visible for some little time, but the mere report that the event had happened was enough to enlighten the most obtuse of mankind as to the meaning of the capitulation of the commander of the army of Northern Virginia. The Confederacy was fairly down with both shoulders on the ground. However ignorant Mexicans might be of what passed outside their own range of vision, one fact was brought home to them with convincing force. It was that some thousands of the Confederates had fled across the Rio Grande del Norte into Mexico. Then there was talk of grand schemes for settling these refugees in the country, and also whatever numbers of others might join them later on. No course more exactly calculated to exasperate every class of Mexican against the imperial Government could possibly have been devised. From the hacendado with his millions of acres down to the Indian "peon" there was one common revolt at the mere suggestion that swarms of Norte-Americanos, or, to use the popular name given them, "gringos," all armed, all prompt to shoot, pushful and overbearing, would be settled among them. All could remember what had come of the settlement of Sam Houston and his supporters in the once Mexican province of Texas. They had been Southerners, and it was precisely the old slave-holding States forming the Confederacy which had brought on the war of 1848 and had robbed Mexico of much of its territory. The suggestion was so ill received that nothing came of it. Nothing came of a not dissimilar

THE RISE TO THE FIRST RANK 89

scheme for settling a French colony in Sonora. But the suggestions had been made, and they were equally offensive to Mexicans and to the United States. Mexicans who had once been disposed to agree with Uraga that their national independence was safe with Maximilian began to think that it was more threatened by him and his French supporters than by anybody else. The Federal Government would tolerate neither French nor Confederate colonies on its borders. Napoleon III. never made a greater mistake than when he permitted himself to think aloud in his correspondence and to tell General Forey that it was his purpose to check the expansion of the United States over Latin America.

There was no concealment of the fact that the Government of Washington was pressing Napoleon III. for an answer to the pointed question when he meant to withdraw his troops. When they were gone there could be no reasonable doubt that the utterly artificial Empire of Maximilian would be brought down like a card castle. There is a close parallel between the Empire of Maximilian in Mexico and the monarchy of Joseph Bonaparte in Spain. The Spaniards would certainly never have been able to drive the French armies from their country by themselves, but if Napoleon had left his brother to fight with no better support than he could get from his Spanish partisans the patriot forces would have made short work of him. Yet if the Spaniards had frankly accepted Joseph, then Wellington could never have forced the French to retire. If the Mexicans had submitted honestly to Maximilian the United States would have had no ground for interference. In both cases native resistance gave the intervention of an allied force the means of proving decisive. Both countries would have spared themselves infinite misery if they could have taken the intruding ruler who demanded their submission. But nations do not live by material advantages, or common sense, alone, and the ages in which any people could accept a lost battle as a judgment of God, and bow for their own ultimate great good to a William the Conqueror, lie far back in the past.

For eight months Diaz remained a prisoner. His relations with his jailers, Austrian officers, were on the whole pleasant. When after a time he found himself placed under the care of Count Thun he was indeed very closely watched, and suffered, he says, some discourtesy. Thun tried to persuade him to write a letter to the patriot General Lucas, who was threatening to shoot certain imperialist prisoners. Diaz refused to comply with a request which would certainly have compromised himself, and would probably have done no service to the threatened captives. The Austrian governor retaliated by making his captivity more strict. He was not even allowed to go to the bath except with a sentinel to watch. Yet his confinement cannot have been very rigid. From his own account we hear of card parties with his fellow-Mexican prisoners and Austrian officers. When he had finally decided to effect another escape he had no difficulty in opening communications with friends outside. His trusted agent was an Indian of the name of Hernandez, who had been a servant of his family. Diaz could rely implicitly on the man's fidelity, but not altogether on his discretion. When the time for making the escape had come he instructed his follower to wait with a horse at a place he named, but did not say that the mount was needed for himself; Hernandez

THE RISE TO THE FIRST RANK

was told that he would be met by a prisoner who was about to escape. In order that he might be sure to give the horse to the right man he was supplied with the half of a visiting card, and told that the other would be presented by the escaping prisoner. If the precaution, which reads like a quotation from the memoirs of some hero of the Fronde, strikes the reader as a needless refinement, he must remember that Diaz knew his countrymen.

When the night fixed for his escape had come, Don Porfirio took a rope which he had provided with the help of a friend—a proof that the watch kept on him was not very thorough—and made his way from the flat roof of the convent of Sta. Caterina in which he was confined to the roof of an adjoining house. Beyond this house was a yard, or garden, enclosed by a wall which ran from the corner of the building. His plan was to let himself down from the edge of the roof to the wall and then drop into the street. The only support he could find for his rope was the lead figure of a saint. He found it very shaky, but calculated that it was fixed, though loosely, on a spike. The rope was tied round the pedestal, and Don Porfirio, who retained his power of swarming up a rope till an advanced age, had no difficulty in letting himself down. The street was empty, and all went well till he got down to the level of the wall. When he let go of the rope thinking to land on the coping of the wall he missed his footing, and fell inside right on the top of a stye full of pigs. He fell soft on the startled porkers, but rolled over and lost the only weapon he carried—a well-sharpened knife, the weapon which by various names of " navajo," " puñal," " curvo," or " falcon " comes kindly to the hand of the Spaniard and the Creole. The squeaking of the alarmed pigs rent the air, but the noise was too familiar to attract unwelcome attention. Diaz picked himself up, found a place where he could clear the wall, dropped into the street, and walking without undue haste, passing civil salutations with the stray night-walkers he met—" Buena noche "; " Vaya Usted, con Dios " (" Goodnight " and " God go with you ")—reached the place where his henchman was waiting for him with a horse. When once he was mounted he lost no time in making his way to the home of the guerrillero, the Sierra. A municipal official whom he met turned out to be a sympathiser, and gave him a useful hint where to meet other friends. The alarm was indeed raised and bells rung, but he was off and beyond reach.

Now began what one biographer, Dr. Fortunato Hernandez, has called the " epic " of Porfirio Diaz. To put it less poetically, the next year of the future President's life may be justly said to give us an exact picture of the rise of a highly capable guerrillero. He meets a few friends who follow his fortune. With them he overcomes a few enemies and takes their weapons. Yet other friends who will use the arms under his direction are soon recruited, and so the ball rolls till, one having become a few, the few become many. The band grows into an army. It is the history of Mina, of El Empecinado, of Chapalangarra, of Julian Sanchez, of José Palarea (called El Medico), of a whole brood of heroes of the Peninsular War, and of Spanish America. It would be amusing enough to follow the apparently erratic movements, the astute stratagems, the surprises, starts, escapes, swift hand-to-hand skirmishes, which make up the guerrillero's career. But we must resist the temptation to dwell

THE RISE TO THE FIRST RANK 93

at excessive length on these adventures. After all, they were not in the case of Porfirio Diaz different from those of other " cabecillas," or heads of guerrillas. There were others—his own brother Felix (El Chato) for one—who played the game as well as he could. He is important to us because he was much more than a guerrillero, because he was an organiser, a general, and a man of government. It took him a year to create a serious force, but when he had achieved the feat he brought to the siege of the city of Mexico not a mere overgrown guerrilla, but an army with a well-filled and well-managed military chest. If we look only at the marches and passages of fight we shall lose sight of the wood because of the multiplicity of the trees. Now the wood which really mattered was this—that during 1866 Diaz drew the south and south-east of Mexico into his own hand, created a Government and a treasury, and convinced friends and enemies alike that he was a man with aims far above the mere acquisition of booty, and faculties of a higher order than are needed to keep a band together in the Sierra and use it to worry a Government. A single incident of those important months says much to explain his final victory over all other forces at work in the hurly-burly of Mexican war and politics. After one successful skirmish with a certain Visoso, then an Imperialist, but later on a repentant Republican, he captured the sum of $3,000. Given, so he tells us, the moral character of some of the elements he had to work with (every guerrilla is of necessity a Cave of Adullam), it followed that the $3,000 was in extreme danger of being divided in the true brigand or piratical way at the capstan's head. If that had been allowed to happen, his band would soon have been no better than so many others, which differed little, or not at all, from downright brigands. But it was not allowed to happen. The $3,000 were collected from grasping hands, and became the nest-egg of a military chest from which Diaz handed over $300,000 to the empty treasury of Juarez when the capital was occupied. His treasurer, Manuel Guerrero, never lacked funds altogether. How he enforced honesty we are not told in detail, but can guess that the secret lay in the fact that he commanded because he was he, and they obeyed because they were they. In the last resort Diaz could when necessary kill his man. And then all knew that he would take care of them.

The taking care could go to great lengths. When nobody else was available Don Porfirio could even tackle a surgical operation : witness the case of the drum-major Rodriguez. The poor man had received a wound on the leg which made amputation unavoidable. It is hardly necessary to say that there was no surgeon attached to the guerrilla. The whole medical corps, such as it was, resided in the person of an American drummer (in the sense of bagman) who was wandering about in Mexico to sell some quack medicine. When he was asked whether he would undertake to perform the operation he began by answering with all the well-known self-reliance of his class and nation that he would. The only instruments available were a razor and a carpenter's saw. It would be idle indeed to suppose that there were any anæsthetics. The lack of these last was, however, made good (as it was in the Crimea) by the administration of a very strong dose of raw spirits. When the moment came to fulfil his promise the American became frightened and whispered to Diaz his confession that he dare not attempt the task of removing the leg. Then the general did what was necessary himself, and with the instruments named. He says —and nobody will doubt his word—that when the leg had been amputated he went away with the intimate conviction that the drum-major must infallibly die very shortly. Yet Rodriguez survived for many years, and lived, not unhappily, on a small pension—a remarkable instance of the American Indian's insensibility to pain and tenacity of life.

The most promising course Don Porfirio could take was to resume his command as general of the Army of the East. He could have served neither his cause nor himself by joining Juarez, who was still being hunted from pillar to post in the northern States. Nobody had been named to succeed him, and the field, though occupied by the enemy, was clear of rivals. The fact that the Army of the East had to be made, and by him, without help from the fugitive Republican Government was not altogether oppressing to a man in the prime of life, and well trained in the conditions of Spanish-American civil war. He might feel reasonably confident of his capacity to do what many of the party leaders of his country had done before, namely, create his army by his own exertions. A nucleus had gathered about him quickly. It consisted mainly of Republican officers who had been left without soldiers to lead through the recent disasters of their cause. We need not deny them the credit of having acted from conviction, but it is also true that they had not much choice. The native forces raised by Maximilian did not offer tempting chances of service. The Emperor had little money, and his troops were but poorly provided for. What resources he could command were devoted first of all to the Austrian and Belgian bands imported to stiffen his Mexican levies, and then to the French officers who entered his service as instructors of native soldiers. These men, who brought with them sentiments of dignity and self-respect formed in a great European army, were apt to treat the Mexican Imperialist officers with scant regard. Patriotic loyalty and political convictions were strengthened for the Mexicans who followed Diaz by resentment for what they not unnaturally considered mere insolence. So they fought as " reformados," to use a military term of Spanish origin once familiar to all Europe—that is to say, they did duty as soldiers because their corps were disbanded or broken up, and until fortune should give them a chance to resume their position.

The Commander-in-Chief of the as yet non-existent Army of the East would have preferred to begin in his native Oaxaca, but he was headed off by the French Colonel Ilon and the Imperialist guerrillero Visoso. There being no opening on that side, he made for Guerrero. This province was one of several parts of Mexico never occupied effectually either by the French army or the Imperial officers. As far as it was governed at all, it obeyed the former hero of Ayutla, who was in fact its cacique and ruled from his ranch at La Providencia.[1]

Alvarez supplied the refugees with arms—at least with a few, some of which are reported to have been

---

[1] Our ranch is known to all men to be the Spanish *rancho*, but the original is not generally used in the sense we give it. In Old Spain *rancho* means a soldier's rations. In most parts of Spanish America the name is given to a small holding occupied by a head herdsman in the employment of a big cattle station, *i.e.*, an " estancia."

flint-locks. General Leyva, Colonels Cano, Segura, and others, joined Diaz in La Providencia and put themselves under his orders. His operations grew more bold as he gathered strength, which he did in pretty exact proportion to the increasing favourableness of the circumstances during 1866. The good peace-loving people of Oaxaca had discovered within a few months, or even weeks, that when they helped Bazaine to rid them of the Republican authorities they did not also free themselves from tax collectors and forced contributions levied by the Emperor's Government, which had urgent need to improve its revenue, nor yet from the exactions of the patriot guerrilleros. They had in fact cause to regret the administration of Diaz, who, by the confession of his enemies, always made a moderate use of his power. And then it soon became a matter of common knowledge that the days of the French occupation were numbered. The Government of the United States offered a steady resistance to clamour for strong measures. It would have done a popular thing if it had sent an army into Mexico. There was a time when Bazaine felt called upon to take measures to concentrate his army in view of the possibility that General Sheridan would cross the Rio Grande at the head of 200,000 Federal troops. But concentration meant evacuation of all the outlying provinces north and south. In the meantime arms, money, and volunteers began to cross the frontier to support Juarez. As the French drew together Republican armies began to spring for the soil. The Republicans who had never reconciled themselves to the intruding Empire came out of hiding or descended from the Sierras to be organised into regular armies. All that element of prudent people who when the broom is to be used prefer to be on the side of the handle began to see that it was much safer to join Juarez than to sit quiet and still more so than to help the Emperor. The agony of Maximilian and his poor wife was beginning.

The southern provinces were less accessible to American help than the northern. But very soon the French posts on the coast and their squadrons in the Pacific and the Gulf of Mexico had to be withdrawn. Then help from the States came to Diaz also. His advance was not continuously successful. Though he had not to deal with regular French troops, but only with Maximilian's Austrians[1] and Mexicans, he was for some time held in check and once badly beaten. But his scattered band soon rallied, and went on growing in force. He fixed his headquarters at Tlapa, and from thence made his excursions either to beat up the enemy's quarters, or *para arbitrarse algunos recursos*—that is to say, to levy money and men among the Mixteca and other Indian tribes.

By autumn he had made himself master of the open country, and had reduced the Imperialist garrison of Oaxaca to a state of blockade. The Government at Mexico, sinking into ever-increasing difficulties, could do but little to help General Oronoz, the Mexican supporter who held the town. At the close of September Diaz overpowered a small body of "Hungarian" cavalry at Nochistlan. He frankly allows that they were only a few, but points out that their undeniable superiority in discipline was an appreciable set-off to

[1] Diaz himself speaks of his European opponents as Hungarians, but I do not feel sure that he used the name only to designate the nationality of the foreigners. "Ungaro" is a Hungarian no doubt, but the sense in which it is most familiar to Spanish-speaking peoples is gipsy, or even only vagrant, tinker. The first gipsies who followed that trade in Spain said, probably with truth, that they came from Hungary.

THE RISE TO THE FIRST RANK   99

their numerical weakness. This stroke exasperated Oronoz, and he sallied from the town with some 2,000 men, resolved to scatter the Republican guerrilleros.

Oronoz may have been zealous for his cause, but he was not quick-witted enough to handle his opponent. He allowed Diaz to lead him into a trap of the most simple if also of the most effective kind. The Imperialist officer advanced, apparently without taking the least precaution to reconnoitre, along a road running through the Indian town or big village Miahuatlan, at the foot of the Sierra de Cuixtla. Diaz, who did keep a sharp look-out, laid an ambush for him. He posted a part of his mounted men in front of the village to meet Oronoz and draw him on. The bulk of his force was disposed to the rear of the village, concealed in " waves of the ground." The function of the cavalry in front of Miahuatlan was to run away through the village and draw the Imperialists into an over-confident pursuit which would carry them headlong into the middle of the ambush in the rear. Oronoz fell into the trap, came helter-skelter through the village, and was fired into from both sides. His force was brought to a sharp stop. The reaction from over-confidence to panic is inevitable with ill-trained troops, and the Imperialists began to turn back. Then Diaz charged and drove them in rout before him. The official, or patriotic, historian of this war, Señor Escudero, talks of the " delirium of battle " in Miahuatlan. Yet it seems that the total loss of the Imperialists was only eighty in a force of well over 2,000. As for the killed, the majority were, as was the custom in Mexican conflicts, shot after the battle. We have the authority of Don Porfirio for the fact that twenty-two Mexican officers whom he captured were shot. He spared the lives of some French officers whom he took. He was nowise given to the Munchausen style. He never indulges in talk about deliriums of battle and so forth. There is a tone of sobriety and an obvious desire to tell the truth in his reminiscences which inspires confidence. He records a detail which a writer more concerned to give an heroic turn to the story would have omitted. He says that the villagers of Miahuatlan, who were " very daring and *were drunk*,"[1] fired into the flanks of the Imperialists and did good service by capturing hack and led horses. The loss of these latter was disastrous for the officers of Oronoz's ill-led column.

The victory at Miahuatlan, which was won October 3, 1866, had a considerable moral effect. It was indeed a mere guerrillero action such as had been fought by the hundred on Mexican soil without producing any consequences worth noting. But it was of immense importance in relation to surrounding conditions. The Republican arrows were now flying with the wind, and all the world could see that unless help came the next step would be the occupation of the city and the total ruin of the Imperial cause in the south and east. Hard pressed as Maximilian's Government was, it could not allow such a disaster to happen without making some attempt to support its officers. A column of 1,500 of its foreign soldiers, on whom it could rely more than on its Mexicans, was sent to relieve Oronoz. A few days after his victory and the retreat of his opponent on Oaxaca Diaz intercepted a despatch from Mexico to Oronoz informing him that the relief was on its way. He was then blockading

[1] *Estaban ébrios*, he says ; and he adds nothing to indicate that they were *ébrios* with patriotic emotion or indeed with anything but aguardiente or pulque.

THE RISE TO THE FIRST RANK

the town closely with the force he had organised and had now brought to fair order, and with the cavalry guerrillas commanded by his brother Felix. He was in some danger of finding himself between two fires. There were three ways in which he could guard against the misfortune. He could try to storm the town before the relieving force could come up, or he could turn on that force itself, or he could raise the blockade. The third course he was resolved not to take, and he did not think his force equal to taking the first. So he adopted the second, and carried it out with military decision aided by a pleasing admixture of guerrillero craft.

The Republicans had already secured a footing in the lower quarters of the town, though they had made no impression on the barricaded, loopholed, and mined upper part of it. Diaz knew that his opponent had ways of learning what was going on in his camp. He had observed in the course of his studies of human nature that if a man wishes his secrets to be soon proclaimed from the housetops he can take no more effectual course than to confide them in strict confidence to well-selected friends. Therefore he informed such chosen persons as he knew would not fail to blab that he meant to assault the upper town on the very next night. As he foresaw, Oronoz was duly warned, and stood to arms prepared to account for any movement he might hear in the lines of the blockaders as being the preliminary of an intended surprise. Then, while the Imperialist waited for the attack which never came, Diaz marched swiftly and in the dark to occupy the point at which he intended to intercept the relieving column. When at daybreak the Republican position was seen to be empty, Oronoz was puzzled. He suspected a trap and could not guess what it was. The despatch which might have enlightened him had, as we have seen, been intercepted. After hesitating and delaying long enough to allow Diaz to lay his ambush for the coming column, Oronoz did come out. But his shrewd opponent played for his head. After posting his infantry and guns he came back with his cavalry to a farm on the road. The mayordomo, or bailiff, in charge was, as he well knew, a strong Clerical partisan. So he made ostentatious preparations to ambush Oronoz in sight of this man, who was not put under arrest nor watched. Of course, he ran off with his valuable information. The Imperialist officer, who had the fear of Diaz in his bones since Miahuatlan, fell into the trap and went in haste back to Oaxaca.

Don Porfirio had decided to wait for the relieving column in a place which was to have a personal interest for him—La Carbonera. He had instructed his subordinate, General Figueroa, to join at that spot with certain Indians of the Mixteca hills who had "risen at the call of patriotism." The call had of course been sounded by the voice and in the tones which usually summoned an "Indiada."

La Carbonera is a small plateau on the road to Oaxaca from the north. It is divided into a larger and higher and a smaller and lower portion by a "cuenca," a shell or dip, through which the road runs. It was wooded, and on the lower portion the bush was thick. This was the part of the ground where the infantry were stationed by Diaz. Colonel Hotze, the Austrian who commanded the relieving force, showed no more judgment than Oronoz. He marched till he was brought up by the Mexicans on the lower ground.

THE RISE TO THE FIRST RANK 103

Then Diaz, who disposed of the greater numbers, turned his flank through the wood on the higher ground and beat him utterly.

The well-managed affair at La Carbonera completed the ruin of the Imperial cause in Oaxaca. Diaz had marched on October 16 and had won his fight on the 18th. On the 30th the town was surrendered by Oronoz. The interval had been largely spent in negotiations. One of the negotiators was the bishop Dr. Covarrubias, whose aim was to provide for himself. He sent to ask the Republican general what treatment he had to expect. Don Porfirio, speaking daggers that he might frighten his man away and so be spared the necessity to use them, replied that it was his intention to shoot the bishop in " full uniform." Dr. Covarrubias did not think proper to embarrass him by giving him a chance of fulfilling his threat, but fled hastily to Mexico along the line of escape carefully left open for him. Yet, as after Miahuatlan, Diaz showed no squeamishness in ordering military executions of traitors. Pablo Franco, the Imperial Prefect of Oaxaca, who endeavoured to escape at the same time as the bishop, was taken (probably because he was more sharply looked after) and condemned to be shot. He appealed for mercy in vain. He had indeed done a thing which made it difficult to pardon him. A known Republican of Oaxaca, Justo Rodriguez by name, had been shot by his orders. Justo's brother, who was a portrait painter, had made a likeness of his body after execution. Diaz hesitated, or was thought to hesitate, as to whether he would allow the execution. The painter sent the portrait to him with a statement of the facts, and Franco was left to his fate. The story stands in the official biography of the President published so late as 1909, and with his approval, by Dr. Fortunato Hernandez, "Un Pueblo, un Siglo y un Hombre." It is allowed that Diaz was, as compared with other Mexican leaders, humane. Yet we see from this episode, and from the slaying of the Mexican officers taken at Miahuatlan, that he was not wholly untouched by the element of pure savagery in which he was born and grew up. In his later days, when he had become the pet of American and European capitalists and " edifying letters " were written about him by persons who had received favours from him and hoped to receive others, details of this kind were suppressed. Yet he had no wish to hide them himself. He was no more inclined than Cromwell to be beautified, at any rate not by himself, and it is most probable that he saw nothing to conceal. He was a governing man, but he was a Mexican. Full of blood and battles was his youth, and full of blood and battles was his age, and in his country it was not given him ever to leave that life of blood.

The fall of Oaxaca was soon followed by the surrender of Tehuantepec, the last Imperialist post in the south. Diaz now received substantial help from the United States in the form, not of money, but of arms. Money he could get by raising contributions, but it would have done him no good if he had had to spend it in acquiring arms. The south being now reconquered for the Republican cause, he could prepare to bring help to his party in the centre. The French troops were being concentrated on the line from Mexico city to Veracruz, getting ready to take ship for Europe. Napoleon III. was naturally much concerned to provide against the risk that the evacuation should be disgraced by some untoward incident. Bazaine was

THE RISE TO THE FIRST RANK 105

no less desirous to come off with a good grace. The atmosphere was favourable to intrigue, and a letter which Diaz wrote at the time to Don Matias Romero records that he was asked to take part in one of a truly extraordinary character. Romero was Mexican Minister at Washington. The Republican officers in the south were cut off from Juarez, who was in the northern provinces, and were compelled to communicate with him through the United States. So it was to the Minister, and not to the President, that Diaz made this surprising statement : " General Bazaine, through a third party, offered to surrender to me the cities which they [*i.e.*, the French] occupied, also to deliver Maximilian, Marquez, Miramon, etc., into my hands, provided I would accede to a proposal which he made me, and which I rejected, as I deemed it not very honourable. Another proposition was also made me by authority of Bazaine, for the purchase of six thousand muskets and four million percussion caps, and if I had desired it, he would have sold me both guns and powder." [1]

The witness for the fact that Bazaine made these proposals is manifestly the third party who reported them to Diaz. Twenty years after the letter to Romero was written (in 1886) it came to the knowledge of Bazaine, who was then living in great misery at Madrid. It provoked him to write an angry expostulation to Don Porfirio, who at that later date had been well established for some time as President of Mexico. The unhappy exile recriminated by a counter-charge that Diaz had written a compromising letter to him in 1865, and asked very reasonably for the name of the alleged agent. Don Porfirio's answer is explicit:

[1] Mrs. Tweedie's "Porfirio Diaz," p. 169.

"With regard to the second point, although some years have now passed, I do not think that you will have forgotten Señor Carlos Thiele. I must tell you, since you ask me, that he was the person whom I sent to you to arrange the exchange of Mexican prisoners who were in your power for those taken by me in the actions of Nochistlan, Miahuatlan, La Carbonera, Tehuantepec and Oaxaca, an exchange which was made with great advantage to the French army, because I sent as a favour all the chiefs, officers and soldiers that were left with me when you had no officers of ours of equal rank to exchange for them. This Señor Thiele it was who, in your name, made me the proposals which I reported in the letter which has aroused your resentment, and who, a few months after the circumstances to which I refer, settled in Guatemala, where he can still be found. I should be very pleased if you could some day persuade me that the whole affair was an imposture on the part of this gentleman, and I would make it known to the public who read my letter; but for this I need Señor Thiele's own declaration, as the knowledge that I have of him does not justify me in doubting his honour."

As for the letter of 1865, Diaz avows that he could not remember its terms, but was sure it could not do him any harm, for he could not call to mind any deed in his life of which he had cause to be ashamed. And there perhaps we may as well leave the matter. That Don Carlos Thiele, when he had been hunted up in his retreat in Guatemala, would have confessed that he was guilty of a mere imposture seems improbable in the last degree. But then it is no less incredible that a marshal of France who had a great career before him at home should have offered to kidnap Maximilian,

THE RISE TO THE FIRST RANK 107

Marquez, Miramon, etc., and hand them over to the Mexican general of the Army of the East. What price could Mexico pay to compensate him for social and professional ruin and dishonour ? Diaz does not tell us what the condition was that Bazaine was said by Don Carlos Thiele to have made. Until we have better evidence than the word of the gentleman now retired to Guatemala to go on it is useless to inquire. The safest course is to dismiss the whole as a story of a cock and a bull. It is true enough that some superfluous arms which Bazaine disposed of before he left Mexico did come into the hands of the Republicans. But then the Mexicans who were armed by Maximilian were always going over with arms and baggage to the enemy. So did the Spaniards who were recruited by Joseph Bonaparte in the Peninsular War. Diaz says he got them by ordering the villagers to bring in whatever arms they had. He no doubt told the truth. We need, however, have no hesitation in believing that Maximilian tried to induce Don Porfirio to join him and sent a certain M. Burnouf to give him the invitation. The poor Emperor was desperate at the close of 1866, and was in a mood to try to make arrows of all wood. It was a matter of course that the offer should be refused. Even if we put all considerations of honour and principle aside (which, obviously, we have no right to do), common sense would have taught Diaz to keep aloof from an adventure which was visibly on the brink of ruin. Even when he was a prisoner at Puebla and the Republican cause was at its lowest ebb, he had steadily refused even to see Maximilian.

All this conflict of insinuations and assertions serves merely as a reminder that the French intervention ended as it began, amid intrigues and delusions. The Mexicans never dared to make an attack on the retreating French troops. Bazaine shipped the last detachment of his soldiers and sailed away with them in the early days of February, 1867. Maximilian, after a short crisis of hesitation, did the one thing which could save his honour. He had committed himself to folly, and all that remained for him to do was to stay and die. His enemies closed on him from north and south. On March 9 Diaz, having now thoroughly organised his Army of the East, began the siege of Puebla. His attack followed the same line as Forey's—from the east and from house to house and barricade to barricade. The defence of the Imperialists was for a time at least resolute. Diaz was once in no small danger from the fall of the blazing roof of a house while he was directing the attack in person. He had the misfortune to be rather severely burnt. Yet the way in which the town fell on April 2 shows, to say no more of it, that the defence was far less resolute than Ortega's had been in 1863. What was said is that the place was betrayed for money, but one has to allow that this is just what would be said.

The fall of Puebla would be a final blow to the Imperialist cause, for when the city was in possession of the Republicans all communications between Mexico and Veracruz were cut. Some effort must unquestionably be tried to save it. The attempt was made by Marquez, the Tiger of Tacubaya, who was now in command at Mexico. If there was any man from whom the most determined exertions in the Imperial cause were to be expected he was this blood-stained partisan. There was that between him and the Republicans which seemed to make it for ever impossible that there could be any question of quarter for him. Yet the Prince of Salm Salm, who was serving Maximilian and was actually present with Marquez's command, believed that he played false. He left Mexico with a force which could, if vigorously used, have raised the siege of Puebla. It included some Austrian troops of far better quality than the Mexican levies, though weak in numbers. But he dawdled on the road, and while he delayed Diaz stormed the town. If the element of treason was absent (and all our witnesses, native or foreign, are far from the truth if it was often unknown in Mexican conflicts), then Don Porfirio acted as did the Duke of Wellington when he knew that Marmont was on the way to relieve Ciudad Rodrigo. " Ciud ad Rodrigo must be taken to-night," was the famous order, and taken it was. Even if there was treason, Diaz was entitled to take advantage of the baseness of his opponents, however much he might despise them. " La traicion place, pero no el que lo hace " (" The treason is acceptable, but not the traitor "), is another Spanish proverb, and military casuistry has always allowed of the corruption of the enemy's officers. Be the truth as it may, Puebla was taken, and not without some fighting.

And now the next step was the pursuit of Marquez. On April 5, on the third day after he had occupied the town, Diaz marched to overtake the " Tiger." He was unable to start sooner because two or three of the outlying forts continued to resist. The way of surrender was made smooth, and on this occasion there was no butchery of prisoners. Don Porfirio found and availed himself of an opportunity to prove that he did not nurse a grudge. When he escaped from Puebla in September a certain Imperialist official, one Escamillo, had made a great display of zeal by offering a reward for the capture of the prisoner. He had talked of shooting. He was now in Don Porfirio's power, and was reasonably nervous till he was relieved by the good-humoured, if rather scornful, words, " It was lucky for me I was not caught."

The pursuit of Marquez was pushed with energy. On April 6 Diaz, who had left his infantry and guns to follow and had led the pursuit with his cavalry, came upon the enemy at San Diego Notario. Marquez made no serious attempt to stand, and he left the Austrian or Hungarian and Polish horsemen, commanded by Kodolich, Wickenburg, and Khevenhüller, to cover his retreat. A clash followed which has, as is not unusual in all accounts of wars, been diversely reported. The Mexican version—that is to say, Don Porfirio's—is that the Europeans were beaten in and the whole body of the Imperialists forced into a run. Prince Salm Salm has it that the Mexicans were beaten off and the retreat of the Imperialists covered. Marquez marched hurriedly for Guadalupe Hidalgo, to the north of Mexico, taking a curve to reach his refuge. Diaz hoped to cut his road at Paso de Tortolitas. He had directed another Republican officer to occupy the pass. This officer, Jesus Lalanne, did make the attempt, and was severely cut up. But he delayed Marquez till Diaz could bring his infantry and guns into action. Finally the " Tiger " got away with the majority of his men by sacrificing his guns and baggage and going off across country in the regular scattered guerrilla style. The Europeans in his army suffered severely; but he and his Mexicans did not shine as fighters.

The ensuing blockade and occupation of the city of

THE RISE TO THE FIRST RANK

Mexico formed the honourable close to the services of Porfirio Diaz in this war. The capitulation of the city on June 20, the day after the execution of Maximilian at Querétaro, was indeed the penultimate date of the struggle. The actual last was the capitulation of the Imperialist garrison of Veracruz on the 28th of the same month. It was the good fortune of the future President of Mexico that he ended this period of his life in circumstances which made it possible for him to combine perfect loyalty to his cause with the utmost moderation. He had no direct connection with the tragedy at Querétaro, for tragedy it was in more than the loose sense of the word. It has been much the custom of historians to draw a distinction between the humanity of General Diaz and the Indian ferocity of Juarez. A biographer is bound in honour to say the best he can for his hero, and there has been and will be much good to say of Porfirio Diaz. But the loyalty of a biographer is one thing and the *lues Boswelliana* is another. It was possible, and even easy, to show humanity at Mexico. It was not so easy, and it was even not possible, at Querétaro. Can anybody give a rational reason why the Archduke Maximilian should not have shared the fate of the Count of Raousset Boulbon? To say that he was a gentleman of illustrious birth and that he ought not to have been treated like a vulgar filibuster is not to give a rational reason, but to make an exhibition of flunkeyism. And apart from that contemptible sentiment, what is there to say of the unhappy Archduke? Napoleon III. was in 1862 the ruler of a sovereign State, and he may be said to have had a right to pursue any line of policy he chose, however unwise. His officers and soldiers obeyed their master as they were bound by military honour and all law to do. But Maximilian was no officer of Napoleon's. He was, with all his great pedigree, simply an adventurer who came to fight for a throne, for he had no sort of evidence that the Mexicans would accept him. When he consented to sign the notorious decree by which he refused quarter to the Republican officers who fell into his hands he put himself on a level with the very worst of the people he was professing to regenerate. If he had won he would have enjoyed his victory in wealth and power. It was the least he could do to stake his life, and when he lost to pay the forfeit. He did so quietly and manfully, and that was best for him. Juarez had a hard part to play, but he did his duty. If he had done less he would only have encouraged other younger sons of royal houses to seek their fortunes in the disorders of Spanish-American republics sword in hand. We need not think that no element of revenge entered into his decision. After all he was a Mexican-Indian. But we have no right to affirm that revenge was his main motive. What Diaz would have done in his place must remain a mere matter of conjecture, but he never explicitly condemned the President's action.

As it was, he had only to wait and watch till the city capitulated. It is highly probable that he might have forced his way in if he had chosen. But the surrender was certain to come, and he was anxious to shed no blood unnecessarily. Hunger would do the work effectually, and the brutality of Marquez could only serve to make the townsmen long the more heartily for the coming of the day of his overthrow. The savage was indeed desperate. He made a furious display of a determination to hold out to the last,

THE RISE TO THE FIRST RANK 113

but the main measures he took were to extort money and scatter lies. Whoever refused to pay the forced loans he demanded was put into prison and allowed the smallest ration which would support life. This kind of energy was quite in the Mexican tradition. Juarez had done the same thing; but Mexicans who had money to lose, and the foreign men of business settled among them, may well have asked themselves what they had gained from the grandiose schemes of Napoleon III. for the regeneration of Mexico. One firm was robbed of $125,000 and another of $100,000. Some part of this plunder—to say the very least of it—was not spent on the defence of the city, but reserved to be carried off when the time should come to run away. Meanwhile Marquez and the Imperialist Press, which repeated what he ordered it to say, kept assuring the townsmen that Maximilian was victorious in the north and would soon come to their assistance. It is only fair to add that on May 6 he did get a message from Maximilian reporting some successes won on April 27, but nobody knew better than Marquez how hollow such victories must needs be. Though the forces of Diaz were as yet hardly sufficient to allow him to beleaguer the city closely, he was master of the open country, and could cut off the supply of food. Early in June provisions were running short and the inhabitants, if not the Imperialist soldiers, began to suffer severely from hunger. The one passage of what can be called fighting took place on May 12. On that date General M. Diaz de la Vega, an Imperialist officer, made a sortie to the north, succeeded in forcing the blockading force back for some little distance, and collecting a useful quantity of forage. The Prince of Salm Salm gives the whole credit for the operation to the Austrians in the garrison. The Mexican authorities deny that any Austrians took part in it.

On May 16 Diaz found means to let the town know that Maximilian had been taken on the previous day. He had the news by telegraph. Marquez continued to deny and to threaten to shoot. But reinforcements began to reach Diaz from the north. On May 24 he was joined by Ramon Corona with 15,000 men, and by his brother Felix with cavalry from the south. Other reinforcements followed, and the lines were drawn closer round the city. Marquez continued to deny and to wrangle, and as the end grew nearer his efforts to extort money became more savage. On May 28 he was persuaded or forced to send out a flag of truce to verify the report of the Emperor's surrender. Diaz showed the officer who brought it the letter which Maximilian had sent to Baron Magnus asking him to come with a counsel to assist in his defence. Still Marquez would not give in, but declared that the government now belonged of right to a regency. The fact was that the man could not surrender. For him there could be no quarter. His only hope was to break out after laying hands on as much money as he could carry and escape to the hills and from thence to the United States. He made his last effort on the night of June 17–18 with 6,000 men, but was met by Diaz and driven back on the city. And now the end came swiftly. The Austrians refused to fight. They had been told by the Minister Baron Lago that the Emperor had written from his prison telling them to resist no longer, and that the letter must have been intercepted by Marquez. They withdrew into their barrack and stood on their guard.

THE RISE TO THE FIRST RANK 115

The conduct of these heroes does not appear to have been calculated to persuade the Mexicans that Europeans stood on a higher moral level than themselves. They had renounced their nationality when they entered the service of the Emperor. But in the general disaster they hurried to seek protection from the Austrian Minister Baron Lago, without making the least effort to obtain terms for their Mexican fellow-soldiers. Diaz, taking the whole responsibility on himself, entered into negotiations with Baron Lago on the 19th, and promised favourable terms of capitulation to the Austrians. They were to keep their personal baggage though they were required to surrender their arms, and were secured a safe conduct to Veracruz. While they were providing for their safety Marquez was taking care of his. He resigned the Government and found means to hide himself, till he escaped to the United States. Other Imperialists who were very badly compromised were not so fortunate. General Ramon Tabera, who replaced Marquez, endeavoured to obtain a capitulation, and, on being told that he must surrender at discretion, talked of fighting to the last. But when Diaz began a bombardment, and made visible preparations for a storm, Mexico surrendered on June 20. The town was occupied next day.

With the occupation of the capital of the Republic we come to the turning-point in the life of Porfirio Diaz, or perhaps it would be more accurate to say the point where he was to be called upon to show whether he had it in him to go further and higher. His action at this time, both during and after the siege, seems to prove that he himself was conscious that he stood at the place where his fate was to be decided.

He acted as if he were consciously presenting himself to his countrymen as one who was fit to rule, and might be trusted to use power without brutality. He confined himself to doing what was necessary to secure the victory of his cause, but he avoided bloodshed as much as he could. He took no personal revenge, and those of the Imperialist partisans who were captured and put to death died by order of the Government, and not by his. If this was his purpose, he succeeded. From the day of capitulation he was a recognised candidate for the place of governor of his country. He had still not a little fighting, successful and unsuccessful, to do, but his purely military life was over and his political career had begun.

CHAPTER V

THE POLITICIAN

AT this moment when we are at the turn of the road we must stop to make an estimate of the man, to endeavour to see what he was in himself, and what his work could be expected to be either in so far as it was the expression of his own capacity, or as it was conditioned by the elements he had lying to his hand. There is a known difficulty in learning what any man was, or is, in himself, and it is apt to be insuperable when we lack, as we do in the case of Porfirio Diaz, the guidance of a great mass of private correspondence. No evidence of that character has been published, nor is it likely that any ever will be. Don Rafael de Zayas Enriquez, author of a bitter-sweet biographical study, has stated that he never learnt to read or write well. The very neat handwriting of certain notes of his published in facsimile vindicates his penmanship, but we may take it for granted that he was no great writer of letters. The autobiographical narrative he dictated in his latter years shows no trace of self-revelations. It is downright and purely historical—at least, that is the case with the published parts; and while it gives the acts it does not dwell on the reasons nor the motives. But we may doubt whether there was anything to reveal. As he appears to the world Porfirio Diaz was a man who had one rule and one great quality. He played the game, and he loved order. The rule and the quality can be so amply displayed in act that autobiographical revelations are quite superfluous. His mind was simple and his will was clear. He had no velleities, but always definite intentions.

This essentially practical and manly mind was lodged in a most fortunately constituted body. He is called tall by one who was himself very short, and of middle height by another who judged by a different standard. All agree that he was remarkably well put together, though he looked somewhat taller in the saddle than he did on foot. From this we may perhaps conclude that, like the strong types of men belonging to the southern, or so-called Latin, races, he was longer in the body than the legs. It is very credible that, as some of his critics have alleged, he liked best to be seen and to be pictured in the saddle. Nor is it anywise difficult to believe that he liked a big horse rather than a small one. He belonged to a race of horsemen. He spoke a language in which horseman and gentleman are synonymous. It is quite likely that he would have seen nothing absurd in the old maxim that the man who is mounted on the great horse is as high above his fellow-men as fortune can place him. A strongly-built frame is a great gift of Nature, but it must be completed by a sound constitution and a freedom from any tendency to disease. That Diaz was favoured in that respect even beyond the fortune of well-endowed men is proved by one patent fact. He lived either in poverty or in constant hardship and exposure for more than half of a life of over eighty years. He was wounded, and badly; he was severely burnt; he was visited at least once by marsh fever contracted in unwholesome bivouacs. These injuries and invasions of germs of disease had no weakening effect on him whatever. They were thrown off and left no evil consequences behind. He died of senile decay when the strong body was worn out.

Other men have had these advantages and have wasted them. We have the testimony of those who hated him, and would have said all the ill they could of him, that he treated his powerful frame and his fine constitution as instruments to be kept in order by sobriety. For the first half of his life the conditions in which he had to work constituted a perpetual training. He had to ride by day and night, when his safety depended on his nerve and his vigilance. But if he had not observed the famous rules of Blaise de Monluc he would not have borne the strain even in his youth.[1]

From the time that he became the political head of his country he made it his aim to keep himself in training. He could not have adopted this rule if he had not been prepared. His habits do not give us the chief reason why he rose, for men of a very different way of life had reached the place, but they do explain better than any other knowledge we have of him why he remained at the head for so many years. All our witnesses tell the same tale, but the only one who need be quoted is the most hostile, Carlo de Fornaro,

---

[1] The four rules of Monluc will be found in the address to the lieutenants and captains of France which he puts at the head of his Commentaries. They do not contain the highest reasons for observing morality of conduct. Blaise would naturally leave them to his brother the Bishop, but, speaking as an old soldier to young soldiers, he talks excellent sense. The passage is too long to quote, but the substance of it is that a man will never become one of those good officers whose services are indispensable to the distributers of promotion unless he avoids certain sins of the flesh which besot and weaken him, so that he will not have at command the clear head, the steady nerve, and the ever active body which can rise to all emergencies by day or night.

author of a typical scream of Spanish-American invective. Observe that Señor Fornaro, in his " Diaz, Czar of Mexico," published in several languages in 1909, speaks in this style of a passage in the history of the President's first term of office : " This was the finishing stroke of the most brutish, the most craven, and the wildest orgie of blood perpetrated in the annals of humanity ; it was an insensate Saturnalia of Gore, the luxurious rage of an impotent, cowardly, sadic old despot."

The event of which Señor Fornaro spoke in these rabid words will be told under its proper date. In the meantime, this frenzy of abuse is a not exceptional example of Spanish-American political polemics. The disputants hurl terms of insult as if they were half-bricks and with an apparent entire disregard to the meaning or applicability of the words they use. About fifty pages further on we get this account of the manner of life of the " sadic old despot " : " His private life for the last thirty years has been spotless, and although surrounded by all the luxuries he has led a life simple as a hermit's : in food and drink abstemious as an Arab ; in a country where everybody smokes he has been an exception ; where alcoholism is rampant he only tastes water ; where everybody goes to bull-fights he stays at home ; does not visit theatres except at official functions ; seldom hunts, and never plays. Private life, personal hygiene, hard work, physical and intellectual economy, have been concentrated for the prolongation of power through the medium of a perfect body."

He loved no plays, he heard no music. The Presidency was to him, not a prize to be enjoyed, but a redoubt to be stormed, and then held by sleepless

THE POLITICIAN

vigilance and the same hard fighting that was needed to win it. Given a man of prompt practical faculty, great physical energy, of steady purpose and strong will, and we can easily understand why he conquered in the midst of the feeble personalities, the social incoherences and the political nullities of Mexico.

When we have made for ourselves a picture of the manner of man he was, we may before entering on his political career endeavour to attain to some conception of what he was likely to be able to do. That he won the Presidency and held it for a period which makes a long reign for a king whose right was not liable to be contested was a feat. But was it to be only the feat of the resolute skipper who, pistol in hand, cows a mutinous crew and keeps it to its duty, or the achievement of a statesman who develops institutions and makes a lasting Government? A few years ago the general disposition would have been to put him with the creative statesmen. There were some who doubted. It is said, and we can believe, that Cecil Rhodes declined to enter into certain enterprises in Mexico because he could find no security that the peace of the country would last longer than the life of President Diaz. He spoke with the understanding of one who knew what government is. The world at large was of another opinion. The difficulty would have been to obtain adhesion to the verdict that the regenerator of Mexico, the creator of a new and better order, would turn out to be only a transient keeper of the peace. Now we all know that the old disorder welled up before the death of the strong man who had kept it down. He seemed to have failed, and those who had been most ready before 1909 to believe that a new heaven and a new earth had been created for Mexico by him were not the least disposed to think that they were disappointed by his fault. Those who were so quick to condemn ought to have asked themselves whether a ruler can be fairly said to have failed if he has achieved a great measure of success in a whole generation of effort to do the impossible.

Gourgaud, who was mentally incapable of inventing it, has recorded a saying of Napoelon's at St. Helena : " J'ai trouve tous les éléments de l'empire. . . . Je ne serais pas venu, qu'el est probable qu'un autre aurait fait de même. . . . Un homme n'est qu'un homme." He said it beyond doubt, and his words were profoundly true of himself and of all the rulers of men. However great a man may be, and in whatever field he works, he is subject to a human limitation. He can handle what is given him to manipulate, but he cannot create his material. The greatest of statesmen can do no more than the sheep-breeders who sell the wool, or the weavers who make it into cloth. They can breed with more intelligence and so improve the wool, or they can improve the process of weaving and therefore produce better cloth. The best of them cannot create the wool-bearing animal. Napoleon did great and lasting things, but then he had great and lasting elements lying ready to be worked on. There is no sort of comparison between the French and the jarring classes of Creoles, half-breeds, and Indians who make up the population of Mexico. But a people may be far below the French of the revolutionary epoch in intellect, and yet offer all the elements out of which a stable polity may be made. They may have ideas, aspirations, dispositions which only need to be combined in order to produce a

THE POLITICIAN

Government, and an Administration which will last for centuries. Those were elements Napoleon found in France, and there were others. The very parts of the Administration he framed, which still governs France, had been rough hewn for him by the monarchy. His Prefect was the old Intendant. His centralisation had been begun by the kings. It never came to full development under them, partly because they falsified it by interference at the bidding of personal whims, partly because it was blocked by the mouldering remains of what had once been real instruments of government. The Revolution burnt the rubbish away, but the indestructible parts of the old Administration were there to be used. All that was necessary was to put them together. It was the work of a constructive statesman. But a ruler as great in capacity as Napoleon, and a wiser than he, could not have created these elements. " Un homme n'est qu'un homme."

Let us make a great effort and assume that the boy who was baptised at Oaxaca on September 15, 1830, had been a Napoleon, what could he have done with Mexico ? He could have kept it quiet, he could have given it some material prosperity, as Diaz did, and that is all he could have done. When he had achieved his utmost the Creole would have still been a Creole, the half-breed a half-breed, and the Indian an Indian. If, indeed, it had been possible for a man living in the nineteenth century in a country bordering on the United States, and in communication with Europe, to get himself accepted as a " Son of the Gods," he might have founded a sacred race and a lasting institution. But that was the impossible of all impossibles. In the age he was born into and in his country, all he could be was to be the constable who kept the peace, and that he could be only while his strength lasted. We cannot, therefore, fairly ask that Diaz should have given more than he gave. He could only be the best of the so-called Spanish-American tyrants. We cannot critically compare him with a Richelieu, a Cavour, or a Bismarck, who had all such widely different elements to deal with. By the side of those statesmen he must needs look but a transient, even a futile, figure. The fair comparison is between him and other Spanish-American rulers who have had the same problem to deal with : Francia in Paraguay, Juan Manuel Rosas in the Argentine, Guzman Blanco, " the great American," in Colombia, or Barrios in Central America. He has no need to fear comparison with any of them.

There are two other conditions which must be clearly realised before we begin to look at his political career. They are the physical limitations of Mexico and the nature of the Indian population.

In some parts of South America the influx of foreign capital, mainly British, and of foreign labour, of which the most valuable part is Italian, has bred a considerable material prosperity. The Argentine is the most conspicuous example. The growth of this industry has made it more profitable for political intriguers to levy blackmail and take bribes than to fight. In these countries the essential anarchy of the community is skinned over, and presents a smooth surface to the passing visitor. This has not been the case in Mexico, and is not likely to be. A great deal is said of the natural wealth of the country, but there is one fact which ought to be a warning to those who are inclined to accept all they are invited to believe on this subject.

THE POLITICIAN

After thirty years—if not of absolute peace, at least of anarchy kept down by the parish constable—the whole trade of Mexico, with its 769,000 square miles of territory and a population estimated at 15,000,000 or so, is not equal to the trade of Cuba, which is little more than a twentieth of its size and has a population of 2,000,000. The estimates of population are but plausible guesswork. No real census has ever been taken in a Spanish or Portuguese American State. Yet the proportion as between Mexico and Cuba may be as 15 is to 2. If the first were really a country of great natural wealth this would most assuredly not be the case. It would at least be on a level with the Argentine. But Mexico is not a country of great available wealth.[1] Old and New Spain have a curious likeness to one another in this respect. Both have a reputation for immense natural resources, yet both have ever been poor, because, though they do possess rich districts and fine mines, they consist largely of barren rock and high tablelands of indifferent soil and ill-watered. The communications of both are obstructed. The tablelands of Mexico are held up by mountain ranges on east and west. The fall to the Gulf of Mexico is precipitous, and that to the Pacific, though more manageable, is steep. Northward from the plain of Anahuac the communications look easy enough. As Humboldt pointed out more than a century ago, it would be perfectly possible to drive a wheeled carriage from the city of Mexico to the valley of the Mississippi. Indeed, the caravan trade conducted in big prairie wagons on the Santa Fé trail

[1] The reader who wishes to see this subject more fully dealt with may be recommended to look into " A Study of Mexico," by David A. Wells (New York, 1890, published by Appleton & Co.).

came from St. Louis, on the Mississippi, by Durango to Mexico.[1] But if the plain is smooth it is broken by districts which are waterless. Irrigation is difficult, because, with the exception of certain breaks in Central Mexico, the mountains do not go beyond the limit of eternal snow. The rivers of both New and Old Spain alternate between being raging torrents, when the winter snows melt on the hills and the spring rains pour down, and dry river courses (barrancas) at other times. There is in fact a great open central road connecting Mexico with the United States, and that may some day prove to be the physical fact which will decide the fate of the country. But the road is not a good one, because it is so easy to starve or die of thirst on it. Therefore Mexico has not had the rapid prosperity of the Argentine and is unlikely ever to attain to that level. Therefore, also, foreign capital has never had the same influence as in the southern republic. Large tracts of Mexico are by nature poor, and when they are mountainous are also very inaccessible. In them is a population which gains nothing by such prosperity as there has been, and which offers a fine recruiting ground for the revolutionary and the brigand.

The position of the Indian population of Mexico when Diaz began his career has already been stated in a general way. But a few further details may be given, because they show what was one problem of government he had to deal with. In the north-west along the American frontier there were certain tribes of pure savages who had never been subdued under colonial rule, and who grew more independent and

---

[1] See J. Gregg's "Commerce of the Prairies," 1844, for an account, by one who followed it, of the old Santa Fé trail.

actually aggressive under the Republic. There were tribes like the Apaches, who were just savages. During the French intervention they took active part against the Mexicans. Over all the north, where the land is held in great estates, the Indians, though nominally free, remained in fact serfs. The Peons (*i.e.*, pawns), or mere day-labourers, of Indian blood continued to be enslaved by their inherited ideas and their improvidence. They have shown a natural disposition for the status of serf. Strange as it may seem, they appear to prefer the kind of fixity of occupation they get by contracting a debt, for which they then pay by their labour. A Peon who wishes to acquire a wife and hut takes a loan from an employer and promises to work it off. He never does, because he is soon in need of food and clothes. Then he has to indebt himself again. A truck system which he is incapable of checking keeps him for ever in debt. One employer may let him go to another, but only on condition that the new master pays his debt. If he can find an employer on these terms he simply passes from the old master to the new. It has been said that during the rule of Diaz the Indians sank from a condition in which all had some estate in the land to one in which nobody had any except the great landowners and capitalists. A good deal of fancy has been expended on this social revolution to the injury of the poor. The " pueblo " Indians whom the Spaniards found were living in a tribal and communal state. The laws of the Indies secured to certain Indian towns a ring of communal land. These lands were not respected when the Church's endowments were secularised, and the Indians suffered. But the fact that some Indians had definite communal rights in specified pieces of land is far from proving that all had rights in the soil. All the evidence goes to show that they were serfs under Spanish rule by law, and have continued to be so through their own inability to rise to a better state. You cannot put a five-fingered hand into a four-fingered glove. The tribal and communal life is intelligible to the Mexican Indian, and no other is. When left to himself he is incurably improvident and idle. Foreign employers in Mexico have thought that the sloth and carelessness of their workmen were due to the low rate of wages, which did not allow them to aspire to any comfort. In the hope of stimulating them to industry they have introduced systems of piece-work by which men could earn twice as much as their rate of pay. They have found that the Indians did do a better day's work for as many days as were needed to earn the equivalent of the miserable old weekly wage. Then they spent the rest of the week drunk with pulque or only just in absolute idleness. In the south among Juarez's people and Don Porfirio's the Indians showed more character because they had kept their old tribal organisation in the mountains—and the tribe had no scruple in using the lash on the drone who was a mere burden.

The whole race has been degraded by serfdom, but not by that only. An ancient Mexican tradition which has at least a mythical truth tells how one of the peoples who preceded the Aztecs on the plain of Anahuac became utterly deboshed by drinking pulque and fell victims to the first invader. Pulque is in fact a terrible cause of degradation. It is easily made, is very abundant, and so cheap as to be within the reach of the very poor. Though not very alcoholic, it has a peculiarly besotting effect when drunk continuously and in large quantities. Those who know Spanish America all agree that while the inhabitants of the low-lying lands are on the whole sober, the mountain populations are much the reverse. Mexico is emphatically a country of mountains and high tablelands, and beyond all dispute it is very drunken. What was to be done with a population degraded to this extent by powerful causes of long standing ? A great deal has been said about the illiteracy of the Mexicans and the good effect which education would produce. But the people of Mexico have not been more illiterate than were the Englishmen of the reign of Elizabeth or the French of the reign of Louis XIV. Their stagnation is due to the intellectual sloth of those who have had a chance to be literate, and the lack of an intellect capable of responding to education in the case of the huge majority of the inhabitants. They can be drilled to perform some simple industrial function in a mechanical way, but they cannot be taught to show the intelligence of a skilled European workman. The faculty is lacking ; and these hopeless human beings of an inferior stock constitute from a half to two-thirds of the population. They are the labouring part of the nation, and they fill the ranks of the army. The political and industrial fabric of Mexico rests on such foundation as they supply.

Within twenty-four hours of the surrender of Mexico Diaz took a step which must needs have, and we cannot but believe was intended to have, the appearance of putting him in a position not perhaps of actual hostility to the Government of Juarez, but of separation from his old chief. He resigned the command of the Army of the East. His resignation was declined, but he insisted, and the President was forced to agree to his wish on July 13. He continued, it is true, to hold the command within the city till the 21st, because he could not be spared a day sooner. It is claimed on his behalf, and cannot be seriously denied, that nothing but his firmness saved the city from plunder and massacre. His army, thanks to his good discipline, which was made possible by his careful management of the money raised in the south, was well in hand. But, as was to be expected, his original force had been largely recruited during the blockade by bands of patriots who did not so much spring from the soil as descend from the Sierras. They burdened him with offers of assistance, which, as he well knew, covered a lively wish to share in the spoils. His most pressing obligation was to keep them out of the city till measures had been taken to forestall their entry. For twenty-four hours nobody was permitted to go in. The interval was long enough to allow of a hasty arrangement between the victorious general and those of the townsmen who possessed ready money, and therefore had the best of reasons for fearing an outbreak of robbery. The first troops to enter were picked among the bands he had brought to a fair state of discipline, and their morality was confirmed by a payment of arrears. When all restrictions were removed, the less trustworthy elements of the patriot army poured in, only to be met by what our Elizabethan ancestors would have called " a cooling card." They found the plunderable parts of the city already occupied by well-placed troops standing to arms, and they saw a plainly-printed notice in conspicuous places to the effect that any man caught pillaging

THE POLITICIAN 131

would be hanged out of hand. They knew their man, and the confidence that was due to his word. Diaz saved his cause from disgrace, and if it was added unto him that he gained the good opinion of the moneyed men that reward was creditably earned.

On July 13 Juarez and his Government returned from their years of exile and wandering in the north. The national treasury was empty, and an army of about 100,000 men, largely armed mobs, was concentrated in and around the city. The $300,000 from the military chest of the Army of the East which Diaz handed over at once to the President represented the whole of the funds immediately available to meet all the expenses of government. The service was great and timely. Moreover, it was not long since Don Porfirio had given a marked proof of his loyalty. Don Benito's term of office as President had run out in the previous year. Some of those about him had seized the opportunity to declare that as the Constitution forbade a re-election of a President he must retire and make room for a successor. " Ote toi de là que moi je m'y mette " is in Spanish America the most universally acted on of all the phrases applicable to politics. It is but just to allow that this sadly characteristic example of Mexican anarchy met little approval. The pushful persons who took the moment when French troops were still on the soil of Mexico and the intrusive Imperial Government had still an army in the field, to stand on the letter of the law and insist on performing the farce of holding a Presidential election were ill looked on. The United States continued to treat Juarez as the legitimate President. Diaz, who controlled the whole south, might have given serious trouble if he had had no more good feeling and political sense than many of his contemporaries. But, though he was by this time well aware where he meant in the end to go, he was not the man to show overhaste. He declared that the Indian who had represented the independence of Mexico during years of defeat and suffering must not be displaced till victory was won. Juarez was formally recognised as President in his camp.

Yet when the two met it was as friends between whom a gulf was opening. Diaz declared in aftertimes that Juarez had begun to be cold to him about the time of the siege of Puebla. He had barely acknowledged the report of its capture and had added no thanks. The explanation of his ill-will is not difficult to find. The mere course of events had made the two rivals. There is everywhere such a thing as serving your cause too well. When he who renders the service puts himself in the superior position it is hard for the person served to feel nothing but gratitude. Now this was what Diaz had done. Others had fought hard and forwarded the cause, but none of them had to their credit the recovery of the South and the taking of Puebla and the capital. He was marked out as a present rival and future successor. Juarez is believed to have been a disinterested man, and yet we must not expect too much virtue even from the best. He was poor, and the loss of the Presidential chair would inevitably destroy his means of support. Cincinnatus can return to his plough when he is Cincinnatus—that is to say, when he is not only a virtuous man, but a patrician who owes his place in the world to his birth, not to his means. Juarez was a lawyer without fortune, for whom the loss of the

THE POLITICIAN 133

Presidency must entail the necessity for beginning life again in his old age. The governorship of his native State might have been a dignified refuge, but he had lost his hold on Oaxaca during the war when he was far away and Diaz was on the spot. How could he feel friendly to the former subordinate who was, not indeed maliciously, but by the force of circumstances, supplanting him?

Moreover, unless we are to dismiss the word of Don Porfirio himself as worthless, he had just done something which outweighed many services. He had given the President a lesson, and a rather humiliating one. When he reported the capitulation of Mexico he received an order to place the French Minister, M. Dano, under arrest and to take possession of the archives of the Embassy. He at once refused, telling Juarez that since they already had the ill-will of Napoleon, they had better not add that of France by insulting its honour. Juarez made no answer. Diaz pressed him to send somebody else to carry out the order, but nobody came. M. Dano, who had obvious reasons for not wishing to be in Mexico when Juarez returned, applied for a safe conduct to Veracruz, and Diaz gave it at once. His prompt resignation of his command of the Army of the East had much the appearance of having been a measure of precaution meant to leave him free to refuse to obey. It was unquestionably a sign that he felt himself strong enough to dispense with official rank.

Yet he tells us that he was at this time hard pressed for money. During the war he had been content to draw from the military chest he himself had filled no more than was enough to provide for his daily needs. He now offered to acknowledge that he had received a third of what was due to him, though as a matter of fact he had taken less. It was not safe to fob off a creditor of his standing, and Juarez offered $21,000 in payment of all claims. Diaz was careful to warn the President that he would not consider himself bound to follow any particular line of conduct laid down for him in consideration of this payment, and he says he added that the issue of the money from the treasury might be stopped if it was to be hampered by any condition. The relations of the President and the General must have been tart indeed by this time. But the $21,000 were duly paid to Don Porfirio's agent, José de Teresa. Diaz had spoken to Juarez of his intention to go into business. The business he did go into took the strange form of gifts of $17,000 to support a newspaper, a rapid and effectual method of evacuation. The balance was stolen in the house of his agent, and he only recovered a half. Though he persisted in resigning his more important commands, he continued at the head of the 2nd Division of the army till 1860, when he retired with the remnant of his $21,000 to a farm called La Noria (Waterwheel), which had been conferred on him by his native State. In estimating these and other sums named in dollars we must bear in mind the effect produced on the currency of Mexico by the depreciation of silver during the latter part of the nineteenth century. The Republic adhered for long to the silver standard, and its money fell in exchange value till the process was stopped, as will be told further on, by the financial measures of Señor Limantour. In 1868 $21,000 made a larger sum than they would have done when the coin had reached its present level of 2s. o$\frac{1}{2}d$. He had married his first wife, Delfina Ortega y Reges, during the siege. We know little of Doña Delfina except that she bore her husband three children and died young. For two years they lived quietly on their farm, and Don Porfirio applied himself to the cultivation of the sugar-cane.

There was in after times no lack of persons who were ready to ask him why he did not rest content to go on planting the sugar-cane. They made it a matter of reproach to him that he too became an agitator in due course, and joined those who perpetuated the disorder of the country by disobedience to the law and the selfish pursuit of their personal ambitions. These critics omit to show what it was incumbent on them to prove—namely, that there was any law in Mexico to obey save in the impotent form of mere words on paper. As for the charge of ambition, it is cheaply brought against every man who in any polity tries to rise to great place. The Earl of Chatham was ambitious, for he believed that he could save the country, and that nobody else could. Holding that faith, he did well to seek power. " For good thoughts," says Bacon, " (though God accept them) yet toward men are little better than good dreams, except they be put in act ; and that cannot be without power and place, as the vantage and commanding ground." The ambitious man stands or falls by what he does with the power when it is in his hands. Diaz would never have had an opportunity to do good to his country if he had waited till a united Mexican people, or even a well-disciplined Mexican party, came to La Noria to interrupt him while he was cutting his harvest of sugar-cane with his *machete* (his cane-knife) and petition him to take the Republic in hand. He had to win the means of doing good, and that by such methods as the society he was born in forced him to use. Chatham could do no other, though he was more happily placed than Don Porfirio. He had to co-operate with men whom he despised, and allow them to help him for their own ends by the use of means which his soul loathed. " The rising unto place is laborious, and by pains men come to greater pains ; and it is sometimes base, and by indignities men come to dignities." Diaz was born in the midst of a blood-stained anarchy, and had to rise by the use of force. He is to be judged by what he did with the power he conquered.

Anarchy is the one name for the condition of Mexico after the withdrawal of the French army and the death of Maximilian, as it had been before. Juarez, it is true, was formally re-elected President at the end of 1867, though re-election was forbidden by the Constitution—a tolerably clear proof of the little respect felt for the letter of the law in Mexico. We must believe that gratitude had a share in confirming him in power, but it is certainly the fact that there was nobody at that moment who could have secured sufficient support to oppose him. Support does not mean votes, which have never decided anything in a Spanish-American republic, but an adequate military force to dictate to the voters over a sufficient part of the country. We ought not to blame Don Benito if his administration failed to restore peace to Mexico. The treasury was empty. Foreign nations had lost all confidence in the promises of the Republic and would lend no money. Indeed, civilised peoples, except the United States, stood aloof from the Republic for a time. The United States could not help, for they were not then able to dispense with foreign capital for their own needs. The country was swarming with broken men, brigandage, and " pronunciamientos." The Roman Catholic clergy, then and for some years to come, were unscrupulous in fomenting disorder. The Government lacked the means to pay a regular force to do the most elementary police work. It was the President's bad fortune that the years of his administration were full of earthquakes, bad harvests, and disease. Yet, when every allowance has been made, it must be recognised that the taciturn Indian patience, which had served Juarez and Mexico well during the years of the French intervention, was but a negative quality. It was after all only a power to endure and more was needed to establish order. Yet it was all that Jurarez had to give.

As his term drew to an end it became clear that the Indian tenacity of the President, his stolid capacity for staying where he was and looking in silent obstinacy at all menaces, was about to be shown by an attempt to retain his seat. In other words, he was preparing to violate the provision of a Convention he had helped to make. There goes a story which at any rate conveys a truth, whether the thing happened exactly as it is told or not. Juarez, so the tale runs, had it out with Diaz between themselves, and said to him by way of closing the interview : " You will be President some day, but not while I live." Whether these words were ever uttered or not, it is not the less true that they state the intention of Don Benito. He would be President while he lived, which, of course, implied that he would make his own re-election by setting his dependent mob of placeholders to work, by bribing, falsifying the lists of electors, threats to use force, and at a pinch by actual slaughter.[1]

It would surely tax the ingenuity of the most ingenious apologist to show that the cause of the President was also the cause of law and order. He was confessedly preparing to violate the law; and there was no means of prevailing on him to stop except by the use of force. In the natural course of things, there were not wanting those who were prepared to avail themselves of the means so familiar in Mexican politics. The name " party " must still be taken to stand for a body of men who hold certain principles and try to carry them out in the conduct of government. But in Mexico nothing was at stake except the question who was to be President. It will avoid confusion if we use another term once familiar enough among ourselves, and say that there were three connections in Mexican politics—the Juaristas, the Lerdistas, and the Porfiristas. The first were the supporters of Juarez, largely place-holders, who have been called Conservatives. They held the places, and thought that all would be well if they could only " conserve " them. The Lerdistas were the followers of that Don Sebastian Lerdo de Tejada whose brother Don Miguel had been Minister of Grace and Justice under Juarez. They called themselves the " Evolu-

---

[1] It is but a few years since a very pretty example was given in Rio Janeiro of the "Latin" American method of consulting the free and independent voter. It was known that the candidate who was not to be allowed to be returned would probably receive a good many votes in a certain district. On the day of the election the approaches to the ballot-boxes were, in the usual way, occupied by "capangas," that is to say, negro bullies armed with cudgels and revolvers. At an early hour a proclamation was published to the effect that in view of the danger to public peace arising from the excited passions of the district the Government had decided to close the poll and to count only the votes given before the hour of closing. Of course they were the votes of the "capangas."

THE POLITICIAN

tionists," and they held the faith that all would be well if only in the process of evolution they could occupy the places. The Porfiristas were, as their name shows, the followers of Don Porfirio Diaz, and they called themselves Radicals. It was their fundamental principle that no good would be done till a radical sweep had been made of the others and they were masters of the situation. The future was to show that they were not mistaken. Where what was at stake was the personality of the future administrator, the cause of the most capable man was the good cause.

The election was to be held in the autumn of 1871, when Juarez's four years, counting from the election in 1867, would be at an end. The Juaristas had, of course, the advantage of the support of the place-holders. But Lerdo de Tejada had availed himself of his ministerial position to plant not a few friends of his own in offices where they could be useful. Diaz had the aid of all who were not provided for by the others, and also, it is said, of not a few old Imperialists who, if they did not love him, hated Juarez and Lerdo. When it came to voting each of the three connections was found to have sufficient local influence to secure the return of its own man in its own territory. We hear, of course, that the power of the Administration was employed to the full; that towns which notoriously contained a population of 2,000 were recorded to have cast 2,500 votes for Don Benito; and, in short, that the force and fraud of a sham election was in full swing. In spite of this vigorous employment of the traditional methods, Juarez failed to get an absolute majority. The votes were 5,837 for Juarez, 2,874 for Lerdo, and 3,555 for Diaz. The decision rested with Congress, which as a matter of course decided in favour of Juarez. It had been made by him in the well-known way. His opponents showed no more respect for the freedom of voters than he did. They applied pressure and made bargains just as he did. He won because his control of the Central Government gave him the best means for applying pressure and making bargains.

It would have been strange if the defeated parties had rested content with this settlement. We are assured that they were honestly persuaded that the re-election of a President was contrary to democratic principles. It is a nice question why the sovereign people, which is alone entitled to choose its ruler, is to be cabined and cribbed and confined when in the exercise of its rights it chooses the same man twice running. The inquiry would be the more unnecessary in the present case, because when the course of events carried Lerdo to the Presidency he began to provide for his own re-election, and when later on the Presidency came to Diaz he was more re-elected than any man in Spanish-American history. It will be right to state what the different connections professed that they were going to do. The make-believe of politicians has always a certain value, for it throws some light on the moral and intellectual realities of the political stage on which the fictions are thought likely to tell on the gallery. But we would treat some things with a respect they do not deserve if we spoke of them as being more than what they were. It would be easy to fill pages with the promises of constitutional improvements made by Juarez when he was standing for President at the end of 1867, and for some time afterwards. But as they were all dropped when they had served their purpose, the enumeration would be merely tedious. The substantial facts which we have to bear in mind in regard to him are that he proved doggedly hostile to the Imperialists, and that he reduced the army wholesale.

His implacability to the Imperialists offended not them only but many Mexicans who thought he simply perpetuated divisions and causes of trouble. An amnesty was passed in 1870, but with exceptions, and not till many Mexicans had been driven into exile, and many had escaped the entire confiscation of their property by the payment of heavy fines. They remained embittered and on the outlook for a chance of taking their revenge. The moderation which Diaz had shown at all times, and more especially when he forced the city of Mexico to surrender, pointed him out as the one leader they could best join. When he hurried, as we have seen that he did, to disassociate himself from Juarez, in June, 1867, he may have, he probably had, a definite intention to offer himself to all Mexicans as the man who would divide them the least.

The reduction of the army was no doubt a necessity. With the best will in the world, Juarez could not in 1867 and 1868 pay, or pension, a force of 100,000 men or so. But the officers and men who were thrown out of employment penniless in a country poor at the best of times, and now disorganised in its industry as in everything else, were not in a position which made it possible for them to look on his action with a cool impartiality. They provided the general staff and the rank and file of all the forces of disorder which kept the country in a turmoil throughout his administration. It was inevitable that they should help to recruit the connections opposed to him, and that the

leader they preferred should have been Porfirio Diaz,
a soldier like themselves, and one who had quickly
and emphatically marked his alienation from the policy
of the Indian President, and who, moreover, had
always taken great care of his own men. We shall
see that when, after a first failure and some years of
conflict, Don Porfirio became President, he made it a
rule to treat the army, that part which had fought
against him as well as that which fought for him,
with consideration. It was a proof of his faculty to
recognise facts that he always dealt with the army as
being the decisive force in Mexican politics. Then
Juarez did a thing which one cannot wholly condemn,
since he was but insisting on his rights, but was sure
to appear invidious to the multitudes of Mexicans,
soldiers included, who were not allowed to do themselves justice. He insisted on a regulation of his
accounts with the treasury, and on the payment of
his arrears. They amounted to $75,000. He was
by general confession neither corrupt nor greedy.
When his opportunities are taken into account he
must be said to have died poor, for he left his family
only about $120,000. But the arrears he took from
an exhausted treasury were more than half the total
sum. In a country where the judgments passed on
public men are less malignant than they are apt to be
in Mexico there would not have been lacking people to
say that he used his official power for his own benefit,
and that if he strove to secure his re-election it was
because he wanted to increase his fortune. Juarez,
as a native commentator on his life remarked, died in
a happy hour for him and before "ingratitude
assassinated him," but he had himself been ungrateful
to those who had served his cause; and we may be

THE POLITICIAN 143

sure that this sententious judgment expressed a very common opinion.

It is insuperably difficult to discover what was the connection of Don Sebastian Lerdo. It was visibly the weakest of the three which divided Mexico. When events which are now to be told carried him into the Presidential chair, he himself treated it with entire contempt. But his odd story must not be forestalled. He was a Creole, an accomplished man, and a lawyer. His brother Don Miguel had been a foremost leader in the fight with the Church, and Don Sebastian benefited by his popularity with the Liberals. But the foundation of his political importance was that he was President of the Supreme Court, and therefore, by virtue of a tradition which, strangely-enough, had survived from the colonial epoch, was entitled to succeed the President of the Republic in case of his death or disappearance for any other reason. We have seen how Juarez himself when in the same position had used this right of succession. It may seem strange that he should have left a political opponent in a place of so much prestige. The probability is that he knew he could not displace Don Sebastian without driving him into active alliance with the Porfiristas; and Don Benito was no bad master of the art of dividing in order to rule.

CHAPTER VI

THE FIGHT FOR THE PRESIDENCY

FROM 1871 to 1877 Diaz was engaged in the struggle which ended by making him President of Mexico. During the first of these six years his opponent was Juarez. For the rest of the time he was in conflict with Lerdo and then with a new enemy, Don José M. Iglesiàs. His course was not unchecked, nor was his victory easy.

When the Congress declared Juarez duly elected on October 12, 1871, Diaz allowed some three weeks to pass before he took open action. The riotous protests made at various towns by his followers could hardly have taken place if he had been known to disapprove of them strongly, but he did not hasten to produce the " plan " which invariably states the case of a Mexican " pronunciamiento," and is the notification to all whom it may concern that a party is in arms. The methods used in the constitutional conflicts of the Republic are not ours, but they have this much in common with the usages of British or American parties, that they include a programme or platform, and a " good cry " with which " to go to the country." There, too, as in countries of less picturesque ways, political action is preceded by consultations of managers, and a leader has to yield to the solicitations of enthusiastic supporters. Don Porfirio states that it was on the urgent appeals of his friends that he finally decided to put himself at the head of a revolutionary movement. The council in which the resolution to act was taken was held at his hacienda, or ranch, La Noria, on or about November 8. The programme was drawn up and the cry was raised. As the first was subsequently revised and reissued at other places, no more need be said of it now than that it was based on the demand for the Constitution of 1857 and freedom of election. The cry adopted has inevitably a somewhat ironic tone when we consider it as having been raised by the strongest administrator who has ever held Mexico in his hand. It consisted of the words "Menos Gobierno y mas Libertades" ("Less Government and more Freedom"). The candid critic who has been freely quoted already, and to whom we shall have to listen again, Don Rafael de Zayas Enriquez, is of opinion that at this stage in the "evolution" of his mind and character Don Porfirio did truly believe that the great need of his country was more freedom. Experience during the years immediately following the promulgation of the Plan of La Noria, in the opinion of the same authority, taught him that Mexico suffered, not from overgovernment, but from the total lack of governance, or the bad quality of such as it had received, and also that it stood in more need of discipline than of greater freedom. The history of the next forty years certainly appears to confirm the judgment of Don Rafael.

The response to the cry of La Noria was loud and widespread. In this case, indeed, action had preceded the word. Don Porfirio's friends had drawn the sword before he blew the horn, for they had seized the Government's artillery and stores in Oaxaca. In many parts of Mexico the Porfiristas, or Radicals, or

Constitutionalists (they used that name also), rose and took possession of the local governments. But, though the revolt was sufficiently formidable to put Juarez in serious danger, its progress was disappointing after the first days. The peaceful elements in the population were frightened by the prospect of a renewal in a still worse form of the troubles of the last years. As it has been the fate of peaceful Mexicans to be sacrificed to armed factions, their fears might have had no power to injure the Porfiristas. But Juarez had an attached following which stood by him and the control of the central Administration. And then the rather patchwork following of Don Sebastian Lerdo, though it was by no means loyal to the President, was far from being disposed to aid the Porfiristas. It did not wish to exchange King Log for King Stork. Then the premature outbreaks which preceded the " pronunciamiento " of November had given Juarez the opportunity to weaken his enemy in detail. He put down a rising in the capital ferociously, and was even able to take the offensive when he heard of the revolt in Oaxaca.

The old President acted with commendable promptitude, and he was helped by the fact that Diaz, after seeing the movement well on foot in Oaxaca, hurried with 100 horse to get his supporters in the centre and north well in hand. The Juarista general, Latorre, marched into Oaxaca, defeated Don Porfirio's lieutenant, Luis Mier, at San Mateo Xindihui in December, and occupied the town in January of 1872. Felix Diaz, who was in command, found himself unable to defend it, and, falling back on his old life, took to the Sierra. His career was, however, short.

THE FIGHT FOR THE PRESIDENCY 147

Before the end of the month he was surprised while almost alone by a party of local enemies from Tehuantepec and murdered. The insurrection in Oaxaca appeared to be wholly suppressed, but in Mexico, as we have seen and shall see, this only means that it had failed to win for the moment. The conditions which produced it were not altered, and continued to produce their normal consequences.

While his cause was at any rate superficially beaten in the south, Don Porfirio was not able to make head effectually in the centre of the country. He reached Zacatecas, to the north of the city of Mexico, in February. It had been already occupied by his partisans, and we are told that he received a great ovation. But it was far from being the case that all was over except the shouting. The Government troops were better armed and better organised than their opponents. They scattered the insurgents easily enough in the open field, winning " decisive " victories at Cerro de la Bufa, reoccupying Zacatecas, and gaining such successes as every Mexican Government claims to win till it crumbles. Diaz, who was not present at any of these engagements, marched with a body of cavalry on Mexico city itself, in the hope of being received by a popular revolt. But townsmen and garrison refused to move, and big towns cannot be taken by columns of cavalry except with their own consent. He had to retire to the State of Jalisco and wander round the central regions still held by Juarez. The rising had not upset the Government, but whole States were out of hand, particularly in the north, where Sinoloa and Chihuahua were hostile, and there were Porfiristas everywhere in sierra and plain. A small defeat in the field would in all likelihood have brought the Government down. The decision came in another way. Juarez died suddenly on July 18. The disappearance of the old leader in a great internal conflict and a struggle for independence appealed to popular emotion. *Sunt lachrymæ rerum*, even in Mexico. All parties were awed for a moment, and combined to give him " a first-class funeral." The kindly regard for the memory of an old foe which Swift grimly noted in Harley and St. John when they were talking of Godolphin, who was dead and could now do them no harm, is a universal human sentiment. The political world of Mexico gave Juarez his first-class funeral, and voted him " well deserving of his country in the heroic degree." Then it went on as before.

The removal of one of the three competitors for power could make no change in the real condition of the country. Yet it simplified the situation and allowed of an interval of at least relative peace. Lerdo became interim President by right of his place as President of the Supreme Court. By retaining the Ministers of Juarez, by keeping his own counsel, by hinting hopes to his own party, by offering amnesty on easy terms, and buying off individual leaders he kept Juaristas and Lerdists together, and he divided the Porfiristas. Diaz held out for a time, but by October he had to recognise that he would only lose by continuing in arms. Lerdo refused to make any further concessions in answer to letters Diaz wrote on August 1 and September 23. In these documents Don Porfirio only proved, I fear, that after all he too was in the year 1872 a Mexican politician. The one substantial word which stands in the midst of a flow of verbiage was the demand that the amnesty should

THE FIGHT FOR THE PRESIDENCY 149

be amended in his favour. The tenth Article of that document declared that officers of the army who had taken part in the late rising were to lose rank and pay, though they were not to be otherwise punished. And this is the appropriate place to note that, in spite of Lerdo's firm refusal at the moment, the rank and pay were restored before long. We may assume that other communications of a private character took place, but were not put on record. These compromises are unavoidable in parliamentary life, even when it is conducted by " plans " " pronunciamientos," and war cries. If the great Commoner was forced to suffer the intrigues of the Duke of Newcastle, it is no less true that the Duke could not have intrigued and corrupted during a certain set of years without the tacit assistance of the great Commoner. All the other parts of Diaz's two letters are concerned with the usual fine sentiments about freedom of election and a warning that unless Government altered its ways the arrangement now in course of being made would turn out to be but a temporary truce. The prediction was a safe one, even if it had not been uttered by a man who was in a position to fulfil his own prophecy.

For the moment the way to the Presidency was closed. Diaz returned to Oaxaca. His ranch, La Noria, had been burnt down by the soldiers of Juarez during the late troubles, and he now established himself at La Candelaria. For three years or so he again applied himself to the cultivation of the sugar-cane, but this time he added a manufacture of chairs to his agricultural industry. The cultivation of the sugar-cane allows of long, quiet intervals between the planting and the reaping. But he certainly did not limit himself to growing sugar-cane and making chairs. He was now the head of a powerful connection, defeated, even scattered, for the moment, but always capable of reuniting if its members found that their ambitions were not satisfied. Don Porfirio, who was a good judge of men, must have known enough of Lerdo to feel sure that he had only to wait patiently for an opportunity which would not fail to come.

Don Sebastian Lerdo appears, from what he did and what we are told of him, to have belonged to a type of man known in all countries, and certainly not less common among Spanish-speaking politicians than elsewhere. There was in him a combination of dignity, not to say gravity, of outward bearing with inward arrogance, and of frivolity of judgment, which is fatal. Mr. H. H. Bancroft, in his "History of Mexico," gives it as his belief that Don Sebastian had a love of mystifying the people about him. Now few of those who indulge in this form of humour are found to be able to keep their enjoyment of the joke to themselves. They triumph, and indeed it is not always possible to hide the mystification from the victim, and it is especially hard when the point of the jest lies in depriving him of a place or keeping him out of one. The sufferer is forced to recognise that he has been made to look like a fool. There is no more effectual way of gaining enemies than to indulge in these feats of ingenuity. The Duke of Wellington, on one of the rare occasions on which he confessed to have made a mistake, said that it lay in having proved another gentleman to be a fool, for nobody likes to be thought a fool. On one occasion Lerdo mystified the whole population of the city of Mexico by holding a premature ceremony of inauguration of the Veracruz railway, with a great flourish of

THE FIGHT FOR THE PRESIDENCY 151

trumpets. The arrogance of the man, and the frivolity, too, came out when he made a public declaration of his belief that he owed his place to constitutional right and was not bound to consider anybody. He was technically right, since he had succeeded Juarez by virtue of his office as President of the Supreme Court, but he was in that place because he was a party leader. It was not wise to tell his followers that he had outgrown the need of their support. And then, too, he had drawn over many of the Porfiristas by giving them to understand that he would choose some of his Ministers from among them. Yet he kept them at arm's length. And he did a still less intelligible thing. He treated his own party as a negligible quantity, and chose his Ministers entirely among the Juaristas. The Lerdistas were naturally angry. He was accused of corruption and of underhand dealings for his own advantage with the foreign capitalists who were now beginning to lay the Mexican railways, as also of sacrificing the interests of Mexico to British creditors. But these accusations were probably the result rather than the cause of his unpopularity. Withal he might have completed his term of office in peace if he had not sought his re-election in the usual way, which it would be unnecessary as well as tiresome to repeat. The time was ripe and Don Porfirio came out of his retirement to conduct another constitutional campaign.

And now we have come to the last "Plan," and as it really did produce some definite and long-lived consequences, it is worth while to look at the thing with some attention. It was in all ways typical of the political world of Spanish America, in its inception, its development, and its result. Lerdo did not forget the part he had played to Juarez, and thought it wise to take his precautions against any possible display of independence by the present holder of the post of President of the Supreme Court, Don José Maria Iglesias. Don José had been a steady supporter of Juarez and had borne the heat of the day during the Imperial interlude. He was an important man in his party, and Don Sebastian no doubt looked upon him as very capable of nursing ambitious views on the national Presidency, to which, as we have just seen, the Presidency of the Supreme Court had thrice served as a stepping-stone. One of the most valued and honourable functions of the court was to decide on the legality of the election of a national President in case any dispute did arise. Now, as Don Sebastian was quite resolved to be elected and to use all means to that end, it followed that he could not lay himself open to the risk of seeing his return quashed for irregularity. The probability that this judgment would be given was strong, for not only was Don Sebastian resolved to be national President regardless of law, but as the President of the Supreme Court was interim President of the Republic *sede vacante*, it was obvious that in the act of declaring the return of another to be irregular Don José would seat himself in the Presidential chair. To get rid of Señor Iglesias and put a person more likely to prove compliant in his place would at the first blush appear to have been the simple course. But it was not simple. The summary dismissal of Don José Maria would have offended his friends, and would have given the Porfiristas, whose opposition was certain, good ground for asserting that the court had been packed and so for disregarding its judgment. Nor was it at all

THE FIGHT FOR THE PRESIDENCY 153

sure that anyone else who might be put in his place would not be tempted to display a manly and profitable regard for the majesty of the law.

Mere dismissal was therefore not to be thought of. Lerdo believed that he had found a more excellent way. He made a new rule with the help of his docile Congress, and it was that the right of examining into the legality of elections ought on all sound principles to belong to the electoral college which directed the taking of the poll. Of course Don José protested against that new little law of the President's, declared it unconstitutional, and offered his resignation. To let him go in these circumstances would have been equivalent to dismissal. So Lerdo refused to accept his resignation. A stormy interview followed. Don José protested that the law was no law, but he kept his place. It was obvious that his presence on the bench must be dangerous to Lerdo, for in the certain event of a denial of the legality of the election the President of the Supreme Court would insist on maintaining that he had jurisdiction. Lerdo must have considered this the lesser danger of the two. He left Iglesias in possession of his place and went on his own way, relying on being able to enforce his will when the time should come. What Iglesias might do would depend on what the Porfiristas could do. If they were beaten it would not be difficult to dispose of him.

The election was treated as the farce which it was by Diaz and his party. He left his farm, La Candelaria, in December, 1875, to open the campaign. On this occasion the course first adopted differed from that followed three years before. Diaz left his supporter, Don Fidencio Hernandez, to begin the rising in Oaxaca. He took ship in the British steamship

Corsica with several friends, and went to Brownsville, in Texas, just opposite the Mexican port Matamoros, at the mouth of the Rio Grande, which is here the border line between the two republics. His purpose was to cross the river and take command in the field at the opportune moment. In the meantime he directed operations from safe headquarters.

The first move was made in Oaxaca with complete success. Don Fidencio Hernandez found no difficulty in scattering the small body of Federal troops which tried to oppose him and the ill-armed " Indiada " he led. The town of Oaxaca was easily taken, Government arms and rifles seized, while the Government troops were incorporated in the revolutionary army. Hernandez observed the traditional forms by issuing the regulation plan at Taxtupec. As it was modified by Diaz himself later, and produced on a second occasion as the Plan of Palo Blanco, no more need be done now than just note its appearance and name. The happy beginning in Oaxaca was well followed up. In a very short time the " banner of revolt " was being raised in all the four quarters of Mexico. As some troops adhered to Lerdo, and as General Latorre, who had been loyal to Juarez, was also true to him, some smart fighting in the Mexican way took place. Diaz himself crossed the frontier on March 22. Don Porfirio found that the Plan of Taxtupec was not wholly acceptable to the anti-Lerdinas. It provided for much they were in arms to secure, the removal of Lerdo being the essential point of the whole. But the Plan also provided that Don Porfirio should be General of the Revolutionary Army and that the right to act as Government should be given to him. Now the Northern leaders were not disposed to accept a chief

THE FIGHT FOR THE PRESIDENCY 155

named for them by Oaxaca. Diaz saw the necessity for a little judicious face-saving and modified the wording slightly. The preamble, which recited the sins of Lerdo, needed no alteration. The Plan as finally settled provided that the Constitution of 1857, with the amending Acts of 1873 and 1874, should be "the supreme law of the Republic." That the ineligibility of an outgoing President should also be a supreme law till such time as it was made a constitutional reform. That Lerdo and all his men were naught. That governors of States who accepted the Plan were to be kept in office. Those who did not were to be removed and replaced by nominees of the General-in-Chief of the Revolutionary Army. Another election for President was to be held within two months of the occupation of the capital by the said Revolutionary Army. That the President of the Supreme Court was to be interim President of the Republic (this was the face-saving clause) provided that he accepted this Plan in all its parts (this was the condition which rendered the face-saving clause quite harmless). That in case of his refusal the General-in-Chief was to be invested with executive power. That the next Congress was to set about the work of constitutional reform and to provide guarantees for the independence of municipalities. That all generals and officers who accepted this Plan—no limit of time being fixed for acceptance—were to be maintained in the possession of their rank and emoluments.

The really important parts of the Plan of Palo Blanco were the clauses which put the President of the Supreme Court " between the sword and the wall," and the last. If Iglesias accepted the whole Plan he put himself in the hands of the General of the Revolutionary Army, who would take care that he should not be elected definitive President for the full term of four years. But this was not Don José Maria's reading of the constitutional law of Mexico. His view was that when the President of the Supreme Court became interim President of the Republic, *sede vacante*, he alone was to have power to replace governors or do whatever else was necessary to make his own election sure. He pointed to the recent precedents of Juarez and Lerdo, and stood on constitutional practice with all the tenacity of the strictest sect of the Pharisees.

For a time he was able to give substantial trouble to Diaz. He left the capital and entered into negotiations with persons of influence. His claim was that from the end of November, 1875, when the term for which Lerdo had been elected closed, he was interim President of Mexico, and government was to be conducted in his name. He found a good deal of support in the North. It was the trouble given him by Iglesias rather than a small check at the hand of Lerdo's troops at Ixcamula which decided Diaz to return to the South in June. He had made good progress, had taken Matamoros, had been joined by partisans, and had collected an army about him. His revised plan of campaign was to go himself to New Orleans and from thence by sea to Veracruz, then put himself at the head of the Oaxacan forces. In the meantime General Gonzalez, on whom also he could rely, was to lead the revolutionary soldiers who adhered to Don Porfirio across country to the hill country of Puebla. Here the two were to meet and advance on Mexico.

And now we have to leave high matters of politics

THE FIGHT FOR THE PRESIDENCY 157

and strategy and return for a last dip into the world of Dumas and Mayne Reid. The coming President of Mexico, a man of forty-five, head of a party and an army, had to go through an adventure such as would become the hero of a boy's book. Diaz recrossed the frontier of the United States and went to New Orleans. There he took passage for Veracruz in the coasting steamer *City of Habana* in the character of a Cuban doctor. The steamer put into Matamoros to pick up passengers and cargo—that is to say, she lay four miles off that indifferent port till they were brought to her in lighters. When the passengers came aboard they turned out to be Lerdist soldiers who had surrendered to Diaz not long before, had been released by him, and knew him by sight. He was of course recognised at once, and knew he was. So long as he remained in the *City of Habana* he was in no danger, but there was every probability that he would be arrested when he reached Veracruz. In this fix he had recourse to a device which might perhaps have suggested itself at one time of his life to Bismarck, but which we can by no effort of fancy make credible in the cases of Cavour, Thiers, or Mr. Gladstone. He took to the water and made a determined effort to swim the whole four miles to the shore. Now Diaz could swim, but a man must be an uncommonly strong swimmer and in good practice to be able to swim four miles. The gallant attempt to reach his friends in Matamoros went indeed near to ending in a disaster. He began to become exhausted. A boat had to be sent from the ship to pick him up. The captain of the *City of Habana* was no doubt a humane man, but he had a strong motive for not allowing Don Porfirio to be drowned. Spanish and

Spanish-American port authorities have a lively passion for enforcing quarantine and for levying fines. If the number of passengers and crew actually on board had not coincided exactly with the list made at Matamoros the steamer would pretty certainly have been detained and a fine levied.[1]

When Don Porfirio was back in the steamer he was again in danger. But luck or good management came to his assistance. The purser of the steamer proved a friend in need. He contrived to conceal the future President in his cabin—in a sofa seat, it is said, a very trying place to hide in during June or July, and in the Gulf of Mexico. At some period in the course of this adventure a bribe passed into the hands of somebody, but the truth is now in all probability past recovery, and the details of the story as it is commonly told are somewhat hard to work out by anyone who knows the routine of a passenger ship and a seaport.[2] The substantial fact is alone important, and it is that Diaz was helped to escape at Veracruz by the officers, or an officer, of the *City of Habana*

[1] The ways of Spanish-speaking officialdom are not ill-illustrated by this little incident which came under my own observation. A British ship had entered the port of Barcelona. The local health officers were taking the number of her crew to see that it coincided with the list. While the call was being taken the captain, who was on the bridge, had occasion to give an order to the deck. He bent over the rail of the bridge, taking off the sun helmet he wore and holding it out at arm's length behind the back of the mate, who was standing beside him. The health officer counted in the sun helmet and accused the captain of having one more on board than he acknowledged in the list. This was of course an excuse for a fine. When the facts were explained the officials accused the skipper of playing a practical joke on them, and he was fined for disrespect to the authorities. The British skipper, it is true, does play jokes of a very irritating character on " the authorities." One of them who was capable of this and greater things, being pestered just when he was about to leave by two customs-house officers who were prowling in search of an excuse to fine or to extort a bribe, inveigled them into his cabin, gave them beer, locked them in, got under way, and carried them with him to his next port, which was on the coast of Africa.

[2] *Cf.* " Porfirio Diaz," by Mrs. Tweedie, pp. 253—255.

THE FIGHT FOR THE PRESIDENCY 159

disguised as a sailor. And then the other fact that leaders of great parties have to go through these adventures in Spanish-American States tells us much of the level at which those communities stand.

In Veracruz he had friends, not only in politics, but in business, and he was personally liked by them for fair dealing. He had, as we know, a varied experience in escapes, and was moreover well acquainted with the country he had to cross. Between what help he found and his own resources, which must have included some money, he succeeded in reaching Oaxaca in July. Meanwhile Gonzalez was working South, and had reached the Tlascala hill country between Mexico city and Veracruz, while Diaz was getting ready to advance from Oaxaca. Lerdo's danger was steadily increasing. Iglesias was threatening him from the North and the Porfiristas were gathering force in the South. Gonzalez was between him and Veracruz and had cut the new railway at three places. Yet events did not move fast. In the climate of Mexico it is the heat of summer rather than the cold of winter which sends armies into quarters. October was well advanced before Diaz had come sufficiently forward to be in a position to effect his junction with Gonzalez and other friends who were in the mountain country of the State of Puebla. Matters had now come to the point when a defeat in the field would mean the total ruin of Lerdo, while a victory might, and in all probability would, be of no more than temporary use to him. The disaster came on November 16.

General Alatorre, with the Lerdist forces, had his headquarters at Teotitlan. This town lies about halfway between Oaxaca on the South, from which Diaz was advancing, and the mountains east of Puebla, where Gonzalez and other Porfirista leaders gathered to the North. These last had just been reinforced by General Tolentino, who with his men deserted the cause of Lerdo. Alatorre had the advantage of operating from the centre to the circumference, and with it the risk that he might be simultaneously attacked on both sides. It was the worst, and not the best of his position which was to be his lot. He tried to intercept Diaz and get the chance to beat his enemies in detail. But Don Porfirio's little force of some 4,000 men was not hampered by much baggage or train, and he had campaigned all over the country for years. It was not very difficult for him to turn Alatorre's position and push for the hills to the North, and so he did. Alatorre followed, and on the evening of November 15 caught him up. But Diaz could now venture to stand, for his friends were near. He took up his position at Tecoac, north of Huamantla. It was too late to begin a battle on the evening of the 15th, and during the night he was joined by some of his friends from the Sierras. Gonzalez, with the main force, was still at some distance, but was advancing. The battle of Tecoac, the crowning mercy of the war, is said to have been very sanguinary—and indeed it must have been if Alatorre lost, as he said he did, 1,900 killed and 800 wounded. Such a proportion of killed to wounded may be said to be unknown to European armies. But little faith is due to Mexican statements of numbers. Don Porfirio was hard pressed, and in some danger of being driven from his position, when Gonzalez suddenly intervened, falling on Alatorre's right flank. The rout of the Lerdists was complete. Alatorre, it is said, was utterly surprised by the onset of Gonzalez, for he had supposed that the troops he saw approach-

THE FIGHT FOR THE PRESIDENCY 161

ing were reinforcements which he expected to receive. Tecoac was therefore a little battle of Waterloo, in which Diaz was Wellington, Gonzalez was Blücher, Alatorre was Napoleon, and the supposed reinforcements may stand for Grouchy. The usual consequences of a Mexican victory followed in a measure. Three thousand prisoners passed over to the victorious side, but Diaz did not shoot the officers he took.

As Lerdo's whole strength lay in the troops who still stood by him, the game was up after Tecoac. He showed that he realised the facts, for on November 20, four days after the battle, he fled from the capital, taking the till with him : $200,000 taken from the treasury and the Montepio (the state pawnbroking establishment) were loaded in the wagons which he took to the coast under protection of an escort of 1,000 cavalry. Accompanied by some of the more hopelessly compromised of his friends, he fled to the Pacific coast, took ship, and found a refuge in the United States.

His partisans could hardly be expected to go on fighting when he had fled, and, indeed, they lost no time in coming over to the victorious side. And now Diaz reaped the first benefits of the final clause of the Plan of Palo Blanco. It provided, we may remember, that all generals and officers[1] who should accept the Plan were to retain pay and rank. The adherents of the eleventh hour were to be even as those of the first. The object of Don Porfirio was to unite all the military factions under himself, and to drive nobody to desperation. When the Lerdist officers were abso-

---

[1] The Spanish formula is " generales, cabos, y oficiales "—that is to say, generals, commissioned officers, and non-commissioned officers. The phrase ought not to be translated by " generals, chiefs, and officers," as it sometimes is.

lutely running in their haste to make their junction with him in time there was nothing to stay the occupation of the capital. He entered it on November 23.

With Don Sebastian in flight and his military forces hurrying to join the conqueror, only Don José M. Iglesias remained to be disposed of. During the advance of Diaz from the South Don José had been in active correspondence with him, and, indeed, letters continued to be exchanged between them, and friends were busy trying to bring them together till November 27, three days after the occupation of the capital. There was, and could be, no novelty in the discussion. Diaz was prepared to recognise Iglesias as interim President till a new election could be held if he would accept the Plan of Tuxtupec—that is to say, be content with holding a purely honorific place for a time, and perhaps retaining his position as President of the Supreme Court. Don José was resolute to be interim President—without restrictions —to "make" his own election as President of the Republic. He was known to intend to keep the revolutionists of Tuxtupec at a safe distance from office. As a lawyer he would have no liking for revolutionary generals. It was characteristic of the pedant lawyer mind at all times and everywhere, and particularly characteristic of the Spanish slavery to mere sonorous words, that Don José Maria does really seem to have believed that he could put a hook in the nose of Leviathan with his windy constitutional theories and mere phrases. He seems never to have doubted that nothing save a hopeless perversity could prevent the general who had upset Lerdo from immediately giving up all he had fought for, and going meekly back to Candelaria, when he was told to respect the august

THE FIGHT FOR THE PRESIDENCY 163

dignity of the President of the Supreme Court. The patent facts that in such a country as Mexico the only possible ruler was a soldier, that Diaz could be beaten only by some other fighting man, and that even if a general from the North got the better of him in the name of Iglesias the real master would be that general, and not Don José Maria, produced no impression on the legal-minded man. To him facts were naught, and words were the only realities. There was nothing to be done with him but to keep him in play till the coast was clear of Lerdo, then clap your hat on, exclaim there must be an end of this, and call in Harrison's Regiment of Musketeers. And this is precisely the course which Porfirio Diaz followed.

For a short time Mexico was in the curious position of possessing two provisional Presidents. Don Porfirio took the government provisionally in hand when he occupied the capital. Iglesias in the North protested that he alone was provisional or interim President, and he appeared to be collecting a considerable force. Querétaro, San Luis, Potosi, Zacatecas, and Aquasculientes proclaimed for him. The general who commanded in Jalisco put himself and his soldiers at the orders of Don José. The Lerdists in the North seemed to be every whit as ready to support him as those of the South were to adhere to Diaz. Each chief formed a Cabinet, and if appearances had corresponded to realities, there would have been every prospect of a war between North and South in Mexico. But as a matter of fact there was no relation between the appearances and the realities. Diaz was master of the capital and of the communications with Veracruz, as well as of the South. He had possession of the richest parts of the territory of the Republic, and he controlled the chief source of its revenue—the custom duty levied at Veracruz. The northern provinces, which Iglesias seemed to dominate, form the largest part of Mexico, but they are the poorest and the least inhabited. Iglesias's treasury was empty, and there was no prospect that it would be filled. Diaz was in possession of whatever Lerdo had left behind, and he had the means of getting more. His character for moderation and probity stood him in good stead. All classes could remember how careful he had been to protect property and keep the peace in 1867. The classes which could dispose of money were not averse to trusting him. And then, too, the hopes of all the peaceful elements in the country were drawn to him because he was the man least likely to divide the country and most likely to make quiet possible in the future. It was true that he was a revolutionary general who had plunged the nation into another spasm of strife, but Lerdo was so thoroughly unpopular that few were disposed to blame the Porfiristas for getting rid of him. On the other hand, it was known that Iglesias wished to suppress the Porfiristas entirely by excluding them from office, not only in the Federal Administration, but in their own States—that is to say, he was supposed to intend to take the very course which was certain to make trouble chronic.

These things being thus, it followed that Iglesias could have no support except from the generals and politicians in the worst sense of the word who were for the time being collected about him. And where were the causes for which they could be expected to go on fighting ? No racial distinction marked the North off from the South ; and as for questions of principle to be fought over, there was only one, and it was as ill-calculated to nerve men to effort or self-sacrifice as could well be imagined. The Northern men were asked to go on fighting in order to give effect to Don José Maria's interpretation of the constitutional rights of the President of the Supreme Court. It certainly was not enough.

Therefore, though Iglesias was supposed to have the support of an army of 20,000 men and Diaz could collect only half that number, when, after naming a governor to act for him in his absence, he marched out of the capital early in December, all opposition to the General of the Revolutionary Army disappeared without a fight. Iglesias did make one effort to oppose him, but only by persuasion. When Diaz entered Querétaro without meeting the least resistance on December 20, he was asked to agree, and did agree, to a final meeting with his rival. The interview took place at the farm of La Capilla (the Chapel), about three miles from Querétaro. Iglesias again laid his case before Diaz and expounded constitutional orthodoxy. But he was no longer of any value as an associate or even puppet. His men, who indeed were starving, were deserting him in troops with their officers. Diaz told him that he had refused to take the interim Presidency on condition that he accepted the Plan, and that he could not expect that the offer should be renewed. Don José abased himself so far as to offer to accept a Ministry named for him by Diaz. But the offer was declined. Then he retired from Silao to Guadalajara, and there on January 2, 1877, issued a final proclamation to the people of Mexico. Having made his last protest, he took ship at Manzanillo, and retired to exile at San Francisco. Diaz made a progress of a peaceful and triumphant character through the northern provinces, and in February was back in the capital, the acknowledged master of Mexico. He was already President, for the election had been ordered to be held by his representative during his absence. The election of electors—on the American principle—took place on January 28. As a mere detail it is perhaps as well to mention that out of 10,878 votes of electors chosen in 181 districts, 10,500 were for Porfirio Diaz. There were other forms to be observed. The actual election of the President, or opening of credentials of the selected electors, and the election of Congress, were fixed for February 11 and 12, just after the President's return from the North. The Congress was to meet on April 1, and on May 2 Diaz was declared by the Legislature to be the duly elected President. His term was to date from the time when he took possession of the Government after the flight of Lerdo. Therefore his four years would be over in November, 1880.

If now the question What, if anything, had been gained for the cause of freedom, good government, and progress by some two years of fighting ? is put, the answer is easy to give. It had been decided that the man who was most capable of giving Mexico at any rate an interval of peace and well-directed administration was to be at the head of affairs, with a fair prospect of continuance in office. The elements of his power can be easily realised. First of all were his personal reputation and his character. There were no doubt men in Mexico, and even several of them, who could have fought the battle of Tecoac, or could have conducted a campaign of guerrilleros every whit as well as he. There was nobody who had the same general reputation, the support of followers in all quarters of the Republic, and the confidence of the moneyed men, native and foreign, who could give financial help at a pinch. His moderation, his capacity to administer, his probity, and his energy were trusted. Therefore all who were tired of anarchy turned to him. The longing for peace and for some chance to enjoy a little material prosperity, which had caused the non-militant part of the population to hold aloof from him during the struggle with Juarez, were now in his favour. He had turned out to be the most promising man after all. But we must make no mistake on one point. All the other forms of support which he could rely on would have been insufficient if he had not won the confidence of the army. He himself had no delusion on the subject, and he shaped his conduct accordingly.

The first speech he delivered to his Congress on April 1, 1878, ends with a passage which is full of instruction on this vital matter. In it Don Porfirio tells Congress explicitly that he had restored the half of all military pensions which Juarez and Lerdo had taken away for reasons of economy. Faith, the President said, must be kept with the army. The Congress was asked to help him to carry out that obligation. It was given to understand, politely indeed, but with precision, that it simply must conform to the will of the President and the army. And not only must pensions be restored to their full figure, but the army on foot must be paid. The problem which this necessity forced on President and Congress alike was hard to solve. Thanks to the "commendable circumstance"[1] that all the armed followings of the two defeated chiefs had come in, and had incorporated themselves in the Revolutionary Army, the national army was now in point of numbers far beyond the limit last fixed by Congress. The emptiness of the treasury was notorious. Yet these men had been promised the confirmation of their rank and continuance of their pay or a secure pension if they would adhere to the Plan of Palo Blanco. They had with very few exceptions adhered, and they must not be disappointed. Some, it was true, who were really in revolt out of pure resentment against Lerdo, had no wish to continue in arms. Some others who had taken arms under pressure on both sides were glad to be off home to their brown wives and the naked children who were tumbling about their patches of sugar-cane or their "magueys." But even when a large percentage had been withdrawn from the army made up of the three lately in the field, there remained a much larger body than the force last voted by Congress. But empty as the treasury then was, and whatever and whomsoever was forced to wait, faith must be kept with the soldiers. It was not only a question of honour, but of elementary common sense. Everybody in Mexico knew very well what had followed the wholesale reduction of the army by Juarez. Even from the merely practical point of view, keeping faith was likely to prove the cheaper course. But there was an obligation of honour and of patriotism to treat the army well. The soldiers of all

---

[1] "Plausible circunstancia" in Spanish. But the Castilian "plausible," though identical in spelling and origin with our "plausible," does not mean the same thing. It inherits direct from its mother "plauso" (applause), and implies "really deserving of praise "—" a specious pretext " in the old and good sense.

THE FIGHT FOR THE PRESIDENCY

parties had just shown a capacity for combined action in the interest of the country such as had never so far been displayed by any body of Mexican civilians. Military government is an evil beyond peradventure, because it demonstrates the total lack of political faculty in all other parts of the State. But it is the least of evils when it is the alternative to anarchy. An army, even one which as a military force is bad, is at least an instrument of government. A mob of wrangling, intriguing, self-seeking politicians and political lawyers—Carlyle's " attorney species "—is a mere generator of anarchy. The firmness Diaz showed in enforcing justice for the army was one of the best proofs he gave of good political faculty. Without a united, contented army there could be no stable government in Mexico. The fact that he succeeded in doing what no Mexican ruler had done before is the demonstration of his better practical faculty, and of his humanity too. By keeping faction from producing its ruinous consequences among the soldiers he gave the land about a generation of peace; and he was able to get this control over the army because he had not shed blood in mere cruelty. In 1878, except for the executions after Miahuatlan, when it could be fairly alleged that the victims were indeed in the full sense of the word traitors, his hands were clean of blood. His government was based on military force because no other foundation could be laid in Mexico.

His administration will be told later on. But the beginning of the story is the most appropriate place in which to consider, what were his method and his spirit. We have already seen with what care Diaz made and kept himself fit to wrestle with the responsibility and the long hours of work which the Presidential office entailed on a man who would not treat it merely as plunder to be enjoyed. Yet Diaz might have worked, and have worked himself to early ruin, if he had been a mere " mandon." But then no man who came to power in Mexico or in any Spanish-American State was less " mandon " than he. The note of that class of person is that he is intoxicated with conceit of his own grandeur and strength. He prefers to order and to overbear. He supposes that because nothing can be done unless some force stands ready for use in case of need and in the background, anything can be done by force employed in a sufficiently ruthless spirit. It is not necessary to know, to think, to look ahead, to learn, to consider others. The order and the application of force are enough. Acting on that principle the Santa Anas, Marquezes, even Don José Maria Iglesias, had waded from puddle to puddle of blood, and amid manifestations of self-will really not far removed from the delusions of a lunatic asylum, till they went headlong over some precipice. Bold Bayard, who lept before he looked because he was blind, had been the prevalent model in the poor, anarchical country. Don Porfirio was never known to leap before he looked. He was the last man in the world to imagine that because you can shear the sheep it is safe to try to shear the wolf. It was said in praise of our own Drake that he was a hearer of every man's opinion, but commonly a follower of his own. When a leader's own opinion is based on the best he can get from others and can combine, no better description of a managing man could well be given. And it is allowed of Diaz that he felt his way and thought his work out. When as President he had obtained full command of the

THE FIGHT FOR THE PRESIDENCY 171

machinery of administration he put out feelers through the Press, and he " tuned his (newspaper) pulpits." When he had especial reason for looking ahead he would appoint competent men to inquire for him and report. He would hear them in private, and he allowed the utmost freedom of speech. For himself he listened patiently, and his questions were pertinent. When he knew all there was to learn he could act for himself.

It would be strange if nobody had ever discovered that Porfirio Diaz was after all a figurehead, and that the merit belonged to some subordinate. Napoleon, as we have all heard, owed his victories to Berthier, and Wellington could do nothing without his Murray. The real brains of Don Porfirio were known by some sagacious persons to be deposited in the head of Justo Benitez, his secretary. But the time came when the President dispensed with Justo—we shall see in what circumstances—and was never a penny the worse for losing him. That he could use the services of others was obvious enough. No man could rule who was unable to employ agents. But Porfirio Diaz is commonly said to have reposed little trust except where he had chosen his man. Mexican politicians who had held a conspicuous place in public life before 1878 found that he kept them at arm's length. Don Matias Romero, who had been Mexican envoy at Washington during the French intervention, and Don Ignacio Mariscal were almost the only exceptions.

Some time passed, we must suppose, before he had perfected his method or had completed his staff. And there were differences between his first term of office and those which followed. Yet he was the same man in 1878 that he was later on—practical, not blinded by self-conceit, ready and eager to work hard, open to hear the good advice and profit by the knowledge of others, but no less capable of forming his own opinion, fixing his line of policy and acting for himself. He stood there ready to do all the good that it was in him to do for his country. If the good he was able to achieve was in the main transient, the fault must be shown to have been wholly his before he is blamed for failure. A far greater man, one who was a teacher and an inspirer, might have raised the moral and intellectual level of Mexico. At least one shrinks from saying that he could not. But we must take Porfirio Diaz as he was, a practical man, a born man of government who could keep order and administer ably. He, we are told—and the facts bear out the judgment—soon came to the conclusion that nothing more was within his scope. " Less government and more freedom" had been his maxim. A short experience convinced him that "Less politics and more administration" was what the country required. Politics in the world he was destined to live in meant intrigue with or without military violence, and nothing more. It was a curse, and from it he tried with considerable success to preserve the land. More administration when the object was a good one and the methods were rational was a blessing for as long as it could last. To it he applied himself, and it called for the strenuous exertion of all his faculties and the firm use of the military force he had gathered behind him. Don Rafael de Zayas Hernandez sums up the general situation of the country in terms which are borne out by the universal testimony of others : " He found the treasury empty, credit lost, a complete lack of confidence, foreign relations either broken off or suspended,

THE FIGHT FOR THE PRESIDENCY

serious difficulties with the United States were pressing, and much judgment and tact, steadiness, and patriotism were needed to avert so much danger and save the national honour."

The most elementary needs of an orderly society were not supplied. The whole country was swarming with bandits, who kidnapped men of means and held them to ransom. The trains from Veracruz dared not leave the stations without a guard. Murder and robbery were of daily occurrence. And all these crimes were committed with impunity, for there was no means of suppressing them. The evil was of old standing. It dated from the rising of Hidalgo in 1810. It had been intensified by the war between Liberals and Conservatives and the French intervention. Nothing, or nothing really effectual, had been done to amend this long permanent anarchy during the administrations of Juarez and of Lerdo. The preliminary to whatever other good was to be done must needs be the restoration—or perhaps we ought to say the establishment for the first time in the history of the Mexicans as an independent people —of security. But the Government was hemmed in by a vicious circle. Without good administration there could be no development of national prosperity. And yet, without the resources which industry and prosperity supply, how was it possible to provide— that is to say, to pay for—a capable administration? In the presence of such a hopeless-looking task clamouring to be performed, a ruler and a whole people might very well think that politics, even of a higher order than what had gone by the name in Mexico, could wait till a good administration had made it possible for work to be resumed. A nation must live before it can philosophise. The problem for Mexico was how it was to live—or rather the problem for the man who assumed the task of finding a solution was how he could enable a country which had no corporate will of its own, but only a plaintive longing for good government, to exist as a community at all.

It was a great misfortune, and an evil inherited from the past, that the President could look for no help from the Church. Its power was still great in many parts of the Republic—in, for instance, the thinly-inhabited Pacific State Michoacan. The wealth and the great lands were gone, but the hold of the Church on the fidelity of the poor Indian, and mostly Indian, population was strong. Its help would have been of the highest value to a Government which desired to raise the standard of morality and industry in the working classes. But that aid could not be given by the Church, nor asked for by the State. The Church had been despoiled and could not forgive the despoiler. The reader who has no personal experience of the relations between the clergy and the State in the so-called Latin countries of to-day finds it hard to realise the depth of the gulf between them. " El Gobierno es un ladron " (" The Government is a thief ") is the compendious formula of the clergy in Spain and in most of its old colonies. They cannot forgive the " el grande latrocinio " (" the great robbery "); neither can they forgive the compulsory civil marriage which was introduced by Juarez and cannot be abolished. They must condemn it on religious grounds, and they do not detest it the less that it was expressly meant to be injurious to them. The high marriage fees exacted by the Church have

THE FIGHT FOR THE PRESIDENCY 175

been said to have been one of the reasons why the Mexican peon indebted himself to an employer. The civil marriage was meant to deprive the Church of this source of revenue also. The compulsory secular education of which much is heard, and something is seen, in Mexico was no less odious. We need not go out of our own country to learn how very offensive to religious people is an education divorced from religion. We need not go to Mexico to know how a clergy resents being deprived of the great opening for good work (that is, when they are pious men) or the immense power (that is, when they are only human) which is conferred on them by the control of education. So because of grievances and on doctrinal grounds the clergy were hostile to the Government of Porfirio Diaz.

Nor was that all. Those who have not lived in the midst of it cannot realise the fury of distrust, hatred, and repulsion which animates those who stand over against the Church. An Englishman may think that his Established Church asks for too much, and gives itself airs. He does not, or he is a very rare exception if he does, grow hot against it as a fount of mental imbecility and moral corruption. Now the anti-clerical of the Latin countries very commonly does. So President Diaz had to endure the reproaches of some of those who had fought with him under the leadership of Juarez. Though he gave back no lands, though he enforced the law which imposed civil marriage, though he would not suffer the clergy to appear in clerical dress in the streets, nor so much as allow the ringing of church bells, they accused him of truckling to the clergy and encouraging the corruption of the people because he did not put a stop to such functions as the coronation of a certain sanctified statue of the Virgin.[1]

Meanwhile the clergy were denouncing him as a persecutor. All through the administration of Lerdo, who was peculiarly odious to the Church because his brother was the author of the law which secularised the Church lands, and then till far into the rule of Diaz, there took place a series of clerical riots in towns and villages. The worst were in Michoacan, but there were others elsewhere. A President who had by the ears two such wolves as the militant clerical and anti-clerical parties had need to keep a firm hold of them.

[1] To prevent the ringing of church bells may look like a contemptible piece of petty persecution. But a church bell may be rung by way of demonstration or counter-demonstration. A few years ago it was my luck to attend a political meeting of a Liberal shade in a Spanish city. It was held in a hall. On the other side of the street was a convent. For al ong time, and until the police struck in, the: onvent bells were rung madly with the very probable intent, and certainly with the result, of rendering the speakers half-inaudible. There was an overflow meeting in the street. The clerical demonstration was resented, and if there had not been a strong force of constabulary on the spot the convent would have been attacked. The constabulary officer in command had to tell the superior of the convent that he was provoking a riot, and to order him to stop the bells.

CHAPTER VII

THE FIRST TERM

Diaz settled himself, not in the official residence of the President, the former Palace of the Viceroys, but in a private house, to struggle with the hopeless-looking problem he had undertaken to manage. Like other tasks, it grew less terrible when resolutely tackled than it had appeared to be from a distance. If we could gain access to the very private and confidential papers of Mexican moneyed men and foreign capitalists whose interests were bound up with the restoration of order, we would no doubt learn how the new Government was supplied with the funds which tided it over its first days. In most Spanish-American political conflicts there are holders of the purse-strings who keep in the background but who provide the military chest. Some body of interested moneyed men no doubt did for Porfirio Diaz what the bankers of Paris did for Napoleon in the interval before Brumaire, when he was as yet only General Bonaparte and not even First Consul. When the immediate need had been met, the difficulty of finding a revenue equal to calls which could not be neglected was not insuperable. The army did not need to be laboriously persuaded before it could understand that a revenue must be secured if it were to enjoy the pay, allowances, and pensions to which it was entitled. It was a fact patent to the dimmest intelligence that as the best part of the national revenue came from the customs levied at Veracruz, the road to the main seaport must be opened and kept open. Therefore the President had the willingly-given help of officers and soldiers in effecting the first piece of work to be done.

Armed men in competent numbers and in a reasonable state of discipline had no great exertions to make before they could establish a fair working state of order in the more vitally important regions. It is true that many of the so-called soldiers were by origin brigands and guerrilleros. But it is also true that most of them had taken to these lines of life because there was very little else for them to do. They were poachers who were quite disposed to adopt the honest trade of gamekeeper. Diaz made prompt and effectual use of their better aptitudes. The organisation of the excellent constabulary known as " guardias rurales " did not begin with Diaz, but it was vastly improved and developed by him. The rurales in their brown or buff uniforms, high steeple-crowned sombreros, well armed and well mounted, were to constitute not the least useful of the President's instruments of government. He recruited them freely among the men who, under himself or other " caudillos " and " cabecillas " of the days of disorder, had learnt all the mountain paths and hiding places they were now to supervise, in the course of years of guerrillero and bandit adventure. They were masters of all the devices they had practised, and now, having decided to exchange a life in which long intervals of sloth and hardship were relieved by occasional and uncertain hauls of booty, for regular pay and a position of social credit, they became a terror to such evil-doers as they themselves had been in their unregenerate days. The perhaps imaginary Irishman who confessed that he and his friends were not afraid of the soldiers but of the police very exactly expressed the sentiments which were rapidly instilled into disorderly Mexicans. A company of soldiers might be befooled, but not a detachment of old practitioners who knew the country as they knew the palms of their hands, who were everywhere, and who knew not only the places but the persons, who would learn at once whether any man was absent from the house where he ought to be, and why. The methods adopted by the rurales may not have been, and indeed were not, what would be suffered in the kindred Irish Constabulary. They were nearer the ways of the Spanish Civil Guard. A practice which in Mexico was even embodied in a law—the " Ley Fuga " (the " Law of Flight ")—gave the rurales large powers of summary jurisdiction. If a man did not surrender at once when summoned, or if when being taken to prison he attempted to escape, they were authorised to shoot him on the spot. As from the nature of their work it commonly happened that there were no witnesses of the resistance to arrest, or attempt to escape, save the rurales themselves, we can understand that summary executions were nowise uncommon. We may take it as pretty certain that when a man was a notorious offender who had given trouble, and particularly if he was one who at any time had injured a member of the corps, he always offered resistance or attempted to escape. But it is not said that the rurales abused their power grossly, or in order to extort an advantage of any kind for themselves. And it is a fact that men who have inherited Spanish blood and ideas are very tolerant of the use of summary methods in dealing with criminals. They trust rurales or civil guards more than they do the civil tribunals which they believe to be corrupt, and they think the summary " quatro tiros " (four shots) of the constabulary vastly preferable to the lumbering procedure of the courts. Within no long period life and property were tolerably safe in the valley of Mexico, on the Plain of Anahuac, and over a broad belt of country on either side of the road to Veracruz. If the police in the towns was not so good, at least there began to be a police of which we may say that it did deserve the name given to the corps to which Diaz had belonged in his boyhood, " Peor es nada." It was a " better than nothing."

There was another kind of predatory creature, who was all the more dangerous because his offences were more subtle than robbery under arms and were beyond the scope of the rurales. The public service swarmed with bribers and blackmailers and thieves. The long disorders which had favoured brigandage were no less friendly to the corrupt official. When even the army could not be paid, nor the interest on the public debt, it followed that the civil officials had to go without their salaries—or at any rate without regular payment. The armed men were allowed to recoup by rapine—an unrivalled training for highway robbery—and the civil officials to gain a livelihood by corruption. The advantages of the position were so great that places under Government were eagerly sought for. Men of influence provided for their trusty followers by foisting them on a public office. It was calculated that when Diaz became President there were 2,000 confessedly superfluous officials in the public offices of the capital. They were, it is true, not entirely free from check. The great men at the head levied a part of their dishonest gains as a consideration for giving them a wide margin of freedom. Corruption had in fact got to the point when it could be flaunted. Mr. Wells, who visited Mexico a few years after 1878, was not unacquainted with graft in his native United States, but he found it avowed, even after the reform had begun in Mexico, with an audacity which was new in his experience. He heard of a countryman of his own who passed for being exceptionally familiar with lobbies and lobbying. This old practitioner had a concession to secure, or some other interest to be served, and he approached the important person whose approval was needed boldly. " If you will arrange that for me," he said, " I will pay you $5,000 and keep the transaction a strict secret." " If you will made it $10,000 you may tell all the world," was the answer. The story in slightly different forms is told of many lands, but it is not thought plausible save in certain conditions of public morality.

The new President did at least charge home on the pest. Having the whole armed force in his hand, and the army being well persuaded that if it was to receive its pay and allowance out of the revenue of Mexico ($17,000,000) some reasonable measure of honesty must be shown in handling the money, he could use the broom freely. It would be rash indeed to affirm that bribery and corruption ceased either then or afterwards. But the staff was cut down to just proportions to begin with. A stronger measure, which only a very firmly planted ruler would have dared to take, followed. A tax was levied on all non-military salaries. In a country where direct taxation was not known save in the form of a poll-tax on Indian labourers and was vehemently hated, the Government officials were subject to income tax. The measure, hard as it was, could not be spared in view of the distressed condition of the Treasury. Don Porfirio set an example of sacrifice by consenting to the reduction of his own salary from $25,000 to $15,000. He lived very quietly in his house in the Calle de la Moneda (Mint Street),[1] and was as unpretentious in his way of life as he was accessible to all sorts and conditions of men. His disinterestedness compared well with the rather grasping action of Juarez, and must have had a wholesome effect. But he did not rely on compulsory sacrifice and good example alone. He knew that life must be made tolerable for those whose services are indispensable. Therefore he began by taking care that the reduced salaries should at least be regularly paid. When by 1896 the revenue had grown, and the sacrifices imposed in 1878 were no longer necessary, the tax on salaries was taken off. At a still later date the scale of pay was raised to meet the increased cost of living. To employ no more clerks than are needed to do the work and to pay them a salary on which they can live decently are the two antecedent conditions of the formation of an honest public service. The truth has been patent for centuries. The misfortune of many countries has been that it was ignored. President Diaz did try to establish these conditions, and it is a credible proposition that the corruption which continued to exist did not go beyond what was normal in England till the end of the eighteenth century.

The simplicity of his life, the accessibility of the President, and his readiness to hear all men who wished to speak to him had much to do with the uni-

---

[1] In Spanish *moneda* is money, *una moneda* is a coin. La Casa de la Moneda, or for short La Moneda, is the Mint.

versal popularity he earned and kept for years. They would have had their effect in any country, but they were particularly valuable in Mexico. They were made possible partly by the general simplicity of existence, but still more by the fact that the people had inherited their standard of manners from the Spaniard at his best. The Spaniard is always willing to recognise rank, but he expects to be " treated like a man " and without " vapours." The neat indications of rank which can be made by the use of the Don, the Señor, or the unadorned Christian name, are understood by all —by Pedro as well as by Don Luis. So there is the less fear that Don Luis will lower himself, or Pedro will presume when they talk together " like men." And because the formulas are fixed and their orthodoxy is undisputed and universally known, the man who has risen from the ranks drops with wonderful ease into the ways and bearing of a " gentleman born." There is no uncertainty as to what is the right thing to do, and therefore but little of the underbred uneasiness of the parvenu. Señor Fornaro will have it that Don Porfirio learnt the dignity he showed in his later years after his second marriage to a lady of a good Creole stock. Señor de Zayas says that in his earlier years he was timid in his bearing. Timidity may be due to an absence of mere self-conceit. Foreigners who saw him were of opinion that long before he was President he had the air of a soldier and a gentleman. It was not only because Mexico is a republic, but because the Mexicans were in part Spaniards, and trained in the old Spanish standard, that the son of the innkeeper at Oaxaca, who had also been farrier in a cavalry regiment, was perfectly at home as head of the State.

In the meantime popularity, military support, and the general longing for peace and freedom to work were none too much to bear Diaz up in the task before him. There were three dangers he had to face. To put them in their order of real importance they were: the relations of Mexico with the United States; the distress of the national finances; and a remnant of armed faction which plotted, agitated, and broke out sporadically for a time. Unless he had averted the first he would have striven in vain to overcome the second and the third. From the day on which he became President till that other thirty-three years later when he sailed from Veracruz amid the downfall of his labours, there can have been few days, and there cannot have been a single month, in which the relations of his country to the United States did not give him cause for thought and anxiety. The great power to the north has hung, and hangs, over Mexico like a mass of snow or earth which some act of folly or accident may turn into avalanche or landslip. Questions of the diplomatic order pressed for solution, and behind them, giving them an almost awful importance, were physical, geographical, social, and financial forces.

It is a literal statement of fact, that for a Mexican ruler the exterior world is divided into the United States and all the rest. If the first is friendly, the second can do him but little harm. If the first is hostile, the second can render no help. In 1878 there was a strong probability that the United States might become actively hostile. Before going further let us guard ourselves with care against the risk of seeming to agree with those critics, of whom some of the most

THE FIRST TERM

trenchant have been Americans,[1] who have said that the United States have been aggressively brutal to their neighbour. Individual Americans have behaved badly to Mexico, but the Government of Washington, which alone acts for the United States, has on the whole shown much long-suffering in its dealing with the unruly and provocative community on its southern border.

The numerous and chronic disputes between them have arisen from two kindred sources—the disorders of the border, and the losses caused to American citizens by or through the internal confusions of the Spanish-American Republic. Putting aside the conditions of the border for the moment, the two sides may be treated together, to begin with, simply because there was always a question of compensation to be paid for wrongs inflicted on individuals. There were cases in which the sufferer was a Mexican ; and then the one claim had to be set off against the other. The Mexican grievances mostly arose from the border, but the Americans had suffered everywhere. There were cases of violence practised on individual citizens of the States in various ways, but the worst of all were the constant extortions of forced levies of military service and money. On paper the Mexicans had often a good case, and their diplomatists, who are by no means lacking in quickness of wit, could frequently seem to put the United States in the wrong. They could, and they did, argue with much verbal force that these levies and contributions did not constitute a true grievance, because they were not imposed on

---

[1] Mr. Wells, for instance, does not mince matters. He declares roundly that the United States have played the part of a great bully to their weaker neighbour, and that opinion is far from being peculiar to him.

Americans alone but on the whole body of the inhabitants. Now it is a tenable proposition that if a man will settle in a foreign country in search of some advantage to be obtained for himself he has no ground for claiming better or other treatment than is shown to the people among whom he has of his own free will chosen to live. But this is only true when the country he lives in offers good guarantees for order and equal treatment in a uniform and legal way. Moralists and sentimentalists may refuse to make a difference between country and country. They may ask why did you go where the kind of treatment you desire to receive was notoriously not to be found ? The answer is perhaps illogical, but it is a good one. It is, we go because the world is so constituted that we do and we must. If the question is why do you make a difference between one country and another ? the answer is perfectly logical. It is that they are different. There is no parity between the obligation to pay taxes, to conform to police rules, to submit to expropriation for public services, or to the compulsory use of property in a time of war, to which an American might be called upon to yield in England or France, and the outrages—the " avanias "—of Turkish pashas and Chinese mandarins. Now the whole case of America was that the wrongs which its citizens had suffered in Mexico at the hands of Santa Anas and Miramóns were of the same nature as the excesses of pashas and mandarins. If Mexico wished to be treated like England or France she must offer the same guarantees, and that she had notoriously never done. Therefore she must expect to be classed with Turkey or China. And in sober fact the United States were right. Since they were they must be allowed to

THE FIRST TERM

have shown moderation. Even if we look back to and beyond the war of 1848 the Union can fairly say that it endured more and retaliated less than European Governments have done. A comparison between their policy to Mexico and that of the Marquess of Wellesley to the Mahratta rulers or of the British Government to China (a much more stable country than Mexico) ought to be in their favour in the opinion of those who condemn the use of force.

After the war of 1848 there had been long discussions which dragged on till 1876. When at last a settlement was made it left Mexico with the obligation to pay \$4,125,622 in yearly instalments of \$300,000 to begin in January, 1877. A rebate of \$150,622 to be deducted from this sum was made for proved Mexican claims. It is not unworthy of notice that the \$4,125,622 was all that remained of 2,000 American claims which amounted to \$556,788,600. The commissioners who examined the accounts presented to them had to reduce to fair proportions whole floods of greedy pretensions, supported by a positive frenzy of mendacity and forgery. The story had a sequel which can hardly be quoted against the United States. Among the claims presented and supported by the United States Government were two made by a Mr. Benjamin Weil and by the La Abra Mining Company for \$487,810 and \$681,041. The Mexican Government protested against them as fraudulent, and they became the subject of litigation in the States. The law's delays dragged the case on till 1900, when the Court decided against Mr. Weil and the company. Then the United States Government both refused to collect any more for them and refunded the payments which had already been made. It should be added also that the umpire chosen by both sides in 1873 was Sir Edward Thornton, British Minister at Washington. In 1877 the demand of the United States for the payment of the first instalment due in January was to be met. The sum of $300,000 was not a heavy one for a revenue of $17,000,000. But the revenue had not been collected when Congress met in April, and further delays would be dangerous. Indeed, there was no regular channel by which a request for time could be made. The Government of Washington treated Diaz as only one military adventurer the more, and did not so far recognise him as lawful President. It is to be presumed that this refusal of recognition was meant to be a form of coercion and a warning, since it is difficult on a survey of Mexican history to see that the election of Diaz was less lawful than those of his predecessors with extremely rare exceptions—if, indeed, there was more than one. The attitude of the United States Government was of course an encouragement to the irreconcilable Lerdistas who were plotting in their places of exile in Texas. The first instalment of $300,000 must be paid off, and it was paid by having recourse to the familiar expedient of a forced loan. Henceforward the payment was regularly discharged till the whole award was cleared off in 1890. In April, 1878, after the second instalment had been supplied, the United States Government did at last recognise President Diaz, and the relations of the two Governments became as friendly as the unending disputes on the frontier allowed.

These last did not end, and have not ended when this page is being written. They are secure of a renewal of life so long as the condition of the country on the

THE FIRST TERM

Mexican side of the line and the population on the northern side remain the same. When after the disastrous war of 1848 Mexico was deprived of all the territory it claimed to hold north of the Rio Grande —more than half the total area of the Republic—the Mexicans remained, as was but natural, angry and apprehensive. It is true that this vast expanse of territory was of little value. Much of it was waterless and barren, but to a far greater extent it was worthless because it was not inhabited by a useful population. A few settlements of Mexican half-breeds were lost in empty deserts, and among tribes of Red American Indians, Apaches, and others only less bestially ferocious than they. Mexico herself could supply no colonists, and the story of those whom she had invited to Texas from abroad was not encouraging either to them or to her. Still, Mexicans could hardly be expected to bear their loss with indifference. It was not possible that they should be without fear of a new American advance. The best and, in the long run, the only effectual defence would have been to settle the country on the right bank of the Rio Grande up to El Paso, and then on the south of the line running westward from El Paso to the Pacific, which together marked the new frontier. But the Mexicans had no overflow of their own to settle in these regions, and they could not draw on the population of Europe. The conditions which have allowed of considerable German and Italian settlements in Southern Brazil and the Argentine did not exist for such remote, and before the construction of railways such inaccessible, regions as Chihuahua, Coahuila, Sinaloa, and Sonora. The peninsula of Lower California and the maritime States both on the Pacific

Coast and on the Atlantic were, it is true, open to immigration from the sea. But the Mexicans were in fear of all immigrants. Schemes for the establishment of a French settlement in Sonora, whether pushed by mere filibusters like Pindray and Raousset-Boulbon, or more peaceful speculations advocated by Jecker or patronised by Napoleon III. during the Empire, were equally repugnant. The Mexicans were suspicious of all " gringos," and were persuaded that these intruders meant mischief to them. They looked with hostility on the pushful newcomers, as did the Gauchos of the Argentine Pampas on the Europeans who displaced them and threatened to rob them of their very " chiripás." [1]

Except on the sea-coast and in a few ports, Mexico was represented in the great belt of territory which stretches from Lower California to the Atlantic by a sparse population of herdsmen, vagabond seekers for " bonanzas," bits of luck in the shape of pockets of gold, half-breeds, and broken men. In 1877 and for some years afterwards the United States had not subdued their own territory to complete order—and especially not in Arizona and New Mexico, which stand over against Chihuahua and Coahuila. Then the half-breed herdsmen and their like on the Mexican side were not the only inhabitants. Where they could not occupy the land, hunting Indians roamed, or Pueblo Indians lived their old communal life. In these conditions it would have been strange if the border had not reproduced all, or more than all, that our own ancestors knew under that name. The

[1] The " chiripá " is the shawl which the riders of the Pampas wrap round the middle of the body as a protection against the cutting winds from the South Pole. An odd and rather indecent story has been invented to account for an article of dress which really explains itself.

Indian tribes on the northern side began to burst into Mexico as they felt the pressure not only of the rifles, but of what was more deadly by far to them, the economic conditions created for them by the advancing whites who broke up or enclosed their hunting-grounds and were exterminating the bison. From Mexico as from a place of refuge they raided back on the enemy who had starved and forced them out. The unfailing products of an unsettled border—the cattle-lifters, half-breed, and white—could not be lacking. In fact they swarmed. Most troopers are agreeably picturesque figures on the pages of Sir Walter, but Willie of Westburnflat or the Devil's Dick of Hellgarth are less attractive when seen in their native characters of cattle-lifter, horse-thief, fire-raiser, blackmailer, and murderer.

There was another personage at work who had been unknown to the Middle Ages—to wit, the land speculator. Northern Mexico was the country of the " hacendados," the great landowners whose acres were counted by the million. But there was land to sell, and it will occur to everybody as but natural that a title more or less good could be obtained in Mexico at a very cheap rate. It could in fact be acquired in Mexico for a few cents an acre. If only the country could be transferred to the sovereignty of the United States the market price would promptly rise to the same number of dollars. Of course there were not a few holders of titles—Mexicans too in many cases— who were perfectly ready to foment any disorder in the hope that the United States might be tempted or provoked to make another advance and annex another belt of Mexican territory. The change of sovereignty would promptly have interpreted itself for them into a very profitable transaction. Nor was there wanting on the American side a lively desire for new land to be settled, or, what was more innocent, for the greater security which would come of the presence of the United States cavalry on the right bank of the Rio Grande. In short, pretext, provocation, speculation, and the just resentment of the Government at Washington might combine at any moment. Therefore it was that the United States hung over Mexico like an impending avalanche or landslip. Indeed it was thought that but for the firmness of President Hayes the whole mass would have been precipitated during Don Porfirio's first Administration, and that, no doubt, was one main reason why he was resolved, and was able, to bring his countrymen to pay the $300,000 a year of indemnity according to the terms of the award of 1876.

There was, however, more to be done. If the Mexicans suffered from Indian and other raiders who came across the border from the American side, the citizens of the United States lost far more by the raiders who came from the south, for the sufficient reason that they had incomparably more to lose. Pursuit of the offenders was useless when they could take refuge across a border and could not be followed. There is no reason to believe that the United States would have wished to send their troops across the frontier in pursuit of Indian or half-breed raiders if the Mexican Government would have maintained a proper ward of the marches. But that it would not and could not do. Like other Spanish American communities, it was far too ready to take advantage of its own wrong, to plead that because it was anarchical, and therefore very poor, it ought not to be

THE FIRST TERM

summoned to perform its elementary functions. When it was shown to be incompetent to the injury of its neighbours, it stood on its dignity. When during the Administration of Juarez it was asked to consent to allow American troops to cross the frontier, it declined. The American Government was honourably patient and took the perfectly fair course of offering reciprocity. Till 1877 nothing was done. In the confused condition of Mexico in these years it was often not as much as possible to say who was the Government, or where was the Government, at any given moment. In 1877, just when Diaz was really beginning to bring the country to order, the condition of the border, especially where it marched with the new well-inhabited and prosperous State of Texas, had reached a point where the sufferers declared that the nuisance was no longer to be tolerated. The reputation of the Texans is that not very much is required to bring them to the fighting pitch. Some among them by general admission were on the same moral level as Mexican cattle-lifters. Every raider was not born south of the Rio Grande. There were some who had first crossed the river from the north, and to whom Mexican territory served as a no man's or debatable land, where they could find refuge. But that is only another way of saying that the Mexican Government did not govern. The grievance was not all on one side, but it was real, and it was worse for the richer of the two countries.

In June, 1877, the United States Government gave instructions to General Ord, the officer commanding in Texas, to cross the frontier in pursuit of Mexican marauders. He was, however, told to act in harmony with the local authorities and to ask their help.

These instructions showed a desire to make compliance as easy for the Mexican Government as the state of the case permitted. None the less the advance of the American troops would have constituted an invasion. The action of the United States, or rather the threat to take action, created a serious difficulty for Diaz. If he yielded, he would have discredited himself in the eyes of his countrymen, and then somebody would have been found to set the old anarchy boiling again. If he had taken a very high tone with the United States, he might, indeed he certainly would, have provoked a war in which Mexico would have suffered grievously. No such result was desired on either side. President Diaz took a line which, while satisfying the susceptibilities of his countrymen, was really a compliance with the just demands of the United States. He sent General Treviño to the frontier with a competent body of troops and with public orders to resist General Ord by force if he advanced. It was generally believed, however,—and the opinion seems a plausible one—that General Treviño was privately instructed not to be officious in putting himself in the way of the American general. This measure was accompanied by a vigorously-worded protest against the proposed action of the United States as contrary to international law. But the protest was followed by the adoption of measures to bring the border to quiet. It was allowed that they were effective and that the marauding was abated. It is not rash to assume that General Treviño and other Mexican officers, acting under the wholesome stimulant applied by America, administered a good deal of Jeddart justice and Halifax law on the right bank of the Rio Grande.

THE FIRST TERM

The trouble did not cease, for it arose from the natural wealth of the soil in such growths. But President Diaz convinced the United States that he meant well, and that if he were not unduly hampered he would do better. After he had been recognised in April, 1878, the two Governments joined to provide a remedy. In 1880 the States asked for an arrangement, regularly recognised and recorded, by which their troops might cross the line in pursuit of marauders. President Diaz, after consulting with his Congress (mainly, one imagines, from politeness and for form's sake), consented to a treaty, not, however, signed till July 29, 1882, when he was not in office. By this treaty the regular troops of each Government were to be authorised to cross into the territory of the other on certain conditions. The entry must not be made on settled land, nor go within six miles of any settlement. It must be notified at once to the local authorities, and the pursuing force must retire when the capture was effected or the trail was lost. Conventions of this kind have since been repeatedly made and renewed. President Diaz had secured for his country equality of treatment, though it was not he who actually signed the treaty of 1882.

The line adopted by the two Governments was the best available, but it is obvious that there was a considerable danger in such reciprocity as this. When one side was impatient and perhaps unduly scornful, and the other was susceptible and not without resentment, collisions were not unlikely to occur. One did in 1886. An American officer, Captain Crawford, crossed the frontier into Chihuahua on a proper occasion with a few United States soldiers and a large proportion of Apache scouts. By a misfortune such as was inherent in the case, a body of the Mexican Chihuahuan guard which was in pursuit of other raiders fell in with Captain Crawford's detachment. Misled, as it alleged, by the sight of the Apache scouts, it concluded that it had to do with a body of plundering Indians. It attacked and Captain Crawford was killed. The incident excited, as may be supposed, much anger in the United States. But a war was not desired, and Diaz, who was now back in the Presidency, had the confidence of the American Government. It recognised that Captain Crawford had not observed the terms of the treaty with exact care. He was entitled to cross the frontier, but only with regular troops. The greater part of his command consisted of Apache scouts who could not be so described. The trouble was smoothed over, but when collisions of this character were likely to occur vigilance and goodwill must have been taxed on both sides to keep friendly relations from being broken.

His first Administration did not give President Diaz the chance of putting the finances of Mexico on a better footing. He was indeed tempted to do them some damage. But they may be allowed to stand for a space while we turn to his struggle with the conditions which had to be subdued if he was to go on doing any measure of good on any side of Government.

The new President had bound himself by all "Plans" issued by him—La Noria, Textupec, and Palo Blanco—to establish the rule that no immediate re-election for the Presidency was to be allowed in future. And this rule was to apply to the governors of the States. He had also bound himself tacitly by the final clause of the Plan of Palo Blanco, and explicitly by definite promises he gave in a public letter published after

THE FIRST TERM

his return to the capital from the north in February, not to govern with or for one party, but for the nation, and with the help of men of all parties who would frankly give their aid. Now nothing was easier than to persuade Congress to pass a nice little law forbidding re-elections. Laws can be made with a light heart in countries where they are but little respected. Nobody in Mexico can have believed sincerely that the new constitutional law would prove to have more virtue than the long series which had preceded it. But to govern without strict regard to party was by no manner of means so easy, for it implied that the President must disappoint some at least of those who helped him to rise to power. And in such a country as Mexico this meant that the disappointed persons would protest with the use of force. Then, too, a patriot President resolved to rule free from the bonds of party was no less sure to offend those of his opponents who would be content with nothing less than all, and it was a matter of course that they would take up arms. President Diaz had to meet trouble from both sides.

Those who have heard how he gave peace to Mexico may be surprised to be told that there was no year of his first Administration in which there was not fighting somewhere. But a year of peace in Mexico was one in which only local conflicts occurred. It would be a wearisome task to go through a long list of these scufflings of kites and crows. Their incidents were monotonous and barren. The characters of the persons concerned were of the poorest. It will be enough to take one example of each class of disturbance, the explosion of disappointed personal ambition and the violent outbreak of pure insurrection.

General Marquez de Leon—no connection with the Marquez who was Tiger of Tacubaya—had been one of the supporters and agents of General Diaz in the north-west. He was a native of Lower California. This man was one of those who considered that the President had not rewarded his services as they deserved. He was of course intent on gaining his revenge, and he had the power to do mischief. In the course of his political activities in previous years he had acquired a useful connection in the State of Sinaloa. Sinaloa is the State which lies directly south of Sonora on the Pacific coast, and the northern end of it is in the Gulf of California, opposite Marquez's native State. Having connections in both, it was possible for him to combine them. And he was presented with an opportunity by a local disturbance in Sinaloa. The governor, Cañedo, had fallen out with his fellow-Sinaloans on constitutional points which the absence of evidence makes it difficult to master. Judging by analogy, we may conclude that what was at stake was the control of the spigot of local taxation. " Pronunciamiento " was in the air, and such a well-practised wire-puller as Marquez de Leon was had no great difficulty in turning a local riot into a general rising. The immediate command in Sinaloa was given by him to one Jesus Ramirez, who was locally popular. He himself passed into Lower California. During the whole of 1879 and much of 1880 these two were engaged in keeping up the banner of revolt by " several pronunciamientos " and " opportune seizures of funds," to quote the demure prose of Mr. H. H. Bancroft. Skirmishes occurred, repulses, captures, the ups and downs of the guerrillero-*cum*-bandit wars proper to those constitutional con-

THE FIRST TERM

flicts. At last Jesus Ramirez was shot in a skirmish by Federal troops, and Marquez de Leon, finding the game was going against him, disbanded his men and fled to the United States. Meanwhile there were other fights for freedom in the same or very similar conditions going on in other parts of the Republic. They were taken as matters of course and treated as of no consequence. In the address to Congress at the beginning of the session of 1879 President Diaz referred to them in terms which show how calmly a state of anarchy in solution and always on the point of precipitating was accepted by the strongest man of government in Mexico : " Some events have occurred in different parts of the country of which, though they have provoked transitory confusion and local difficulties, it cannot be said that they affect the general peace of the Republic or menace established order."

Each by itself these outbreaks were but little more dangerous than strike riots. The wide extension of them and their persistence was none the less a menace to " established order," for it showed that anarchy was bred in the bone of the Mexicans. In the speech with which he prorogued the Congress in September, President Diaz made a dry and laconic reference to another manifestation of this same evil which had occurred at Veracruz. It was the event to which Señor Fornaro referred in the screech of fury quoted above (see p. 120). It was far too characteristic of the country, too significant of the conditions with which a ruler who would keep order has to deal, and it touches the personal character of President Diaz too closely to be lightly dismissed.

Our story has already shown that Veracruz was a point of peculiar importance, because it was the main port of entry for Mexican trade, and the place where the bulk of the customs was collected. For that reason it was always guarded by Government with exceptional care. But for that reason also the seizure of the town was always a great object with insurgents of all colours. They were not likely to forget that Juarez had won against the Conservatives and Miramón very largely because he had been able to occupy and hold the port. If the place could have been captured the Government would have found itself deprived of funds at a critical moment. There was no lack of intriguers in Mexico who were capable of making this simple calculation. Irreconcilable Lerdistas were ready to combine with disappointed agitators of the stamp of Marquez de Leon. In the spring of 1879 a conspiracy was undoubtedly on foot. It may have been ineptly contrived, for the Lerdistas generally were clumsy conspirators, but it was genuine. The plan was to bring about a mutiny in two Government gunboats lying near Veracruz, the *Libertad* and the *Independencia*, and then act in combination with Lerdista conspirators on shore who had returned secretly from their exile in Texas. The fighting leader was to be Mariano Escobedo, a veteran of the French war, and he had with him " some colonels of known dash—Lorenzo Fernandez, Bonifacio Topete, Carlos Fuero, José B. Cueto, and others." There were other intriguers of the wire-pulling rather than of the fighting order within the town.

President Diaz was too well aware of the vital importance of keeping a tight hold on the place to have neglected the precaution of putting it in safe hands. The governor was the Luis Mier y Terán to whom he had entrusted the command of his following in Oaxaca at the time of the rising against Juarez. Terán[1] had gone through various fortunes. He was a prisoner when Lerdo fled from Mexico, and it was he who brought the news of the flight to Diaz. He was devoted to Don Porfirio. Don Rafael de Zayas describes him as a perfectly illiterate rough diamond of jovial temperament and breezy popularity hunting manners. He was commonly known as El loco Terán (Rattlepate Terán)—a description answering to our " good old So-and-so," and implying more condescending approval than respect. Perhaps the reputation of the man as a kind of noisy buffoon misled the conspirators into underrating the danger of incurring his suspicions. They were to discover that all this genial hail-fellow-well-met outside covered a capacity to be ferocious in the most extreme Mexican style.

It may very well be the case that some of those engaged in this particular plot entered into it because they found conspiracy almost as exciting as the gambling for which most Mexicans have a furious passion. Even among more sober peoples men have been known who found an irresistible attraction in the game of conspiracy. The French Royalist Hyde de Neuville tells a story of the famous Chouan, George Cadoudal, which he gives as being by no means an instance of idle talk. They were escaping together in an open boat, and were on their way across Channel

[1] The reader may perhaps not always know what is the meaning of such a name as Mier y Terán—that is, Mier and Terán. The second surname is that of the mother. Diaz himself, for instance, was Diaz y Mori. Whether the two names are habitually used depends on whether they are easily pronounced together and other considerations, such, for instance, as the convenience of being able to distinguish Señor Ramirez y Lopez from Señor Ramirez y Sanchez. A man sometimes prefers to use his mother's surname, and this was the case with Mier y Terán, who is commonly spoken of as Terán only.

to England. In the middle of the night Cadoudal suddenly asked him if he had reflected on what was the first thing the King ought to do when he was restored. Then he supplied the answer. It was to shoot them both, for, said the Chouan, they had become so wedded to this kind of life that they would never be able to lead any other. And Hyde acknowledges that the humorous judgment of George had a basis of truth. There were certainly not a few Mexicans with whom plotting and "pronunciamientos" had become a habit. They followed their bent lightly and they talked too much. Terán became aware that some trouble was brewing and laid hands on one of the "characterised" members of Lerdo's party. Martial law had not been proclaimed in Veracruz, and the governor thought it best to observe the forms. He applied to Don Rafael de Zayas, who was Federal judge of Veracruz at the time, and asked him to commit other prisoners. Don Rafael, from whose narrative these details are taken, declined to comply with the governor's request. Terán was angry, and did not hesitate to accuse the judge of tepidity in the cause of public order.

The arrest of the "caracterizado" may perhaps have stimulated the fighting element in the conspiracy to immediate action. The gunboats which were to be seized were lying, not in the poor roadstead of Veracruz, but at Tlacotalpam to the south-east, where the Papaloapam and the Alvarado rivers run together and form a species of delta and a lagoon. The anchorage is connected with the sea by a narrow passage. The town of Alvarado stands on the north-west side of the entrance and Tlacotalpam on the inner side of the lagoon. The proposed coup was only partially successful, but the *Libertad* was seized during the absence of her captain, who was ashore, and by a party from Alvarado. The captors made off with her to the eastward and took her to Carmen, at the end of the Lagoon de Términos in Yucatan. Here while the leaders of the plot were ashore in search of " fortunate seizures of money " the boatswain and the loyal part of the crew retook the *Libertad* and brought her back.

In the meantime Terán had been promptly informed of the seizure of the *Libertad*. He telegraphed at once to the capital for orders and received for answer the words " Fusilalos en caliente " (" Shoot them hot and hot," or red-handed). Terán did not wait for a second order, but at once shot a whole batch of the Lerdistas he suspected, and buried them immediately. He seems himself to have been aware that this summary execution would be blamed, for he reported to the Government that an attack had been made on the barracks at Veracruz, and that assailants nine in number had fallen in action. In view of what followed it is not easy to see why Terán put himself to the trouble of lying. The truth was notorious. The execution caused more excitement than might have been expected in a country where shooting of prisoners had been so common. But hitherto the firing parties had been busy with the officers of defeated armies. In this case those who had suffered belonged to families of substance and to the class which had kept in the background to pull the wires and work revolutions for their money. Their families insisted that an inquiry should be held. The Government was slow to meet their request, but at last, on July 13, some three weeks after the execution, the bodies were exhumed. It was then found that they were tied with ropes, which of course showed the absolute falsity of Terán's assertion that they had fallen in open fight.

Having obtained this amount of concession, it would have been, on the face of it, easy, one would think, for the families to force the Government to bring the general to a real trial. Yet they failed. It is true that he was brought before the grand jury in the capital in May, 1880, and that his case was put before Congress more than a year afterwards in November, 1881, when the President's first term was over. Both bodies declared they were incompetent to try him. He was never punished by the law. There is no honest reason for concealing the manifest truth that if he escaped punishment it was because Don Porfirio did not choose to allow him to be punished. But, that being so, we naturally wish to understand why, in spite of public emotion and newspaper clamour, the President's popularity was not in the least diminished by an act for which he must be held responsible, and which was as savage as any recorded in Mexican history.

Writers who have undertaken to draw Diaz as of blameless walk and conversation according to an approved European model have passed over this episode in silence. Others who wished to show a certain measure of independence have endeavoured to prove that the famous "Fusilalos en caliente" only meant that Terán was to shoot the mutineers on the *Libertad* if he could catch them red-handed. This is the kind of apology for which no human being could really be grateful. It endeavours to save Don Porfirio's moral character at the expense of his

THE FIRST TERM

common sense. If that was what he meant he could easily have said so in terms which could not be misunderstood. He knew Terán well. His telegram was worded, not in the official and polite third person singular, but in the familiar second, which is never used except between very close friends or relatives—" fusilalos," not " fusilelos." It was a personal encouragement from one old friend to another to hit hard. Knowing the man as he did, Diaz must have been woefully lacking in judgment if he failed to foresee that Terán would take the message for a direction to do some such thing as he did.

There are only two ways in which such an incident as this of the massacre at Veracruz can be judged. Either there was no excuse for it, or it needed none, as being one of those actions not laudable in themselves, even cruel, which were none the less done for the good of the State. If Mexico was a country in which the Government could move with a strict regard to law, then Terán was a murderer, and Diaz, who undeniably aided him to escape punishment, abetted the murder. But if Mexico was not such a country, but one in which there was no respect for the law, and where many men, greedy, self-seeking, or feather-headed, were for ever trying to let loose the forces of anarchy and bloodshed which had just been chained up, then there was no murder nor abetting of murder. There was a merciful rigour which at the expense of nine lives averted far greater slaughter.

The fact was that for two years before the summary shooting at Veracruz the unhappy country had been worried by local outbreaks and raids from across the frontier, all frivolously undertaken, all ill-conducted, all encouraged underhand by wire-pullers who laid plots and advanced money. Escobedo, who was to have co-operated with the Veracruz mutineers, had been taken in 1877 and had been allowed to go free on parole. Yet he was scheming again. If the country was to attain to a lasting peace there must be an end of this. Since moderation and persuasion could not bring that end about by gentle means, then an example must be made. The people who intrigued between four walls, found money and pulled wires, must be taught that there was some danger in being too busy. They were taught once and for all. It is allowed that the terror produced by the blow struck at Veracruz was profound and lasting—so lasting that it was felt thirty years afterwards. The intriguers realised that for the future no half-measures would be taken with them. They cowered down, and from that day "pacifism" became possible. Diaz could afford to be moderate because the disorderly elements had learnt that they must keep quiet.

Yet his hand was always heavy on recalcitrant minorities. In his later years possible competitors for the Presidency used to vanish into prison, and did not always come out. Governors of States whom he could trust were kept in office for life in spite of the Constitution. Only a blindly obedient servant could hope to be appointed or retained as "gefe politico" of a district. Spies and informers were used without scruple.

CHAPTER VIII

AN INTERIM

THE first Administration of President Diaz was timed to end in November, 1880. He had spent the first year of the four which constituted his legal term in fighting for his position. The three which followed were spent in clearing the ground and in laying down the lines on which his future government was to be conducted. The first process has been sufficiently illustrated by the story of Marquez de Leon and the Veracruz conspiracy. But it is necessary for the full understanding of the subject to add that the President showed a most consistent determination to shake himself free of all bonds of party or connection in his choice of men to serve the State. He made many changes of Ministers and he took, one after the other, several who had served his predecessors. Ignacio Mariscal, an accomplished diplomatist and linguist; Rubio, who had been one of the followers of Lerdo, and had fled with him to the United States; Berriozabel, who had been Minister of War with Iglesias, and others, were reconciled to the new ruler. They were joined with his secretary, Justo Benitez, with Gonzalez, who had decided the day at Tecoac, and other Porforistas of the early times. By this policy of judicious selection the President gained a double advantage. He provided himself with a staff of capable agents, and he deprived other parties and connections of their ablest leaders. In his case, as in that of all men, death of others and mistakes of rivals had helped him to fortune. Juarez was gone ; Lerdo had made himself odious ; Iglesias had taken no hold. No one else rose above the crowd sufficiently to counterbalance his popularity. But of him also the maxim *Faber fortunæ quisque suæ* holds good. He had known how to take advantage of the chances which fortune put in his way. And as he rose step by step he persuaded an ever-increasing number of those Mexicans whose support was valuable, and, what was quite as much to the purpose, of those foreigners whose aid was needed by every Mexican ruler, that their interests were safer with him than with any other. The Mexicans were those who longed for peace and an opportunity to attain to prosperity. The foreigners were capitalists whose financial aid was indispensable in so poor a country, and one where so much was to be done in the way of public works.

When we inquire what it was that the President aimed at above all else during his tenures of the Presidency we cannot hope to find an answer more conveniently, or in more satisfactory form, than in the pages of the two volumes somewhat largely named " The Authentic History of the Administration of General Diaz." The licentiate Ricardo Rodriguez, who published this compilation in 1904, went too far when he called it a history. It is a collection of the speeches which the President made at the opening and prorogation of Congress at the beginning of every April and in the middle of the following September of each year. These " discursos " are akin to the messages of the Presidents of the United States, though they are never framed on the same ample scale. They show every sign of being the President's personal work, if only because of the great similarity of their style to that of the biographical notes from which quotations have been made above. Like these notes, the speeches are singularly free from the faults of garrulity and mere rhetoric which are so commonly to be found in Spanish and Spanish-American political oratory. The President tells Congress what is to be done, what has been done, or what it would be desirable to do, in plain, straightforward sentences, unhampered by involved parenthetical clauses and inter-locked gerunds in "ando" and "iendo." The style we know is the man, and it is part of the biography of Porfirio Diaz that he was silently contemptuous of formulas and that his mind went directly to things, and to the work which the eye can see and the hand touch. Though he was neither a man of letters, nor desirous to be one, he by mere virtue of clearness of head and directness of mental aim, did not seldom attain to command of the well-knit short sentence and the alert prose of the Spanish writers of the good epoch. He was not, to be sure, Mariana, nor Lope de Vega, whose prose was an example to Europe, but he can stand with the explorers and the captains of Charles V. and Philip II., who were both manly and sober.

Now when we look at the matter of these speeches we find that what predominates is public works. Other things are there, the advantage of getting rid of the abuses which had grown from the old practice of farming the Mint and of the destructive form of tax named "Alcabala," and so on; but in the main the President presses on the attention of Congress such substantial things as railways, roads, drainage, bridges, afforestation, the dredging and construction of ports—in short, the equipment of tools without which no country can make use of its resources. And, as this was what the peaceful and industrially inclined part of the population of Mexico knew to be most necessary, the prominence the President gave it in all his measures and speeches tended to root the confidence felt in him more deeply.

Yet his first term of office could see only the promise, or at the utmost the beginning, of the good work, and in Mexico there was then, and we now see that there still is, but the poorest of security for the continuance of any good work apart from the personality of the dominant administrator.

This serious consideration was in fact forcing itself into the minds of a good many Mexicans by the year 1880. In 1877 Congress had embodied the great principle of the " Plans " published by Diaz himself at various times and at La Noria, Textupec, or Palo Blanco in a law. It had then provided, as far as the law could, that no President, nor governor of a State, could be re-elected at the conclusion of his term of office. Such re-election was, it seems, contrary to democratic principles. The President or governor must retire and wait his turn. He was not disqualified for ever, but his terms of office must not be consecutive. It is needless to say that in the act of making this law the Congress assumed that elections for President and governor were formalities in Mexico, or else that it tacitly confessed that the people did not consider re-election undemocratic. If the sovereign people did hold that faith and was free to choose, what compelled it to re-elect any man ? But Congress knew very well that elections were mere

AN INTERIM

matters of form, and that such words as " elector,"
" voter," " sovereignty of the people," " democratic,"
and so forth, had no meaning for the huge majority
of Mexicans. They stood for institutions and ideas
borrowed from abroad, and applied to creoles, half-
breeds, and Indians, to whom they were completely
alien, and with whose real sentiments they had no
sort of organic connection. They made a mere mask
which in moments of passion or sincere emotion was
thrown aside as artificial and as useless. The law of
1877 was simply one of many other attempts to
provide a paper-barrier which should restrain the
actual tenant of office from turning himself into a
tyrant in the proper force of the term. A really
beneficent ruler was the most dangerous of all
" tyrants " in that sense. He was exactly the man
who was least likely to be met with opposition when
he took measures to perpetuate himself in office, and
thereby to block the road to those who wished to
enjoy their turn. How far Diaz did at any period
of his life believe that a mere Congress-made rule of
this kind would prove to possess any virtue of its own
is a question which he might himself have found it
difficult to answer in his later years.

Before his first term was over he must have learnt
that there were many in Mexico who would have been
glad enough to see the Congress undo in 1880 what it
had done in 1877. If Diaz had lent himself to their
wishes there can be no doubt that the Legislature
would have done as it was told, and that he would
have been re-elected at once. But the law had been
so recently passed, and Diaz had so repeatedly
declared against " the principle of re-election," that
he would have discredited himself, if not in Mexico,

where declarations for or against principles had never had much meaning and had come to have none, then at least in the United States. Moreover, as we shall see, it was not absolutely necessary for him to retain office in order to keep control of affairs.

It is a truth which if men were not in practice so blind to it would be a platitude, that in politics no paper Constitutions, or other constructions of words printed and called laws, are of the slightest avail against the facts of the case. Power in Spanish America has resided, resides, and will continue for long to reside, in some person or connection of private persons who can coerce rivals by armed force. Their power is personal, however it is obtained, and it either overrides Constitutions or finds some way of evading them. The Constitution of the United States is a reality, and the American people has an inherited respect for law. Yet we know what has become of the attempt made by the fathers of the Republic to arrange for the choice of a President by a process of double elections. The constitutional law made by the Mexican Congress in 1877 has had the same fate. It was one of many made in Spanish America to prevent any particular man from perpetuating himself in office, and they have always proved equally futile. When they have not been set aside by force a coach and four has been driven through them.

The first of the two processes needs no explanation, but a few words will not be wasted in accounting for the second. They are in fact necessary in order to render the next stage in the life of Porfirio Diaz intelligible.

We have within the last few years become acquainted with the political term "rotative." It came from

AN INTERIM

Portugal, where it seems to have been invented, but the thing is common to the whole Iberian peninsula and its colonies, and is also ancient. Don Rafael Altamira, the most learned of contemporary Spanish historians, has found traces of it in Biscay and in the Middle Ages. It is simply an arrangement by which two persons or connections agree to "rotate" in office. The reader must not be misled by memories of Republicans and Democrats, Whigs and Tories, Liberals and Conservatives, when considering this Iberian institution. There is no question here of an appeal to the country with or without a dissolution, of a victory of a party at the polls, and of a transfer of office from a defeated to a victorious side. The election is always made by the politician in office as an alternative to the more destructive, and not less corrupt, method of calling the troops into the streets and the guerrilleros to the hillsides. We may say that it marks a distinct progress from a state of anarchy to one of constitutional order. The rotative system was highly developed in Spain, and worked, on the whole, well during the reign of Alfonso XII and the regency of the queen-mother Maria Cristina. Don Antonio Cánovas went out and Don Mateo Práxedes Sagasta came in. Then Don Mateo went out and Don Antonio came in. In every case the incoming Minister "made" his own Cortes, care being taken that the "outs" should be allowed a becoming proportion of seats.

Wherever a Spanish-American republic has attained to a state of peace it has been by the adoption of a rotative system. Absolute smoothness of working is perhaps not to be looked for. The outgoing connection may find the door effectually locked behind it by the rotators in office who will not keep to the spirit of the bargain; or, again, the "ins" may try to lock the door and fail. In either case there is trouble and a reversion to the old rough method of "pronunciamiento." But in many cases the arrangement works. The President whose term is drawing to an end, and who is forbidden by the Constitution to seek for immediate re-election, selects a safe man to succeed him. He superintends the election and gives his personal support to his friend. Four years later the parts are reversed. Guzman Blanco brought this essentially Iberian adaptation of constitutional government to great perfection in the Republic of Colombia. With or without the guidance of his example, and perhaps by the light of his own sagacity and that of his advisers only, Diaz prepared to perpetuate his personal influence and to prepare his own return to the Presidency at the end of four years by a rotative arrangement. A safe man was to be chosen, and to him was to be entrusted the duty of continuing the work begun, on the distinct understanding that he would repay the service when the time came to clear off the debt.

The choice of a trustworthy *locum tenens* presented difficulties. The best associate would be one who would carry out the bargain in the letter and the spirit of his own free will and mere motion. But such perfect harmony of brotherhood was hard to find. The next best resource was someone who would not be able to break the bond if he should be tempted to play false. He must be one who had no dangerous amount of popularity and influence of his own. Yet a mere figurehead, a mere nonentity would not suffice. Diaz wished to serve the interests of his country too honestly to be prepared to leave them at the mercy of a bungler, simply in order to smooth the way for his own return to office by showing that he was indispensable. The President for the next four years must in fact be qualified to allow good work to go on, and yet not quite equal to making an independent position for himself. Tact and insight were much needed for the task of selecting " a safe man."

Those who profess to have been well-informed affirm that the President began by making choice of his secretary, Don Justo Benitez. They had fought together in the dark days of the French invasion. Benitez had worked hard for his chief during the struggle with Lerdo. It is true that he had not always avoided giving offence in quarters where Diaz looked for support. But he had been loyal, and the very fact that he had committed errors of management in dealing with persons tended on the whole to show that he would not be a dangerous substitute. So he was chosen, and in order that he might be put in a position of sufficient prominence to appear worthy of the Presidency he was to be sent on a mission to Europe. But Don Justo broke down under the test. A lively French contemporary who was employed to negotiate with Wolsey has recorded that the cardinal began by saying " The King." Then he said " The King and I," then the formula became " I and the King," till at last he took to using the bald first personal pronoun. Don Justo had no doubt heard persons of insight say that he was the " intelligent soul," the *alma pensante* of his chief, and had come to look upon himself in that light. He soon showed too much independence, and spoke too much in the *ego et Rex meus* tone. Such haste in claiming the first place was a warning and Don Justo was dropped. Then, so it is said, President Diaz's thoughts turned to Terán. But the outcry raised over the general's fierce dealings with the Veracruz conspirators rendered him dangerous as a *locum tenens*. The President did indeed prove that he would not allow the general to suffer for displaying excess of zeal in carrying out the order " Fusilalos en caliente "—if excess of zeal there had been. But he could not take too much of Terán's unpopularity with some of the Mexicans on his own shoulders while the scandal was fresh, and attempts to bring the general to a genuine trial were still being made.

Whatever the true truth as to the tentative selections may be, we know that the candidate finally chosen was Don Manuel Gonzalez. He was the general to whom the President had entrusted the command of the infantry of his army during the struggle with Lerdo in the north. His timely appearance on the right flank of Alatorre's line had decided the battle at Tecoac. He had been for a time Minister of War for Diaz. The President could rely on his loyalty, and his position was such as to justify his candidature. The election was held and passed off peacefully because Diaz kept order, and also because four other candidates, one of whom was Justo Benitez, were allowed to canvass freely and to receive a decent show of support. But the influence of the President was thrown openly on the side of Gonzalez, who was elected by an immense majority. The Congress declared him duly returned on September 25, and he entered on his term of office on December 1, 1880. In the speech which closed the session of that year Diaz congratulated Congress on the good order which had reigned during an election, though the public had taken

AN INTERIM

unusual interest in the contest. All constitutional government requires the aid of fictions, and Mexico has its own.
The real character of the transaction is sufficiently displayed by a single fact. Diaz offered his active support to the new Administration, and was invited by his successor to take a portfolio in the new Cabinet. It was characteristic of him that he took the department of Public Works. In that office he was able to apply himself to what was of most interest to him, while keeping a watch over the whole administration. He showed himself particularly attentive to the new harbour and railway works at Tampico. They were not without a certain political interest. The Gulf coast of Mexico is ill-provided with ports. Hitherto the interior tableland had been wholly dependent on Veracruz, which is but a narrow anchorage between the rocky little island of San Juan de Ulloa and the mainland, and the route inland has to climb a very steep ascent. Tampico lies to the north by west of Veracruz at the mouth of the Panuco River, which is navigable for a short distance, and close to the lagoon of Tamaulipas. It is just at the southern point of the State of that name. The natural harbour is not a good one for large ships, but it is on the whole better than Veracruz. By improving the port and connecting it with the capital the Central Government would free itself from the dangerous old dependence on what had been the sole outlet and entry place for trade. We can therefore easily understand why Don Porfirio, who looked forward to his own return to office, should have shown a special desire to forward the works. In fact, the whole question of "works" was becoming predominant in Mexico, and whoever had the general

direction of them stood fair to be the most important man in the country.

Though the statement may appear to be rather in contradiction with what has been said above, it was probably the very importance of the post which induced Diaz to retire from the Ministry at the end of a year. He gave as his reason for withdrawal—and it must be allowed that it was a plausible one—that he found some of his colleagues were of opinion that he overshadowed them. They were certainly not wrong, and it must be allowed that his presence in the Cabinet was too well calculated to emphasise the real nature of his relations to the new President. The general rule in Spanish America is that the outgoing rotator pays a visit to Paris. The sailors have a saying that an old mainstay makes a bad foresheet. A man who has once been skipper is an uneasy first mate, and that is particularly likely to be the case when there is an understanding that he is to resume command of the ship in the future. Diaz must have felt himself awkwardly placed before the year was out; and moreover he must have foreseen coming trouble arising out of this same question of works. He was to have his hands free of it. The story may be left till it can be treated as a whole. In the meantime Diaz withdrew from the Cabinet and returned to his native Oaxaca, where no doubt by previous arrangement he took up the governorship.

Oaxaca, as we know, was not only the State to which he belonged by birth, but it was that one wherein he had been " cacique." Influence there had been the foundation of his power. Of late he had not seen much of his home, but the time might be at hand when he would need Oaxaca again. The laws of 1877 had

AN INTERIM

limited a State governor's tenure of office to a year. Diaz, as was usual with him, played the game strictly. He spent twelve months on the Administration of Oaxaca, which had, as can easily be believed, fallen into considerable confusion since he issued the Plan of Textupec. The question of works followed him here, and his tenure of the governorship was made notable by strenuous efforts to promote the construction of the railway across the isthmus of Tehuantepec from Santa Cruz on the Pacific to the port with the rather unmanageable Indian name Coatzacoalcos on the Bay of Campeachy. Coatzacoalcos was officially deposed in favour of the easier, if less characteristic and sonorous, Port Mexico. When his twelve months were over he returned to the capital, and took up his residence in Humbolt Street, in a house which became his own and was afterwards occupied by his son Felix.

For a short time, and in so far as retirement was possible for one who was known to be about to resume the Presidency, he lived apart from politics. But the interval was filled for him by an event of the first consequence for his future life. He had become a widower during his first term of office. We know little of the lady whom he married during the siege of Mexico. But the second Señora de Diaz was to be almost as conspicuous a figure of the political and social life of the country as her husband. A certain reserve must be used in speaking of a lady who is still alive, even when there is nothing but good to be said. The facts which can be mentioned without risk of intrusion are that his second wife was much younger than himself and was by birth a lady who had received and had profited by a more serious education than has usually been given to the daughters of Creole families. Doña Maria del Carmen Romero Rubio was the daughter of Don Manuel Romero Rubio, who had been one of the Ministers of Don Sebastian Lerdo,[1] had gone into exile with him and had returned. He was afterwards one of Don Porfirio's Ministers.

La Señora de Diaz (for why should we say Mme. Diaz ?) has confided to Mrs. Tweedie that she had had a girlish admiration for Don Porfirio, and had, in fact, regarded him with the sentiments which Desdemona felt for Othello. The President who had been and was to be was nowise insensible to a homage which we are given to understand was not disguised. His attentions—so his biographer, Señor Godoy, records—were noted in Mexican society. Nobody was surprised when his marriage was announced and took place in November, 1882. It was a happy one in private and public ways alike. Don Porfirio never showed the least tendency to fall into the folly of some of his predecessors who tried to surround themselves with a sham court. He maintained a " republican simplicity " of life. But there is room in the simplest life for dignity and good breeding. Indeed, there is none in which those qualities can be shown with greater merit. To dress richly and well is comparatively

---

[1] Spanish feminine names are not always clearly understood by us, and a few words on the subject may not be amiss. The full married name of the President's wife would be Maria del Carmen Romero Rubio de Diaz. In social life the full name is reduced to Carmen de Diaz. It is safe to say that every Spanish woman is baptised by the name of Mary, though she may have and may prefer to use another Christian name—or font name, " nombre de pila." But it is usual not to give the mere name Maria. One of the personifications, or attributes, or qualifications of the Virgin is added: " Maria del Carmen," " Maria de los Dolores," " Maria de la Concepcion," " Maria de la Incarnacion," " Maria de la Asuncion," " Maria de las Nieves," or local virgins, as " Maria del Pilar," " Maria de Guadalupe," " Maria de la Peña de Francia," and many others. Some of them have familiar abbreviations—" Concha," for Concepcion, or " Blanca," for Nieves (" the Snows ").

AN INTERIM

easy. To dress very simply and very well is a test of good taste. It was part of the exceptional position which President Diaz took among Spanish-American rulers that his household was presided over by a lady who would have been at home in the society of a great European capital. The education of women in the different Spanish-speaking communities has a tendency to develop a somewhat narrow form of piety which shows itself in an excessive deference to the clergy. Whatever the opinions of the master of the house may be—and in the educated class they are generally those of indifference to religion—the wife is, except in rare cases, a " clerical." It is believed that the education of La Señora de Diaz had been of a kind to save her husband from this source of lack of sympathy.

Shortly after his second marriage General Diaz enjoyed the only visit to a foreign country which he was able to make as a pure holiday in his life. It was certainly not for mere reasons of convenience, nor of economy, that he went to the United States. It would have been at least as easy for him to have crossed the Atlantic to Paris. But the city which has so strong an attraction for most Spanish-Americans did not draw him. Even on a honeymoon he obviously did not forget that the Union is far more important to Mexico than all the rest of the world. We may take it for granted that he was in search of more than rest and amusement, that he wished to see and become known to the influential people in a country with which he was to have close relations. General Grant visited Mexico in 1880. He did not come for any political purpose properly so called, though he may be said to have come in connection with matters which entered largely into the international relations of the two republics. In 1880 the public career of General Grant was over and he was beginning to enter into those unhappy business ventures which embittered his last years. What he represented when he came to Mexico was the growing conviction of American capitalists that Mexico was becoming a country in which investments might be profitable because they would be safe, and that President Diaz was the man to secure the safety.

During the year of his visit to the States and the Exhibition at New Orleans matters had been ripening for a change in Mexico. The administration of General Gonzalez had begun in peace and amid every appearance of content and of nascent prosperity, only to end in a very different state. It has been said that the first two years were a golden age, but were followed by such an outburst of waste and corruption as had never been seen even in Mexico. The blame was freely laid on the shoulders of President Gonzalez. Rhetorical phrases of this stamp inspire distrust. We ask ourselves how and why the general should have violated an ancient maxim by suddenly becoming *turpissimus* between the end of the second and the beginning of the third year of his administration. It is not enough to say that he was generally and fluently abused. Gonzalez may not have been perfectly disinterested, and in fact it is allowed that when he retired from office he had provided for himself. Mr. H. H. Bancroft, who writes in the most friendly spirit to him, has to make a concession of a rather significant kind : " It was said that the source of his fortune, which has been grossly exaggerated, was due to peculation ; when the fact is, that at a

AN INTERIM

time of such material development as Mexico derived from the administration of Gonzalez, it was an easy matter for any intelligent and shrewd man to acquire wealth in enterprises of recognised utility to the country, as was done by many others, some of whom were not at all friendly to the President." The apology is rather of the nature of a paving-stone which, when used to squash the calumnious insect, falls on the head of the person to be defended. President Gonzalez was the ruler of the country in which enterprises of recognised utility were being carried on by foreign capitalists who stood in need of countenance and sometimes of subventions from the Government. In such cases a shrewd and intelligent man who has the power to give or withhold may indeed easily make his profit by accepting what Mr. Pepys called compliments, without going over the blurred line which divides indelicacy from bribery pure and simple. But he has need to be careful if he will keep himself untouched by the accursed thing. As Gonzalez was not known to have had means of his own to use for purposes of speculation, it is to be feared that the fortune he took away with him from office, which, though it might well be grossly exaggerated, was confessedly not a pure invention of the enemy, had its origin in compliments made to him by the moneyed men. We need not make too much of this. Many others did the same beyond all doubt. That office should lead to fortune was as well understood in Mexico as it was in the England of the seventeenth and eighteenth centuries. President Diaz, who was born in poverty, and whose official emoluments were never great, acquired a fortune, and it would be difficult to say how he did so except by a very similar use of shrewdness and intelligence. If one must find an explanation for these things, it can be found without doing violence to probability, in the supposition that the best of Mexican rulers entered into transactions of the same character as those investments of navy balances in Indian funds, and for his own benefit, which have such an ugly look in the trial of Lord Melville. Yet Melville was the friend of Pitt and the patron of Sir Walter Scott, who defended him fiercely. Moreover, he made a good head of the navy at a great crisis in our history.

Gonzalez might have taken the compliments and might have speculated safely with balances, and yet have retired without reproach, if certain troubles for which he was nowise responsible had not come to a head in the latter part of his Administration. They all had their origin in " public works " and financial distresses, and they ran their courses in close connection with one another.

President Gonzalez might complain with entire justice that the difficulties which overwhelmed him in the last year of his tenure of office had their origin in the Administration of his predecessor. We have seen that President Diaz was intent on developing the resources of his country, and showed himself very well aware that the first step to be taken was to make them accessible. Therefore the indispensable preliminary to all else was the construction of railways. Nothing could well be more true. But Don Porfirio had not learnt from Benjamin Franklin that there is such a mistake as " paying too much for your whistle." Railway construction, except along the plain which rises gently from the Rio Grande to the valley of Mexico, is bound to be costly. The rise from Veracruz to the capital is one of 7,000 feet in a distance of 263 miles : 2,500 feet of this rise have to be overcome within 12 miles—at the edge of the Plain of Anahuac, where it falls almost in a precipice to the Tierras Templadas. The construction was a great engineering feat, and one we may be proud of, for it was carried out by a British firm. But the working expenses were high. The outlay was hugely increased by a piece of jobbery. Don Antonio Escandon, the *concessionnaire* of the line, added $6,743,938 to the cost of construction by causing the line to be increased by 120 kilometres (85 miles) in order to serve certain mills and lands of his own. The subvention he received from Government was $7,056,619. In order to cover interest on capital and working expenses the freights were high, though they were much below the cost of carrying goods on mule-back, the only method hitherto available. The Veracruz line had been completed in 1873, and President Diaz was not responsible for the extravagance or the jobbery. His error was that he did not take warning by the history of this enterprise, but granted subventions to projectors of new lines on a colossal scale. In the last year of his Administration he promised $64,000,000—a huge sum for a Government to engage to find, even by instalments, out of a revenue which in 1880 had just risen to $24,000,000 from the figure of $17,000,000, at which it stood in 1877.

It is commonly said that when Diaz's first term ended in 1880 he left a balance in the treasury, and that when he returned to office at the close of 1884 he found nothing. Such a statement as this must have been made in reliance on the lack of knowledge among those to whom it was directed. That there was money not yet paid out of the exchequer may be believed. But there was no part of the revenue, either in hand or likely to be paid in, which was not earmarked, and far more than covered by obligations which were about to mature. The railways were not the only claimants. Subventions had been promised for drainage works and harbours. All the schemes which swarmed at the end of 1880 were not as much as begun to be executed. A good many were put in execution and carried far enough to give the projectors a claim for part of their subventions. Then they were left unfinished. Not a few of these undertakings were, in plain English, " bubbles." They had no commercial nor industrial foundation. It was true that on the whole the railway-making of this period did in the end profit the country, and it is not less true that the revenue rose from $24,000,000 to $33,000,000 in about four years. But in the meantime the expense was out of all proportion to the returns, and the growth of the revenue was largely fictitious. It represented the customs dues levied on the material imported for these as yet unremunerative works. The amounts which were going out in the form of subventions largely exceeded what was coming in as customs dues. And these dues were of course added by the importer to the price of the material for which in the end the Mexicans were to pay. For the moment the Government appeared to be in the enjoyment of a handsome surplus. The working expenses of the administration (which for a reason to be given did not include payment of interest on the debt) were estimated at $22,000,000. As the revenue had risen, on paper at least, to $33,000,000, it would appear that there was a surplus of $11,000,000. But this sum was about a sixth part of the subventions promised to railways alone in one year of Don Porfirio's first term. And then it must not be forgotten that, as Mexico was quite incapable of providing the capital for all these works herself, the creditors were foreign capitalists. The debtors, who were called upon to pay sums far in excess of their resources, were the native Mexicans.

One does not need to be a profound financier in order to be capable of understanding that as his term of office drew to an end General Gonzalez found himself in the position defined by the colloquial Spanish phrase as " between the sword and the wall " (" entre la espada y la pared "). There was not enough to pay everybody. Therefore somebody must go unpaid. It has been counted for pure righteousness to the General that he decided not to impose any sacrifice on the capitalists who were demanding these subventions. They were paid to the full, and in order that they might not suffer he stopped the payment of all the salaries of all the civil officials of his Government. The soldiers, who had at command very convincing arguments why they should be satisfied, continued to receive their pay. We can easily believe that the foreign capitalists applauded the President's tender regard for the national honour. It is the easiest thing in the world to say that the Mexicans ought not to have incurred obligations without considering whether they could fulfil them. An extremely modest critical faculty can point out that if parliamentary government had been a reality in Mexico the Congress would have put an impossible barrier in the way of the speculative temerity of President Diaz. If a country cannot force its Government to act with good sense, it must suffer for its weakness. All this is the most obvious of the obvious. Whether the foreign capitalists, who were not unacquainted with the financial and industrial condition of Mexico, and who had every means of learning that the contracts they made could not be carried out without injustice to somebody, were blameless for the wrong done is too big a question to discuss here. The Mexican officials who were deprived of their salaries considered themselves as robbed for the benefit of the foreigner. They were not the less angry because they could see that General Gonzalez was accumulating a modest fortune by a shrewd and intelligent participation in works of public utility. They did not take a large view, but simply said that he had been bribed by foreign capitalists to satisfy their greed at the cost of the hapless civil officials. If there was an outbreak of corruption and pillage at the close of the General's term, one reason is perhaps that so many of the agents of his Government had been deprived of all other means of subsistence. If President Gonzalez had inherited trouble from his predecessor, he repaid the ill-service by leaving him a no less serious difficulty to overcome.

When an important and vocal section of the Mexican community was in this excusable state of irritation, the President added two other grievances to the causes of the unpopularity which overwhelmed him. One he could not well help; the other was the result of mere bad management. The first was the long-drawn-out dispute over the British debt; the second was a Mexican version of our " Wood's halfpence "—the exasperating blunder made with the nickel coinage. Both were to be left for Diaz to settle.

The debt was a sore of some sixty years' standing,

AN INTERIM

for it dated from 1824. It had been founded by the Federalist agitators who with Santa Ana at their head had upset the " empire " of Augustin Iturbide. The Mexican Government issued bonds for £3,200,000 at 5 per cent. The whole was taken up by a London financial house (B. A. Goldschmidt & Co.) at 58. The figures are sufficiently eloquent as to what was thought of the security, which was the whole revenue of Mexico. The Republic got in fact about £2,000,000 and had to pay 5 per cent. on £3,200,000. That the bargain was not a good one mattered little to those who controlled the spigot of taxation in Mexico for the time being. They would not have to answer for the payment, and in the meantime they handled £2,000,000. Neither, presumably, did the future weigh much on the minds of the financiers, who passed the stock on to the too confiding investor. The security was bad, and the usual sequence of events was unrolled. Next year the Mexican Government was in the market with another loan of £3,200,000—this time at 6 per cent. It was taken by another financial house (Barclay, Herring & Co.) at 86¾. Then in due course came the inevitable irregularities of payment, reductions of interest, capitalisation of arrears, and so forth. The same old bad debts were rearranged and renamed. Somebody was paid for services, or, in English-Chinese phrase, took " squeezes," but the bondholders were paid by fits and starts and very ill or were not paid at all. If the protecting shade of the Monroe doctrine had not loomed in the Gulf of Mexico the Republic would probably have been taken in hand very much as Egypt was to be. But the Monroe doctrine did stand in the way, and the sorrows of the bondholders never got beyond the stage of being the subject of diplomatic correspondence. If the holders of the bonds lost their investments Mexico obtained no good from the money. The fortunes accumulated by Santa Ana and other politicians alone remained to show where it had gone. As the anarchy grew worse the ways of Mexican politicians grew more violent. The culmination of the whole miserable story was the forcible seizure in the British Embassy by Miramon of a sum of money set aside for the payment of British creditors. This was the last provocation which stimulated the British Government to join with France and Spain to enforce some attention to their claims. The common action of the three was dissolved when the designs of Napoleon III. were revealed. If British creditors received any satisfaction it was because they were able to intercept part of the loan raised in France under the patronage of Napoleon III. and for the benefit of Maximilian.

When Juarez by virtue of the protection of the United States issued victorious from the struggle in 1867 he declared that all the Governments which had recognised the archduke had thereby declared war on the Republic. War dissolved all treaties and obligations. He expelled foreign Ministers with the exception of the representative of the United States. Little by little and step by step relations were renewed. The North German Confederation set the example in 1869, and when France resumed diplomatic intercourse in 1880 the only Power which still sent Mexico " to Coventry " was Great Britain. When it is remembered that during these years a British company completed the Veracruz to Mexico Railway, and that British men of business prospered in the country, it would seem that the lack of a Minister did no harm.

AN INTERIM

The fact, of course, is that the more serious among Mexican politicians were perfectly well aware that they could not afford to offend the capitalists of the great creditor nation, however high might be the tone they allowed themselves to take with its Government, from which they had nothing to fear thanks to the protection of the Monroe doctrine.[1] In spite of many loud complaints of ill-usage and occasional injury by common criminals, or officials who lose their heads in fits of greed or rage, foreigners in general, and British subjects in particular, suffer incomparably less from the vices of Spanish-American government than do the natives.

By the time that Gonzalez became President the debt had rolled up in snowball fashion till it had, what with original capital and arrears of interest capitalised and further arrears of interest on what had been capitalised, reached the figure of £18,383,761. Though Mexico seemed to get on very well without holding diplomatic relations with the British Government, and though British capitalists showed no

---

[1] An incident which happened in another Spanish-American republic may help to explain the comparative unimportance of Ministers and Consuls to those British subjects who are in the service of great financial concerns. An engineer in the employment of a British-made and managed railway took upon himself to give first aid to a native " peon " whose leg had been accidentally broken in a railway station. When the native doctor was called in he asked indignantly who had dared to perform a surgical operation to the detriment of his monopoly. When he was told, he caused the engineer to be arrested. If the good Samaritan had had to wait for help from Minister or Consul he would have waited a long time while the correspondence was following the proper course. Fortunately for him another resource was used. The local manager telegraphed to headquarters. The chief of the company in the province went to the governor. In a few minutes the governor's secretary was on his way to the local station in a special train. The company's representative had simply told the governor that its servants must not be treated in this style. The officials were suspended and the engineer was released. Nor did he hear any more about the matter, though he had undeniably laid himself open to a fine for performing a surgical operation without a diploma.

reluctance to risk money in the Republic, yet President Gonzalez and his advisers could not but be aware that Mexico could not go on for ever without regulating her relations with the great money market of the world, and Great Britain was aware that she could not keep Mexico " in Coventry " for ever. Of course, the settlement of the debt dispute was to be the preliminary to better relations in the future. Approaches were made on both sides; unofficial consular visits were made by Great Britain. Sir Spencer St. John, a diplomatist who knew Spanish-America well, came to Mexico to arrange for the resumption of diplomatic intercourse. Don Ignacio Mariscal came to England from Mexico on a similar mission. Settlements were proposed, discussed, rejected, taken up again. The main purpose of the Mexican Government was to consolidate the debt and raise more money with which to carry on, and meet the first coupons when they became due. By the final arrangement, which was maintained by President Diaz, Mexico was to contract a consolidated debt of £17,200,000, of which £14,448,000 was to be acknowledged to the bondholders and £2,752,000 was to be set aside for " expenses of conversion."

The President had probably made as good a settlement as was possible, but at the end of his Administration when the transaction was completed he was so unpopular that he was sure to be blamed for whatever he did. The Mexican public said that they were being burdened by a debt vastly in excess of any sum the country had ever received. They did not consider that the greater part of the sum represented interest which Mexico had promised to pay and had not paid. They accused the President of intending to steal the

£2,752,000, and they resented certain new taxes which he had imposed with the consent of Congress to enable the Government to meet its obligations. The last days of his Administration were disturbed by riots, and he left the burden to be taken up by his successor.

In all these matters Gonzalez had found confusion provided for him to deal with. But in the matter of the nickel currency, he made trouble for himself, and bequeathed it to his successor. There was a lack of small currency in Mexico. Something smaller than the old gold and silver coins was needed. As the country had its mints and abounded in metals, nothing would appear to have been more simple than to make the necessary small change at home. The course taken was certain to arouse distrust. Nickel coins were made in the United States and sent to Mexico to be stamped. From the first there was a pretty manifest suspicion that some swindle lay behind the introduction of these coins. And it is not to be denied that, whatever the intentions of the Government may have been, the nickels lent themselves to swindle. They were divided into one, two, and five cent pieces. The sizes were so ill-judged that it would have paid dishonest officials well to melt down the one and two cent pieces and recast them as five cent pieces. No limit appears to have been fixed to the amount for which these pieces of token money were legal tender. The limit put on the total amount to be struck, some £400,000 (about $4,000,000 Mexican dollars), was believed to be a mere blind. It was thought that vastly greater sums of nickel would be issued. It followed that if a creditor or an employer was free to pay debt or wages in these coins the creditor or workman would find himself in possession of nothing better than a handful of tokens of no intrinsic value.

The nickels were rejected from the very beginning. Stronger Governments than the Mexican have failed in the attempt to force a distrusted currency on a whole population. Peoples who will submit to extreme degrees of religious and political oppression have been known to revolt against this form of attack on their pockets. However docile the bulk of the Mexicans may be, they showed a disposition to take a violent course against the nickels, and President Gonzalez's Ministers thought it would be prudent in them to try to insinuate these coins into circulation by gentle methods. If there was no element of fraud in the device they chose, their moral character can be vindicated only at the expense of their intelligence. They sold large quantities of these tokens to merchants at discounts which in some cases went as high as 25 per cent. As the Government could not refuse to take its own money in payment at the nominal value without utterly destroying its credit, and as no limit was put to the amount for which the nickels were legal tender, the obvious result followed. The astute men of business presented them in payment of customs dues. The coins were soon back on the hands of the Government after inflicting a loss on the revenue in the course of their brief tour out and home. As for the mass of the population, after a preliminary period of protest and agitation it fairly broke into riotous assembly. Even if the Government could have relied on the soldiers it would have been beaten. But the rank and file of the army were like to be as great sufferers as any other class. There could be but one end to such a conflict between any Government and

AN INTERIM

the instincts of human nature. The nickels were howled down, and President Gonzalez had to go to Congress with a request that it would help him to withdraw them in some decent manner.

If Diaz had ever entertained a doubt whether his *locum tenens* would keep to the understanding between them he must have been reassured by the course of events at the end of 1883 and throughout 1884. Gonzalez had become so utterly unpopular that he could not have broken the compact if he had tried to play false. Nobody in the country had the least interest in supporting him unless it were the capitalists, and they had nothing to gain, but, on the contrary, a great deal to lose, by helping him to launch on an adventure which would soon have plunged the country back into all the troubles of Lerdo's time. A President of Mexico can do a great deal in the way of imposing a dummy successor on the country, but not when he has offended all the civil servants, when he has no certainty of support from the army, and when all the elements of the population are banded against him. The fact that there was no general rising and that no " Plans " were promulgated in any of the States showed that the increase of employment due to the introduction of foreign capital to be spent on railways, harbour works, etc., was turning the attention of the Mexicans to more profitable forms of activity than " pronunciamientos." But the fact that apart from a few street riots in the capital and some towns the peace was kept is best explained by the universal conviction that Diaz would soon be back in the Presidency. Nobody appeared against him, and when the election was held in September he received 15,999 votes of a total of 16,462 delegates.

There is no reason to suppose that Gonzalez made any attempt to prevent the return of Don Porfirio. He was, it is true, accused of attempts to poison the President-Elect, and also to kill him by engineering an accident on the Irolo Railway, on which Diaz was travelling. But these are the little vivacities of Spanish-American political controversy. Nobody believes such accusations, and least of all those who make them. President Gonzalez retired to enjoy his fortune in peace, and President Diaz took up the reins in December, 1884, to hold them for twenty-seven years.

CHAPTER IX

PRESIDENT FOR GOOD

THERE is no reason for breaking the narrative by any further accounts of Presidential elections in the life of Don Porfirio Diaz. Elections there were in a purely formal way. But everybody in Mexico knew well that they meant nothing. First Congress amended the law which forbade immediate re-elections. Then it removed all restrictions. Then in 1904 it prolonged the President's term of office from four to six years. No competitor appeared in any of the elections so called of 1888, 1892, 1896, 1900, and 1904. An opponent did come forward in 1910, but the end was then at hand, and the story must be left till we reach its date. It is enough to say here that for about twenty-seven years he was by common consent, and, to judge by appearances, to the satisfaction of all, the master of Mexico. Francia, the Despot of Paraguay, governed for nearly as long, and did in one way more than Don Porfirio, for he died in power, and he founded a kind of dynasty. No other Spanish-American tyrant has achieved as much as either of them, and Francia had a far easier task than the ruler of Mexico.

During those twenty-seven years, or rather during twenty-six of them, Diaz was the Government of Mexico. It was not because Congress approved that he was re-elected and his term was not prolonged. Congress approved because its master directed it to give its approval. In other words, the Government of Mexico was, in the technical sense of the word, " a tyranny." A single man had taken to himself all the powers of the State, and was not a whit the less tyrant because he used them to the best of his ability and with the help of the wisest advice he could obtain for the general good. No great event, or succession of events, divides these twenty-six years of rule into periods. Their history cannot be told chronologically —or at least nothing is gained, and some quite unnecessary repetition is incurred, if we follow the mere order of time. We have one single subject to deal with—the manipulation of Mexico by President Diaz. It may be divided under heads for purposes of convenience and for its better understanding, but it cannot be intelligently arranged by mere dates. And the subject is the sincere effort of a strong-willed and clear-headed man to cure a chronic anarchy, by police repression, by the spread of mere school education, and by the development of material prosperity. It will be interesting to see how far he succeeded. The spectacle of a strong man resolutely engaged in " getting things done " is always to be looked at respectfully. But the political instruction of the story, and even the true meaning of it, are to be sought rather in the reasons for his failure. For, as we now must confess, he did fail. He would not have succeeded, even if he had died in possession of power, as Francia did, and the anarchy had broken out after his death. But it burst forth while he was alive, and drove him into exile, from which he never returned. After all he had done for Mexico he came to the same end as some of the least sympathetic of Spanish-American despots—Juan Manuel Rosas, for

PRESIDENT FOR GOOD

instance. What, then, did he really do? And was it his fault that his work bore so little fruit? The answer to the second question can wait, and, indeed, cannot be given till we have replied to the first.

We may begin by allowing that he did all that lay within the power of a strong, resolute, and very laborious man who commanded a sufficient armed force to endow his country with all the material instruments capable of being used to produce material prosperity. It was a considerable feat, and well deserving to be studied. But in the face of what we are forced to see to-day one becomes a little impatient with the effusions of writers who but a few years ago were assuring us that because of the roads, railways, drainage, mining, and new harbours which were already made or in process of being made, because of a growing revenue, and recurrent surpluses, a new heaven and a new earth had been created in Mexico. The races who ran their courses on the great central plain, in Oaxaca, or Yucatan before the Spaniard came executed public works, which may have been "strangely magnified" by uncritical writers, but were none the less far from contemptible when they are considered as the achievements of peoples who had not the use of domesticated animals, and were forced to work with stone and copper tools, and yet they lie overgrown by tropical forest, or crumbling amid the degraded descendants of the peoples who had once the energy and ingenuity to build them. The Spaniards constructed "obras de romanos" while they ruled in " the Indies," but we know how their colonial empire ended. And these vanished Indian communities and their destroyers did their great works by themselves. They were not left in debt to foreigners when the work was done.

Mexico was so indebted. The work was done for her by foreign skill and capital. Every mile of railway represented an increase of the hold which the foreigner had on her land and her resources. Everything, therefore, is not said when we are asked to note that whereas there were only 567 kilometres all told of railway when Diaz became President, the mileage had risen to 16,285 kilometres by 1906. We want to know what she paid for this increase in her means of communication and to what extent her people profited individually. We hear that the national revenue trebled without any great increase in taxation, and that the surpluses were frequent and large. In 1906—1907 the surplus reached the remarkable figure of \$29,209,481 out of a revenue of about \$88,000,000. With these figures alone before us we do not expect to find that the national debt has increased in the same proportion. And yet it has. The traveller who finds the streets of Mexico city greatly improved, parks laid out, a national opera-house built at great expense, sees the proofs of increasing civilisation. But he sees them only because he does not look below the surface, or because he keeps entirely to a few towns. A national opera-house in a very fine style of French architecture has been built out of municipal funds in the city of São Paolo in Brazil. When one of the authorities was asked why so much money was spent on a theatre when the people of the town have little liking for this form of amusement, and rarely leave their houses at night, he replied that the building would impress foreigners with an idea of the opulence of São Paolo and would in short be a good advertisement. If the foreigner who is to be impressed goes for an hour's drive out of the town he will find the population living

PRESIDENT FOR GOOD 241

in huts of thin mud walls with but thatched roofs, and in conditions which preclude not only comfort but even common decency. There is not a little of such civilisation as this in Spain and Portugal themselves, and there is far more in Spanish and Portuguese America. Whoever goes but a very short way out of the towns goes centuries back in civilisation ; and he goes from the outward appearance of opulence to a reality of dire poverty. The prosperity which is shown in public works, increases of revenue, French fashions, and buildings in the towns does not seem to affect the mass of the population in the least. Even a rise in wages seems to do no good, for it is accompanied by, or is the result of, a rise in prices.

In order to begin doing what it was given him to do, President Diaz had to start his second term by bringing the finances back into order, and to do that he had to make what was in fact a confession of error. He had swamped the revenue by granting subventions to the contractors—foreigners all of them, even when there was a Mexican figurehead to the enterprise. General Gonzalez had met the difficulty, as we have seen, by sacrificing his own employees and paying the foreign capitalists. He may or may not have had personal reasons for maintaining the national honour at such a cost, but it is certain that he put the Mexican Government on the road which must infallibly lead to a renewal of revolts and anarchy. President Diaz boldly reversed his predecessor's course and did not shrink from making what was in fact a practical confession of his own errors. He restored the salaries of the civil servants, but with the abatements already mentioned, which were for the moment put as high as 25 per cent. The figure was lowered after a time to 10. The means to do this act of bare justice were found by suspending payment of the interest of a floating debt, and by withdrawing the subventions which he had promised to give when he was in office before. This was, of course, neither more nor less than a partial bankruptcy, but the drastic measure did not hurt President Diaz in the estimate of the capitalists. They must have known that the measure was necessary; they had profited much already, and they foresaw large advantages in the future if only the peace could be kept. So long as the President did provide Mexico with a working Government, capital and labour between them could do the rest by drawing vast quantities of marketable materials from the soil of Mexico.

Industry asked for defence from mere violence while it was engaged in obtaining and transporting the material, and that the President did give. We have seen how he had begun the work during his first term. He had not then been able to do more than make a good start, and there had been a fall from the standard he then reached during the Administration of General Gonzalez. Mexico was still a land of brigandage. We who have never quite succeeded in putting a stop to dacoity in India ought not to reproach the memory of the Mexican Government of that time if it took years to get the upper hand of the bandits. In a thinly-inhabited country full of hiding-places, with a very poor population who have no cause to fear the robber, and can even sympathise with him, brigandage is a very difficult pest to cure. It was particularly hard to suppress in Mexico because the most valuable part of the national produce was still bullion, the most desirable form of portable property to the highwayman. Until railways had been much developed, and President Diaz had had time to extend the action of the " rurales " to all parts of the Republic, the transport of the gold and silver from the mines to the ports was never quite safe. Indeed, it was not until the police had been brought up to the level of their task that the trains themselves were secure. They were occasionally stopped and robbed.

The bullion was carried to railway stations or ports in convoys or caravans known as " conductas." This word applied originally not to the " recuas " or strings of mules which carried the booty in earlier days, or the wagons which came to be used afterwards, but to the armed guard sent with them as a protection. Even an escort was not always enough in a country where the brigands operated in bands which might be numbered by the hundred and the roads ran through mountain passes or through bush. The mine owners adopted a device to improve their own chance of escaping loss and to puzzle the bandits. They took to sending the bullion in iron wagons which were heavy to drag along, but were for that very reason troublesome to carry off across country. They were elaborately barred and locked so as to be hard to open. The calculation was that the brigands would be unable either to carry them off or break into them before an armed force could be brought up to recover the spoils. When Mexicans were reproached with the little security their country afforded to the honest trader they were apt to reply that the care the Government took to provide escorts was the best proof of its desire to protect life and property. The desire was no doubt sincere, but the execution was defective till President Diaz's " rurales " were in full working order. But it is allowed that by the close of his second term the settled parts of Mexico had become safe. And this, it must be confessed, was the condition antecedent to every other kind of improvement.

It was also far easier than the task imposed by ancient fiscal error on the Government of Mexico. A valuable trade can be conducted without any measure of Government protection where the traders can go armed in bodies and defend themselves. The once-flourishing trade of the prairies in the Santa Fé trail owed nothing to the police either of the United States or of Mexico. There was none, and the traders who carried their goods in the prairie wagons defended them against wild Indians and robbers alike with their rifles. But a bad system of taxation produces a universal and pervasive evil, which can only be overcome, and that but partially, by another evil all but as bad as itself, which is smuggling. There was smuggling in Mexico, but mainly on the northern frontier, and its operations did not extend southward across the belt of desert which divides the north from the centre of the Republic. The rest of the country suffered from a system of taxation inherited from the old Spanish colonial Government. It was of a nature to be destructive to all industry. A reformation which should sweep it away and replace it by something more rational was quite as necessary as either public works or public security if Mexico was to reach the level of prosperity attainable by its poeple. But it was far more difficult to obtain. Any Mexican, official or unofficial, who had average commonsense and was an honest man, would see easily enough that without facilities for transport there could be little or no trade, and that without security for life and property there could be no industry, or but little. It was equally easy for him to see that roads and railways would provide the facilities, and that a good constabulary would establish the security. But when the matter to be considered was the reform of an old-established system of taxation, to which everybody was accustomed, and in the continuance of which many were interested, there was no chance of the same unanimity as in regard to such simple questions as roads and police, and the remedy was likely to be hard to find. There was no mere question of the suppression of a recognised evil. One system of levying a contribution from the pockets of the taxpayer was to be replaced by another, and somebody was sure to be afraid that the change would do him a damage. There were indeed three classes of great influence in Mexico who would certainly oppose any effective reform. The problem was so continually prominent during the whole Administration of President Diaz that any account of his government in which it was passed over would be most incomplete.

The substance of the whole question may be divided under two heads. There were taxes in Mexico which by their very nature were destructive of all industry, and therefore could be properly dealt with only by total abolition. There were taxes which, though reasonable in themselves, were so unfairly apportioned that they did about as much harm as the others, and failed to produce an adequate revenue.

The tax-exacting devices which were so bad that they could be amended only by abolitions were the "alcabalas," the "portazgos," and the internal customs barriers. All three had been imported from Spain, where they had produced their full effect by killing the nascent industry of the country, and they had continued their destructive course in Mexico. The first has always been quoted as the very perfection of a thoroughly bad tax. It was an excise levied on goods sold in the market or by public auction. In spite of its Arabic name it was of Roman origin. Of course it was not always equally heavy, nor levied with equal severity. Mexicans got off more lightly than the Spaniards of Old Spain. In the mother country the alcabala (or alcavala) went as high as 14 per cent. of the price of the goods at one time, and the country was sensibly relieved when it was reduced to 6. When in 1885, the first year of Don Porfirio's second Administration, Congress voted the general alcabala for all the Republic, it fixed the rate at " one half of 1 per cent. upon the value in excess of $20 of transactions of buying and selling of every kind of merchandise, whether in wholesale or retail, in whatever place throughout the whole Republic." The same impost was put on " all sales and resales of country or city property ; upon all exchanges of movable or immovable property ; on mortgages, transfers, or gifts, collateral or bequeathed inheritances ; on bonds, rents of farms, when the rent exceeds $20.00 annually, and on all contracts with the Federal State, or municipal Governments." One-half of 1 per cent. does not sound like a heavy impost. But this was only the Federal alcabala. The States and municipalities levied others to provide their local revenue. Sometimes they levied an *ad valorem* duty, sometimes they imposed a fixed charge on the article. Whatever the rule was the alcabala was a killing pest, because it required for its collection a swarm of officials and an endless fuss of inspection. Of course, it tended to have the effect which, as Adam Smith pointed out, was inseparable from such an impost. " Through the greater part of a country in which a tax of this kind is established nothing can be produced for distant sale. The produce of every part of the country must be proportioned to the consumption of the neighbourhood." It is obvious that this must have been the effect. The alcabala was levied on the ox when it was sold to the cattle-dealer. Then again when the dealer sold it to the butcher, on the hide when sold to the tanner, on the tanned hide when sold to shoemaker or saddler, and on the saddle when sold by the maker to a tradesman, or by a tradesman to the customer. At every step there was an inspection to be undergone, forms to be filled, stamps to be fixed. No circulation of goods was possible under such a perpetual downpour of officialdom and taxation.

It is not enough to say that such a system of taxation would ruin any industry. It could not be applied in a country in which active industry existed without producing universal rebellion. On the only occasion on which an attempt was made to apply the alcabala to an industrial community—when the Duke of Alva tried to impose it on the Spanish Netherlands—it did what political oppression and religious persecution had failed to do—it united all the Netherlanders, Protestant and Catholic, in one universal rebellion. The Duke, arbitrary and brutal as he was, and his King, Philip II., who was as stiff-necked as the general, were forced to withdraw. The " alcabala " could be levied in Spain because there was little, and in most parts of the country there was no, movement of trade. Each district used up its own raw material, and the goods passed direct from the handicraftsman to the purchaser. In such an unindustrial state of a population it is indeed difficult to see how the vast majority are to be made to contribute to the revenue except in some such way. A bad tax must be imposed because no other would have any effect. If we need a proof we can take the case of British India. Our salt tax is a bad one, but it is only by the use of an impost of this character that the huge majority of the inhabitants can be made to bear a part of the taxation. But the salt tax is a long way short of an alcabala. If, however, we can see how this Spanish adaptation of the Roman "Vectigal Rerum Venalium" came to be fixed on Spain and its colonies, we are also forced to see that when imposed it had an invincible tendency to petrify the population in its stagnancy.[1]

The "portazgo" was another inheritance from Rome. It was a charge imposed on all ships which entered a Mexican port, and was paid for a licence to trade. It was in proportion to the value of the goods brought, but it did not release them from the obligation to pay the alcabalas. The natural result was that it tended, not only to limit commerce, but to prevent the rise of a coasting trade. For instance, all goods brought into Lower California across the Gulf from Sonora or Sinaloa, or *vice versâ*, paid the portazgo as well as the alcabalas. If brought in by land from the north, they only paid the alcabalas. So it actually suited a Mexican trader better to bring in his goods

[1] The alcabala was more like the Roman "vectigal," because in the ancient world so large a part of the population lived as slaves or serfs on the vast estates. Slave handicraftsmen worked up raw material supplied by slave agriculturists and herdsmen. The community was self-sufficing. The same conditions prevailed on the great landholdings in Mexico and in some parts of Spain. And on that fact we may base an observation for which many other supports could be produced. It is that no other country has inherited so much directly from the Roman Empire, and has so carefully preserved what it inherited, as Spain.

from the United States across the border than to buy from his own countrymen. The portazgos were more limited in their incidence than the alcabalas, but within their scope they were quite as fatal.

The internal customs barriers are not so strange to us as the alcabalas. We, in fact, had one till Lord Randolph Churchill swept it away—the shilling a ton tax on coal imported into London. If few noticed it while it lasted, or now remember its obscure existence, most of us knew the French " octroi," and many of us have heard of the Spanish " consumos." They are municipal impost duties levied on whatever is to be eaten, drunk, worn, or burnt within the town.[1] But these municipal dues were not all. There were customs barriers between province and province. There were in France under the monarchy, and in Spain till recent times. They survived in Mexico, and in spite of all attempts at reform they go on because the local authorities must have a revenue, and also because a part of the money is taken for account of the central Government. A piece of goods imported across the

[1] As an instance of how the " consumo " works I give this experience of my own. Some years ago an English merchant in Madrid sold a huge steam threshing machine to a landowner in Granada. It had been exhibited at an agricultural show. In order to move it across Madrid from one railway station to another the merchant had to hire a team of oxen—twelve in all. Now oxen when introduced into Madrid for the meat market are subject to " consumos." This team was not to be slaughtered, for it was brought in from the country outside to drag the weight. But the story of the machine and the transport across Madrid might be a fraud. So the town council insisted on the deposit of the consumo as a guarantee of good faith. The sum of 1,000 pesetas, say £40, was paid on the understanding that it was to be refunded so soon as the draught cattle had gone out again. Here was a ceremony not tending to the facilitation of business. But this was not all. The town council liked to show the best possible revenue; so it was very punctual in insisting on the deposit of the money, which went duly down on the receipt side of the balance. But for the same reason it put off the repayment as long as it possibly could. The merchant had to " hacer antesala " (dance attendance in ante-rooms) for some time before his deposit was refunded; and was lucky if he had not to oil the wheels of the official machinery with palm oil.

frontier or at a seaport would be taxed over and over again before it could reach the customer. No wonder if an article priced at $30 on the frontier costs $100 when sold to the customer in an inland city. Sydney Smith's famous joke on the British taxation of his day was an under-statement of the Mexican fiscal system. There was hardly a transaction of daily life which had not its corresponding tax—not even a marriage, a christening, a dance, or a funeral. To make all safe the tariff of a Mexican town might, and at least in some cases did, contain such a clause as this : " All articles which are not contained in the present tariff remain subject to the pleasure of the authorities of the city of Guerrero to levy upon them a contribution which they think right and just."

We are by no means at the end yet. A licence was required for the practise of any trade. In a country in which the journeyman workman rarely earned more than 20 or 25 cents for his day's work he had to pay a monthly poll tax of 12 cents. This was the old Spanish " pecho," or breast tax, levied on all who were not " noble." It was just the " karrach," or tribute levied by the Arabs on all Christians. The only difference was that whereas they took it from the unbeliever the Christian States took it from the tradesmen and the poor and exempted the gentry.

And with that detail we come to what was not the least destructive, and still less the least unjust, feature of the Mexican fiscal system. It has been noted already that the landowning class in Mexico claimed to reproduce the " brazo militar " of the mother country—that is to say, the nobles who were exempt from personal taxes, and to an extent variously fixed by custom or royal privileges from the "alcabalas." The Church was of course equally favoured. Now it is calculated that the whole of the land of Mexico was held by about 6,000 persons. This figure does not include the Indian communities, which in out-of-the-way places went on living their old communal life, tilling their bits of ground and dividing the produce according to rules older than the Spanish conquest. But it did cover by far the greater part of the country. These masters of the land were able to defeat the humane Laws of the Indies to a great extent. They would combine to protect their own profits if for no other purpose. The King's laws, as a favourite phrase of theirs had it, were to be "obedecidas y no cumplidas"—obeyed, but not carried out. They went on the statute-book, and they went no farther. The same power which enabled them to render the laws meant to protect the Indians of little effect was used to save themselves from taxation. The secularisation of the Church lands made no difference. The plundered property passed into the hands of intriguers, who got it for nothing, or purchasers who paid derisive sums, and they continued to escape taxation. There were land taxes, but they were low and were dishonestly assessed. Land not in actual cultivation—of which there was much in the vast Mexican estates—escaped taxation altogether, even though it was appreciating in value. There are no countries in the world in which a smart undeveloped land tax is more urgently called for than in the former colonies of Spain and Portugal in America.

More might be said without exhausting the subject, but we have already seen enough to enable us to understand why the mere construction of railways or the improvements of ports might fail altogether to better the condition of the mass of the population of Mexico. They enabled mine owners to gain easier access to the metal and carry it to the ships for export. They enabled the merchant who imported such goods as the richer classes could afford to buy to bring their imports more rapidly, and also more cheaply, to the small market open to them. But while alcabalas continued to be levied on the scale defined by Congress in 1885, and customs barriers stood round every State and every town, the mass of the population would be never a jot the better save for such day's wage as they could earn in the capacity of mere labourers. This was a temporary gain. For the rest the very large majority of Indians and the mestizos would go on as before—dressing in goat-skins warranted to last for years, the roughest of cotton shirts, blankets woven by their women folk, and wearing sandals made of a sole of leather and tied on by thongs which they fixed themselves. The revenue grew by and for the capitalist. The people could not buy nor sell without bringing a flight of tax-collecting vampires down on them. Their small balance of money went mainly in the pulque shop. No wonder if Mexico possessed in the "Léperos" one of the very worst vagabond populations in all the world.[1] A wailing song went about in Mexico at the very end of Don Porfirio's rule. "The negro of Cuba," so it said, "is free and lives by his day's pay. Only the Mexican Indian eats little and lives ill. He lives in a poor hutch.

---

[1] The similarity of the word Lépero (to leper) must not deceive the reader. A leper in Spanish is "leproso," or popularly "gafo." "Lépero" is a word of uncertain origin, and is supposed to be an adaptation of an Indian word. Lepers there are in Mexico, but they are usually known as "pintados" (painted or blotched).

R. W. H. Hardy, R.N., a gentleman who had taken part in the conquest of Java and in the expedition to New Orleans, and who in the times of peace and no employment was prospecting for pearls in the Gulf of California. And this is his judgment on them : " The Yaqui nation is spread over every part of the province. They are miners, gold-diggers, pearl-divers, agriculturists, and artisans ; and in the arts of peace, by far the most industrious and useful of all the other tribes in Sonora." Other witnesses bear out Lieutenant Hardy. They note that the Yaquis succeeded in cattle-breeding, and that they came in numbers to plant and take in the harvest in parts of Sonora occupied by white settlers. When they had earned their money they went back to the valley which, by right of occupation dating back for centuries and by the written records of Spanish colonial authorities and Mexican Republicans, was theirs. We need not picture the Yaquis as mild children of poetry and nature. They could fight hard for their rights and, like other fighters, could strike from passion. If some were stout-hearted, some, in the fallen state of human nature, would probably be quarrelsome and arrogant. But men do not hold their rights because they are of unspotted virtue, but because they have a title recognised by the law. Now by all the laws of God and of Mexican men the Yaqui Valley belonged to the Yaquis. " Qui terre a guerre a," says the French proverb. There were disputes between them and their kinsmen the Moyos over boundaries, and in a country where the law was so feeble as it has long been in Mexico these disputes led to broken heads. They have produced the same consequences in more civilised lands. The Indians

Señor Limantour was by birth a Frenchman, and had not been naturalised till he was twenty. It is true that Constitutions are subject to revision in Spanish America, and that Congresses will commonly revise or do whatever other thing they are bid to do.[1] But in 1904 the anti-foreign feeling was rising, and the selection of a financier of alien origin might have been dangerous.

The understudy chosen was Don Ramon Corral. Don Ramon has been made the theme of an immense amount of abuse in the best style of Spanish-American polemic or of renaissance literary blackguardism. All that may be left standing on its own basis. It is enough to say that he was connected with land company speculations in Sonora, was associated with American capitalists, and was not in good health. As an " Americanised Mexican " he was peculiarly repugnant to the patriotic sentiment of the north of Mexico and not a *persona grata* in the south. If the choice was due to the influence of " foreign plutocrats " and of " Wall Street " it afforded a wondrous example of the extent to which business men can be besotted by their reliance on the " power of money."

There was a peculiar reason why the creation and nomination of a Vice-President should be carried out with great tact in the choice of the person. The measure was a most intelligible warning that steps were being taken to perpetuate the " system of Diaz." The view taken of it is quite lucidly explained by Don

---

[1] It was only the other day that a President of the Argentine Republic, finding his Congress inclined to be sulky and to go on strike, arrested a quorum, marched them to the House in charge of the police, and stood over them till they did as they were told. The same sort of thing might happen in any part of Spanish or Portuguese America, except in Chile, where the power is in the hands of a species of oligarchy of landowners.

PRESIDENT FOR GOOD

They pay him with aguardiente, to make an end of his race. All the world knows it, my heart; all the world knows it." It is "a doleful song"—"steaming up a lamentation and an ancient tale of wrong."[1]

There was a clear understanding in Mexico of the evil consequences of the fiscal system. A conference on the subject had been held in the capital during the Administration of General Gonzalez. The delegates were competent judges, and, as the Spaniards would say, "they talked pearls." One and all agreed that while the alcabalas and the internal customs barriers remained in existence the country was doomed to beggary. But they were equally unanimous in declining to propose a remedy. They said, and with truth, that, whatever the vices of these barbarous old methods of taxation might be, they provided the only means by which the States and municipalities could raise a revenue, and they were the sources of a good part of the receipts of the Federal Government. This was the vicious circle in which the Government was confined. The taxes kept the country stagnant and poor, but abolition would render all administration impossible. It would for one thing entail the disbanding of the army, and that, of course, meant anarchy. There were, no doubt, men in Mexico who

[1] I add the Spanish. Even a reader who does not know the language, but will give the vowels the broad sound, will be able to catch the "doleful" lilt of the lines :—

> "El negro de Cuba es libre
> Y vive de sa jornal.
> Solo el Indio Mexicano
> Come poco y vive mal
> Vive en un pobre jacal.
> Le pagan con aguardiente,
> Pa que la raza se acabe,
> Lo sabe toda la gente mi vida,
> Toda la gente lo sabe."

were quite well aware that the remedy was to impose a just land tax and house tax and income tax ; to take the alcabala off everything else and quadruple it on pulque ; to lower the outrageous import duties imposed on manufactured goods for the benefit of a handful of mills which produced bad cotton shirts to be sold at a high price. But to do all this implied a land valuation, a huge amount of work, and the command of time. It implied something more—namely, that reform would deeply offend the caciques who controlled the Governments of the States and the municipalities, as well as the swarms of officials who lived on tax-collecting—and bribes for not collecting—together with the owners of houses and land who had hitherto contrived to escape taxation nearly if not altogether. This last class might be politically useless—and indeed had proved that it was—but under the Republic, as under the old Spanish monarchy, it could act to defend its pocket. It could, as it often had done, pay for a pronunciamiento. That this was no imaginary peril is proved by one single fact. When, after many years, there came a revolt against the " autocracy of General Diaz," the immediate cause of the rising was that a certain family in Northern Mexico, whose members owned among them 20,000,000 acres of land, spent £250,000 in financing the outbreak. In the end they brought murder on some of themselves, but in the interval they had plunged Mexico back into anarchy.

This was, if a threadbare image may be used again just for once, the Augean stable which President Diaz had to clean if Mexico was to attain to its possible level of prosperity. The attempt was made and persevered in, but, it is to be feared, with something far short of complete success. Accurate information of what was really done is hard to obtain. Nothing, indeed, is easier than to find from "The Authentic History" of Señor Ricardo Rodrigues, or the life of the President by Señor José F. Godoy, that the abolition of the alcabalas was the constant care of the Government, and that steady progress was made in the good work. But it is to be remembered that neither of these books makes as much as a pretence to being critical or complete. The first is a collection of the President's speeches to Congress published when he was standing for his prolonged period in 1904. The second is an electioneering pamphlet published in New York in 1910, when he was standing for the last time, and was addressed rather to the American than to the Mexican public. The Federal Government might renounce the alcabala so soon as the growth of the national customs allowed, but that the different States dispensed with the old familiar method of obtaining money is not proved. The fact, no doubt, is that they continued to be levied within the different States, or at any rate some of them, and to produce all their old bad effects. The inter-State customs barriers were certainly not wholly swept away, and if they have not reappeared during the recent troubles the conduct of the adventurers and caciques who have been tearing the poor country to shreds has been contrary to nature.

Finance would in any case be likely to be the weak side of a Spanish or Spanish-American Government. Nothing in the training of Don Porfirio was calculated to turn his thoughts in that direction. He confessedly managed the funds he raised in the South during the French intervention with probity and success; but that was a simple business. The merchant shipper of the old times carried a bag with him to sea. He put into it what he received for freights and took out of it what he had to spend for the expenses of the voyage. What remained was the profit. A partisan leader could do as much, but to understand the principles of good taxation was another and a more complicated matter. The Spanish mind does not turn readily to the study of finance. It was possible for the President to find a good Home Secretary in Señor Rubio, his father-in-law, and a good Minister for Foreign Affairs in Señor Mariscal. But it does not appear that he had a good financial adviser at his elbow till he found one in Señor Limantour, the son of a French man of business, born in Mexico, but not naturalised till he was twenty years old. In spite of all obstructions, the mere maintenance of peace, even with an accompaniment of local disorders in the States—which, let it be noted once more lest we forget, never ceased entirely—the making of railways and so forth, the development of mines, and some improvement in agriculture, produced greater well-being in some classes and a growing revenue. The world thought that Mexico was on the way to an industrial development which would bring prosperity and orderly habits with them; and continued to believe so till the crash came.[1]

[1] I am conscious that much is lacking here for a full account of Mexico's financial and industrial position, but can only say that the real truth is not to be obtained. Travellers who have been in Mexico since 1911 have found signs of prosperity, and have been told that times of trouble are not so bad, because in peace so much was taken away to be spent out of the country which now remains at home. Does this mean anything except that Mexico, being a debtor nation, had to export in peace to pay its debts, whereas in time of trouble it repudiates and keeps the things for which it went into debt? That gives an air of prosperity for a time.

Yet while we recognise, as we must, that much in the work done by President Diaz was transient and superficial, it would be most unfair to deny that, even so, his achievement was honourable. In no other Spanish-American State has a ruler been able to increase the revenue by the growth of industry and to secure a succession of real surpluses. In 1896, and for the first time in its history, Mexico could show a revenue of $50,000,000 and an expenditure of $45,000,000. The surplus made it possible for the President to relieve his officials from the heavy deductions made from their salaries. The revenue continued to increase till it reached $101,385,000 in the financial year 1908—1909. In the year 1906—1907 the surplus had been $29,209,481. During this period his treasury had had to contend with difficulties which affected all Governments but were peculiarly severe for Mexico. The depreciation in the value of silver hit a country which still retained the white metal as its standard, and allowed free coinage, very hard. Its currency was discredited, and the chief of Mexican exports fell in value. Silver had been freely coined in the eleven private mints which farmed the privilege of coining money from the State. The coins were an article of export brought by other nations for use in the Chinese trade. This flood of money which was depreciating rapidly threatened to make the exchange ruinous for Mexico. The Republic was steered through the crisis partly by stopping the mints, and partly by the adoption of the gold standard in 1902. It does not in the least detract from the credit due to President Diaz that the actual manager of these financial operations was the Franco-Mexican Señor José Limantour. An admiral or general who sees the wisdom of some suggestion made by a subordinate and acts on it is entitled to all the credit of whatever measure of success it may achieve. It is to his credit that he sees the wisdom of the advice, and it is by his authority that the right thing is done. To him belongs the honour of turning what was but an idea and mere words into a profitable act. The chief in war or peace who will not take advantage of the capacity of his subordinates, lest he should be supposed to be influenced by them, makes an exhibition of gander vanity; and moreover he is not doing his best to fulfil his duty. Now it has always been a great fault of the Spanish character that it has lacked the capacity to see and give free play to the capacity of subordinates. The " mandon " will do everything himself, and will do nothing that may appear to come from another lest his dignity should suffer. The type of this too prevalent Spanish littleness is the immortal Don Gregorio de la Cuesta, who hampered Wellington during the Talavera campaign. He refused to move his army at the English General's suggestion for fear that his soldiers should be led to doubt his wisdom when they saw him act by advice. In a very brief space he was ignominiously bundled out of the position he had refused to leave when he might have moved freely. There was nothing of Don Gregorio in President Diaz. He never gave a better proof of his fitness to rule than when he detected and utilised the financial capacity of Señor Limantour.

Critics who were enlightened by the course of events after 1910 have blamed Don Porfirio on the ground that the surpluses shown by the revenue in the last years of his Administration were largely gained by making dangerous reductions in the army. But it is more than doubtful whether the evils which followed the revolt financed by Madero in 1910 could have been averted by the maintenance of a larger army. What if the army did as it had often done before in Mexican history—what if it divided against itself ? The smaller army did so divide, and a larger would probably have behaved in just the same way. A tendency to disorder and a lack of national sentiment are bred in the bone of all Mexico, of which the army is but a part, and will out in the flesh. This supposition that a stronger army would have kept the peace for ever is but a mere guess.

It is, on the other hand, a fact that such measures as the purchase by the State of railways and the drainage of the Mexico valley represented in different degrees lasting gains. By every purchase of a railway the country did to some extent free itself from tribute to the foreign capitalist. It was far too poor to free itself entirely. These transactions appeared to give promise that the days when Mexico was looked upon as a species of booty, and when it granted concessions wholesale in order to attract foreign capital, and in many cases to speculators of very indifferent character, might be passing away. The purchase of the Veracruz-Pacific line in 1904 was a case in point. This line, which must not be confused with the Veracruz-Mexico, was built by an American company. The builders got into difficulties and suspended payments in 1903. As the line started from Córdoba, on the Veracruz-Mexico route, and ran south to the railway across the isthmus of Tehuantepec, it was of importance to the Government for the purpose of maintaining communications with and its hold over Oaxaca. And then it provided a connection between the Gulf and the Pacific. A certain element of politics or of self-defence supplied a motive for the measures which the Mexican Government took to acquire control of the Central and the National lines. Both were built by American capital, and they connected Central Mexico with the United States. The first crosses the frontier at El Paso del Norte on the Rio Grande and reaches the capital by the great plain. The National enters the Republic at Laredo in Texas and runs to the capital. It was completed as a narrow-gauge line in 1888 and widened by 1903. In this case the Government of President Diaz acquired a commanding interest and the control of the lines in order to protect itself against possible dictation on the part of American capitalists. Of course the chance that such measures as these would prove of lasting benefit to the country depended on how far it could continue to possess an honest and businesslike Government.

The drainage of the valley was a gain pure and simple if only because it resulted in an immense saving of life. The actual work could be adequately described only by an engineer, or by one not ignorant of the engineer's art. Yet without that skill we can all of us look at a mechanical achievement of this order from the point of those for whom it is done. The valley of Mexico is a great bowl of which the rim is formed by mountains. The water drains from the mountains into the valley and has no natural exit. When the Spaniards entered "The Valley," as they called it, *par excellence*, the soil was still largely covered by forests which held the water and delayed evaporation. The Aztec "pueblo" Tenochtitlan, on the site of which the city of Mexico now stands, was surrounded by what the Spaniards called a lake, but what appears to have been in reality a very watery swamp, which after a rainy season and the melting of snows was entirely covered, and became navigable by vessels of shallow draught. Within a few generations of the conquest the Spanish hatred of trees which has desolated large parts of their own country had begun to produce its effects in " The Valley." The forests began to go, the balance of water, and of wood to absorb and hold the water, was upset. Being no longer confined as it had been, the drainage from the hills flowed more rapidly where the slopes gave it free way. The position of the lasting deposits of the waters which drained from the hills shifted. The alternations between the lowest and the highest levels of the lakes became more violent. The city came to stand not in, but on the side of, its lake, which was the lowest of the three in the valley. So it was increasingly menaced at the times of high floods. Apart from this chronic peril, the city, because of its position, was subjected to another and perhaps a worse evil.

It stood almost on the level of the lake into which it was drained. The sewers had a very slight fall. Therefore the refuse was not carried well clear. What was borne away went to fill up the lake and create a further obstruction for the drains. At last the city stood on a vast network of cesspools. Only the extreme dryness of the climate, due to the height of the valley above the sea, preserved the population from being wholly destroyed by disease. It escaped this fate because refuse when exposed to the air dries hard. Even so the death-rate rose to sixty in the thousand, or more than twice the figure of Bombay. The Spaniards are not a provident people. If they had been more in the habit of looking ahead carefully, Hernan Cortes, who was one of the wisest of them, would not have allowed himself to be tempted to found his city on the site of the Aztec " pueblo." He would have chosen a higher position, of which he could have found many and good in " The Valley." Pride and a wish to plant his foot on the very neck of the conquered pagan misled him. By his decision the city which was for long the greatest in the New World was doomed to perpetual danger and disease. In the first times of the seventeenth century the necessity for taking precautions had become so pressing that the task was taken in hand. But it was not taken in the right way. Dams were built round the city to keep out the floods, and of course they blocked the exit of the drainage. A great attempt to provide an outlet for the overflow of " The Valley " waters—a true " obra de los Romanos "—was promoted by the viceroys. It was the huge cutting of Nochistongo. The cutting is used by the Central Railway, but it never served the purpose it was meant for. The viceroy's Dutch engineer Maartens, who transliterated his name to Martinez, misjudged his problem. The work was done in the too common Spanish way—by spasms of feverish activity under the stimulus of recent disaster, alternating with long intervals of neglect. Multitudes of Indians perished by forced labour and bad management, and " The Valley " was not drained. The Republic and Maximilian's Government found the problem still to be solved. Plans were made, foreign engineers were called in, but resources were lacking. They were not available till after President Diaz had been firmly seated in 1884 ; and then twenty years passed before the outlet which now drains " The Valley " to the north and into the bed of the Tula river, which reaches the sea at Tampico, was completed. The work was at first entrusted to a British firm, and when the enormous cost of keeping their works clear of water as they went on compelled them to withdraw, it was completed as a State undertaking at an expense of $9,000,000. A canal 35 kilometres long running from the north of the city carries the water to a tunnel of ten kilometres which opens on the valley of Tequixquiac. It was a great date in the modern history of Mexico when President Diaz in 1903 broke through the last screen of rock with a pick and could say that after more than 180 years of labour, error, and delay the work was done. Even then a price had to be paid for the original mistake of the Conquistador. When during the Administration of President Lerdo or of President Juarez an American firm of engineers was consulted, they doubted whether the drainage could be carried out at all, and they added that if it ever were the withdrawal of so much water from the soil would probably bring the city of Mexico down in ruins through the shrinking of the ground and the settling of the foundations. Their fears and doubts were excessive; but the soil has shrunk and the foundations have settled, so that much of the city is out of the perpendicular.

Finance is confessedly of vital importance for all nations at all times, but in telling the life of statesmen and rulers of the nineteenth century it is not often necessary to dwell on their patronage of public works. In the great settled States of the modern world it is no more necessary to insist on their merits in that way than on their achievements in the slaughter of savage monsters. Yet there was a time when the leader of men had need to be a mighty hunter before the Lord, because superiority had to be established over the wild beasts which contended with the human animal for the dominion of the earth. A ruler of Mexico was first bound to see that his country was provided with the instruments of industry, which in a settled, prosperous State are the products of the normal activity of the community. When Carlyle was writing his admirable essay on the Despot of Paraguay, Francia, he rebuked one of his authorities who had laughed at the South American " Perpetual Dictator " for publicly using a theodolite in the streets of Asuncion. " O Robertson," he asks, " if there was no other man who *could* observe with a theodolite ? " President Diaz was better helped than Rodriguez Francia, but in the main his position in an anarchical Spanish-American community was the same. He had to stand over everything and see the work done. His enemies have asserted that his merits in the matter were small, for the needful roads, railways, harbours, and drainage would have been without him. How do they know ? The palpable fact is that through him they were done—and the rest is guesswork.

CHAPTER X

THE INDIAN PROBLEM

To have brought the finances into good order, and to have provided the Republic with the means of attaining to the level of prosperity at which a recurrence of the old disorders would be intolerable, was much. But it was far from being enough to secure the future of Mexico. What remained to be done was to inspire the whole population with an understanding of the value of order, and a desire for prosperity. A strong ruler who could rely on the army could do the first. But no strength of personal character, and no military force, could do the second by themselves. They required the co-operation of the people who were to be governed. And in Mexico that co-operation was lacking, not altogether, but very largely. Señor Limantour is reported to have said that the great obstacle in the way of the development of the prosperity of Mexico has been that a bare 20 per cent. of the Mexicans care for those material advantages which are desired by more developed or more ambitious races. And this is what is meant here by the Indian Problem. The name does not imply, and is not meant to imply, that 80 per cent. of the population of Mexico is of pure Indian blood. Whatever the proportion may be (and the facts are very ill known), it is not so high as that. But a large number of the mestizos are far more Indian than white, not only in blood, but in ways of thinking and of life. They are part of the Indian problem, and that is just this : " How are you to persuade men, who do not value what civilised Europeans or citizens of the United States consider as indispensable things, to work in order to gain them as the European will, and to desire what he desires ? " If they cannot be persuaded, how are they to be forced ? For if Mexico is to become orderly and industrial they must needs be brought to give their aid. They are the rank and file of the whole industrial army, and without their co-operation nothing permanent, nothing which will raise the whole body of the population, can be done. It is hard for us to realise that there are peoples who would not value the things we value if only they had the chance of knowing them, and yet it is true. We must not suppose that because an Indian here and there might rise as Juarez did, or as a few had done in the Church under colonial rule, the whole of them had any desire to change their way of living. The contrary was the case. Neither are we to suppose that because they were unhappy and believed themselves to be oppressed (as they did) they wished to enjoy the kind of existence acceptable to prosperous white men. Their grievance was that they were not allowed to live in their own ways. Of these there were two—the way of the wild Indian, who was a hunter and a raider ; the way of the tame Indian, who would, if he could, have lived a communal life in his traditional style. Until this great and torpid obstruction to a healthy national life is removed, Mexico will not only not be entitled to take a place among civilised States, but it will not even be the home of a real nation.

If President Diaz made no attempt to conquer this hostile condition to his country's true welfare he must stand condemned as a statesman. A mere interval of

THE INDIAN PROBLEM 267

internal peace maintained by a vigorous police is a good for so long as it lasts. But it may go and leave nothing behind it. A statesman is a ruler who does leave something done for ever, and something not merely material, not only roads or bricks and mortar. If all Diaz was able to achieve were measures of violence which intensified old evils and perpetuated old and cruel injustices, then he stands ill as a statesman and as a man. Now it is a fact which his biographer is bound to face that Diaz has been accused both of failing to try to improve the lot, and with it the character, of this vast Indian population of Mexico, and of acts which intensified injustice and cruelty. The floods of praise, often fulsome in tone, poured out by his admirers, official and voluntary, have had a counterpart of invective. The tone of these hostile judges does not indeed inspire full confidence. They are too much addicted to mere shrieks of invective, and they show absolute credulity in accepting every tale of cruelty or corruption they may have heard. Their rule of criticism is too often no more than this, that whatever is said to the credit of Don Porfirio is a proof of the sycophancy or the self-seeking of the witness. Whatever is said in the way of abuse is to be accepted with confidence because it is hostile. Yet there are certain facts which are not to be denied. The plantations of Yucatan cannot be hidden, nor can the fate of the Yaquis. If they are what we are told, and if President Diaz was responsible for perpetuating the first and for bringing about the second, a very great deduction must be made from the measure of praise which ardent admirers have considered his due. Such things could not stand alone. Exceptions of that kind are not heard of in countries where a Government hates iniquity. They stand out because they are extreme examples of a prevailing condition.

A few sentences must be enough to deal with the case of the true wild Indians. They did not constitute a serious difficulty except on the northern frontier, where they were represented by the Apache race in all its many subdivisions. Good kind-hearted people are apt to be shocked when they hear it said that there is nothing to be done with such human beings as these cruel red men were but to suppress them. And yet it is the unhappy truth. They were our fellow-men, and they were what they were because they had been produced by very ancient conditions. But these same ancient conditions had so fixed them that they had lost the power to change. In the great human family they represented those individuals who are to be found everywhere who are born callous and greedy and incapable of recognising their obligations to others. Every society has to suppress them, if not by the swift process of capital punishment, then by segregating them and leaving them to die slowly within four walls. It was not the case with these untamable Apaches that they could not but be what they were. In the country over which they roamed to plunder and murder there were kindred red men who built "pueblos," tilled the soil, and used arms only to defend themselves against the Apaches. For generations the province of Sonora was protected against them by the valour of the Opatas, who were "'pueblo" Indians. The people of the pueblos learnt something from the white men, even if it were only to breed cattle. They listened to the priest, and if all they learnt from him was superstition the fault was not wholly theirs. The Apache took nothing but what must needs be

THE INDIAN PROBLEM 269

used for evil. All the subdivisions of the race were not equally malignant, but as a rule the Apache took only what would increase his powers to kill. If he learnt to use the horse, that was because he employed it to raid farther and faster. If he acquired any manufactured article, it was one that would serve for war. When, therefore, at the beginning of his second Administration President Diaz did enter into cooperation with the United States troops to suppress the Apaches by downright killing, or by confining them to reservations where they withered in pauperism and hopeless competition with the industrial superiority of the white man, he was only discharging the elementary duty of a ruler.

The case of the Apaches along the northern frontier was a very simple one. But there were other wild Indians whose case was nowise simple. The long anarchy which began in 1810 had completed the destruction of those ecclesiastical missions—Jesuit and Franciscan—which had honestly, for some generations, done their best for the Indians. The best they could think of was to keep them in a state of perpetual childhood because they were not *gente de razon*, not rational creatures, and because " of such is the Kingdom of Heaven." Even before the suppression of the Jesuits the missions had, in the judgment of their critics, somewhat declined from their first standard. By the constant inculcation of childishness they had themselves become childish. After the suppression the missions declined still further under the rule of the Franciscans. The revolution ruined them, and in the frightful confusion which ensued their flocks reverted to savagery of a vagabond order. How to bring them back to a settled life was the great question which pressed on the honour and the conscience of the rulers of Mexico. They were scattered about in many parts of the Republic, but mainly in the northern regions. The painful facts are that for long nothing was done, and that very little has been done to this day. The remedy which suggests itself as the best available would have been to collect them, or entice them to collect, in conditions which as nearly as might be would represent the kind of orderly life they understood—that of the " pueblo " Indians. But if that was to be done those " pueblo " Indians who still survived in a fair state of order and prosperity must be justly treated. The treatment they received is but too fairly represented by the story of the Yaquis. As it is typical, and as it touches the reputation of President Diaz very closely, the tale must be told at some length. Writers who made it their business to praise everything the President did without stint have spoken of these Indians as bloodthirsty savages. Let us look at the facts.

This Indian people came first in contact with the Spaniards in 1533. Cortes was still in the country and was sinking a large part of his great fortune in voyages of exploration to the north-west in search of the passage which, as he believed, must exist between the Atlantic and the North Pacific. Some of his rivals were engaged in the same work. One of them, Nuño de Guzman, pushed up by land through Sonora in search partly of the passage, partly of gold mines. The first Eldorado of the Spaniards was in " Quivira," a fantastic kingdom placed by imagination in the modern Arizona or in New Mexico.[1] In the course of

---

[1] The Quivira which did come into existence was a later Spanish settlement in New Mexico.

his advance he crossed two rivers which run from the Sierra Madre to the Gulf of California—the Moyo and, north of it, the Yaqui. Two peoples known to the Spaniards by the names of these rivers occupied their valleys. They were settled people who lived in pueblos and raised crops, and they were kindred. The Yaquis were the most numerous of the two. They offered a stout opposition, and, though defeated by the better arms of the invaders, they inspired the Spaniards with a certain measure of respect. The two came to terms. The Spaniards acknowledged the Yaquis as the owners of the valley. The Yaquis accepted a priest and a mission. Throughout the whole colonial period they lived on tolerable terms with the Spanish rule, though not without an occasional brush. The cause of conflict was always the same. The Yaquis resented the intrusion of white prospectors for mines and other intruders into their land. When provoked by these aggressions, they fought, and on the whole with success. They ended by falling out with the missions, but only when the missionaries became too grasping. When the colony became independent they took all they heard about the rights of man and equality and so forth as being really meant. They soon discovered that the Mexican Republicans did not consider that those fine principles applied to " pueblo " Indians, and they found that they were assailed by new aggressions on their valley. So they defended themselves, as before, under a leader known as " Bandera " because he carried about a banner with a picture of the Virgin on it, which he had taken from a church and which, he said, had belonged to Montezuma. At this time (1825—1828) the Yaquis were seen by our countryman, Lieutenant

THE INDIAN PROBLEM

resented the intrusion of white trespassers, and if they had not they would have been robbed. But though human and therefore liable to passion, they were an industrious people and helpful to their white neighbours. We can well believe that the task of dealing at once firmly and fairly with such a population was not without its difficulties. An experience of three centuries had rendered the Yaquis suspicious and touchy. They were on the outlook for aggressions, and prepared to repel them by the only means of defence which had been effective in the past. But an honest and humane Government would not have failed to understand that the one condition on which the Yaquis could be kept in peace was absolute justice of treatment, and that was impossible unless their claim to the sole possession of their land was recognised. It is only too certain that this condition was lacking. When Mexico settled down to comparative peace during the first Administration of President Diaz and his successor, General Gonzalez, a great revival of agricultural, mining, and other industry began in Sonora. The State had been half-depopulated during the early days of the gold-mining development in Upper California. The white inhabitants had swarmed over the border to share in the wealth to be drawn from the mines. The Indians were left alone. After 1880 the tide of immigration set in again. Sonora was known to possess great natural resources. The French enterprises of Pindray, Raousset—Boulbon, and Jecker had aroused interest in the country. Mexico was naturally enough desirous to possess a California of her own, and very soon the Yaquis saw that they were again menaced in the enjoyment of their lands.

The full truth as to what happened during the last twenty years of the nineteenth century is hard to learn. Impartial observers were not likely to be present. There is much unsupported assertion and much heated rhetoric on both sides. But the main fact is not to be denied. The Mexican Government took a course which had for its inevitable end the destruction of the Yaqui people. It and its admiring advocates have asserted that these Indians were a horde of savages. Against this is to be set the testimony of American railway-makers and foreigners of several nationalities interested in Sonoran mines and land which agrees entirely with the words of Lieutenant Hardy quoted above. The fact appears to be that the Mexican Government had no idea how to develop the resources of Sonora otherwise than by making huge concessions of land to " concessionnaires " who were often its own political supporters. These men intruded, prospected, marked out claims, and so forth, without the least regard for the rights of the occupiers of the soil. The Yaquis took up arms, and then followed a war which lasted from 1886 to the first years of this century. It cost the Mexican Government a sum estimated at $51,000,000, and it entailed the destruction of the most industrious part of the Indian population of the whole Republic. For a time the Yaquis made head, but when the Mexican troops were re-armed with the Mauser rifle they were overpowered. A remnant held out in the Bacetate Mountains, in the background of that valley. The great majority were reduced to slavery. They were not even enslaved in Sonora. They were transported in gangs under escorts of soldiers and rurales to the sisal hemp plantations of Yucatan or the tobacco plantations of the Valle Nacional and there sold, under certain hypocritical disguises, as slaves.

The traffic reached its highest level after 1904, and was as open as ever was the trade of the African Slave Coast at its worst. The captives were shipped at Guaymas, the chief port of Sonora in the Gulf of California. Thence they were taken by steamer to San Blas, on the Pacific Coast in the State of Jalisco. From San Blas they marched over rugged ground escorted by soldiers and rurales in what was known as a " coffle " (*i.e.*, *cafila* = caravan) in the days of the African slave trade, to San Marcos the farthest point then reached by the Pacific branch of the Mexican Central Railway. The train carried them—men, women, and children—to Veracruz, where they were shipped for Progreso in Yucatan. The co-operation of the police and the troops disposes of all pretence that this vicious traffic was a matter of private fraud carried on without the knowledge of the State. The Government of Mexico was as much concerned in the trade as ever was a negro " king " in the kidnapping of the miserable creatures who were brought down from the interior to the slave ships lying to receive them in the Bonny river. When delivered in Yucatan $60 a head was paid for them by the sisal planters. They were not called slaves. Slavery is abolished by the Constitution of the Mexican Republic. The theory was that they were " peones," field hands, who, like others of their class in Mexico, were working off debts due to the planters. The debt was the $60 paid to the Government for the command of their enforced services.[1]

[1] The world was shocked when the story of the Yaquis was told by Mr. John Kenneth Turner, of California, in his " Barbarous Mexico." He was

This is surely a most deplorable story of a failure to govern humanely and in the interest of the whole country. There is worse to be said of it, but for the moment, and until we are done with other stories akin to that of the Yaquis, it is enough to note the administrative ineptitude of the thing. In Mexico, which is burdened by a great population Indian, or nearly pure Indian, in blood, thriftless, degraded, half savage, or, what is worse, formed of once tamed Indians who have reverted to savagery, no wise Government would have tolerated the destruction of a community of men and women who worked freely and well, and who lived an orderly life, raising crops of maize and sugar-cane within its own borders, and eking out its poverty by labour on railways and by taking in harvests. It would have borne with the natural suspiciousness of the Yaquis, and while it suppressed the excesses of individuals among them it would have abstained from ruining the whole community. To enrich a handful of political hangers-on and speculators it took the very opposite course. And that is not all. The sins of the Yaquis, real and alleged, were made the excuse for a similar persecution of other " pueblo " Indians—Opatas, Punas, and so forth. The number of " bond servants " dragged

accused of hysteria and of being animated by a personal grievance. Mr. Turner does indeed write as if the zeal of the Lord's house had eaten him up. It is not credible that Yucatan planters should have shown not only utter indifference to, but absolute glee over, the high percentage—a third or so—and the very early date of the deaths among their purchases. Men of business who had paid $60 for the labour of a Yaqui "bond servant" cannot surely have rejoiced over his or her death before the price paid had been worked off. Yet I accept Mr. Turner's account of the trade as substantially true—in the first place because it is borne out by other testimony, and in the second place because it is perfectly consistent with the recent Brazilian rubber forest scandal, and with what I know, from the testimony of credible witnesses given to me in the countries themselves, to be the case in other Spanish-American countries.

THE INDIAN PROBLEM

from Sonora to Yucatan and some other places far exceeded the Yaqui population even if it had lost none of its members in battle and a remnant had not saved itself in the hills. If the fate of this hopeful race stood alone it would be a shameful blot on the government of Mexico. But it was not. It was only the most odious example of similar offences against humanity and true statesmanship which were committed all over Mexico.

The henequen or sisal hemp plantations of Yucatan were not supplied with forced labour from Sonora only. They were helped to provide themselves with bond servants from among the native Indian population, the Mayas. In this case there was some shadow of an excuse for the brutality shown to the victims. The Mayas, to judge by the buildings they have raised during centuries, and long before the Spaniards appeared on the coast, were endowed with a better natural intelligence than other native races. But they had been utterly barbarised during their long conflict with white intruders. There is only one name for the whole history of Yucatan since it was first visited by Pánfilo de Narvaez. It is disgusting. It is one long record of brutal aggression and bestial retaliation. What the Spaniards did not teach the natives was taught them by English logwood cutters in Campeachy, a gang of buccaneers, pirates, armed smugglers, and kidnappers. The Mayas proved very apt pupils. As much of the country was covered by dense tropical forest, they continued to possess fastnesses into which their enemies could never penetrate. They defended themselves—and the miasmas of their swamps helped to defend them—against invasion. They sallied out to raid and massacre. The long tale of mutual slaughter grows nauseous. At times the Spanish settlements appeared to be on the verge of extinction. Then the white race regained ground. As mere slaughter was accompanied by the capture and subjugation of women, a half-breed race was formed. The planters as a rule belong to this class of mestizos. They would prefer independence to union with Mexico, and they do demand with success a very considerable measure of local self-government. But they need the support of the Republic, and so profess a certain loyalty. According to what has been the rule in all Spanish America, these mestizos are more merciless to the pure Indian race than the Spaniards themselves. The outcome of centuries of cruelty has been for Yucatan the domination of a small class of half-bred planters who grow rich by the forced labour of Indian serfs. If the possession of better weapons and a great show of municipal improvements in their pet town, Mérida, constitute civilisation, then Yucatan is civilised. If the sacrifice of a whole population to the interest of a few, if cruelty and slave-driving, are barbarous, then Yucatan is in a state of barbarism. If a planter is a humane man, he treats his slaves better than does a mere brute. But a condition in which decency of behaviour depends wholly on the virtues of individuals, and is not enforced on all by the law, is one of barbarism. And the most humane of planters does not live on his land, but in a fine house in Mérida. He has an agent, an "administrador," who manages for him, and has an office in the town. The plantations are ruled by overseers ("mayordomos") who are expected to get the work done. The treatment given to the bond servants depends on these men, who are

THE INDIAN PROBLEM

bound to show a profit. All experience teaches us how they have ever been wont to secure the desired gain.[1]

Between these two extremes of Mexico, Sonora to the north-west and Yucatan at the south-east, there were varieties and degrees in the treatment given to the " peones " and the weaker portions of the inhabitants of Mexico. In the Valle Nacional, to the south of Cordoba on the Veracruz to Mexico line, there was a reproduction of the conditions which prevailed in Yucatan. In this case the plantations were devoted to growing tobacco. The bond servants were largely provided by the industry of a class of agents known as " enganchadores " (crimps : *gancho* in Spanish is a hook), who corresponded exactly to the rascals once well known in the West of England as " the Spirits." Their business was to hire labourers for the West Indian and Virginian plantations. They made lying promises, and when their dupes reached their destination they found themselves in a condition of slavery. The " enganchadores " worked in this way for the tobacco plantations. The Valle Nacional is long, is shut in by steep hills covered with tropical forest, and well watched at its entry and exit by the police. The bond servants who tried to escape were commonly captured and brought back. A fine was imposed for the attempt to break their contract, and it was added to the debt they were working off. Some, however, did escape and told their tale. The character of the Valle Nacional was well known. In addition to the bond servants who had been obtained in this way there

---

[1] I do not dwell on certain details of flagellations, the treatment of the women, etc., etc., on which eye-witnesses have been copious. Such abominations are incidental to slavery wherever it exists. There are Bluebooks and other sources of knowledge to tell us what was done in Jamaica by British men and women who were alive not very long ago.

were others obtained in another fashion. They were simply crimped by the police under pretence that they had committed minor offences. Sometimes they had committed them, and were punished by the magistrates by being sent into slavery. It may be added that many of the tobacco planters in the Valle Nacional were Spaniards. That fact helps to account for the massacre of immigrants from Old Spain which occurred after the fall of Don Porfirio in 1911.

The judicious reader of such stories as these finds, and rarely fails to use, an opportunity to express doubts as to their exact accuracy. He suspects exaggeration at least. And often he is right. The witnesses who have been revolted by the spectacle of wrong and misery do not stop to look at the other side, to note the cases where those who have power exercise it with moderation, nor do they always remember that those whose misfortunes are the result of their own misconduct can invent plausible tales of oppression. Yet the substantial truth of the pictures drawn of Yucatan and the Valle Nacional is certain, and in a wholesome state of society the errors or even the sins of men and women are not punished by turning them into mere instruments for money-getting, to the advantage of small bodies of employers who happen to be useful to the persons who command the public services for the time being, and who dignify themselves by the name of " the State." If judicious persons cannot believe that the police and the judicial authorities can lend themselves to such bad practices as have been mentioned above, their knowledge of Spanish and Portuguese America must be greatly to seek. It may be laid down as a rule to which there are few exceptions that no man who approaches the courts in those countries can hope, we need not say so much as for justice, but for a bare leave to state his case, unless he comes with money in his hand. The money, it must be understood, is not for the payment of lawyers' fees, but as a gift to the judge, in order to obtain his attention. The fees will have to be paid in due course. Again it must be borne in mind that in these countries what ought to be judicial acts are often performed by administrative officers. Fines can be arbitrarily imposed; no protest will be listened to till the money is paid; there is no way in which a single man can enforce a hearing of his grievance, and while he continues to complain, the authority goes on imposing fines. If he fails to pay, he is arrested, and then it is a short step to send him to the tobacco plantations of the Valle Nacional or other penal settlement. A distinguished Argentine statesman who was paying a visit to Europe was asked by an illustrious personage whether there was any administration of justice in his country. He answered laconically " Algo " (some, or just a little), and he put the case as high as he could.[1]

[1] Such charges as these ought not to be made without evidence to support them. I would not repeat them unless they seemed to me to be proved. My experience goes to show that they are true. I heard on the best authority in Buenos Ayres of a case which shows what ill-use can be made of an administrative officer's power to fine. A commissioner of police for one of the districts of the city wished to make a mistress of the daughter of an Italian tradesman. As she would not consent, and the father supported her, the commissioner ruined him by a succession of fines, and he was driven to go to another town. But for the fear of giving too much offence to the Italian Government, the man and his daughter would probably have been arrested as anarchists and would have disappeared from sight. It may be remembered that a few years ago the Italian Government did forbid the engagement of its subjects for labour in the Argentine. It was the only way short of a declaration of war by which to put a stop to outrages of the kind just mentioned and worse. There is no obscurity at all as to the use which is habitually made of the " anarchist " law in the Argentine. The son of a large employer of labour told me frankly that it was " terrible," but very useful. " For," said he, " when my father has trouble with one of his men,

Where such administrative and judicial conditions prevailed it is easy to understand how the great Indian, or nearly Indian, population of Mexico might have bitter grievances at all times, and also how their sufferings might be intensified under the rule of President Diaz, and because of its very virtues. This may sound like a paradox, but a few moments' attention will show that it is a mere statement of intelligible fact. Under the old colonial rule, and during the long anarchy which began to be suspended for a time about 1877, Mexico was a very torpid country. The Indians might have no rights, but apart from the forced labour of the mines, which was of long standing, nobody profited by demanding much from them. The land everywhere to some extent, but to a very great extent in the north, was too big for the people. The peon could squat on and work a little piece of ground for his small needs. He might be unable to produce a title, but he interfered with nobody. It did not pay to drive him, for a greater production would have been of no advantage when there were few means of making a profit by sale. Except those hacendados whose possessions were immense, everybody was poor, and, save a few tradesmen, everybody was idle.

A great change began when the country settled down. There was a Government in power eager to develop its resources and compelled to invite the co-operation of the foreign capitalist. This being so, the land grew to have more value as pasture, for culti-

---

he says to the police ' That man is an anarchist,' and they take him away." What this means is that the employer pays the police a yearly sum for their good-will. It also means that a man so arrested is sent to one of the islands on the Argentine coast and left to support himself by fishing. He generally dies of starvation in about three months. Yet the Argentine Republic is more orderly and less brutal than Mexico.

vation, and for mining. And now it became the interest of people who could enforce attention to their wishes because they held the purse-strings to insist on a sharp examination of the titles by virtue of which the land was used. The case was complicated by the fact that, land having been superabundant, and water in the greater part of the country rare, what had been thought sufficiently valuable and disputable to be made matter of record were not titles to land, but water rights. Land could be found anywhere. Water to irrigate it had to be obtained by industry. It follows that if there was to be a general inquisition into titles, a *quo warranto*, nothing could be easier than to show that very much, perhaps the greater part, of the land in the Republic was " tierra baldia," that is to say, unowned land, and therefore domain of the State, and at its disposal to give or to sell. A no less obvious consequence would be that the purchaser or grantee of the land could within his own bounds cut off access to the water. A water right was of no value to a man who could not use the adjacent land. In these conditions it might well happen that grave injustice might be done, and done with punctilious attention to a law. All that was needed was that the law should allow a prospector to peg out and claim unoccupied land and require it from the State, all land which was not held by a producible title being counted unoccupied. And this was the course taken. By the land law of 1886 anyone was authorised to " denounce "—that is to say, to point out—a space of land as " tierra baldia " and to claim to acquire it on payment of a small due to the State. The burden of proof that it was not " tierra baldia " was thrown on those who were making use of it, and occupancy was not accepted as a title. There was no Statute of Limitations in Mexico, and there was on the part of the State—*i.e.*, the politicians in office—a very firm grip of the principle *nullum tempus occurrit regi*. When, therefore, we hear in the President's addresses to Congress of the marking out of " tierras baldias," what is to be understood as implied is that somebody poor, obscure, and mostly Indian was squeezed out of the corner he had looked upon as his, to be worked for himself. We hear, it is true, that care was taken to provide " ejidos " for Indian villages, and if this had been done fairly, and under the protection of an independent judiciary, it would have been the better for Mexico. But that which depended for its just execution on the honour of Government officials and the independence of the courts was not done at all, or was very ill done. As a matter of course only the small men suffered. The great landholders, whose titles were often very doubtful, could take care of themselves. They could make use of interest to avoid inquisition into what they wished to conceal, or they could acquire a title at a cheap rate, or stand in with the speculative capitalist.

As Mexico had to look abroad for capital, schemes for development of the resources of the land had a consequence which in the end proved very injurious to the popularity of President Diaz. It was inevitable that a large part of the " tierra baldia " which was sold to " denouncers " passed into the hands of foreigners, of whom the majority came from the United States. A jest much repeated in Mexico tells how a countryman expostulated with the President on the readiness he showed to allow Americans to acquire land, and how he answered that they would have it all some day, and might as well be made to pay while payment could still be demanded. The serious part of the jape lies in its inclusion of the fact that these foreign purchases were lawful only with his consent. His readiness to agree to them must be taken as proof of his approval and of a policy he pursued for years. It goes with other actions of his which had a disastrous effect. He encouraged European colonists to form land settlements, and, though the results were but meagre, the little done in this way was enough to rouse much angry feeling. The poor little colonies, mainly of Italians, were considered as a menace by the natives. And then the President at least allowed of an attempt to introduce Chinese and Japanese labour. The attempt was equally offensive to Mexicans and Americans. Though not much was done, yet that little also was enough to provoke ill-feeling. The very industrial virtues of the Chinese made them odious in Mexico, as in the United States and our own colonies, though not for exactly the same reasons. It would have been hard indeed even for Chinese thrift to lower the standard of living of the labouring classes of Mexico. But the fear was that they would displace the native. After the fall of the President a dreadful massacre of Chinese was made at Torreon, on the Texan border. The immediate cause was the unfounded belief that certain Mexicans had been poisoned in a tavern kept by a Chinaman, but the real cause was the hatred felt for the whole race. Their industry was their chief sin, but it is also a fact that the floggers and bullies employed to terrorise the bond servants in Yucatan and the Valle Nacional were often Chinamen, and that the women on the plantations were compelled to live with them for the purpose of breeding little slaves.

Against all this evil we have to put the fact that the outlay of foreign capital in Mexico did give increased employment and raise wages. Indirectly it helped the " peones," who were not subject to the plantation system; and that, too, was a gain as far as it went. But a very general experience shows that the discontent born of oppression is more loudly expressed when the sufferers begin to experience some relief. As they gain in strength their fear diminishes, their desires grow, and their claims increase. Of course, they are accused of ingratitude, as the Mexicans have been. The critics should remember that the improved lot may still be bad, and that old memories rankle. Nor do the better wages of a time of industrial expansion always last, while the vices of a social system are apt to endure. Mexicans of the labouring class had always before them the spectacle of the caravans of Yaquis who were carried right across the country into slavery in Yucatan or the Valle Nacional, and the expelled squatters. If they did suspect their white masters of a wish to exploit them, or even get rid of them to make room for Chinese labour, their distrust cannot be said to have been absurd.

In so far then as this Indian population, which was often not the less Indian because of a slight admixture of European blood, was concerned, there is nothing to show that the long Administration of President Diaz did any lasting good or supplied any promise of improvement. There is not even evidence that the President as much as wished to raise its moral and intellectual level. This neglect of what ought to have been treated as an elementary duty cannot surely be counted to him for righteousness. But before we join those who condemn him wholly let us remember that "a man is only a man." He cannot shake himself quite free from the inherited dispositions of the society he lives in. If he could he would only become alien to it and incapable of governing. It may look discreditable to Diaz that though he was largely of Indian descent himself, and could profess pride in his Mixteca ancestry, he did nothing for his red kinsmen. But Juarez was a pure-blooded Zapoteca, and he did no more. He, too, married a Creole wife, and forgot his people and his father's house. The truth is that the Mexican Indian who has risen in the world, and the mestizo, who is half, or more than half, European, alike wish to be even as the Creoles of Spanish descent—to rank as whites. And what else could they be expected to wish? Juarez has been absurdly blamed for not turning Mexico into an Indian republic. If he had made the attempt he would have banded against him all the Creoles and all the mestizos who wished to rank as Creoles. In face of their hostility he would not have lasted for a week. Even if we make the wild supposition that he had tried and had succeeded, what could he have done? He could have won only by a general massacre of the dominant classes and by turning Mexico into an Indian Hayti. The conquerors would have returned to the tribal state with its unvarying conditions—perpetual war between "pueblo" Indians and wild Indians, and the domination of the softer tribes by the more ferocious. Long before it had come to that the troops of the United States would have been in possession of all Mexico.

Juarez could not wish for an Indian republic; and still less could Porfirio Diaz. What he was bound to wish for was the closer assimilation of Mexico to the standard of a civilised European State by the development of its industry and the maintenance of peace. In order that he might succeed he had need of money; and money was to be obtained only by the help of the foreign capitalist. Nothing was more natural than that he should be chiefly concerned to satisfy those whose aid was indispensable to him, and that in this struggle for industrial prosperity the Mexican Indian should have been treated as a mere tool. That is not what would have happened if the man had been greater and the society about him more healthy and higher-minded. In that case the governors of Mexico would have understood that nothing of real lasting good was to be obtained by perpetuating a great cause of anarchy. This Indian population had always been the instrument of adventurers and insurgents because it was torpid subjected and so miserably poor that it did not lose by being drafted into guerrillero bands and rebel armies. So long as it remained as it was it would always serve that purpose. But Diaz was not a great moral and political reformer. He was a vigorous Spanish-American " tyrant " who strove to keep good order and promote material well-being in such ways as his own upbringing and the elements he disposed of allowed. Before he could take in hand a great work of social reform in Mexico he must have had command of a clean-handed, competent administrative staff—some equivalent, in fact, for our own Indian Civil Service, and an independent judiciary, prepared to try to do justice. He had no such aid, and therefore could not have done the work even if he had wished. That he never showed the wish deprives him of all claim to rank with the greater statesmen. It leaves him a strong administrator and nothing else.

THE INDIAN PROBLEM 289

Whether he could have done more if he had tried to do justice to the Indian population is a speculative question. We know that he had to learn before he died how little it avails a country to put money in its purse for a time at the cost of nursing and increasing the rage, hate, envy, and the sense of wrong which provide the rank and file of anarchical armies.

CHAPTER XI

ANARCHY WELLS UP

THOSE of us who have never felt the temptation to cling to power may wonder why few rulers of men have known how to leave the world before the world left them. What satisfaction can it be to struggle on " Bankrupt of life yet prodigal ease " ? In 1904, when his sixth term of office came to its end, President Diaz was seventy-four. He was still enjoying the vigour of body which he owed primarily to an excellent constitution, but in no small measure to the stern discipline he imposed on himself. None the less, he was old, and extreme age lay just before him. His place was no ornamental sinecure, but a heavy toil. He is known to have expressed a wish to retire and to visit Europe, which he had never seen, while it was still in his power to enjoy travel. Yet he stayed, and when his seventh term of office, which had been prolonged from four to six years, ended, also in 1910, he again stayed. Why ?

Astute persons who believe in nothing but their own capacity to see quite through the deeds of men are ready to provide an explanation. It was greed ; it was the love of power ; and all professions to the contrary are but the purest hypocrisy. And no doubt it is the fact that those who have held command are unwilling to pass into the ranks again. We may suspect, without pretending to sagacity, that Diaz did listen, with a predisposition to believe, to foreign envoys, his own ministers, and those about him who are known to have told him that he was indispensable and to have implored him to stay. Yet we can now see that they were right. He alone stood between Mexico and anarchy. He was tied to the stake and must bearlike fight the course. By staying he put off the day of danger, and a space was given in which to prepare for the time when his place must needs be vacant.

The election, so called, was not quite as others had been. There was no opposition, and the part of the electors did not vary. But up to this time there had been no Vice-President in Mexico. The President of the Supreme Court stood ready, as we have seen in the cases of Juarez and Lerdo, to take the accidentally vacant chair. But in 1904 it was felt to be no longer safe to rely on the lawyer who happened to preside over the Supreme Court. A politician trained to the work must be provided to stand by the President ready to replace him if he died, and to succeed him if in 1910 age should have deprived him of the capacity to hold the reins. The precaution was wise, but the choice made was unfortunate. His understudy and successor was expected to continue the same " system "— to keep the peace, to promote industry, and to protect foreign capital. In order that he might be able to fulfil this programme he must have a certain measure of popularity, the confidence of the capitalists, and the capacity for hard work. There was a time when it was assumed that in the new industrial age the most appropriate successor for Don Porfirio would be his Minister of Finance, Don José Limantour. But there was a difficulty in the way. The Constitution provided that the President of Mexico must be native born, and

Francisco Madero in his little treatise " La Sucesion Presidencial en 1910." Señor Madero is a person who will play a considerable part in the last stage of the life of President Diaz, and it is well to know who he was before we listen to what he said.

The Madero family was of Spanish origin and, as it seems, of rather recent settlement in Mexico. It possessed much land in Coahuila, the border State which lies next to Chihuahua to the east ; and it was very wealthy. Francisco, who was still very young when he came forward in Mexican politics during the seventh term of President Diaz, had been educated partly in the United States and partly in Europe. In the course of his travels he is said by those who profess to know and to admire him to have adopted some of those opinions which more sober-minded people call fads. He was a vegetarian and a spiritualist.[1] It is obviously not quite safe to accept the testimony of a man of credulous turn. Yet Señor Madero may be trusted when he says that the creation of a Vice-President and the choice of Señor Corral mark the starting-point of a definite movement of opposition. There were, he says, Mexicans who thought that a time had come for a change in the " spheres of power." But up to 1904 they were prepared to wait till age and fatigue or death should remove Don Porfirio. When they saw that steps were being taken to perpetuate

[1] If we can trust some of those who praised him, he would seem to have been in the habit of consulting the crystal, or the cards, or some other form of divination. It is said that when he had the now notorious Zapata in his power, and might have shot him according to all Mexican precedent, he let him go. The reason given is not that he thought such an act brutal, or was reluctant to execute without form of law. It is that he had been magically " told " that his own death would follow Zapata's within twenty-four hours. This is the sort of story which would be told of such a man, and I would be sorry indeed to vouch for the truth of the tale. But the stories told of a man are in their way evidence. Nobody would have invented or believed such gossip (if mere gossip it was) of Santa Ana, or Juarez, or Diaz.

the possession of office by those about him, they felt that they must act, which means that they must conspire. They might have had patience if they had known that the disappearance from the scene of President Diaz would leave the field clear, but if it were only to mean that another and perhaps heavier hand were to control the same machine they must resist. Nothing could well be more likely, and the course of events during the next six years would be enough to prove that many felt in this way even if we had not the direct testimony of a witness. Even if Señor Madero tells us only what he thought, then, in view of the part he took, his statement has a substantial value.

On the surface all looked well to those who saw the Republic from abroad, or if they came to it came only as visitors to look at the improvements and report astonishing progress. Between 1904 and 1906 there appeared quite a crop of books full of the most hopeful descriptions and predictions. It came to be a commonplace that the evil times were over for Mexico. In 1907 Mr. Elihu Root visited the capital, and many festivities were held and fine speeches were made. The eloquent American praised President Diaz as the greatest of living statesmen. Mr. Root struck a note which was echoed far and wide. At the end of a book published in New York in 1910 by Don José Godoy, the author publishes a long collection of what really sound like testimonials to the efficacy of some invention or patent medicine. They are examples of all the laudatory things said of President Diaz. Señor Godoy's book was in fact an electioneering puff, and one feels in regard to many of the other books that they represent what business interests

ANARCHY WELLS UP

would wish investors to think of Mexico and its Government, and very little else. When in 1909 President Diaz met Mr. Taft at Paso del Norte the toasts and the ceremonies were those which we are accustomed to hear of when Sovereigns hold an interview. In short, there was no failure in the flow of official assurances that all was well with Mexico within and without.

While persons whose first purpose was neither to see nor to tell the whole truth were saying smooth things the unrest of Mexico was growing more acute. It is a significant fact that just when the " coffles " of enslaved Yaquis were beginning to defile across Mexico in shameless publicity—that is to say, from 1904 onwards—the Socialists grew very restive. It is not a whit less significant that just before Mr. Elihu Root came in 1907 there had been a very long and very savage anti-American agitation in Mexico. It was said in a picturesque way that an American " Sicilian Vespers " was averted with great difficulty. When Mr. Taft met his brother President at Paso in 1909, one of the subjects of their unreported conversation must have been the recent flight of exiles from Mexico and the trouble they gave Governments. Everybody who cared to learn the facts knew that only the vigilance of Washington prevented the territory of the United States from being used as a basis of operations for a rebellion in Mexico ; and even this guarantee for peace was not at all times sufficient It is all but impossible to guard every part of a frontier seventeen hundred miles long of which much is not, or is barely, inhabited. In 1908 there was an outbreak in Coahuila which had notoriously been prepared in the States.

There is always an extreme difficulty in getting at the whole truth of events which have happened very recently; and yet we may venture to assume that not much is to be learnt about the insurrection which finally drove President Diaz to Europe beyond what appears on the surface. The reasons given in the last chapter why the peace he had kept for a time unprecedented in Mexican history should at last be broken are also sufficient to account for what in that country and in the circumstances was a natural event. If anything needs to be added, it is that as Diaz came near his eightieth year he could no longer work as he once did. Don Francisco Madero asserts that this was the case. It follows that he fell into the hands of those about him. They intercepted the truth, so Don Francisco asserts, and it is consistent with probability. It is the fatal defect of all purely personal government that it grows old with the ruler before it dies with him. In a monarchical country what descends to the grave with an Elizabeth or a Frederick the Great is a personal method of using an institution. But what of necessity went into exile with the President of Mexico was all government.

Don Porfirio could quote this fact in answer to the question why he decided to re-elect himself once more in 1910. He had had many warnings from 1904 onwards that by persisting in office he would provoke trouble. Open disorder, Socialist or Liberal, had been repressed with apparent success. The " acordada " (secret police) kept watch. Those who threatened to become dangerous were arrested and sent to the castle of San Juan de Ulloa, or driven to escape over the American border. There the United States kept an eye on them, and, instigated, so we are assured, by

Wall Street, repressed their plots. But though a smooth surface was preserved by these vigorous measures, there were signs which could not be ignored that mere police vigour would not be enough. The Press of Mexico is free only by the letter of the Constitution, and as the electors are free. Yet even the Press began to say strong things about the "caciquismo" of the President's rule. The great re-election theme began to be discussed. It was a sign of the times that a very curious compromise found favour with some. They were ready to consent that the President should be chosen again in the old way—in other words, that the voters should do as they were bid in so far as he was personally concerned. But they had a device for introducing true liberty of election. It was that the electors should be absolutely free to vote for or against the Vice-President, Don Ramon Corral. The compromise was infantile. Don Ramon had been selected as President's understudy precisely because he was expected to continue the so-called Diaz system with the same men as colleagues or agents. If he were to be defeated at the polls—and on the supposition that the election was to be free he most assuredly would be—the system would be defeated too. Don Porfirio would be reduced to a figurehead. It was not a position he could be expected to accept; nor ought he to have accepted it. Mexico is not a country which can be governed by a figurehead. The so-called compromise broke down at once when tested.

The fact that everything was at stake became more apparent in 1909 when the Central Democratic Club produced a scheme of reform. It contained a great many generalities, and not a few sentiments, but there was one proposal in it which was undeniably substantial. This was that the office of Jefe Politico should be abolished, and that the Jefes should be replaced by an elected board or committee. Of course this change would have taken away the whole foundation not only of the "Diaz system" but of the edifice of government in Mexico. The novelty was to be accompanied by electoral reform at large—free election for governors and President. Anyone who knew what government meant in Mexico could see at once that the practical result of such a constitutional device must infallibly be a fight in the literal sense of the word in every district of every State in the Republic.

What Porfirio Diaz may have thought or decided *in foro interno* is mere idle speculation. We know with sufficient accuracy what he did. When the time for the new election of 1910 drew near he said he would not stand again, and he broke his promise. That is the substantial fact. Did he break his word from mere longing to retain office, and was his promise a sheer hypocrisy? Or did he decide to continue in office simply because he must? There are good reasons for thinking that the last is the true explanation. The reader is asked to excuse a repetition of the statement that there was but one choice for Mexico—namely, between a vigorous personal government by some one man, working with a trusty staff of agents, and anarchy. Since this was the fact, as the events of the last five years have amply demonstrated, was Diaz to blame if he refused to retire before he could leave the country in strong hands? It is at least a tenable proposition that he would not have been justified. Even if he saw no chance of finding a competent successor, he was to be excused for endeavouring to put off the evil day so long as he could.

In 1969, before the election was formally open, a proof was given of the resolution of some Mexicans to break down the "system." The opponents of Don Ramon Corral decided to oppose his re-election—they did not so far openly oppose the President—and they chose General Reyes as their candidate. General Reyes had been for some years Governor of the State of Nuevo Leon. He was therefore a part of the "system." But he had been a popular governor and had local influence. From all that can be seen of him from this side of the Atlantic, the General appears to have been a moderate man of a kindly disposition, but of not much force of character. He did not, so it seems, exactly put himself forward as an opponent of Don Ramon, but his friends, or the party which thought he would be useful to them, did it for him. Of course this was opposition, and, if it was allowed, would set a bad example. Measures were taken to suppress the agitation, and the Reyista party (a Mexican party nearly always names itself after a person, rarely after a principle) retaliated by riotous demonstrations. The demonstrations were put down and General Reyes was sent on a mission to inquire into the military systems of Europe. It was not harsh treatment, but Reyes had many friends in the army. He went, and before leaving America he gave an interview to newspaper reporters in New York which leaves nothing to be desired as a profession of faith in the virtues of Don Porfirio and the necessity of retaining him as President.

The disappearance for the time being of General Reyes left the field free for Don Francisco Madero.

One cannot but have a certain compunction to speak unkindly of a man who came to such a shocking fate. And yet if he had not been butchered with a barbarity exceptional even for Mexico, it would be hard to keep one's hands off Francisco Madero. Enthusiasts have been found to call him " a star " and what not equally laudatory. Yet, to anyone who will take the trouble to read his book " The Presidential Election " and to learn his actions, he appears to have been neither more nor less than an example of the " ligereza "— the feather-headedness of a certain stamp of Spaniard. He was the pitiable victim of his own errors, and so we may prefer to say all the good we can of him. It is honourable to him that his little book is free from the foul scolding so common in the political journalism of his and kindred countries. But a man needs more than some sense of decency before he is justified in letting loose a civil war. He must have ideas and a cause to fight for. Now it is impossible to make out from Señor Madero's statement of his case that he took up arms for anything except the sacred principle that the places of dignity and emolument ought to go round in a truly democratic country. There is not a trace of any attempt on his part to face the dominant fact that Mexico is not a democratic country nor one in which the choice of rulers, upper and under, can be left to the free and independent electors. The theory of the orthodox democratic doctors, says Madero, is so and so, and we must apply it regardless of facts, conditions, and experience. The man was, in short, a pedant. It is characteristic of him and his unhappy class that, while he speaks with a humanity which must be credited to his honour of the cruel treatment of the Yaquis and other Indians, he gives no sign of having thought out any definite plan for righting their wrongs, nor to have reflected on the principles which ought to guide a Government in dealing with such a population. He has nothing to offer but sentiments and the promise that, if only there is a change of persons in the Presidency and the governorships of the States, all will be well in Mexico. It is said that he was kind to his own Indians, but it is not said that the truck system, which by its very nature worked for evil, was rejected on the Madero estates. There is something suspicious in his candid-looking confession that his family had no private reason for disliking the " system " of President Diaz. Whenever the Maderos had occasion to appeal to the courts or the Administration at the capital their interests had always been treated with equity. What this may very well mean when translated into the language of mere truth is most probably nothing but just this— that the courts and the Administration were always ready to meet the views of an influential family. The Maderos were quite as well disposed as any other wealthy connection to make use of the much-abused system for their own ends. We need not be surprised to hear that when Don Francisco did become President his " good nature " made it impossible for him to check the rapacity of his relatives. There is a kind of good nature, as well as of good intention, which paves the road to hell.[1]

[1] I am not quoting Dr. Johnson, but a Portuguese proverb which says that the road to etc., etc.—a far wiser saying than the Doctor's famous explosion. It is not perhaps of much use to refer the reader to books which he can only obtain by writing for them to Mexico or to Havannah, but if he by accident comes across a book by the name of " La Parra, la Perra, y la Porra " (" The Wild Vine, the Bitch, and the Cudgel "), he will see a fine example of the mere froth of words which surrounded the whole Madero adventure. La Parra was the name of Madero's hacienda.

If there had not been general discontent in Mexico with more than the clinging to office of Don Porfirio and his connection, such a man would have had no opportunity to play a part. And if he had not had command of a long purse he would probably not have cut much of a figure even as it was. But, the two going together, he was the man who hastened the day when Mexico was to return to anarchy.

Before the movement in favour of electing General Reyes had been quashed, and the General had sailed on his mission to inquire into the military systems of Europe, Madero was simply a " joven distinguido " (a youth belonging to an opulent family). But he now came forward as a candidate for the Presidency itself. It is quite unnecessary to spend words in saying what this implied in Mexico. What it meant for Don Francisco was that he was arrested shortly before the election was due, in July 1910. The charge was first that he had helped to protect one Estrada, a partisan of General Reyes, from arrest; then it was altered into a charge of insulting the nation. Finally he was accused of insulting the President. This at least was the account given by his friends. The formula preferred was of no consequence, and any other pretext would have served for a measure which had no end but to silence a politician who threatened to give trouble. The enemies of President Diaz have been put to it to explain why Madero was not shot. They have cleared up the mystery by describing a pathetic scene in which La Señora Diaz implored and persuaded her ferocious husband not to add another to the already long-drawn-out list of his murders. This is precisely what would be said by anyone with a moderate inventive faculty. Madero was not shot, but preserved to be butchered by one or several of the wild beasts he had helped to let loose on his country. He was only kept in jail and out of the way of doing or suffering harm till the election was over.

It being clear that no real election would be tolerated, and as the Government disposed of an adequate armed force, President and Vice-President were declared duly returned by the unanimous voice of the people. In September President Diaz presided over the last peaceful ceremony he was to witness in Mexico, the celebration of the independence of the country, which has been made to date from the rising headed by Hidalgo. We have seen what that emotional priest had really done. A spectator who knew the facts of the state of the country might well have asked himself whether the revival of that memory was not ominous. His doubts would have been justified, for the rule of President Diaz had not then a year to live.

The mere events of his fall need not be recorded here. That Madero took up arms in Chihuahua in January and that by May the " Diaz system " had collapsed are, with one other about to be named, the essential facts. There were no encounters deserving the name of battle. No faculty and no energy were displayed, either in attack or defence. The *régime* which had given Mexico some thirty years of growing material prosperity and the appearance of order fell to pieces, and this happened (here we come to the third fact which is to be kept in mind) because the man on whom all depended had himself broken down under the pressure of age. Don Porfirio bore up gallantly, keeping himself upright by sheer strength of will, speaking of his intention to take command of the forces in the field, if the rising became really dangerous, till his body failed him. On May 1 he was still insisting on a compromise by which he and Madero were both to retire, and a desperate bid for popularity was made by a change of Ministry. But the long fight had ended in defeat. Anarchy was bubbling up on all hands. The United States were threatening intervention. The insurgents could safely refuse to listen to any terms and could insist that the unconditional retirement of the President must be the preliminary to every other measure. Porfirio Diaz himself was prostrate, and the acts of his Government were as the blows of the exhausted athlete which have lost their force. He was confined to bed and his strong body was showing the first signs of senile decay. He could see no one outside of his own family save Señor Limantour, who alone of his old ministers remained with him. On May 18 his resignation was announced to the Congress in words which cannot have been his, and he prepared for exile. There were still among the soldiers, whose interests he had always considered, loyal men enough to see to it that the old President should not be subject to insult or outrage while he was leaving the country. He, his family, and those of his associates who had no choice but to go into exile with him were protected on the way to Veracruz, where they took ship for New York. General Huerta, who was to succeed him, to avenge him vilely on Madero, and in the end to join him in exile, saw to the safety of the party. It was assailed on the way to the seaport, and the escort had to fight it through. On the pier Diaz listened, hat in hand, a pathetic figure, to the last words of farewell spoken to him on his native soil.

From New York he sailed to Europe, and from that time forward his life passed into the privacy of his family, where we have no right to follow him. After spending some time in the south of Europe, he went to Paris in May, 1914. He died there on July 2, 1915, amid the roar of a storm which left the world with but little attention to give to a fallen President of Mexico.

This book has been written to no purpose if it is necessary to spend words in summing up the career and the character of Porfirio Diaz. If a final verdict is to be given it must be something like this. He showed the world what was the utmost that his country was capable of doing in order to qualify itself to take its place among civilised and progressive States. All it has been able to do has been to produce a resolute, heavy-handed man who could keep an incurable anarchy within bounds for an unprecedented period of years. That man had no other nor higher aim than to develop resources, build public works, enable foreign capital to promote industry and make profits for itself. All this he did, and an admiring world took him for a great reformer whose work would last. But, much as it seemed to be, it was naught if we look beyond the outward and visible things which money and labour can produce between them, and try to pierce into those inward and spiritual things which alone make the health of a nation, and without which all the triumphs of industry are but pearls on the swine's snout. He rose to rule a country which could not possess real unity save if it had been endowed with a strong monarchy and a capable aristocracy. Monarchy was impossible, and there were not the most beggarly elements of an aristocracy. Police order for a time he could give, and nothing more. Under cover of that police order the outer world put its hand on Mexico and brought the country appreciably nearer the day when the huge and growing mass of power on its northern border will spread over it — by what movements we do not know, but as surely as water flows from a higher to a lower level. At no period in man's history has a chronic, sanguinary, brainless anarchy been allowed to live for very long beside order and political capacity and thought. He could not even add strength to the mere mechanical unity of his country, for he lived to see the northern provinces in process of being torn away by a mere brigand, while his own nephew was erecting an independent power in his native Oaxaca. He failed, perhaps because he was not great man enough, but more surely because he had not to his hand the elements with which more could be done. *Un homme n'est qu'un homme.*

BIBLIOGRAPHY

Bancroft, H. H. " History of the Pacific States of North America." 34 vols. San Francisco. 1882—1890. The " History of Mexico," 1517—1857, forms vols. iv. to ix. of the whole work. The Histories of the North Mexican States—Texas, Arizona and New Mexico—are in vols. x., xi., and xii. Full, impartial, well informed, with many quotations from documents, and copious references to authorities.

" Datos Biográficos del [Biographic Data of] General Porfirio Diaz." Published in the office of the *Patria* newspaper. Mexico. 1884. Official and partisan, but contains useful documents.

Escudero, Ignacio M. " Apuntes Históricos de la Carrera Militar del [Historical Notes of the Military Career of] Señor General Porfirio Diaz." Mexico. 1889. Partisan, but full of details.

Zayas Enriquez, Rafael de. " Porfirio Diaz, La Evolucion de su Vida " [The Evolution of his Life]. New York. 1908. A critical and not always friendly study by a well-informed writer.

Rodriguez, Ricardo. " Historia Auténtica de la Administracion del [Authentic History of the Administration of] Señor General Porfirio Diaz." Mexico. 1904. A collection of the President's addresses to Congress.

Hernandez, Fortunato. " Un Pueblo, un Siglo, y un Hombre " [A People, an Epoch, and a Man]. Mexico. 1909. An answer to Zayas Enriquez—inspired by the President.

Garcia, Genero. " Porfirio Diaz, sus Padres, Niñez, Juventud " [his Family, Childhood, and Youth]. Mexico. 1906. Useful details of early years (largely supplied by Porfirio Diaz).

DIAZ

Fornaro, Carlo de. " Diaz, Czar of Mexico." No place of publication is given, but probably New York. 1909. An invective.

Godoy, José F. " Porfirio Diaz, President of Mexico." New York. 1910. The work of an official and a partisan.

Madero, Francisco J. " La Sucesion Presidencial " [The Succession to the Presidency]. Mexico. 1911. A party pamphlet, but a useful statement of the views of opponents of the re-election of Porfirio Diaz in 1910.

Tweedie, Mrs. " Mexico as I saw It." London. 1901. " Diaz." London. 1906.

Turner, J. K. " Barbarous Mexico." London. 1911. A book inspired by passionate indignation, but well informed and the work of an eye-witness whose spirit was honourable.

Niox, G. " Expédition au Mexique." Paris. 1874. A good narrative of the French intervention by an eye-witness, and based on official papers.

CHRONOLOGY

1810. Rising of Hidalgo in Mexico.
„ Beginning of revolt of Spanish colonies in La Plata.
1820. Revolt of Spanish army at Cadiz.
„ Mexico declares her independence.
1821. Iturbide proclaimed Emperor.
„ Is expelled by Federals.
1823. Ferdinand VII. of Spain restored by French army.
„ British Government recognises independence of Spanish colonies.
„ Monroe President of U.S.A., propounds Monroe Doctrine.
1830. (Sept. 15.) Porfirio Diaz baptised, probably born, at Oaxaca.
„ Andrew Jackson President of U.S.A.
1833. Santa Ana President of Mexico.
1835. Rosas becomes Tyrant of Argentine.
1837. Accession of Queen Victoria.
1838—1839. French send naval expedition to secure redress from Mexico for outrages on French subjects.
1845. J. H. Polk President of U.S.A.
„ Beginning of war between Mexico and U.S.A.
1848. Diaz volunteers, but sees no service.
„ (May 19.) War ended by peace of Guadalupe Hidalgo.
„ Mexico cedes territory beyond Rio Grande, and California.
„ Revolutionary movements in Sicily, France, Germany, Italy, and Hungary.
„ Gold discovered in California.
1849. First Panama surveys made.
1850. Clayton-Bulwer Treaty.
1851. Napoleon III. Emperor of French.
1852. Rosas expelled from Argentine.

1853. Santa Ana Dictator in Mexico.
1854. Revolt against Santa Ana.
„ General Álvarez issues Plan of Ayutla.
„ Diaz joins guerrilla of Herrera.
1855. Panama Railway made.
„ Diaz sub-prefect of Ixtlan.
1856. Civil war in Mexico.
„ Álvarez and Comonfort successively Presidents after expulsion of Santa Ana.
„ Diaz captain in militia of Oaxaca.
1857. New Constitution of Mexico.
„ Legislation against judicial privileges of clergy and army.
1858. Clerical and military revolt against the Constitution.
„ Comonfort turns against his own Government. Driven into exile.
„ Benito Juárez becomes interim President of Mexico.
„ Diaz Governor of Tehuantepec.
1859. Government of Juarez at Veracruz.
„ Civil war between Juarez at Veracruz and Clerical party, led chiefly by Miramon.
„ U.S.A. Government favours Juarez. Buchanan President.
„ Diaz supports Juarez in Tehuantepec. Promoted lieutenant-colonel and colonel.
1861. Juarez recovers capital and expels Miramon.
„ He rejects claims of Great Britain, France, and Spain for compensation.
„ Spanish troops under command of Prim land at Veracruz.
„ Abraham Lincoln President of U.S.A.
„ Beginning of War of Secession.
1862. British and French forces join Spaniards at Veracruz in January, but the British and Spanish withdraw in May.
„ The French advance into the interior.
„ (May 5.) Diaz, now brigadier, takes part in repulse of French at Puebla.

CHRONOLOGY 311

1862. Lorencez superseded in command of French forces by Forey in August.
1863. Puebla besieged and taken, March 29—May 18.
„ Diaz a prisoner, but escapes.
„ Promoted general of division.
„ French enter Mexico city on June 5.
„ Diaz leads expedition to Oaxaca in October.
1864. The Archduke Maximilian accepts offer of the crown of Mexico in April, lands at Veracruz in May, and enters Mexico on June 12.
„ Civil war in U.S.A. at its height. U.S.A. Government continues to recognise Juarez and refuses to recognise Maximilian.
„ The French, after defeating Juarez in North, begin advance on Oaxaca in autumn.
„ Austria and Prussia invade Holstein and Schleswig and take them from Denmark (January and February).
1865. (Feb. 8.) Diaz, finding no support in population, surrenders Oaxaca. Remains prisoner till he escapes in September.
„ (April 9.) Surrender of Confederate General Lee at Appomatox.
„ (April 15.) Assassination of Abraham Lincoln.
„ U.S. Government press the French to name date on which they will withdraw.
„ Diaz resumes his command in south and south-east of Mexico.
1866. Diaz gains ground in Oaxaca. Retakes city on Oct. 30.
„ French begin to evacuate Mexico.
„ War between Prussia and Austria.
„ (July 3.) Battle of Sadowa.
„ (Aug. 23.) Peace of Prague.
1867. French complete evacuation of Mexico in February. The Republican forces gain ground on all hands.
„ (April 2.) Diaz takes Puebla.
„ (May 15.) Surrender of Maximilian at Querétaro.
„ (June 19.) Execution of Maximilian.

CHRONOLOGY

1879. International Congress to discuss plan of Panama Canal held in Paris.
„   War between Chile and Peru.
1880. End of Diaz's first term as President.
1881. (Jan. 31.) Formation of company directed by Lesseps to work the Wyse concession for Panama Canal.
1882. Arrangement made between U.S.A. and Mexico allowing the regular forces of either State to pursue marauders over border.
1884. Riots in Mexico caused by treaty to settle foreign debt and the issue of nickel coinage.
„   Diaz becomes President for the second time. Settlement of foreign debt confirmed.
1888. Ruin of Lesseps' Panama Company
„   Congress authorises the re-election of Diaz.
1889. Revolution in Brazil. Pedro II. deposed and republic established.
1890. The indemnity due to U.S.A. by Mexico is paid off.
1892. Diaz is re-elected President.
1894. New Panama Company formed.
1895. Settlement of Mexican frontier dispute with Guatemala by friendly offices of U.S.A.
„   Grover Cleveland President of U.S.A.
1896. Re-election of Diaz.
„   The Venezuelan frontier dispute creates strained relations between Great Britain and U.S.A.
1898. War between U.S.A. and Spain.
„   Spain loses Cuba and Porto Rico.
1900. Re-election of Diaz.
„   Hay-Pauncefote Treaty signed.
1901. Death of Queen Victoria. Accession of King Edward VII.
1902. (June 19.) The New Panama Company cedes its rights to U.S.A.
1903. The drainage works of the Valley of Mexico are completed.
1904. Re-election of Diaz for term of six years. Office of Vice-President created and Ramon Corral chosen.

1906—1907. Popular outbreaks against U.S.A. in Mexico.
1909. (Oct. 16.) Meeting of Diaz and President Taft at Paso del Norte.
„ First signs of revolt against the Government of Diaz in Mexico.
„ Diaz announces his intention not to stand again.
1910. Re-election of Diaz.
„ Centenary of Independence of Mexico.
„ Madero, his opponent for Presidency, rises in revolt.
„ Death of King Edward VII.
1911. The revolt spreads.
„ The health of Diaz breaks down, he resigns in May, and leaves for Europe.
1914. (Aug.) Outbreak of European War.
1915. (July 2.) Death of Diaz in Paris.

INDEX

ACULTZINGO, Pass of, forced by French, 60
Alatorre, General, supports Lerdists defeated by Diaz at Tecoac, 159—160
Alcabalas, Mexican excise, 245 *et seq.*
Alvarez, General, President, 43; aids Diaz in Guerrero, 96
Amélie Charlotte, wife of Maximilian, comes to Mexico, 74
Apaches, suppressed, 268—269
Appomatox, capitulation of Confederates at, 88
Argentine Republic, cause of prosperity of, 124

BANCROFT, H. H., quoted, 53
"Bandera," Yaqui chief, 271
Bazaine, General, afterwards Marshal, defeats Mexicans in San Lorenzo, 72; Commander-in-Chief, 73; prepares to occupy Oaxaca, 80, 81; takes, 85; anger with Diaz, 86—87; correspondence with Diaz, 105, 107; evacuates Mexico, 108
Benitez, Justo, secretary to Diaz, 79; supposed to inspire Diaz, 171; why rejected as successor to Diaz, 215
Blanco, Guzman, President of Colombia, and the "rotative compromise," 214
Brazo Militar, what meant, 27
Brincourt, French General, opposed to Diaz, 81

CACIQUE, what meant, 29; of Poyais, *see* Macgregor, Gregor.
Candelaria, La, Diaz's second ranch, 149
Carbonera, La, action at, 102
Cerro Borrego, defeat of Mexicans at, 62

Cerro de la Bufa, action at, 147
Chalchicomula, San Andrés de, 59; explosion at, 60
Church in Mexico, reasons for opposition to Diaz, 174 *et seq.*
Cobos, General, Conservative leader, wins battle of Ixcapa, 44; defeated at Jalapa, 45; defeats Diaz, 48—49; is defeated, *ibid.*
Colonies, British and Spanish compared, 7, 9
Comonfort, President, his erratic policy and exile, 43
Consumos, Mexican octroi, 249
Corona, Ramon, General, joins Diaz, 114
Corral, Ramon, elected Vice-President, 292; re-elected, 296; opposition to, 297, 299
Crawford, Captain, U.S. Army, killed in Chihuahua, 195

DANO, M., French Minister, protected by Diaz, 133
Debt, Mexican public, 228 *et seq.*
Detrie, Captain, defeats Mexicans at Cerro Borrego, 62
Diaz, Felix (El Chato), younger brother of Porfirio Diaz, his birth, 3; aids his brother, 34—37; reinforces his brother, 114; in arms with his brother, 146; murder of, 147
Diaz, José de la Cruz, father of President Diaz, 1, 2, 3
Diaz, José de la Cruz Porfirio, *see* Diaz, Porfirio.
Diaz, Maria del Carmen Rubio Romero, Señora de, second wife of President Diaz, 219 *et seq.*
Diaz, Porfirio, birth, 1; education, 2, 3; volunteers in war with United States, 4; enters seminary, *ibid.*; refuses to enter Church, 5;

studies for the law, *ibid.;* communicates with Marcos Pérez in prison, 34—37; votes against Dictator and becomes guerrillero, 39; Sub-Prefect of Ixtlan, 40, 42; raises company of National Guard, 44; wounded at Ixcapa, *ibid.;* Governor of Tehuantepec, 45, 48; defeated at Mitla, 48; hides in Ixtlan, 49; helps to retake Oaxaca, *ibid.;* colonel in regular army and deputy for Ocotlan, 50; services in field, *ibid.*, 51, 52; takes part in defence of Puebla, 61; quoted, 62; promoted General of brigade, 63; Governor of Veracruz, *ibid.;* his policy for the defence of Puebla, 65; defends San Marcos and San Agustin in, 69; quoted, 70, 71; becomes prisoner of war, 72; escapes, 73; appointed to command Army of East, 76; his march to Oaxaca, 77; assumes government of, 78, 79; operations against Bazaine, 81; ill supported, 82; refuses to join Maximilian, 84; forced to surrender, 85; threatened by Bazaine, 86—87; sent prisoner to Puebla, *ibid.;* refuses to intervene on behalf of Imperialist prisoners, 90; escapes from Puebla, 91, 92; forms new Army of East, 93, 96; performs surgical operation, 95; defeated by Imperialists but gains ground, 98; his victory at Nochistlan, *ibid.;* and at Miahuatlan, 99; his skilful operations, 101; victory at La Carbonera, 102; takes Oaxaca, 103; rigorous measures at, *ibid.;* completes recovery of South and East, 104; correspondence with Bazaine, 105—107; refuses invitation of Maximilian, *ibid.;* besieges and takes Puebla, 108; operations against Marquez, 109, 110; begins siege of city of Mexico, 112, 113; surrounds city, 114; his conduct during siege, 115; estimate of his character and capacity, 116, 121; his separation from Juarez, 129 *et seq.;* protects French Minister, M. Dano, 133; his financial position, 134; retires to La Noria, *ibid.;* his first marriage, *ibid.;* reported conversation with Juarez, 137; opposes Juarez in election of 1867, 139 *et seq.;* heads revolt against Juarez, 144 *et seq.;* has to yield to Lerdo de Tejada, 148 *et seq.;* retired to La Candelaria, 149; heads rising against Lerdo de Tejada, 151 *et seq.;* goes to Texas, 153 *et seq.;* invades Mexico, 154; his difficulties with local leaders, 155; takes Matamoros, 156; returns to United States, *ibid.;* sails for Oaxaca, and his adventure on the way, *ibid. et seq.;* takes command in Oaxaca, 159; his victory at Tecoac, 160; occupies city of Mexico, 162; marches against Iglesias, 165; elected President, 166; insists on keeping faith with army, 167 *et seq.;* his method of government, 170, 172; difficulties of his position, 173 *et seq.;* hostility of Church, 174 *et seq.;* reform of public services, 181; simplicity of his life, 182, 183; relations with United States, 184 *et seq.;* settlement with, 187 *et seq.;* recognised by, 188; difficulties on frontier, 188 *et seq.;* approves action of Terán in massacre at Veracruz, 200—206; First Administration ends, 207; matter and style of his addresses to Congress, 209; on end of his first term takes Ministry of Public Works, 217; resigns and takes Governorship of Oaxaca, 218; second marriage, 219 *et seq.;* visit to United States, 221; probable origin of his fortune, 223; his error in regard to financing of public works, 225; re-elected President, 235; subsequent re-elections, 236 *et seq.;* beginning of his second term, 241; choice of Minister of Finance, 257; makes reductions in army, 259;

INDEX

purchases of railways, 259—260; charges of inhumanity brought against, 267; co-operates with United States to suppress Apaches, 269; favours capitalists and land companies, 284 *et seq.*; re-elected in 1904, 290—291; meets Mr. Taft on frontier, 295; his strength begins to fail, 296; decides to be re-elected in 1910, *ibid.* and 298; struggles to maintain his position, 303; his strength breaks down, 304; resigns and leaves country, *ibid.*; death in Paris, 305

Dominguez, Canon, afterwards Bishop of Oaxaca, godfather of Porfirio Diaz, aids in his education, 4

ESCANDON, ANTONIO, concessionnaire of Veracruz line, 225

FOREY, General, besieges Puebla, 65—72; occupies city of Mexico, 73; superseded by Bazaine, *ibid.*

Fornaro, Carlo de, abuse of Diaz, 120

Franco, Pablo, Imperial Prefect of Oaxaca, executed by Diaz, 103

Fuero militar and eclesiástico, what meant, 27

GONZALEZ, General, left in command by Diaz in North, 156; elected President in 1880, 216 *et seq.*; his Presidency, 222 *et seq.*; retires, 235

Gourgaud, Baron, his quotation of Napoleon, 122

Grant, General Ulysses S., visits Mexico, 222

Guardias Rurales, reorganised by Diaz, their origin and functions, 178 *et seq.*

HARDY, Lieutenant R. W. H., R.N., his account of Yaquis, 272

Hernandez, Fidencio, commands for Diaz in Oaxaca, 153 *et seq.*

Hidalgo, priest, his revolt, 22; death, 23

Huerta, General, protects Diaz, 304

IGLESIAS, José Maria, 144; President of Supreme Court, 152; conflict with Lerdo de Tejada, *ibid. et seq.*; his pretensions, 155 *et seq.*; supported in North, 156; his opposition to Diaz and defeat, 162 *et seq.*; escapes to United States, 166

Indiada, meaning of term, 40, 41

Indians, Mexican, causes of their poverty, 126—128; why prosperity of Mexico did not benefit them, 282 *et seq.*

Ixcamula, action at, 156

JECKER, and Jecker bonds, 54, 55

Juarez, Benito, President of Mexico, is Professor at Oaxaca, 5; his influence in Oaxaca, 29; exiled, 31; Governor of Oaxaca, 42; resists French intervention, 63 *et seq.*; passes Ley Juarez, 43; becomes President, 44; leaves city of Mexico, 73; behaviour to Maximilian, 112; re-elected, 131, 136; tries to perpetuate himself in office, 137 *et seq.*; his death, 148

LAGO, Baron, Austrian Minister, arranges capitulation of city of Mexico, 114, 115

Lépero, vagabond class, 253

Lerdo de Tejada, Sebastian, President of Supreme Court, his party, 138; stands as President, 139; becomes President on death of Juarez, 148; his character, 150; political errors, 151; overthrown, and escapes to United States, 161

Lerdo de Tejada, Law so called, 51

Ley Fuga, its purpose, 179

Limantour, José, financier, 135; becomes Minister of Finance, 256; Minister of Finance, 257;

quoted, 265; indicated as successor to Diaz, 291—292; adheres to Diaz, 304
Lorencez, General, commands French troops in Mexico, 58; defeated at Puebla, 61—62

MACGREGOR, GREGOR, Cacique of Poyais, 53
Madero, Francisco, his origin, 293; opposes Diaz, 299 *et seq.*; his opinions, 300; imprisoned, 302; revolts, 303
Magnus, Baron, assists in defence of Maximilian, 114
Marquez, General, called Tiger of Tacubaya, Conservative leader, 51, 52; his defence of city of Mexico, 112 *et seq.*; endeavours to relieve Puebla, 108, 110; defends city of Mexico, 113 *et seq.*; his escape, 115
Marquez de Leon, General, revolts in Sinaloa and Lower California, 198
Matamoros, taken by Diaz, 156, 157
Mateo Xindihui, San, action at, 146
Maximilian, Archduke, Emperor of Mexico, his character, 57; reaches Mexico, 74; resists claims of Church, 75; recognition of refused by United States, 75; painful position of, 89; his fall and death, 111, 112
Mayas, Indian tribe of Yucatan, 277 *et seq.*
Mexico, Republic of—colonial period, 10—22; first civil war in, 23; declares its independence, 24; anarchy in, 25; condition in 1859, 53 *et seq.*; its physical deficiencies, 124, 125; city of, besieged and taken by Republicans, 113, 115; drainage of, 260 *et seq.*
Miahuatlan, action at, 99
Michoacan, disturbances in, *see* Church
Mier y Terán, Luis, *see* Terán.
Miramon, General, leader of Conservatives, 44; borrows money from Jecker, 55

Mitla battle, 48
Mori, Patrona, mother of Porfirio Diaz, 2; widowed, 3
Moyos, Indian tribe in Sonora, 271

NAPOLEON I., Emperor, quoted, 122
Napoleon III., Emperor of French, reasons for his intervention in Mexico, 56
Nickel currency, story of, 233 *et seq.*
Noria, La, Diaz's ranch, 134; proclamation of, 145; burnt, 149
Nuño de Guzman, Spanish explorer, discovers Yaquis, 270

OAXACA, State and City, Porfirio Diaz born in, 1; taken by enemies of Dictator Santa Ana, 40; retaken, 41; taken again, 42; taken by Republicans, 49; surrendered to French, 85; risings in, 144, 153; Diaz becomes Governor of, 218
Ord, General, instructed to pursue marauders in Mexico, 193
Ordaz, Republican General, killed, 48
Orizaba, defence of by French, 62
Oronoz, General, Imperialist Governor of Oaxaca, 98 *et seq.*
Ortega, Doña Delfina, first wife of Diaz, 134
Ortega, General, Governor of Puebla, 65 *et seq.*

PALO BLANCO, plan of, 154 *et seq.*
Pérez, Marcos, Professor, patronizes Porfirio Diaz, 29; imprisoned, 33; in civil war, 49
Pin, Colonel du, commands French counter guerrilla, 63
Pindray, Comte de, filibuster, his death, 54
Portazgos, ship taxes, 245, 248
Prim, General, commands Spanish troops in Mexico, 56 *et seq.*
Puebla de Los Angeles, repulse of French at, 61; siege of by French, 65, 72; Diaz takes, 108

INDEX

QUERÉTARO, siege of, 111
Quivira, supposed Eldorado, 270

RAMIREZ, JESUS, revolts in Sinaloa, 198; shot, 199
Raousset-Boulbon, Gaston Raoulx, Comte de, filibuster, his career, 54
Reyes, General, chosen as candidate for Vice-Presidency, 299; exiled, *ibid.* and 302
Rhodes, Cecil, his view of Mexico, 121
Root, Mr. Elihu, visit to Mexico, and his praise of Diaz, 294
Rosas Landa, General, Republican leader, his misconduct, 49
Rotative compromise, meaning of, 212, 214

SALIGNY, M. de, French Minister in Mexico, 56; misleads General Lorencez, 59
Salinas, General, Republican leader, his failure, 48, 49
Salm Salm, Prince, quoted, 109, 113
Santa Ana, Dictator of Mexico, his character, 31
Sherman, General, occupies Savannah, 88
Sonora, Province, mines of, and raids of filibusters on, 54

TABERA, RAMON, General, surrenders city of Mexico, 115
Taft, Mr., President of United States, meets Diaz on frontier, 295
Tecoac, battle of, 160
Tehuantepec Isthmus, 45 *et seq.*
Terán, Luis Mier y, General, supports Diaz, 146; Governor of Veracruz, his character and brutality, 200—206; rejected as successor to Diaz, 216
Textupec, plan of, 154 *et seq.*

Thornton, Sir Edward, British Minister at Washington, arbitrates between the United States and Mexico, 188
Tierra Baldia, meaning of, 283
Tolentino, General, joins Diaz, 160
Torreon, massacre of Chinese at, 285
Treviño, General, instructed by Diaz to restore order on frontier, 194
Turner, J. R., author of "Barbarous Mexico," quoted, 275

UNITED STATES, their patience with Mexico, 184, 187
Uraga, General, goes over to Maximilian and attempts to seduce Diaz, 82—83

VALLE NACIONAL, tobacco plantations of and slavery on, 279 *et seq.*
Vega, Diaz de la, General, makes sortie from Mexico, 113
Veracruz, headquarters of Republican party, 44; massacre at, 200 *et seq.*; railway from to Mexico, 225; Pacific railway line purchased by Government, 259

WALKER, filibuster, 53
Wyke, Sir Charles, British Minister in Mexico, 56

YAQUIS, Indian tribe, story of, 270 *et seq.*
Yucatan, Province, 275; sisal hemp plantations of, 277; slavery on, 278 *et seq.*

ZAPOTECA, Indian tribe, their character, 30
Zaragoza, General, defends Puebla, 58 *et seq.*; his death, 65

923.172
D543h